Also by Carolyn Haines and available from Center Point Large Print:

Booty Bones
Bone to Be Wild
Rock-a-Bye Bones
Sticks and Bones

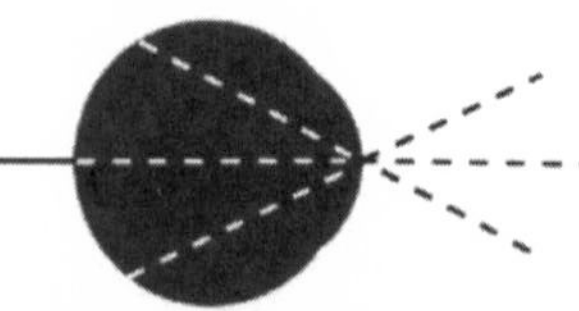

This Large Print Book carries the Seal of Approval of N.A.V.H.

Charmed Bones

A Sarah Booth Delaney Mystery

CAROLYN HAINES

Center Point Large Print
Thorndike, Maine

This Center Point Large Print edition
is published in the year 2018 by arrangement with
St. Martin's Press.

The text of this Large Print edition is unabridged.
In other aspects, this book may vary
from the original edition.
Printed in the United States of America
on permanent paper.
Set in 16-point Times New Roman type.

ISBN: 978-1-68324-893-4

Library of Congress Cataloging-in-Publication Data

Names: Haines, Carolyn, author.
Title: Charmed bones / Carolyn Haines.
Description: Center Point Large Print edition. | Thorndike, Maine :
Center Point Large Print, 2018.
Identifiers: LCCN 2018018888 | ISBN 9781683248934
(hardcover : alk. paper)
Subjects: LCSH: Large type books.
Classification: LCC PS3558.A329 C53 2018b | DDC 813/.54—dc23
LC record available at https://lccn.loc.gov/2018018888

For Christy Cofield—friend and animal lover

Acknowledgments

Sarah Booth and the cast of characters from Zinnia have become like family to me and many readers. To that end, I'd like to thank all the readers, librarians, and booksellers who spread the word when a new Sarah Booth mystery appears. The world of Zinnia grows and thrives thanks to all of you.

Special thanks to Kelley Ragland, Elizabeth Lacks, Hannah Braaten, and Martin Quinn—the fab four of St. Martin's. And, as always, to my agent, Marian Young. This is the eighteenth full-length Sarah Booth mystery, it's been a wild and delicious ride, and there are plenty more adventures to come.

1

Tucked under an heirloom double wedding ring quilt on my comfy sofa, I listen to the wind howl outside Dahlia House. A winter freeze is pushing across the Mississippi Delta bringing ice, hail, and frigid, blustery winds. It's a night for hot toddies and a fire—both of which I have. I hope to finish my February indulgence before the ice storm brings the power lines down and renders my television useless. I'm watching a movie from 1939. My favorite movie of all time.

The green face of Margaret Hamilton leers on the screen. "I'll get you, my pretty. And your little dog, too." Even though I'm fully grown and have seen this movie at least a thousand times, I cringe. The witch's malevolence is tangible.

The Wicked Witch of the West disappears in a puff of smoke as I snuggle against Sweetie Pie, my remarkable red tick hound. *The Wizard of Oz* is an annual event at the house that has sheltered more than seven generations of Delaneys. I always watch it as the February winds blow cold over the raw earth of the Mississippi Delta. When I was a child, I'd snuggle between my parents and drink hot chocolate frothy with marshmallows, safe and secure from the witch's evil intentions.

Dorothy and I share more than I'd ever admit to anyone—a desire to go home. In the movie, she accomplishes that goal. In real life, such a journey is never within reach. Time can never be reversed, and the home of my childhood is far in the past.

On the TV screen, the witch shakes her broomstick and whirls about. The Munchkins cower in the face of such green evil, and I am glad for Sweetie Pie's warm body and the purring of Pluto the black cat, who has my back, literally. It's silly that at my age the witch can still frighten me, but she can.

Not five feet in front of me, orange smoke explodes. In the swirl of vapor, I discern the black and green image of the witch—right in my very own den. She leers at me and shakes her broomstick. "Beware, my fine lady. I may not attend you here and now, but you can't escape me."

I push back against the sofa as the hair on Sweetie Pie's back bristles. She barks and growls. Pluto, on the other hand, jumps from the sofa and saunters toward the witch.

"Away with you." The witch waves the broomstick at Pluto, but the cat is not deterred.

I realize then that Jitty, the resident ghost of my family plantation, has come to devil me again. This is no manifestation from Oz, but the spirit of a former slave who survived the Civil War with my ancestor, Alice Delaney. She is both blessing and curse. "I'm trying to watch a movie," I tell her.

"Give me the ruby slippers and I'll let you live."

I know she is a ghost, not a witch, and can't conjure ruby slippers out of thin air, but I pull up the quilt and check my feet just to be sure. Nope. Plain old gym socks stuck on the ends of my legs so that I look like a sad Raggedy Ann doll.

"Get out of here. You're making me miss the Munchkins. The Lollipop Guild is one of my favorite parts."

"Where's that strong lawman? He should be here, protecting you from the big bad witch. Bringing some strong and upright sperm with him."

"Coleman is working." Jitty is right about one thing. It would have been cozy having Coleman Peters to snuggle up to. An armed robbery at a convenience store has him out working late on a bitter winter night. As sheriff of Sunflower County, Mississippi, he doesn't get to pick and choose his hours. He's a 24/7 kind of lawman.

"You should be out in the patrol car with him, ready to shuck off those ugly sweatpants to help him pass the time while he's doing surveillance. You need a job, Sarah Booth, and that would be a good one."

Jitty's goal in life is to get me pregnant so she'll have a Delaney heir to haunt. "He isn't on surveillance; he's investigating. The last thing he needs is some Lustful Lucy trying to seduce him."

"Sarah Booth Delaney, I know you aren't so unimaginative that you can't figure out a way to be useful to the sheriff *and* get pregnant. Use that thinking cap, Missy. Then use your money maker!"

"Go away." I pause the movie and get up to make more popcorn. It's a futile effort to escape Jitty. She only follows me to the kitchen, where she continues her harangue.

"You were this close to having Coleman," she says, referring to a recent moment when Coleman and I—buck naked—had been headed upstairs to my bedroom. Tinkie Richmond, my partner in the Delaney Detective Agency, slammed through the front door, catching us red-handed and withering our mutual desire. Since then, we've made several attempts to lock out the rest of the world, but life has a terrible way of intervening. The truth is, I'm almost as impatient as Jitty to close the sexual gratification deal—but I'll never let her know it.

"What I need is a new case, not a sperm donor. Now back off or I'll dump a bucket of water on you."

She whirled around once and disappeared in

another poof of orange smoke. She was getting way too good at dramatic entrances and exits. The phone rang and I picked it up as I waited for the butter to heat in the bottom of my skillet.

Tinkie was on the horn. "Whatever you're doing, stop! You have to get over to the Sunflower County Board of Education meeting."

"Why?" I paid my school taxes but I didn't have children so I didn't closely follow the issues of the public schools. In Mississippi, those issues were almost insurmountable as the state legislature cut and cut and cut the school budget. Most of the local school board members were good ol' boys who had about as much business dictating school policy as I had flying jets.

"A trio of witches are in the meeting right now. They're applying for state recognition for their Wiccan boarding school, which they are opening in Sunflower County. Folks are all upset."

"What witches?" Sunflower County had a lot of strange inhabitants, but I'd never come across boarding-school witches, not even in the farthest reaches of the cotton fields and brakes.

"Sexy witches."

Tinkie's response left more questions than answers. "What are you talking about?"

"Get your sassy self down to the school board meeting. You are missing the whole thing, so hurry. I have to get off the phone. I think the school board meeting is about to go postal. Man, I have to film this for Cece." She hung up.

I turned off the stove and raced upstairs for my jeans and a warm sweater. If witches had moved to Sunflower County, I wanted to watch the action unfold. Like all small towns, Zinnia had a few people who'd set themselves up as moral leaders and those who knew best for everyone else. The schools had become the battleground in many instances. Witches! It was going to be interesting.

The wind keened around the eaves of Dahlia House as I opened the front door. Sweetie Pie and Pluto, normally my constant companions, each took one look outside and ran back upstairs. It was for the best. I'd have to leave them in the car and it was a bitter night. I locked the door and drove to town.

The school board meetings were held in an old World War II brick building a block from the courthouse, so I wasn't surprised when I arrived and saw a patrol car parked outside. Things must have gotten rowdy in the meeting, and I knew Coleman Peters well enough to be able to predict his ire if the school board attendees had wasted his time with misconduct.

I slipped into the overcrowded room and took a seat in the back. Tinkie and Cece Dee Falcon, the best reporter in the Southeast, were in the front and therefore had a much better perspective. The room roiled with tension, and the place was so jam-packed I had difficulty finding the source of all the controversy. When at last I saw the witches, I was a bit disappointed. Three very attractive young women sat at the table with the members of the school board. The women were close in age and as Tinkie had noted, oozed sexuality. Blonde, brunette, and redhead—they covered the range of hair colors. Their sense of style was a little risqué, but there wasn't anything sinister about them in the least.

The brunette stood. "Our paperwork is in order. Renovations on the old dairy are already underway. We anticipate accepting our first-term students in August. As you can see, our curriculum has been approved by the state board of education."

Nancy Cunningham, one of the town's most uptight citizens, rose. "Our county will not tolerate this Wiccan foolishness. You will not receive state funding, and certainly you will not be allowed to use state education vouchers. I will see to it."

The battle lines were drawn.

"You have no say-so," the brunette said. "The Harrington School of Nature and Wiccan Studies has approval. There's nothing you can do to stop it."

"We'll see about that, Ms. Harrington." Nancy's hand swept the air, encompassing all three young women. "We will not have the dark arts in a Christian county."

The other two young women also stood. "Our meeting here was a courtesy. If you'd like to tour our facility, please stop by. Otherwise, stay out of our way and out of our business. We're going to bring education back to Mississippi. Our students will understand the role of nature in the world today. You can thank us in twenty years when the best and brightest begin to rule this country and save our planet."

As they marched toward the door, Kitten Fontana stormed into the room and barred their way. "Sit back down. You aren't going anywhere." Kitten was Snooki with a drawl. She even had the ball of teased hair at her crown and the huge earrings that might pass for skinny girl hula hoops. She was one generation removed from brawling in back alleys with a girl gang, but she was loaded. Or at least her husband was.

"Kitten, just stay out of this." Bob Fontana was chairman of the school board, and Kitten was his wife. Fontana Construction and Development had lately gotten a number of bids for work on school facilities—a conflict of interest that seemed to upset no one but me and my friends.

Kitten had no intention of listening to her husband. She had the floor and knew how to use it. "Corey, my son, is missing." She pointed to the witches. "And you are to blame. What have you done to my baby boy?" Kitten was also well known for hurling accusations without any facts to support them.

The woman beside me mumbled, "Whoever has him will bring him back. That boy is destined for a life of crime." Indeed, Corey had a reputation for bad behavior.

"We don't know anything about your son," the brunette said.

"You have him. I know you do. If one hair on his head is harmed, I'll see that you burn like your ancestors."

"I wouldn't make idle threats against us," the redhead said. "We don't like that."

"I don't give two hoots what you like or dislike," Kitten said. "I want my son. What have you done with him?"

"Asked and answered," the redhead said. She turned away to retrieve her purse. Kitten ran toward the witches and just as she lifted her hand to slap the blond one, she cried out in pain and crumpled. No one had touched her—but something was causing Kitten pain.

"Stop! Make it stop!" Kitten cried out. Suddenly she slumped over as if a hard grip had released her.

"I'd be careful of that tennis elbow," the blond witch said. "Now get out of our way. We don't have a clue what you're talking about. If you can't control your child, you shouldn't try to blame it on someone else. At Harrington School, our children will be accounted for and under control at all times. From what I've heard around town, that boy of yours is a menace. Keep him off our property—or else."

Kitten's face contorted and her hands formed into claws, the red-painted talons of her fingertips extended in a classic cat-fight pose. Bob leaped up from the table and grabbed his wife around the waist. "Kitten, control yourself."

"They have Corey. He went over to the dairy to play a prank and he hasn't come home." Kitten grunted with exertion as she fought against Bob's hold. I definitely didn't want to be near their home when all of this came to a head later. Kitten Fontana brooked no constraints when she wanted to express herself. She'd made a fool of herself numerous times at various board meetings and gatherings, and no one was going to stop her from doing the same here.

Tinkie edged up beside me. Cece was snapping photos. "Who are these witches?" I asked.

"Hope, Faith, and Charity Harrington. They're sisters. And powerful witches." Tinkie sounded like she was reading a fairy tale.

"Get real." I'd been inoculated from such foolishness by Jitty.

"They're allegedly very powerful. And they cast spells and sell potions."

Three days ago, I'd noticed a little shop that

had opened on a country road where Musgrove's Dairy used to sell whole milk and homemade butter and cheeses back in the 1970s. As far as I knew, the dairy had been out of business a long time, and the eccentric owner, Trevor Musgrove, a renowned artist, was a recluse in the old manor house that was part of the dairy. As I thought about it, I realized the dairy and manor were a perfect setup for a boarding school and gift shop. The Harrington sisters might not have witchy powers, but they had something better—brain power.

"Tomorrow, let's stop by Pandora's Box and buy some spells." Tinkie was as wide-eyed as Dorothy in the Emerald City.

"I wonder if they have Corey Fontana somewhere on the premises. The boy is a juvenile delinquent who's never paid a price for his destructive behavior. Kitten always buys him out of trouble." I'd heard gossip about some of Corey's activities, such as tossing watermelons off the overpass onto cars. He'd nearly caused several wrecks, but the Fontanas' expensive lawyer had managed to keep him clear of punishment.

"One day he'll get into something she can't get him out of." Tinkie had been a child of privilege, but she'd been held accountable for her conduct.

"Let's meet at Millie's Café for breakfast and we can take a jaunt out to the old Musgrove dairy and see what's what." It was time to leave the school board meeting. The fireworks were over and the board would be back to dull issues like school bus routes and leaky roofs.

As we made our exit, we were joined by the Harrington sisters. I took a moment to introduce myself, discovering that Hope was the brunette, Faith the redhead, and Charity the blonde. They had come to Sunflower County via Lafayette, Louisiana, where they'd run a very successful Montessori school, which had whetted their appetites to try something bigger with more potential impact.

"Mississippi gives any school with a religious foundation the right to apply for state vouchers. I don't think they were anticipating a Wiccan school, but we are a recognized religion. No different from the Baptists or Catholics." Charity flipped her silvery blond hair over her shoulder. "I just have to wonder how some of these people get elected."

"The younger generation has no connection to nature," Hope said. "We have to reconnect or the attacks upon the planet will continue and the future of the human race will be in jeopardy. Without clean water and air, we have nothing."

"Wouldn't a science-based boarding school create less . . . controversy?" Tinkie was always the peacemaker. "Folks around here get a bit uptight about religion. And witches."

"Contrary to what is currently being taught in public schools, religion, nature, and science aren't in conflict. The Wiccan religion is very loving and based on the science of balance with nature. It's not like we worship the Dark Lord and say the Bible backwards." Charity had a merry laugh that matched her blond curls. I couldn't tell if the vivid array of hair color among the sisters came from bottles, but the shades complimented each woman's complexion. And possibly her personality.

"If you don't worship the Dark Lord, what do you worship?" Tinkie asked.

"So glad you want to know." Faith opened her huge purse and pulled out printed material. "This is the Wiccan Rede. It's the basis of our beliefs and a call for ethical and careful behavior. We believe in protecting Nature and the helpless. We believe in sisterhood, the moon, the power of white magic to heal and help, and the benevolence of the Goddess. We can cast spells, but only those that bring light. We make potions, but only those that bring about love and healing."

"Think Glinda," I said to Tinkie. My viewing of *The Wizard of Oz* had been interrupted, but now I found myself in a real-life confrontation of a trio of sexy witches.

"Do we look like Glinda?" Hope asked.

"Maybe if you traded in your leather miniskirt for a ruffled pink gown . . ." I smiled to let them know I was teasing. These were modern witches, and as Tinkie had described them, sexy. They wore black leggings, skinny jeans, miniskirts, and the latest provocative styles. I could definitely see where they might cast a spell on a man.

"What do you know about Corey Fontana?" Tinkie asked.

"The little bastard spray-painted 'Burn, Witch, Burn' on the wall of the dairy. That's what I know," Faith said. Her temper seemed to match her red hair. "I ran him off. I did chase him through the fields and woods, but I didn't hurt him. I didn't catch him. As far as I know, he went home."

"How old is Corey?" Tinkie asked.

Faith shook her head. "Maybe seventeen or eighteen. I didn't get a good look at him, but I know his reputation. He and his mother have been stewing about us for weeks now. Ever since we came to town in December and started renovations. I'm pretty sure she sent him over to deface our property."

"Your property?" I asked.

"We're buying the dairy, manor, and grounds from Trevor. He'll remain living in the manor. There's plenty of room for us and a boatload of students, artists, and teachers."

"I can't believe Trevor's actually selling the property." It had been in the Musgrove family for close on two hundred years. Like my ancestors,

Trevor's had gradually bought pieces of land until they owned a tract of more than a thousand acres. "Is Trevor at the manor now?" I asked.

"On the third floor. He seldom comes downstairs. Charity is going to handle the international sales of his artwork for him. He'll remain on the third floor as long as he lives."

"His work is fantastic," Charity said, already wearing her marketing hat. "His series of ancient goddesses are stupendous. And the nudes as iconic religious figures—now that created such a scandal, but those paintings sold for six figures in Italy, Spain, and Brazil." She nudged Faith.

"He isn't that old," I said. Trevor Musgrove wasn't even sixty. "He could live another thirty years. I can't believe he's going to be a tenant on his own family's property."

"He won't make sixty at the rate he's going," Faith said. "Women march up and down those stairs at all hours of the day and night. His models, or so he says. More like his paramours. He's doing a lot of activity besides painting, if you get my drift. You know, it's interesting that this county gets up in arms about a school, but they don't say a thing about Trevor and his sexual escapades. He's banging half the under-fifty wives in the county."

"It's the whole witch thing." Tinkie held up her hand to stop them from commenting. "You have to teach the public what you represent and stand for. The word *witch* has a lot of negative connotations. Eye of newt, bat wings, spells, consorting with Satan, plagues, famines—black magic."

"How perfectly medieval," Hope said, and we all laughed.

I wasn't certain the Harrington sisters would fare well in Sunflower County, but I respected what they were trying to accomplish. The idea of a school focused around nature and healing seemed like a much-needed area of education—and if a Protestant- or Catholic-based school could get state funding, the Wiccans should be able to have it, too. Besides, if the younger generation didn't value the planet, there would be a terrible price to pay. Even I could see that.

"This school voucher thing," Tinkie edged toward the hot topic. "Do you really believe the state will give students money to pay for your school?"

"They have to. The legislature opened the door to this when they began to allow parents to use vouchers or education credits to pay for private schools. We're a recognized religion. What they do for one, they must do for others." Hope's grin was more than a little wicked. "We wouldn't want the federal government down here messing in the schools again, would we?"

"I might," I said under my breath. The state politicians were certainly making a mess of it. "Okay, good luck, ladies. I have a date with

Dorothy and Toto. I was in the middle of *The Wizard of Oz* before I came here." I was ready to head home. The wind was biting into my face and hands as we stood outside the school board meeting, and my pets were waiting for me. I'd been roused from my evening plans by a tempest in a teapot.

"Watch out for the green witches," Hope called out. "They're the most dangerous." And then she gave a perfect imitation of Margaret Hamilton's cackle. It made chills dance along my skin.

I'd reached my car when Kitten Fontana came bursting out of the building calling my name and Tinkie's.

"I'm hiring the Delaney Detective Agency to find my son," she declared. "Corey went over to the dairy and hasn't returned home. Those witches are up to something and he was going to prove it. They must have caught him or he'd be home. He didn't have any dinner and he's not answering his phone. He's just a kid, and I just know they've done something terrible to him. Here's a check for ten grand. That's your retainer, correct?"

We didn't have a retainer fee, but I took the check. Taxes were due. As much as I wanted to go home, business was a priority.

"Let's head over to the Prince Albert for a libation and a chat," Kitten said. "I need a vodka to clear my head."

I was a little stunned that a drink was Kitten's solution to a missing child, but then again, Corey did have a reputation of driving people to drink. Tinkie waved goodbye to the witches and fell into step with me and Snook—Kitten.

The wind almost took our breath away when we stepped out of the lee of the building and into the street. We put it in high gear and hustled to the Prince Albert bar, where I lost no time ordering a dirty vodka martini with multiple olives. It was a martini kind of night. Kitten went straight for the cream with a White Russian, and Tinkie played it safe with white wine. Someone had to be responsible.

I was a little curious that Kitten jumped on her barstool, kicked off her shoes, and sighed with contentment. The night was tanking—temperature-wise—and the mercury was on the verge of freezing. Her teenage son was missing—she'd written a check for ten grand for us to find him—and she was drinking cocktails. I wondered if Bob was out looking for the boy or if they'd simply had enough of his bad behavior and the worry it caused. Or maybe she knew exactly where her kid was and she'd come to the school board meeting to cause trouble for the Harrington sisters.

"Do you really believe those women are witches?" Kitten asked.

"You tell me. You were going to slap one of

them and you stopped." I was dying to hear this explanation. "What happened?"

"It was like someone grabbed hold of my hand and bent it backward. Almost like they were going to break it at the wrist. The pain was excruciating."

She had doubled over, as if she were in actual pain. But Kitten, like all women who made their way pleasing a man, was a great actress. I'll bet Bob Fontana believed he was the best lover alive. Ego was always the weakness of men like Bob. He had a talent, but it wasn't sensitivity or brains.

"And the pain stopped as suddenly as it began?" I asked.

"It did. It was very curious. You don't think—" Her eyes widened. "She was protected by a spell!"

"I didn't say that."

"It would certainly explain it." Kitten whipped out her phone. She couldn't wait to spread the news that the witches could cast spells.

Tinkie snatched her phone. "Don't do that. You have no proof and you're going to get those women hurt. Some people will get hysterical about the idea of spells and such."

"Have you been to Musgrove Manor?" Kitten eyed her phone but she didn't attempt to grab it. Tinkie had won, for the moment. "There are cats everywhere. Everyone knows witches have cats as familiars."

I could only roll my eyes. "I have a black cat."

"I've always wondered about you, too," Kitten said, deadly serious.

"Please, if I had the power to cast spells, you'd know it. The only reason the dairy is overrun with cats is because Trevor was too lazy to get them spayed and neutered. Totally irresponsible."

"Trevor is a great artist. He shouldn't worry about vermin." Kitten sipped her drink and licked her lips, just like a cat. I had visions of neutering her.

"Where do you think your son is on this bitter cold night?" Tinkie asked, inserting the ice pick and giving it a little twist.

"Those witches have him. I know it in my heart."

"Now if they were into voodoo, he might be a great human sacrifice," I said, draining my martini. I'd had enough of her company. Her check might be good but her soul was rotten. To the core.

"They wouldn't dare harm a hair on his head." Kitten lapped her drink and gave me a knowing look. "They'll default on that property, Bob will buy it, and soon Sunflower County will have an exclusive subdivision built around a world-class golf course. Those broomstick riders will fly right out of the county."

She was pretty certain of her predictions, and I wondered why.

"We'd better get busy looking for Corey," Tinkie said. "It's freezing outside. If he has injured himself and is out in this weather, he could face hypothermia."

"He has the finest outdoor gear. Vest, coat, socks, boots, hand warmers." Kitten slipped into her heels and stood. "He's probably hiding out at a friend's."

"But you just gave us ten grand to find him. If you think he's safe . . ." This wasn't about Corey or finding him. This was the beginning salvo in the Fontanas' plan to get their hands on Musgrove Manor and the dairy. The golf course subdivision wasn't just big talk, it was the future as envisioned by Kitten and Bob.

"We'll report in tomorrow," Tinkie said, grabbing my elbow and steering me toward the door. She knew I was about to explode. "Daddy needs a new Cadillac," she whispered to me as she forced me to the exit. "Hold your tongue. Daddy needs a bright red Caddy." Tinkie's brand-new car had been destroyed in our last case, and she did need a new one.

"Okay, okay." I shook free of her and continued out of the hotel. In the shadow cast by the front of Hoffman Furniture, a woman lurked, blending into the storefront. I nudged Tinkie. "Who is that?" Tinkie knew everyone in the county.

"I don't recognize her, but I can't see her all that well either."

The woman was staring right at us, but she didn't step forward. She was trim and wearing stilettos that looked like a whorehouse special—the kind of shoes we used to call knock-me-down-and-screw-me shoes, which led me to believe she might be a friend of Kitten Fontana. She had that Snooki thing going with her hair, too. Hadn't they ever heard that roaches would nest in teased hair that was shellacked to madness with hairspray?

"I'll bet she's waiting on Kitten to come out." Tinkie tried to hustle me away from the hotel door.

When I looked back inside the bar, Kitten was on the phone. Judging from the animation on her face and her excitement, I'd be willing to predict that spellcasting would be the town buzz by daybreak. Tinkie and I race-walked around the corner and pressed ourselves against the wall. And waited. When we heard voices, we looked back.

Shadow Woman had stepped under a streetlamp and Kitten rushed out the door to speak with her—after casting furtive glances around to be sure she wasn't seen. She should have been safe; the town was quiet. But she hadn't counted on us.

Tinkie inhaled sharply. "I know who that is. It's Esmeralda Grimes, the tabloid reporter from Memphis. She's on a lot of those entertainment shows where they dish the dirt on celebrities.

Millie is going to have a field day." She was about to squeal with delight when I put a hand over her mouth. Tinkie was correct—Millie Roberts, café owner, was addicted to celebrity and entertainment gossip—but we were snooping and had to stay quiet.

Oh, I knew who Esmeralda Grimes was. "She's that crazy . . . person who writes for the *International Report* and does those stories about live births of half-sheep-half-human babies, alien abductions, conspiracy theories about members of the royal family and their connections to Appalachian baby sales."

"That's her! And she's meeting with Kitten. Those two are up to no good."

And that was the first major understatement of the new year.

2

Instead of going home, as any smart detectives would have, Tinkie and I left her rental car and I drove my mother's antique Mercedes Roadster to the U-Tote-Em, Zinnia's all-night emporium of rolling papers, wine, cigarettes, pork skins, and cardboard pizza. And, best of all, the latest issue of the *International Report*.

While I picked up two packs of cashews and some sparkling water, Tinkie grabbed two copies of the tabloid. We were off into the night. It was one of those rare evenings when Tinkie wasn't ready to go home. Nothing against her husband, Oscar, but our detective blood was up. We had work to do. And I suspected she hated driving the rental car, which looked like a cube on wheels. Tinkie's elegance bone was offended.

Sweetie Pie and Pluto greeted us at the front door of Dahlia House as we hurried inside. I rustled up some drinks and popcorn to go with the cashews and we went to our office to study the tabloid. It didn't take much study. The headline screamed zinnia witches conjure dead elvis.

The whole front page was an image of Faith,

Hope, and Charity flying around a bubbling cauldron on broomsticks. Rising from the pot was gold-lamé Elvis. The picture was so obviously Photoshopped I wanted to laugh. How many rubes would take this as literal evidence the Harrington sisters were raising the dead? Not to mention flying on broomsticks.

"Satan selling Popsicles," Tinkie said. "This is an outrage."

And suddenly we were both laughing. And we knew exactly why Esmeralda Grimes was in town. Kitten had money to burn, and she was determined to rid Musgrove Manor of the witches. One way or the other. Slander and libel would be as effective as a house fire. Kitten was a devious and determined woman.

We read the story, which held little factual content and a whole lot of speculation about the sisters and why they had left Lafayette, Louisiana. Still, it was a good lead for us to follow up on, should Corey Fontana fail to appear in the next few hours. I felt certain the teenager was only helping his mother foment fear about the witches, but I'd learned never to count my chickens before they hatched.

Tinkie and I drank, ate, and talked until the sun came up. We made a list of places to check for Corey, including classmates, hangouts, and area jails—the boy was a known juvenile delinquent. But mostly we talked. It had been a long time since we'd pulled an all-nighter just sharing. And we were ready for action at first light. Tinkie brought out a pair of sweatpants and sneakers from her desk drawer. We'd vowed at the first of the year to walk and work out at least three times a week. Needless to say, her clothes were still clean and unworn. But they'd come in handy now.

I raced upstairs to change into hiking boots. Our breakfast at Millie's would have to wait. I grabbed flashlights and my gun. Again, I didn't anticipate shooting anyone, but it was better to be prepared. Just as the sun peeked over the horizon, Tinkie, Sweetie, Pluto, and I were on the way to Musgrove Manor to search for the missing teen. Chablis, Tinkie's little Yorkie, was going to be angry at us, but we didn't want to risk waking Oscar by stopping by Hilltop for her.

My cell phone rang and Coleman's warm and sexy voice buzzed in my ear as he teased me with, "Ready for some company in that big bed?"

"Only if you don't consider three a crowd. Tinkie is with me. She said she had a hankering to stand naked on the stairs at Dahlia House." I could still make him blush at the mention of Tinkie and sex in the same sentence, and though I couldn't see Coleman I knew he was blushing. When Tinkie had caught us both naked on the stairs, she'd gained the upper hand over Coleman Peters. And I was glad to help her keep it.

"Sarah Booth, just understand that there's a price to be paid for not playing fair."

It was definitely a threat. "I'll take my chances."

"I'll wait until Tinkie isn't around. We'll see how tough you are when you don't have your protector."

"I can take care of myself." But my heart was racing, and I felt a little light-headed. "So did you catch the robbers?" Turning the conversation was the only smart thing to do.

"I did. I heard from DeWayne that you're working for the Fontanas." He was all but laughing. Kitten's reputation preceded her.

"Her kid is missing. Maybe. I think she's stirring up trouble for the Wiccan school."

"Corey Fontana is trouble. He's been associated with some real crime in the county. I haven't been able to pin anything on him, but he's got a streak of violence. Be careful."

"I think the kid is at home playing video games. This is a ploy."

"Bob Fontana wants to develop the Musgrove property. I'd say your instincts are right on," Coleman said. "Still, be careful."

"Tink and I are headed out to search the woods for the missing boy. Just in case he's hurt."

"Shall I join you?"

"You get some sleep. If you're going to bring me to heel, you're going to need all of your strength." I hung up before he could respond. Baiting the bear was safe only for a limited amount of time.

Tinkie was grinning like the Cheshire Cat when I glanced at her. "Shut up."

"I didn't say a word." Her grin widened. "I should have taken that photo of you two looking like 'possums in the headlights. I'll never again let decency and friendship overrule a chance for power."

"Coleman would put you in jail."

"And Cece would print that photo. Then where would our pistol-packing sheriff be?"

Tinkie had the upper hand. The best I could manage was a graceful retreat. "Look, there's the dairy. Shall we start on the grounds or go to the manor house and wake them up?"

"Do witches need to sleep?" She answered my question with a question as I pulled into the parking area. She leaned over and pressed hard on the horn. "That should do the trick."

A frisky Tinkie was a dangerous creature. The horn roused about two dozen cats of all colors and descriptions. They came out from under the porch of the house, out the windows in the dairy barn, jumping out of trees and off the porch roof. Cats were everywhere. And Pluto was standing at the car's front window, all alert and eager.

"What if they haven't had their vaccinations?" I said to him.

"Meow." He waited for Tinkie to open her door and he was out like a shot. Pluto was a curious fellow.

"No more stray cats dumped here," Hope said as she came out the door tying a gorgeous oriental wrap around herself. The reds and blacks were perfect for her coloring.

"He's my cat. He's only here on official investigative purposes." Once Corey Fontana was found and returned home, I'd speak with the Harrington sisters about a trap, neuter, and release program for the cats. Or maybe they could just do a sterility spell on the colony. Wouldn't that be convenient?

Hope sat down on the porch steps and ran her fingers through her black, tousled hair. "Cat detective. Backwoods Mississippi. Nothing surprises me. Does he talk? Maybe bartend?"

"No, but he can sniff out a villain," I said, handing her the folded tabloid.

Her response when she opened it was a long belly laugh. "This is great. And yes, I have Elvis upstairs in my bedroom. He's my sex slave. He's got it going on." She stood up and struck an Elvis pose complete with leg shake and a few bars of "Whole Lotta Shakin' Goin' On." She had a great voice.

Tinkie burst out laughing and I had to join in. Brunette witch had a good sense of humor.

"So Esmeralda Grimes is in Zinnia," Hope said.

"I'm happy to see she never lets the facts stand in the way of a good story."

"The *International Report* believes in alternative facts," Tinkie said. "I wonder if alternative facts would fly with paying my taxes?"

"I wouldn't risk it," I said. "Now let's talk about Corey Fontana."

"Why don't you come inside and have some coffee?" Hope stood and opened the front door. "It's freezing and I need caffeine if I'm going to talk sensibly. Bring your dog inside, too."

She didn't have to ask twice. I let Sweetie Pie out of the car and we all rushed the front door, where we were met with a wave of delicious heat. In the back of my mind I had a thought for Corey Fontana. I hoped the boy hadn't spent the night outside. He was a delinquent, no doubt about it. But if he was fooling around and ended up injured and exposed to the elements, he could lose fingers, toes, or even his nose.

We found Faith and Charity in the kitchen. The delicious aroma of fresh-brewed coffee made me sigh with pleasure. Hope picked three mugs out of the cabinet and poured coffee for us. When we were all seated at a sturdy farm table, I brought the conversation around to Corey Fontana.

"Like I said in the school board meeting, the kid defaced our barn," Charity said. "I'm sure his daddy will pay to have the paint removed. I saw the boy doing it and ran out the door yelling. He dashed off into the woods, and Faith and I chased him for a little ways, but I didn't have a jacket or gloves and it was freezing. I gave up and came back home."

"How did you know it was Corey?" I asked.

"He's been snooping around here since we arrived. Sometimes he hangs out in the tree line and watches us with binoculars." Faith laughed. "One of these days he's going to get a real surprise."

I was about to ask her what she meant by that, but Faith picked up Tinkie's hand. "We can help you with your problem."

Her words were so out of context with anything that had been said that I was stunned to silence.

"What problem would that be?" Tinkie asked.

"The child you want." Faith held her hand even when Tinkie tried to withdraw it.

"I don't think that's funny." Tinkie's dander was getting up.

"It's not a joke," Faith said.

"We can help you," Charity added. "We can cast a spell, do an incantation. There are some herbs you can take. You'll have a baby before the year is finished."

"That must be some kind of spell," I said sharply. "It's already February. She'd have to conceive virtually this week."

"It can happen," Faith said, her green gaze steady.

"Really?" Tinkie bit hook, line, and sinker. She'd wanted a baby more than anything for a long, long time. But there were fertility issues. Medical issues that couldn't be wished away.

"Tinkie, don't be foolish. You've been to the best doctors in the nation." I couldn't bear the thought of Tinkie's disappointment—again.

"This isn't about medicine," Faith said. "It's about the power of love. The power of motherhood. The need for a child. And a little bit of magic. I'll get a potion from the shop. We just stocked everything fresh."

I stood up and slammed my coffee cup on the table. "This is wrong. You know it's wrong."

Tinkie reached out and grabbed my arm. "What would it hurt to try?"

"We aren't charging," Faith said. "It's our gift to you."

It wasn't money. Tinkie and Oscar had enough to light bonfires with it if that's what they wanted to do. It was about my partner's heart and spirit. "What time was Corey Fontana here?" I meant to finish my business with the sisters and leave. Tinkie would have to go with me; I was driving.

"It was just after school let out." Faith went to the cabinet and got several unusual boxes of tea. She began to mix a concoction while she heated water on the stove. "I was making some extract of dandelion weed when I saw him spray-painting the wall. I ran out, he ran away. Charity and I gave chase and when we couldn't catch him, we came home." She poured the hot water over the tea and put the mug in front of Tinkie. "Let it steep a few minutes. You should probably give up coffee and alcohol."

"Tinkie, I need a word with you." I wasn't about to let her drink whatever that was. I grabbed her arm and almost lifted her out of her chair. In a moment, we were out of the kitchen and in the hallway. "What are you doing?"

"I want a baby. I don't care how I get one." Her lips were thin and pressed tight. "Stay out of this, Sarah Booth. I mean it. This probably won't work, but if there's even a one percent chance, I want it."

"You're only going to get hurt."

"I have a right to take any risk I choose."

This was old, familiar ground, but I was usually the one arguing for the right to risk-take. Most often against physical injury. And Tinkie defended that right. Even against Coleman, who felt it was his personal duty to keep me safe.

"Okay." I had no right to stop her. "Try it if you have to."

We returned to the kitchen and Tinkie drank the tea, which she said was surprisingly good.

"We should go," I said. "We need to find Corey."

"We could dowse for him," Hope offered.

"Dowse?" I'd heard the term and knew it was a

magical search, but I'd always associated it with looking for water. "I'd like to see that."

Hope left the kitchen and returned with a property map of Sunflower County and a crystal pendant on a silver chain. "I'll concentrate on where Corey is and allow the pendant to swing over the map. When it pulls down, it will show me where Corey is."

"Really?" Tinkie was impressed. I was skeptical.

Hope held the chain and set the pendant to swinging. She said a few incantations in a language I didn't understand, then finished with, "Corey Fontana, we seek you."

The pendant twirled and gradually stopped moving. The crystal actually seemed to tug Hope's hand down as it struck a point on the old Crenshaw property next door to Musgrove Manor.

"He should be right there." Hope looked troubled. "I honestly thought he'd gone home and Mrs. Fontana was just staging a drama."

I studied the map. The Crenshaw plantation had been abandoned for a long time. If Corey was there, he might be injured. We had to search for him. "Would it be okay if we cut across your property to see if we can find any traces of Corey?" I asked.

"Knock yourselves out," Hope said. "That boy is full of the very devil. And, trust me, witches know the devil when we see it." She grinned.

I couldn't help but like her. She had a wicked humor. "Thanks."

Faith leaned over and whispered something in Tinkie's ear. She smiled and nodded her agreement, but she followed me outside without complaint.

With Sweetie Pie and Pluto leading the way, we left the manor house. We cut through an impressive herb garden that was tended with great love and headed through the fields toward the woods. Some of the pastures remained cleared and planted in alfalfa and Bahia grasses that were harvested for hay. A lot of the once-cleared land had grown up in thick woods. When we left the open fields and entered the woods, the temperature dropped at least ten degrees.

Tinkie and I walked side by side. I waited for her to break the silence.

"If we find Corey on the Crenshaw place, will you believe the witches have powers?" she asked.

"No. I'd be more likely to believe they knew where he was because they put him there."

She laughed. "You have no faith in magic, Sarah Booth."

It was a statement I'd have to study. I had a family ghost haunting my home who sometimes brought me messages from the Great Beyond. Why couldn't I believe three sister witches had the power to make Tinkie fertile? Until I had an answer, I vowed to keep my mouth shut.

Movement to our right made us all freeze in place. Sweetie Pie's ruff bristled and a low growl came from her throat. A ripple of energy, like a dark shadow, raced through the trees. Tinkie drew closer to me. I'd never been afraid of anything in the woods, but my heart was pounding with fear. "There's no such thing as the boogeyman," I said, though I hadn't meant to speak aloud.

"What was that?" Tinkie asked. Pluto arched his back and turned to face the direction we'd come from. In the distance, branches snapped and a long, extended howl seemed to ricochet off the tree trunks.

"Let's get this finished," I said. We were almost to the Crenshaw place. If we didn't find Corey, we could take the long route home along the roadway. I wasn't walking back through the woods. I didn't care how ridiculous I sounded. Something was there. An intelligence. And it watched us.

"There's the old house." Tinkie pointed and I could make out the shape of the former plantation. The white paint was long gone and the gray boards blended with the drab winter grounds.

We came to the edge of the woods but were met by a thicket of blackberry stalks. The thorny vines were almost impenetrable.

"Sleeping Beauty," Tinkie said, expressing my exact thoughts.

"We won't find a princess. If we do find Corey, he's more like a bad apple. Speaking of which, I wonder if the Musgrove apple orchard still has fruit. Those were some delicious spring apples." I wore a thick jacket and sturdy jeans, but I didn't relish wading through a field of briars.

"There's a path." Tinkie had found a narrow dirt trail through the worst of the briars. We set out toward the old Crenshaw plantation. The sun had risen and the day was warming, promising a blue sky and temperatures that were tolerable.

"Corey!" Tinkie yelled out his name.

"Corey!" I joined her.

We left the briars behind and stepped onto the front porch of the abandoned dwelling. "Corey!" we called through a broken window.

No answer.

"Corey!" I put a hand on Tinkie's arm to halt her. On the east side of the house it sounded like someone scuffling. "Corey!" we yelled again.

"Help!" The word was small and muffled, but clearly a request for assistance.

We jumped off the side of the porch and spread out to explore the raggedy lawn. Volunteer oak trees grew up in the middle of heritage camellias and the dead limbs of bridal wreath and hydrangeas. This had once been a gorgeous lawn that framed the graceful architecture of the old house perfectly.

"Corey! Where are you?" Tinkie called out.

"Here! In the pit."

His voice was clearer now. We moved toward the eastern lawn. About twenty yards from the house we came to the edge of a pit where tree limbs and leaves had been piled. Something moved beneath the leaves. It was like the stirring of a long untouched grave, and I grasped Tinkie's hand.

"Corey?" If it wasn't Corey, we were going to set a land record getting out of there.

"Help me."

A la *Carrie*, a hand reached up through the leaves.

Sweetie Pie went crazy barking and growling and Pluto dashed up a nearby chinaberry tree.

"Oh, shit!" Tinkie reeled backward and tripped over a big stone. I grabbed for her and lost my footing, too. In a moment, I'd fallen on top of her and we both rolled down the slope of the pit.

"Awwwghh!" was the only utterance I could get out.

We crashed to a halt on top of the hand, and Tinkie let out a squeal. "It pinched my bottom! The hand pinched my bottom!" She leaped up, stepped on my head, and vaulted out of the pit. Good thing she was petite or my skull would be crushed.

"Hey, you're suffocating me," the body beneath the leaves said. "Help me out."

I flipped over and dug down into the leaves

with my hand and caught hold of another hand. A warm, human hand. "Corey, is that you?"

"Get me out of here. I fell in and my leg is caught."

I glanced at Tinkie, now composing herself on the edge of the pit. "Get your cell phone out and call Coleman. Tell him we need help rescuing Corey Fontana."

"I vote we just leave him." Tinkie wasn't kidding. "He scared ten years off my life. And he pinched my butt. Hard."

I started laughing. I couldn't help it. We'd spooked ourselves and nearly suffocated Corey. "Make the call. We just earned ten grand for two hours' work. It's worth a few scratches and some leaves in your hair."

"So say you." But Tinkie whipped out her phone and made the call while I began to clear away the debris. Corey appeared fine, and he'd been smart to bury himself in the leaves to stay warm. We'd need a chain saw and some strong men to get him out. I could only hope the little juvenile had learned a lesson, but somehow, judging by the smirk on his face, I doubted it.

3

James and Elroy Wilson put away their chain saws, took the money I offered them—and would be reimbursed for by the Fontanas—and left Tinkie, Corey, and me sitting on the front porch of the old plantation. Coleman had sent the brothers to cut Corey out of his pit, and they'd done a fine job. Kitten had been alerted that her son was safe and she was on her way to retrieve him.

"How in the heck did you fall into that pit?" Tinkie asked. She was still a little miffed at the grabby juvenile. Corey was maybe late teens, but he had the attitude of a privileged twenty-something.

"Something was chasing me through the woods." He smirked. "It was big and black and evil. It had to come from the witches."

I didn't believe Corey for a minute, but once again, the sensation that we were being watched washed over me. Sweetie Pie was asleep beside us on the porch, but Pluto walked sentry duty around the perimeter of the yard. He was on guard for some reason, and I trusted the feline's instincts. Something was out there.

"Some*thing* or someone?" Tinkie pressed.

"It moved too fast to be human, but it was no match for me." Corey obviously didn't have sense enough to be worried if he had been pursued by a supernatural being. He was flexing his muscles and striking poses for Tinkie's benefit. As if she'd be interested in a spoiled rotten high school senior.

"Did you see it?" I asked.

"I heard it. First it was behind me, then to my left, then in front of me. It moved through those thick woods without any trouble. That's why I don't think it was human. Those witches have brought something evil to town."

Corey was seriously creeping me out. I had no reason to be so jumpy, but I couldn't help it. I had a sense that something was brewing over at Musgrove Manor and it wasn't just education. The whole dowsing thing with the crystal, the fact we'd found Corey exactly where the witches said he would be. Of course, the logical explanation for that was because one of the sisters had pushed Corey into the pit.

"Did you fall into the hole or were you pushed?" I asked.

"I was running as fast as I could and I knew if I could find the driveway to the old Crenshaw place I could get out on the road. I didn't like being in the woods."

The boy couldn't answer a question if his life depended on it. "Were you pushed?"

"Maybe. It all happened so fast. That thing was gaining on me and then I was falling through all those branches and leaves. It knocked the wind out of me and when I caught my breath, I could hear something above me. It kind of snorted and grunted, like it might be an animal."

"There aren't any bears or big cats left around here. Do you think it could have been a deer?" I grinned as I asked the question. "Yeah, maybe a killer deer."

"It wasn't a deer. Those witches. They sent something after me."

"And why would they do that?"

"Because they're witches. Duh! Read any fairy tales or was your childhood barren of culture?"

OMG, the little pissant sounded just like his brain-dead mother. I considered pushing him back in the hole and leaving him, but I needed the paycheck.

"Let's get him back to his mama before you wring his neck," Tinkie said, sliding off the porch. "We'll wait for Kitten on the highway."

By the time I let Tinkie off in Zinnia to pick up her rental car and stopped by the Piggly Wiggly for some food supplies, I felt like I'd been run over by a road paver. The surges of adrenaline had taken a toll on my winter-plump body. I'd learned a valuable lesson over the cold months—pumpkin might be a great source of fiber, but if you loaded it up with eggs, sugar, cinnamon, and cream and baked it in a piecrust, it was also fattening. But oh, so satisfying.

I arrived at Dahlia House just in time for a second breakfast, as Bilbo Baggins would suggest. And, in my defense, I'd skipped the first one for some aerobic exercise in the Musgrove woods. Walking up the front steps, my mouth was watering at my plans for a delicious sweet red pepper, onion, and soy sausage frittata. The front door stopped me cold. Huge claw marks raked down the wood, scoring the new paint job. Whatever had clawed my door had meant to get in, and the marks indicated a paw of enormous size. I whipped out my cell phone, took some photos, and messaged them to Coleman.

His response was instant and gratifying. He was on his way over.

Before I could pocket my phone, it rang. To my dismay, I saw that Kitten Fontana was calling. I'd delivered Corey to her car—and her clutches. To my surprise, I'd had a pang for the boy as Kitten lit into him about how much time and money he'd cost her. Not a word about her concerns for his safety. But Corey was safe; I had no clue what she wanted now. As far as I knew, my business with her was done. Nonetheless, I answered. She could stop payment on her check and I wouldn't put it past her.

"I want you and Tinkie to poke into those witches."

"To what purpose?" I didn't mind another case, especially one that would allow me to scratch the itch of my natural curiosity, but I suspected Kitten had an agenda. Like most manipulative people, she didn't mind trapping the innocent in her machinations. I preferred not to be crushed.

"Sunflower County is a God-fearing place. We can't have a bunch of Wiccans teaching the local schoolchildren."

I still had the Wiccan material that the sister witches had given me at the school board meeting and I picked it up from the hall table. I was within eyeshot of the wet bar and talking to Kitten really, really made me want a drink. It was too early in the day to start drinking. Besides, Coleman was on the way over.

I picked up the Wiccan Rede. It was a simple rule: "An it harm none, do as ye will." The Harrington sisters had provided a brief explanation. The goal of every Wiccan was to live a life that harmed no living thing, including the planet. Wiccans worshiped nature and the seasons, the natural world of time and place. They honored the three stages of life for the female: maiden, mother, crone. And they worshiped the Earth as the Mother Goddess.

"They don't really look dangerous to me," I said to Kitten. "If you don't like the school, don't send Corey there."

"I've notified the Anti-Satan League. They'll be paying a visit to Sunflower County. They'll root out the Satanic tentacles of those witches, and you'll see. When you worship the devil, there's always a price to be paid."

"You're sounding a little stressed out, Kitten." I couldn't help myself.

"I'm on the front line of saving this community from hellfire and damnation."

"Why not give the witches a chance?" I said. "Some new blood in Zinnia. Certainly education in Mississippi could use a boost. I like the idea of science and nature-based education."

"You would." She spat the two words like bullets.

"What is it you want me to find out about them?"

"What are they really up to? I saw the tabloid story saying they were raising Elvis from the dead."

"Kitten, that's impossible." I didn't mention I'd seen her with the author of that ridiculous article.

"There was a photo of them flying around on broomsticks."

Dear God, Kitten was either dumb as a rock or getting ready to work this angle for her own benefit. "That was Photoshopped. I would have thought since you know Esmeralda Grimes you would know that."

Silence greeted my statement, and I had a moment of satisfaction.

"Those women are up to no good. You can count on that."

"What do you want me to find out?"

"Where are they getting their funding? That would be a start."

"I'll need another retainer." I didn't feel bad at all for hitting her pocketbook.

"I'll drop a check by the bank as soon as it opens."

"Perfect."

The rattle of the windowpanes in the parlor alerted me to something going on that had nothing to do with Kitten Fontana. I was expecting Coleman, and my heart did a little triple beat. "Gotta go," I said. "I'll prepare a report when I have some information."

"You're on my dime now, so get busy."

I hung up without responding. I didn't trust myself not to be snarky. Besides, someone was in the front parlor of Dahlia House and I had to find out who it was. I eased to the front parlor and stopped.

"How would you like to spend your wedding night with a bullfrog?"

Endora, the witch and mother of Samantha from one of my favorite old TV shows, *Bewitched*, stood at the wet bar making a dirty vodka martini. Her chartreuse gossamer dress floated around her as she walked toward me. "That Darren was such a namby-pamby, but Coleman Peters, now he could get my broomstick in high gear. You'd better jump on that ride and shout hallelujah before some other woman snatches up the goods."

I knew exactly who stood in my parlor. "Jitty, you are death to romance." I walked past her and made myself a Jack and water. I needed it. To heck with the fact it was barely noon. I'd fallen into a pit with a juvenile delinquent, interviewed witches, and dealt with Kitten Fontana. I deserved a drink.

"A little early in the day for hard liquor, wouldn't you say?" Endora asked as she raised her martini glass in a toast and then drained it. I had to admire her upswept hairdo. It was lacquered into place. I was reminded of some fashion tips I'd read in magazines from the fifties—women were advised to wrap their hairdos in toilet tissue at night so they didn't get messed up.

"What was that in your hand?" I indicated the martini glass. "Distilled water?"

"I'm a witch. And I'm dead. I'm impervious to the effects of alcohol."

"Remind me never to die. Alcohol is the only tonic that allows me to put up with you." I didn't bother to hide my sarcasm.

"Time is marching right over you," Endora said. "Have you noticed your earlobes are bigger? You realize your nose and earlobes keep growing until you die. Then in the coffin, your hair and fingernails grow and curl."

"What tangent are you on?" She was truly driving me mad. I didn't want those images in my head. "I can avoid all of this by donating my body to science."

"That might be the only chance your body has to do a good deed. You act like a cloistered nun. When you gonna jump that man's bones and seal the deal?" As she talked, she slowly shifted from Endora to Jitty.

"Couldn't keep up the classy witchy act for long, could you?" I had to get rid of her. Coleman was on the way over, and if I had my druthers, we'd say our hellos while doing the horizontal mambo. Jitty was always gigging me because I couldn't get laid, but the truth was, Coleman and I were both willing. It was the rest of the world—Jitty included—that wouldn't cooperate. Folks wouldn't give us an hour of peace so we might get our locomotion going. And the idea that Jitty might be sneaking a peek at us was enough to shrivel my desire.

"I promise to leave you alone." She grinned as if she'd read my thoughts.

"I'm not sure I believe you." I swallowed half my drink.

"You have my word of honor. If you get that man in your bedroom, I won't peek. I'll even guard the door from your partner. That last encounter was a fiasco."

She was right about that. "Coleman is on the way over now."

Jitty swirled around, her dress a green blur, and she was gone.

Had I known getting rid of her would be that easy, I might have backed off the drink. But it was too late now. I finished it off just as Coleman's cruiser pulled into my front drive. When he got out of the car, my heart pounded so hard I thought for sure the house would vibrate. It wasn't just sex, though I'd anticipated making love with Coleman for so long now that I thought I might burst into flames at the very idea of it. Taking this step was a journey from which there was no backtracking. If the romance failed, the friendship would die. I didn't know if I could face my life without Coleman in it, even if it was only as a friend.

I heard his tread on the front steps. He crossed the porch and paused to examine the claw marks. I opened the door. For a moment, looking into his blue eyes, I couldn't breathe. And then it didn't matter. I was in his arms, swept away by his kiss.

We'd learned our lesson about unlocked doors, and even though Tinkie had a key I knew she wouldn't use it if she saw the patrol car in the drive. I locked the door anyway. Taking Coleman's hand, I led him up the stairs to my bedroom. There wasn't a single sign of Jitty. There was nothing or no one to interfere.

I still had my doubts, but more compelling were my needs. I loved Coleman. Given a chance, that love would grow and expand in many directions. I had no doubt, though, that he was a man who could match me, season for season. This was the second chance I'd been offered, and I meant to take it.

Our last thwarted encounter had been hot, delirious, and deliciously frantic. This time, I set the pace at a crawl. Button by button, I undid his starched shirt. "One of the things I love about you is this shirt," I told him. "I can smell sunshine and my childhood whenever you're close. It reminds me of a time when I was safe and the days stretched out before me like a golden path. You were a part of that, though most days I thought you were more of an annoyance than an asset."

He kissed my fingers and then his lips moved to my neck. "I always knew you'd eventually see me in a romantic light."

Of all the men in my life, Coleman connected me to the past and to the land. Those were places where my heart dwelled, places where Coleman's smile lingered and I could still hear his laughter on a riverbank as the sun set. We'd grown up riding horses and cruising in convertibles with the radio blaring. He'd known my parents, and the circumstances that had stolen them from me. He'd been at their funeral, a lanky teenage boy who hadn't tried to comfort me with empty words.

I'd loved Coleman for as long as I could remember. A deep love forged in a time and place that had vanished from the Delta I loved with my entire soul. Now, we were taking that love into the future. Would it be strong enough to sustain us? Only time would tell.

I kissed him, letting him know how much I hungered for him. When he picked me up and put me on the bed, I was done with the teasing and tantalizing. I wanted to make love without delay.

He'd just unbuckled his pants and slid out of them when both of our cell phones began to ring.

"No." I grabbed his phone and mine and tossed them under the bed. "Whatever it is can wait for half an hour."

"Damn straight." He unzipped my jeans and pulled them down my body in one swift motion. My shirt and bra followed. "You're a beautiful woman, Sarah Booth."

I felt as shy as a maiden as I held out my arms to him. We kissed and whatever worries I'd had a half hour before disappeared. There was only Coleman's touch, our bodies skin to skin.

Outside the door Sweetie Pie set up a raucous howl and several car horns began to blare.

"What the devil?" Coleman had great powers of concentration but neither of us could ignore the fray. Coleman walked to the window and peeked out the curtains. I was treated to an extraordinary view of a fit man in the prime of his life.

"Quit staring," he said, without even looking at me.

"Quit posing," I replied.

"Hellfire, DeWayne is coming around the house to try the backdoor."

That motivated me to jump from the bed and find my jeans. "I can't believe this is happening," I said. "We are cursed."

Coleman picked up his clothes and dressed in silence. "Saturday night, have a bag packed. We're going to Memphis where no one can find us."

"It's a date," I said as I pulled my shirt down. Together we walked down the stairs and to the front door. When we pulled it open, Tinkie and DeWayne were waiting for us.

"Sorry," DeWayne mumbled, though he couldn't stop grinning. "There's a protest against the Wiccan school brewing. A busload of protesters are on the way out to Musgrove Manor to picket."

"You have got to be kidding me," Coleman

said. “Do we really care if people protest? It’s a First Amendment right.”

“Alvin from the pawn shop said some of the protesters were in there buying paint guns and ammo. Some had real guns.”

Coleman sighed. “If they take any aggressive action, we’re going to arrest them and they’re going to jail. We’ll hold them as long as we can.”

“I’ll meet you at Musgrove Manor,” DeWayne said, turning back to his car. As he passed Tinkie, she gave him a high five. Coleman followed DeWayne, giving Tinkie the stink eye.

When the lawmen were gone, I cast a long look at my partner. “You really don’t want me to consummate this relationship, do you?”

“Honey, I do. But you have the worst timing on the planet. Did you ever consider making love when the sun has gone down—not in the middle of a workday?”

“I thought you were more of a ‘strike while the iron is hot’ kind of gal. And if you’re going to get pregnant, you and Oscar are going to have to put in some time making love.”

“I got my booty call.” Tinkie was full of herself. “In Oscar’s office. At the bank! Oscar may not approve of the idea of a spell cast by witches, but he is certainly not opposed to a little hot action on his desktop.”

“Your daddy would fire him and disown you.” I was shocked. I couldn’t help it. Proper ladies didn't have sex on the bank president's desk—even if they were married. And Tinkie was the leading lady of the Delta, the Number One Daddy's Girl, the keeper of the rulebook.

"You're just jealous." Her laughter was like tinkling bells. Whatever she'd gotten from Oscar had put her in a delightful mood. "Let's go to Musgrove Manor. You won't be getting any loving from Coleman and I want to see who shows up at the protest."

She was right. Any chance of *amore* had fled. Again. We might as well indulge our curiosity, and I needed to gather some info to earn another paycheck from Kitten. I rounded up the critters and stopped at the front door. Gone was the ugly rental car and in its place a Chinese red Cadillac touring sedan. Oscar had pulled some strings to get one for Tinkie to try out, and it was a five-star beauty. Whatever she'd done on the desktop, Oscar had gotten busy finding this car for her.

We tore down the road to Musgrove Manor and arrived just as a busload of people unloaded in front of Pandora's Box, the gift shop the Harringtons had opened. The protesters, many of them carrying signs saying witches go home, or ban witchcraft, or no spellcasting here picketed in front of the gift shop. I recognized a few of the local townspeople who either didn't have jobs or who might be on the protest organizer's payroll. That would be one Kitten Fontana, who sported a T-shirt that said witches must die. At her side was Esmeralda Grimes.

"This could get ugly," I said, calling Cece at the newspaper. When she answered, I told her what was happening. "Pick up Millie, please. She can't miss this." Millie would be heartbroken if she missed the scandalous fun. She'd love this showdown.

"Roger that, Local Gumshoe."

"What's going on?" I asked.

"Just trying out some old CB talk. I figured that would have been your handle, *if* you'd had a CB radio."

"That's a really big if, as in not ever. Cece, I really don't want to know how your mind works. Just step on it and get over to the old dairy. Bring a photographer."

"Ten-four, Big Mama."

Tinkie and I parked a good distance away and walked to the manor house, where the three sisters were sitting on the steps. They wore wicked little flirty skirts, black hose, pointed shoes, and black-and-white polka-dot sweaters. They were high-fashion witches.

"What's going on?" Hope asked us.

"Apparently, Kitten has organized a protest against you."

"For what? We haven't done anything." Hope's mouth quirked up. "Yet. But tonight we're planning on a moon dance."

"To what end?" I asked.

"To honor the Goddess and the full moon. It's a time when women are in their power. Hecate shines on all of us, influencing the tides, our cycles, the seasons. It's all about the power of women. You should join us."

"I'll be there," Tinkie said. "I'm feeling very feminine and very powerful."

"And soon you'll be very pregnant," Faith said.

"I know. I can't wait."

Tinkie's certainty was like a spike in my heart. She was bound to get hurt with this foolishness about fertility spells. Before we left the property, I'd have a talk with Faith. It was one thing to play at being witches and wear sexy little outfits and sell lavender-scented potions and concoctions in colored bottles designed to bring love into a lonely person's heart. It was something else to promise my partner a baby.

"It might be wiser to hold off on moon ceremonies until Kitten Fontana simmers down." I wanted to word my warning a lot stronger, but I realized I was spitting in the wind. These sisters were going to do whatever they wanted and the consequences be damned. It was almost as if they were flaunting their beliefs in the hopes of starting trench warfare.

"We aren't harming anyone."

Except maybe my partner, if she got her hopes up over a baby she'd never be able to conceive.

"Doesn't matter. You can have all the rights in the world, but if you stir up some of the people who are afraid of you, you're still going to pay the price. Let things calm down. Or hold your ceremonies privately."

"Part of our reason for coming to this community is to teach the people here about what the Wiccan religion really is. We don't consort with Satan or hurt people. We're all about respecting others and caring for Mother Earth. How can anyone view that as harmful?" Hope's passion was easy to see.

"None of that matters if you're hurt or dead. There are people in this county who are terrified of anything other than exactly what they knew growing up. You need to excite their curiosity first. Make them want to know about you. Knocking them over the head with it won't help you." I was shocked at my reasonable argument, because I understood Hope's point. She was free to practice her religion. That was what America was all about. But it couldn't raise her from the dead if someone killed her, and I doubted if magic would be helpful in such a case.

"People don't change unless they're forced to," Charity said. Her big blue eyes misted over. "Why can't people just try to get to know us?"

I shook my head. The answer was way too

complex for me. I didn't have a chance to answer anyway. The protesters came marching down the driveway, chanting "Witches Go Home."

"Should I call the law and have them removed?" Tinkie had her phone in hand. "They are trespassing."

"Let them get it out of their system," Faith said. "We aren't afraid of them."

I herded the sisters into the house and called Coleman to come watch over the protesters to make sure they stayed orderly. When I closed the front door, I had a question for the Harringtons. It went to the financial aspect of the Harringtons and their school. "What does Trevor think about all of this?"

"He's up on the third floor," Charity said. "He may not be paying attention. When he's in the middle of a painting, he forgets to eat. He's seriously involved in his art. The project he's working on now is so interesting. Nude women as tree trunks. Eerie and exquisitely beautiful. He contours the wood grain to give the women their curves and shapes. Who knew a cedar trunk could be so sensual?"

"Let's go talk to him," I said to Tinkie.

"You go. I'll get some info from Faith, Hope, and Charity about their school and such."

More like she'd get another spell or potion or enchantment for her baby. But I couldn't stop her and I had work to do. If I could find out how the Harringtons were funding their school and the purchase of the dairy and acreage, I'd have something to report to Kitten. The sooner I found information, the quicker I was done with Queen Fontana.

4

The Musgrove Manor staircase was dark mahogany with a dragon motif carved into the banister and railings. I had to admit it was perfect for a witch school, very Harry Potter. The house had elegant and Gothic touches throughout, and I would have enjoyed walking around exploring if I'd had more time.

At the third floor, I was filled with a sense of foreboding so strong I halted. The landing was furnished with a comfortable-looking sofa and two chairs. The lighting was soft but serviceable. There was no reason for the sense of dread that filled me. And then I heard it. The soft scrabbling sound of something moving down the hallway behind a closed door. Toenails on wood. The hair on my arms stood on end. Was this the creature that had scored my front door?

"Mr. Musgrove." I had to force his name out past my fear. "Mr. Musgrove?" I hadn't really spoken to the eccentric artist since a long-ago school visit to the dairy. He'd been wildly handsome—dark and brooding, like a proper hero.

The door closest to me burst open and a handsome man in a beautiful paisley silk smoking jacket and tailored black slacks popped out at me. "Who might you be?" He sized me up. "I don't have a model coming today, but I can work you in." He grabbed my arm and pulled me into the room he'd come from, which turned out to be his bedroom.

The unkempt bed and the empty wine bottles on the floor told a familiar story. One that warned me to watch my step. Trevor Musgrove was a very handsome older man in his late fifties, and he had a well-earned reputation as a lothario.

Torn between a confrontation with a tipsy artist and whatever I had sensed in the hallway, I decided to take my chances with Trevor. He was a seducer, not a rapist. "Would you mind answering a few questions?"

"Would you care for a glass of wine?" he asked.

"No thanks, Mr. Musgrove. I'm working." I tried not to sound prim and proper but I wasn't certain I was successful.

"What kind of questions?" He found a corked bottle on the floor and filled a Waterford Crystal wineglass. He was a study in contradiction of sloth and taste.

"About your property here. What made you decide to sell it?"

"I've exhausted the area women willing to

model. I want to end my days in a big city, in a place with . . . amenities like good health care and clean air. I have no heirs, that I know of. No one to carry on the Musgrove name. I might as well enjoy spending my last years as I wish. Yes, a big city calls to me."

"New York?" I asked.

"Heaven's no. Stockholm. Or perhaps Copenhagen."

"You're going to move there?" I was a little surprised. I didn't often hear of Delta residents moving to Scandinavia, but he had a point. Best health care and education systems, and a terrific support network for artists.

"I need a new perspective. The land here is lush and so . . . humid. I thought perhaps a cold climate would give me new ideas for my paintings."

I didn't really understand. The bedroom walls were covered in fantastic paintings of nude women in various poses. I wasn't an art critic but I could see the paintings were rich in detail and the earthy colors of the Delta. The landscape was as sensuous as the female models. "But you paint nudes." Stating the obvious was a talent of mine.

He glanced around the room. "My summer series. Their bodies are as generous and fertile as the Delta soil. That was my inspiration. I wonder how I'll view the human form in a frozen terrain."

Trevor's take on his art was fascinating and I really would have liked a chance to study the paintings to see which of his models I knew, but I'd come for financial information. And I was worried about what Tinkie might be getting into. The witches seemed to have co-opted her reasoning ability.

"Have you signed a contract on the dairy with the Harrington sisters?"

"There was a time when a gentleman's handshake was enough." Trevor was savvy like a fox.

"So true, but I doubt three businesswomen would begin renovations without a contract."

He smiled. "They're very pretty, aren't they? Each one exquisite."

"Mr. Musgrove, Trevor, this could really help me on my case."

"Sorry; poking into my business shouldn't be your case."

Well said. "You could have sold the property long ago for development. I've heard Bob Fontana has been hot to buy it for years. Golf course, exclusive subdivision, a real appeal to the upper crust, and close enough to Ole Miss for football games and alumni functions."

He shrugged. "Golf doesn't interest me. Our educational system needs a shake-up, and if the Harringtons can get state vouchers for their school, that will give people something to think about. Vouchers are an attack on the public school system, but if the state is going down that road, then I want to be sure there are diverse schools for students to choose from. Those witchy women are going to stir the pot. Or the cauldron." He chuckled.

"Yes, indeed they are. And some of the people getting stirred are protesting right outside this manor."

He flicked his fingers. "Let the gnats buzz."

"If you'd confirm the details of the sale of the property—"

"It's no one's business but mine if I gave them the property." He refilled his wineglass. Holding the bottle, he nodded toward a door. "Step into my studio."

Curiosity made me fall in behind him. And when he opened the door onto the long room with a vaulted-glass ceiling, I couldn't stop the sharp intake of breath. The room was stunning, filled with winter light. The view was of well-maintained pastures still in hues of brown and tan, but soon the spring would turn the vista green. I could see his inspiration for the summer series.

Once I'd had my fill of the view, I turned to the paintings that lined the back wall. I noticed several of my former classmates—who were married to prominent businessmen. Many were women I didn't know. All were magnificent.

"Let me paint you," Trevor said. He'd filled a

glass with wine and handed it to me. My fingers closed around it of their own volition.

"I'm not a model." And I had no intention of taking my clothes off.

"It's an experience every beautiful woman should have. To model for a man who appreciates the female form. I paint my models as goddesses."

And he did. Gazing on his paintings, I saw a total appreciation of the female form in all of its varieties. The women were sirens, seductresses, femmes who owned their power.

"I'm really here to ask some questions."

"Which I don't intend to answer." He stared unflinchingly at me. "It's no one's business."

"It's my job, Trevor."

"Posh and fuddletops. I'm not answering. Think about modeling. My paintings sell mostly in Europe. My religious icon series sold at well over six figures a painting. You might grace the wall of a Swiss château or a villa in Italy. Your bone structure is so . . . the way the light strikes the planes of your face." His smile revealed the true source of his seductive ability. He liked women and he loved painting them. He was almost irresistible. Almost.

"Thank you for your time. You're a talented painter." I put my wineglass down, untouched, and found the door to the hallway by the stairs. Whatever presence I'd felt earlier was gone, but

I noticed claw marks on the floor that I didn't recall seeing. I hurried down the stairs to find my partner sitting in a chair surrounded by the three sisters. They were chanting something and blowing aromatic smoke onto her.

I'd arrived not a moment too soon.

I ran into the huddle like a linebacker and snatched Tinkie out of her chair. "We're going home."

"It's fine," Faith said. "We're done." She turned her full attention to Tinkie. "Within three days you'll conceive, if you make love with a virile man."

"Oscar's fine. We've had his sperm count checked," Tinkie said matter-of-factly. "The problem is me. There was scarring."

"And that problem is resolved." Faith radiated confidence.

I gave them all a mean glare and took Tinkie's arm. "We have to go."

Without further conversation, Tinkie and I left the manor. Outside, the protesters had dispersed and Cece had returned to the newspaper after snapping a few photos. Coleman, strangely, had never shown up.

Tinkie freed her arm from my grip and faced me. "The Harringtons told me they came to Mississippi with a nest egg to put into the school. It had to be a considerable sum, maybe an inheritance." She'd done her work toward finding the answers Kitten wanted. "Sarah Booth, you have to stop treating me like a child," she said. "I'm capable of managing my own life."

"Tinkie, I can't stand to see you get hurt."

"And you have no right to interfere. I mean it. Back off." She didn't wait for a response but went to her car and drove away.

The protest march of the anti-witch forces had been short-lived, but the day was bitter cold and since the sisters didn't come outside for the hecklers to torment, the event had turned boring. I wasn't worried at all that the witches would be run out of town by Kitten and her cohorts. My concern rested squarely on my partner's heart and how easily it could be broken by false hopes.

After Tinkie's abrupt departure, I loaded the critters up in my car and made a beeline for the bank. I wanted a word with Oscar about Tinkie, and I also needed a moment's consultation with Harold Erkwell, a man I cared greatly for.

Before I went to the bank, I stopped at Millie's Café. I ran in and ordered a hamburger steak and broiled catfish to-go for Sweetie and Pluto. Because my pants were tight, I got a chicken salad plate for myself. I ate at the counter and talked to Millie while the kitchen made the food for my pets. As I predicted, Millie was agog at the fact Esmeralda Grimes was in town, and thrilled at the prospect that the witch sisters had resurrected Elvis. She let me know that the protest had been a dud. "Cece and I got there and snapped maybe three photos and then everyone packed it in and left. What kind of protesters do that? They don't have any grit or perseverance. They're just pantywaist protesters."

"I'm just glad they didn't shoot the witches."

"I'd really hoped to see Elvis," Millie said with a measure of wistfulness. "You can't imagine the impact Elvis had on my aunts and older cousins. He was this rebel, this handsome boy who gave people Cadillacs because he could, this sexy man who treated women like princesses. And he could sing in a way that made shivers run over their bodies. I think every one of them was in love with him."

Millie had swept me up in her memories. The King of Rock and Roll had captured my mother's heart, too. "He was a handsome man," I agreed. Every Mississippi girl had at one time or another fallen for Elvis. He'd been an icon for another generation, but his charm and legendary kindness still lived on, forty years after his death. "My mother taught me to dance playing his records."

"If those witches could really bring Elvis back, maybe he could push Mississippi into the future."

"Maybe." Millie believed her idols were capable of all kinds of magic. Who was I to step on her dreams?

"Do you think you could set up an appointment for me with the witches?"

I turned my head so fast I almost got whiplash. "You? Why?"

"I have some important decisions coming up in my life. I might need some assistance."

"Millie, surely you wouldn't trust your future to three women who pretend to be witches?" I couldn't believe it. Maybe Kitten and the Anti-Satan League had a point. Everyone in town was acting like a spell had been cast over them.

"How do you know they're pretend witches?"

I didn't have evidence one way or the other. Yet. "I'll find proof. And then you and Tinkie can snap out of it. If Tinkie doesn't get pregnant, her heart is going to break. All of that because those women are playacting." I sounded hot and I was. I picked up the to-go order and prepared to leave. "If you care about Tinkie, don't encourage her to believe this foolishness. And please don't tell her you're thinking of going to the Harringtons for advice."

"I won't. I'd never do anything to harm Tinkie."

I felt a rush of remorse. "I know you wouldn't. I'm just worried sick that she's going to realize this is all pretend and then she's going to grieve all over again about a baby."

Millie nodded. "You're right about that. If she doesn't get pregnant, it's going to be bad."

• • •

Oscar shared my concern about Tinkie's investment in a magic potion to guarantee pregnancy, but his long years of marriage had taught him a valuable lesson—sometimes he had to step back and let things play out.

"I can't forbid her from believing something," he said. "Belief and faith, Sarah Booth, they can't be conquered by rational thought. That's why so many people believe some crazy things."

He was right. No argument. "So how do we minimize the damage?"

"We remind her how much we love her, and we make her remember how worthwhile life was before this unrealistic obsession cropped up." He pushed back from the huge desk he sat behind and stood up. I had to work hard not to visualize Tinkie and Oscar working their mojo on top of that desk. He continued talking. "I'll do everything I can to try to convince Trevor to abandon this sale of the property to the Harringtons. Trevor is notoriously hardheaded and eccentric."

So, Oscar wasn't as Zen as I'd feared. His method of helping Tinkie involved getting the witches to move on down the road. "Right. If the witches leave town, maybe we can minimize the damage. Tinkie said the witches had come into some inheritance. Have you heard anything about their funding?"

"They haven't opened an account here."

That was as much as I would get from Oscar, but it was at least a fact I could trust.

"Maybe you can have some sway with Trevor. That property is worth a fortune. I just don't see how three women selling salves, potions, and spells could come up with the funding. Maybe they will move on."

"For now, that's the plan."

I left Oscar's office and stopped by Harold's. The décor reflected my friend's artistic interests. Harold bought a lot of local art to support potters and painters, and his walls and shelves were covered in interesting work. I could have spent four hours just examining everything he'd collected, but I'd come for a different reason.

"Sarah Booth!" The anticipation faded from his features. "I gather you haven't come to tell me I've finally won your heart."

He could read me like a first-grade primer, and I got right to the point. "I'm going to give Coleman a chance." Harold and I had flirted on and off for the past two years. No one could have asked for a better friend, and though he'd made it clear he wanted more, he'd respected my boundaries. Of all my suitors, he knew me—and accepted me, warts and all.

"I see." When he smiled, I felt my heart crack a little. "Coleman is a good man. I've known all along you had unfinished business with him. I think it's best to resolve that."

He was one of the most generous and kind men I'd ever known. "Thank you."

"You deserve everything, Sarah Booth. Don't settle for less."

"I won't."

He motioned me to a chair. "I'm worried about Tinkie."

"I was just here to speak to Oscar about the whole . . . baby thing."

"I saw her down at the baby boutique. Remember when she kept the little redheaded baby and bought everything in the store for her?"

I nodded. I remembered that very well. Tinkie almost fled the country with the infant she'd named after my mother, Libby.

"She's doing it again. She's so certain she's going to have a baby she's refurbishing the nursery at her house. Oscar can't reason with her."

"Do you have a suggestion?" Harold loved Tinkie as much as I did.

He shook his head. "Tinkie is one of the smartest, most reasonable people on the planet. It's only on this subject that she can veer off the rails in a big way. I only know we have to help her."

"Has the sale of the Musgrove dairy gone through or do you know?"

"My understanding is that Trevor and the

Harrington sisters had an agreement drawn up by a lawyer and signed. There's been no financing through the bank, but they could have used any number of financial institutions."

"Do you know any local lawyers who drew up the paperwork?"

"I've mentioned it to several, just in casual conversation. As far as I can tell, neither Trevor nor the witches have hired any of them to do this."

"Is zoning at the dairy good for a boarding school?"

"It is. As far as I can tell, the sisters have crossed every *t* and dotted every *i* in regard to state laws for an educational facility. The only hitch I can see is the community reaction to a Wiccan school. Most people don't have a clue what Wicca really is—they're opposed on the surface. They associate Wicca practitioners with the old witches from movies, fairy tales, and Halloween stories. The spell casters who try to destroy the fair princess."

"It's very easy to stampede people into fear." As much as I loathed the idea of using fear to run the Harringtons out of town, I had to protect my partner.

"You can't do that, Sarah Booth. Not even to save Tinkie."

Sometimes Harold was a better conscience than even Jitty. "I have to do something."

"You can't use people's ignorance and fear against those women."

I sighed. I could, but I wouldn't. My father had taught me better than that. James Franklin Delaney had been a man who believed in Justice with a capital *J.* The Harringtons had as much right to live in Sunflower County and open their school as I did. It wasn't the Harringtons who were dangerous but my partner's expectations.

"You're right. That would be unethical."

"And possibly immoral." Harold's smile took the sting out of his response. "Look, Tinkie has to deal with her issues of infertility once and for all. This is an opportunity for her to do that."

"It could break her." I clearly saw the risks.

"Don't underestimate Tinkie. She's powerful and strong. And deep down, she knows a potion or spell or enchantment can't give her a baby."

He was right, but it didn't make it any easier for me to watch this play out. "Do you know anything about the Harringtons? Kitten has hired me to dig into their finances, and since I can't find anything current, I need to excavate their past."

"They lived in Lafayette, Louisiana. That's what I know. They ran a Montessori school is the gossip I heard. Why not check with the State Department of Education there?"

"Genius." I stood. "Thank you, Harold. I never

underestimate what your friendship means to me."

"I love you, Sarah Booth. I can love you as a friend. I don't want to lose that."

When I walked out the door I wondered if I'd ever known a smarter man.

5

My thoughts were on internet investigative techniques when I turned down the driveway to Dahlia House. To my surprise, Pluto put his front paws on the Roadster's dash and bristled like a porcupine. Sweetie Pie, too, sat up and stared toward the house, which was visible through the bare limbs of the sycamore trees that flanked our path.

"What's going on with you two?" As I drew closer, I didn't see any vehicle in the drive that might support such animosity from my pets. But they were clever animals, and I had learned not to discount their reactions.

I stopped at the front steps and got out slowly, moving to the trunk of the car to get my pistol. Tinkie was by far the better shot, but I knew how to use a firearm and I would protect myself. The animals raced up the steps and Sweetie Pie started howling and barking at the front door. Pluto arched his back and danced sideways, as if an enemy were near.

The beautiful wood had earlier been scored with claw marks, and a tremor of foreboding shot though me. What in the hell was running loose all over Sunflower County? But the damaged wood wasn't the worst. My front door, which I knew I'd locked, stood open. A chill raced up my back and I felt again the dread that had swept over me in the woods at the dairy. "There's no such thing as a witch," I said aloud.

"Deny not what your eyes witness."

The voice came from behind me and I almost tripped over Sweetie Pie as I whirled around to confront the Red Witch of child burning, wars, demonic impregnation, and other horrors from the TV show, *Game of Thrones*.

"Melisandre," I whispered. Her ambitions knew no bounds.

"We all must choose. Man or woman, young or old, lord or peasant, our choices are the same. We choose light or we choose darkness."

In the February sunlight on my front porch in the Mississippi Delta, the Red Witch held me in a trance. I couldn't move. Sweetie and Pluto were caught in the same spell.

"Witches aren't real," I said.

"Explain real. Reality is but perception." She clutched the necklace of red stones at her throat. "Am I old? What do you perceive?"

"You need to leave." At last I'd found my tongue. And my spine. "Get off my property."

She brushed a hand over the gouges on my door. "And leave you alone with this?"

The hint of a slow Southern drawl had crept into her voice.

"Jitty! Damn it." Relief flooded through me and with it a desire to slug her. She'd truly scared me. The whole witch thing—built on top of my fear of Margaret Hamilton as the green witch in Dorothy's Oz—had really gotten to me.

Slowly Melisandre morphed into Jitty, who still wore the red gown and necklace. She was even more beautiful than the television Red Witch.

"Why are you scaring me?" I asked. "Who's been in the house?" Gun at the ready, I stepped inside. Dahlia House was still and quiet. If anyone had been there, nothing was disturbed, but I did a quick tour, checking empty rooms and closets. Jitty was on my heels the whole way, with Sweetie Pie and Pluto in line like ducklings. "You should guard Dahlia House while I'm away." Jitty needed a job.

"Nobody has been here," she insisted.

But the open door was a contradiction of that fact. I'd locked it, yet it was open. It made me doubt my own actions—and my memory. "Are you sure?"

"No livin' person has been here. Can't say about anything else."

That wasn't very comforting.

Jitty continued. "You have to stay alert, Sarah

Booth. There are worlds beyond the one you know. Fantastical worlds. For those who believe, the rules of your reality don't apply."

"Are you telling me those Harrington women are real witches and they sent something over here that went into my house?"

"I'm tellin' you to consider the implications."

I took a step back—literally and figuratively. Jitty was pushy, demanding, annoying, and downright troublesome. But she loved me. "If those women have real powers . . ." The possibilities were scary. For Sunflower County, but also for Tinkie. Call me superstitious, but I was a big believer that gifts from the dark side always came at a terrible price.

I put in a call to Coleman and left a voice message inviting him to drop by. I'd tell him about the open door when he arrived, and this time he couldn't accuse me of not keeping him informed of dangerous situations. When darkness fell over Dahlia House, it might be nice to have two-hundred-plus pounds of muscle and bone in bed beside me.

I went to the Delaney Detective Agency office in the wing off the music room and called Tinkie. She didn't answer. She always answered. This did not bode well. She must be really mad at me. I sat down at my computer and went to work on tracking down the Harringtons' past lives. It didn't take long to find newspaper stories about the Montessori school in Lafayette. Though the reviews of the school were mostly five star and some parents raved about the wonderful education the two sisters gave, there were articles of protests. Also, only Hope and Charity were involved with the school. There was no mention of Faith.

I called the Lafayette newspaper and spoke with Cheri Sistrunk, who'd reported on the school. As it turned out, Cheri's daughter had been enrolled and she had nothing negative to say about the school or the Harringtons' approach to education. "Hope and Charity hold teaching degrees from a major university. They followed all the health-code rules. They taught my daughter more in two years than she's learned in the public schools since."

"And the third sister, Faith?" I asked.

"She wasn't involved in the school. It was just the two."

"Do you know why they left Lafayette and moved to Mississippi?"

"Not for a fact, but there was a rumor."

Rumors were notoriously unreliable, but I wanted to know. "Please."

"An inheritance. I don't know how much or from where, but they were supposed to come into some money."

That was interesting and useful, actually, since it spoke directly to their financial situation and also confirmed another rumor I'd heard. "What kind of inheritance?"

"Just a lot of money. I know the Montessori school didn't bring in big bucks. Their tuition was very reasonable. But I heard they'd bought an extensive property in Mississippi, so it had to be a nice bundle of cash."

She made good sense. If the witches bought the property outright, all it would require would be a deed transfer. "But why did the sisters relocate to Mississippi?"

"I assumed it was for the property. And to get away from hurricanes and flooding. Lord knows I wouldn't mind moving inland."

She had a point. "Do you happen to know how they found out about Musgrove Manor in Sunflower County? I mean the place was never advertised for sale, and most people aren't driving around the Delta looking for a piece of property."

"Hope was excited about the prospects for her boarding school. She said Mississippi had the easiest route to getting state vouchers for private schools. From what she said there are hundreds of private religious schools and home-schooling agencies, and in Mississippi almost anyone qualifies to get state funds through the voucher system. Freedom of choice is more important than quality education."

It sounded almost as if the Harringtons had set

out to game the voucher system. Almost. And that wasn't a crime. Plenty of other people did it.

"But you said the Harringtons provided a quality education."

"Oh my, yes. I didn't mean to imply otherwise. They are fabulous teachers and, even with the little ones, they made connections between the world today, the past, and the future, in science, history, geology—you name it. I'm actually thinking of sending my two children over to Mississippi next fall. That's how great I think they are."

A high recommendation—unless there was more to the situation than met the eye. I'd known a few kids who had been shipped off to boarding schools and education wasn't the reason. Distance was. The parents wanted the kids as far away as possible.

"The whole Wiccan thing doesn't bother you?"

Cheri laughed. "I grew up in an area where people go to *traiteurs* for healing. Some areas practice voodoo, which is also a misunderstood religion. If everyone in the world practiced Wicca, we wouldn't be fracking and mining and destroying the balance of nature. I have no problems at all with what the Harringtons teach. I hope my children learn and become part of the solution, not more of the problem."

Someone had really drunk the Kool-Aid. Or been enchanted with a spell. That thought was like a shadow passing across the sun. Was it possible the witches had powers? I had a vision of Sunflower County with all of the residents smiling and agreeable as they went about their daily chores. I pictured an elegant Victorian house in the middle of town. Ensconced in a turret was Bette Davis. The young people of town paraded down the street, and she watched them. As she looked out the window, she picked the sacrifices for the next harvest ceremony.

I snapped myself out of it. Yeah, I'd watched way too many horror shows and *The Dark Secret of Harvest Home* was another favorite.

"Ms. Delaney, do you have any other questions?" Cheri was ready to get back to her day.

"Not for the moment. May I call again if I do?"

"Absolutely. And give Hope and Charity a hello from me. I'm sure once you get to know them, all of your fears will be set aside."

The next few hours zoomed by as I navigated old reports of strange behavior and the history of the Harrington sisters, who claimed to come from a long line of witches.

I found only one incident of negative publicity, where Hope Harrington was accused of stealing another woman's husband. It was a lawsuit filed in the Evangeline, Louisiana, civil court. The small town was several parishes over from Lafayette. In the divorce proceedings, Lurleen

St. Pe named Hope as a co-respondent in her suit against Kenny St. Pe.

The interesting part was that Lurleen had claimed that Hope put a spell on her husband and forced him to be unfaithful. I could imagine the shock value of that trial, and I saw that the date came only six months before the sisters moved to Mississippi. The timeline began to make a lot more sense.

I called Tinkie again. Still no answer. Now anger began to mingle with my concern. If Tinkie wanted to shut off our friendship, she could at least tell me to my face. There was no help for it. I was going to have to drive to Hilltop and confront her. We'd had disagreements in the past, but Tinkie had never shut me out of her life in this way. I couldn't let it continue.

My fingers grasped the car keys when the phone rang. Relief! I answered instantly and the voice on the other end was like a slap.

"Trevor Musgrove is missing. Those witches have done something to him and it's on you. You should have found something to run them out of town." Kitten Fontana was practically spitting with fury.

"How do you know Trevor's missing?" I asked.

"He missed an important appointment with me, and I have my sources, which obviously you do not. What kind of private investigator doesn't have any good sources?"

"The kind who's going to quit if you keep being a bitch." I needed the money, but not enough to take Kitten's claws.

"Find out where Trevor is." Kitten hung up. I couldn't help but wonder what kind of appointment Kitten might have had with Trevor—probably trying to buy the manor and land out from under the witches. If she was telling the truth, which I'd give a fifty-fifty chance.

I picked up my keys and headed out the door. My fingers were dialing Coleman on the cell phone as I walked. What was going on with my friends? Tinkie was dodging me and Coleman had failed to appear.

"I haven't forgotten you." Coleman answered his phone with a statement that made my heart pulse.

"What's going on?"

"Kitten Fontana says the witches have murdered Trevor Musgrove to get his property."

"I know. She called me, too. She wouldn't say how she knew Trevor was missing, only that he'd missed an appointment." Kitten had a way of co-opting the "truth" as her own version of reality.

"I have to check it out; it's my job." Coleman didn't sound enthused. "He's probably up in that attic painting away."

"I'll meet you there." It seemed if I wanted Coleman time, I was going to have to find a way to see him on the job. Jitty's lascivious recommendations came to me and I felt heat creep up my neck. I was ready to take the action to the front seat of the patrol car, if necessary.

"Maybe afterward we can take a ride over to the river." Coleman managed to keep his voice innocent.

The thrill of a possible high school make-out session left me breathless. "Going to the river" had been code for those long, intense sessions of kissing and longing that every Delta teenager knew so well. If we were ever to have some alone time, it was obvious we were going to have to find it away from my house. Our rendezvous at Dahlia House seemed cursed.

The minute I thought the word, a darkness passed over me. Damn. The witches were working on me and I knew better!

"See you there," I said to Coleman and ran across the porch to the steps. Sweetie Pie and Pluto weren't going to be left behind, and I was glad for their company. I was surprised to see the day had slipped away from me. I'd been so absorbed in the witches that I'd lost all awareness of time. Now the sun was setting, and along the western horizon a bank of clouds was limned in pinkish gold. Another Cecil B. DeMille moment of gorgeous Delta landscapes. And still no word from my partner.

The weather had been cold and dry, a true relief

from the swelter of summer. But if rain came, February could be a brutal month for livestock and those who worked outdoors. I stopped along the drive to watch Reveler, Miss Scrapiron, and Lucifer frolicking. Horses have a method of communication that fascinates me. They all rush forward and cut right as if their play has been choreographed. The way they moved told me they had a psychic connection—one that I shared with those horses. It was the ultimate bond between equine and rider, to move and think as one.

Pluto put his paw on the car horn and let me know that idling in the driveway was doing nothing to solve my case. And Coleman was waiting. I put the pedal to the metal and roared toward Musgrove Manor.

I tried once more to call Tinkie, and at last she answered. Her voice sounded muffled and weird, like she was in a tin can. "Where are you?" I asked.

"Working the case."

The way she said it, I knew she was lying. Why was Tinkie doing this? "Where are you?" I asked again, this time with a cold anger.

"Headed to Musgrove Manor."

"Good. Me, too." I hung up, letting my hurt feelings get the better of me.

6

Coleman and I weren't the only people gathering at Musgrove Manor—though Tinkie was nowhere in sight. Kitten Fontana and the half-dozen members of the Anti-Satan League were back on the property, picketing the gift shop. Esmeralda Grimes was there, too, broadcasting a live feed back to her trashy newspaper's website, which was the photo op for the protest.

Esmeralda all but declared Trevor dead as she went into a lurid description of the property and the slaves that once worked it, claiming all sorts of atrocities. None of her facts was true or had anything to do with Trevor's disappearance. She painted a picture of enchanted trees, demons roaming the woods, a family with Gothic and perverse secrets, and the feral cats as familiars with magical powers.

I listened to her broadcast until I thought the top of my head might pop off and then drove past all of them and went to the front door. The horde of feral cats was nowhere in evidence. Even they had sense enough to get away from Kitten, Esmeralda, et al. Pluto, though, was growling deep in his throat. He was eager to get out of the car, and that made me concerned. If something untoward was going on at Musgrove Manor, I didn't want my kitty injured. Also, I'd heard rumors that Kitten had been poisoning feral-cat colonies around Zinnia, saying they destroyed property values. If Coleman caught her doing that, she'd be charged with animal cruelty, notwithstanding the irony of her name.

Complaining loudly, Pluto remained in the car along with Sweetie Pie, while I knocked on the front door. Faith didn't look pleased to see me, but she invited me in. Her red hair caught the golden rays of the setting sun, and I was reminded of Jitty's appearance as Melisandre, the Red Witch, a woman who claimed to be in service to the Lord of Light, a deity that seemed to be a very dark lord. Were these three young women truly in the service of a dark force? I had to find out.

I pushed such fantasies away and focused on what was happening in the manor. The three sisters were sipping cocktails, totally unperturbed by rumors of Trevor's disappearance.

"May I speak with Trevor?" I asked.

"If you can find him, by all means," Faith said. Her drink was a pomegranate martini if I knew my cocktails, and I did. Hope sipped a Black Russian, and Charity had what I guessed was a Blue Long Island. The drink choices were telling.

"Does he often disappear?"

"Sometimes we don't hear from Trevor for days at a stretch," Hope said. "When he's in a frenzy painting, he loses touch with time. He drinks 24/7 and he doesn't eat. Then he'll exhaust himself, fall out, and when he wakes up hungover and hungry, he'll come downstairs for us to make him a meal."

"How did you discover he wasn't in his room?" I asked.

"One of his models called, looking for him. Said she couldn't get him on his phone, so I went and looked. The third floor is empty." Faith put her glass down. "May I make you a cocktail?"

"No, thanks. I just want to get some info about Trevor. And my partner is here?"

They all three shook their heads. "Haven't seen Mrs. Richmond," Hope said. "Trevor has a separate, exterior staircase from his wing of the manor. His models use that to come and go, so we often don't see them. Truthfully, we wouldn't know he was up there most of the time. He keeps to himself." She frowned, and I wondered if it was annoyance or concern for Trevor.

"I hate to ask this, but was the sale of the manor and land finalized?"

"What do you mean?" Charity asked. Her blue eyes widened. "Of course it was finalized." She turned to her sisters. "Right?"

"That's right," Faith said. "Signed, sealed, notarized, and filed."

"What about Trevor's will?"

"He isn't dead," Charity said, sitting forward on the sofa. "He's just gone somewhere. You're acting like he's dead."

Guilty as charged. "I'm sorry. I just have to touch all bases. Have any of his ex-wives been visiting him?" Trevor used to tell people that all of his exes lived in Texas, but it wasn't true. At least three still lived in Sunflower County, and they weren't shy about talking about what a bastard he was.

All three shook their heads. "We don't think so, but we can't say for certain, because we don't keep up with his visitors," Hope answered. "And we don't know all of his habits. Perhaps he went to Memphis to buy painting supplies. We just don't know."

"Does he have a vehicle?"

"No," Hope said, pondering that information. "But he could have called a ride or had a friend pick him up."

"Nothing was disturbed in his rooms or studio?"

"Nothing," Faith said. "Though it's hard to tell if you aren't accustomed to the clutter. As far as I know, the only thing missing is Trevor."

I had a few final questions. "Did you see Kitten Fontana over here?"

"Nope." Hope wasn't really interested. "Like I said, his models use the exterior stairs in the back."

And now for the pay dirt. "Did you pay cash for the manor?"

Hope was suddenly very interested. "I like you, Sarah Booth, but that question is just too damn personal. It's nobody's business but ours and Trevor's."

She was right about that, but I still had a job to do. I would ask Trevor when I found him.

Night had fallen around the manor, and I had no legal right to search Trevor's rooms. But I did have one more question. "Who was the model who reported Trevor missing?"

"I don't know her name. She was really upset. She said something about how she couldn't be involved in anything untoward. I called Sheriff Peters, and he asked me to check upstairs. Sure enough, no sign of Trevor." She shrugged one shoulder. "Trevor will likely turn up."

"I'm sure Coleman will be here to search further, unless Trevor does appear. Please don't go in his area. I mean if there is foul play involved, don't muddle with the evidence."

"Sure thing, Nancy Drew," Faith said. "If there's nothing else, we'd like to finish our cocktails before we begin the moon dance."

"Do you think it might be smart to cancel a moon dance? There are protesters outside."

“All the more reason to dance,” Faith said. Her red hair was a true indication of her fiery nature. “We won’t be bullied by those sheeple. They don’t know anything about who or what we are, but they’re out there protesting us because someone told them we’re evil.”

She had a point, but it had nothing to do with Trevor’s disappearance or the financial status of the Harrington sisters, which was what I was being paid to look into. I did have a personal bone to pick. “Listen, I’m asking you to stop this foolishness with Tinkie about getting pregnant. She believes you, and when she finds out she isn’t, it’s going to break her heart.”

They all three looked at me like I’d grown another head.

I wasn’t about to let it drop. “What you’re doing is cruel.”

“Just because you don’t believe something doesn’t mean it won’t happen,” Hope said. “Why don’t you give it a chance? You might discover that there are things beyond ordinary logic that can happen. The Goddess can be compassionate. She can heal people.”

Doc Sawyer, the local M.D. who also served as coroner and had taken care of me my whole life, had been pretty clear that Tinkie had physical fertility problems. She’d been to a dozen specialists. All had told her she’d never conceive and even if she did, she couldn’t carry the pregnancy to term. I didn't believe a goddess could produce that kind of miracle.

"If my friend is hurt by this, I'll hold you all accountable. False hope is cruel. There's no other way to describe it."

A yowl from outside made the sisters jump to their feet and I was right with them as we rushed to the front door. I was afraid Kitten Fontana was up to her old tricks of killing cats. And my cat was on the premises, though safely in the car. Not. Pluto was sitting on the hood of the Roadster while all around the car the feral cats had gathered. It was a kitty clowder camp meeting! The Anti-Satan League stood at a respectful distance, awed by the cats' behavior. By tomorrow morning the gossip would be that my black cat Pluto had connections with the devil and that I had joined up with the witches.

"Go home!" Faith yelled at them. "Unless you want to participate in a Wiccan celebration of the moon, you'd better clear out."

The protesters backed up as if her words carried physical force.

"Ladies, when the sheriff arrives, please ask him to give me a call," I said as I picked up my cat and put him back in the car. It was impossible that he'd gotten out, and yet he had. "Remember what I said. I don't want my partner hurt. And when she finally gets here, tell her not to bother calling me."

"She won't be hurt," Hope said. "Have a little faith."

As I drove toward Dahlia House, I pondered faith and my lack of it. Life had not given me a lot of reasons to trust that divine entities, be they Christian, Buddhist, or Wiccan, would solve the problems of my life. I didn't expect miracles, and I wouldn't tolerate cruelty.

I'd just poured a Jack Daniel's when Tinkie's car stopped at the front steps and my cell phone rang with Coleman's number. The two of them seemed to bird-dog me in tandem now. I wondered if the witches had given Tinkie some kind of sixth sense that let her know when I was trying to jump Coleman's bones.

I answered the phone as Tinkie came up the steps and knocked at the door.

"Sarah Booth, can you surveil the witches' ceremony for me tonight?" Coleman wasn't kidding. I could hear the earnestness in his voice.

"Sure. Why?"

"Some guy named Malvik has checked into the penthouse of the Prince Albert. He told the desk clerk he's a warlock and he's come to preside at the witches' sacrifice."

That was a whole lot of information to take in all in one gulp. I went for the obvious. "Have the witches captured Kitten? If she's the sacrifice I won't intervene."

"Not amusing, Sarah Booth. I'm shorthanded, and I need your help. I've got to hire another deputy."

"You've got it. What did you find out about Trevor?"

"No evidence of foul play. He has no family left, so the Harrington women said they would notify me when he returns. There's no reason to believe anything has happened to him."

That was good. "I'll help you on one condition."

"Name it. And I hope it involves handcuffs."

My knees jellied, but I pressed my demand. "After the ceremony tonight, and when you finish whatever you're doing, we meet at Dahlia House at midnight. We turn off our phones and lock the door."

Coleman groaned softly. "You are killing me. There's not a chance we'll be left alone. Not a single chance. You know it, too. I never believed in spontaneous combustion, but it might happen to me."

I couldn't help but laugh as I opened the door for Tinkie. One look and my heart dropped to the top of my cankles. She looked like hell. "Is it a deal?" I asked Coleman.

"I accept your terms. Just keep an eye on things and make sure the witches aren't sacrificing any small animals, and that the Anti-Satan League stays back on the road and away from the manor.

DeWayne is busy, so if you need help, call Junior over at the bail bonding office. He said he'd back you up, but he's getting up in years."

"Got it. I have to go." I was staring into Tinkie's marbled-looking blue eyes and seeing something very upsetting.

"At midnight," Coleman said.

"Before the stroke of twelve." I slipped my phone into my pocket. "You look like shit." I saw no reason to mince my words. I'd been calling her all day, and she'd managed to ignore me.

"I've had terrible dreams," she said. "Night-mares." She began to weep. "My body doesn't feel like mine anymore. What if I am pregnant and it's a . . . a . . . a monstrosity? What if black magic gives me a demon child?"

I wrapped my arms around her and pulled her tight into me. "Stop it. You could never have a demon child. You're too good. And the Harrington witches are good witches." I didn't believe that at all, but it was important that Tinkie believe it.

Tinkie slumped against me and I realized what a toll the last few days had taken on her. It felt like the Harringtons and the problems they'd brought with them had been hanging over Tinkie and me for at least three years.

"Are you sure?" Tinkie asked. "I was going to meet you there an hour ago, but I couldn't make myself face them. What if my child is evil?"

"Not happening." I remained calm and confident. "I promise."

"You're sure?"

"Very sure." I grasped her shoulders and forced her to stand tall. "Coleman has asked me to watch over the Wiccan moon ritual. Want to come? Oh, and we're hired to find the financial info on the Harringtons for Kitten. Another ten grand and I've already found out some interesting stuff."

Tinkie nodded. "Can I still be your partner? I know I've disappointed you."

I nudged her with my elbow. "Of course. Don't be foolish." I maneuvered her out the door and into the car. I needed to be on the move if I intended to fulfill the job Coleman had given me.

I put the heater on full blast and took off down the drive. Even though the car windows were up, I could smell the freshly turned alluvial soil. The old saying was that the dirt smelled like money, because it could grow anything. The inky blackness of the Delta settled around us and we rode in silence for ten minutes.

Tinkie sighed long and loud. "I have to put this baby issue behind me. I have to. It's like I start thinking about it and I spiral down into this place where it's all I can think about. I know it isn't healthy."

She was leading herself to water and drinking. Best to keep my lip zipped. I changed the subject.

"By the way, Trevor Musgrove has been reported missing."

"Really? Faith told me he never left the third floor. Or almost never."

"Well, he's gone now."

As we drew closer to Musgrove Manor, I could see torches burning in the night. Witches or protesters? Was either option really a good one?

"Kitten should just climb on her broomstick and ride into the moon," Tinkie muttered when we got close enough to see the half-dozen protesters. What a pathetic lot. They milled around, accomplishing nothing. They each held a torch, and I thought of Frankenstein's monster. A creation that hadn't asked for life but only wanted to be loved. The villagers had pursued him with lighted torches, intent on burning him to death. Mobs with torches were never a good thing.

"Oh, dear Goddess," I said when I caught sight of the sisters. They danced nude in their front yard around a fire pit. Flute and drum music came from a speaker on the front porch. The sisters' lithe bodies—and they all three had excellent figures—spun and twisted in an Alvin Ailey-ish modern-dance interpretation that left me in awe. They were trained dancers. Truly trained.

The flames from the fire pit cast their shadows against the walls of Musgrove Manor, demonic silhouettes that writhed and contorted. It was a hellish scene designed to scare folks half to death.

"I don't think this is smart of the Harringtons," Tinkie said softly.

Understatement of the century. The protesters had torches—they had mobile fire. And a bellyful of fear. No wonder Coleman had been concerned. I checked to put Junior's number on speed dial. In fact, I gave him a call and told him things were "heated." No pun intended.

"I'm finishing up with a client, but call if you need me," he said. "Fact is, I'll stop by the local fish-wrapper and tell your buddy Cece what's going on. Sometimes the media can quell a mob. They don't want to be held accountable and photos are hard to dispute."

"Good idea." Thank goodness Junior had his thinking cap on.

"What's the purpose of the moon dance?" Tinkie asked. She was sitting in the passenger seat of my old Roadster, looking like a lost child. "Last time I talked with them, I suggested they cancel the moon dance. No deal. They are hardheaded women."

"They dance to honor the moon, the feminine, the cycles of time, the tide, the seasons." I ran down the list. I couldn't remember what applied, but some of the items did.

"Sarah Booth, the Harringtons are good people. We can't let them be harmed."

"I know. Let's park here and make our presence known."

It wasn't until I opened my door that I realized Pluto, the devilish black cat, had stowed away in the car. He was out the door like a shot, headed for the manor and the feral-cat colony that had magically appeared on the porch. The cats were lined up like a blockade. All shapes and colors and sizes. When Pluto arrived, they fell into a column and walked behind him as he disappeared, heading toward the dairy.

"What the hell is that?" Tinkie asked.

"I don't know, but I don't like it." I would deal with Pluto later.

"Thank goodness the sisters aren't really naked," Tinkie said. "Look, they're wearing flesh-colored leotards. They only *look* naked."

Their nakedness was the least of my worries, but Tinkie was right. They wore dancer's togs that made them appear nude. Which had to be a deliberate effort to arouse the ire of the locals, making my job harder than it had to be. At the moment, I was more worried about what Pluto was into than what might happen to three very provocative women who set out to create hardship for themselves.

"I'm going after Pluto," I said. "If they start throwing stones at the Harringtons, call Junior to come."

"I'll hold the ground here," Tinkie said. "If I yell, come running."

"Got it." I skirted the dancing witches and

hurried behind the dairy. I found the cats, all in a line, heading across the back field. It was a visual that chilled my blood—like a kitty funeral procession. Pluto was in the lead and I had no choice but to push my reluctant body into a sprint. I was going to nab him and take him back to the car.

But Pluto was elusive, and the cats picked up their pace. The faster I moved, the faster they goose-stepped in a march that only cats can pull off. I ended up at the old apple orchard. I had fond memories of the spring apples at the Musgrove orchard. My mother had made fabulous pies from the small green apples.

In the light of the full moon, the trees were twisted into grotesque shapes, leafless and barren of all fruit. Not a good omen. I recalled the sensation of something powerful and evil watching me. I felt it again, that disquieting sensation of someone with malevolent intent spying, hoping for a chance to do harm.

Gertrude Strom came full-blown into my imagination. My nemesis. The woman who held a ridiculous grudge against me because of some imagined slight from my mother decades back—but one who had also tried repeatedly to kill me. She was no joke, and she was still on the lam. While there hadn't been reports of a sighting of her in several weeks, I knew she was still stalking me. She'd left a message to that effect.

Feeling exposed out in the open, I ran into the apple orchard after the colony of high-stepping cats. Anything was better than standing like a perfect target in the open field. Or so I thought. I darted through the trees, dodging the crooked and grasping branches. This brought to mind the terrifying apple tree scene as Dorothy journeyed to the Emerald City. I never should have started that movie and I wouldn't have if I'd known I would be consorting with witches.

I nearly tripped over a pretty little calico who'd stopped in the path. As I stumbled forward, trying to slow my momentum and regain my balance, I saw something lying on the ground. Something about the size of a body.

Whatever it was, dressed all in black, didn't move. In the semibrightness of the full moon, I slowly advanced. What if the thing began to crawl toward me, jaws snapping? What if it was playing 'possum until I was close enough to grab?

"Damn," I whispered as I tried to slow my pounding heart. Though I wanted to turn tail and run, I advanced. Very carefully. The cats formed a semicircle around whatever it was and waited. "Hello?"

There was no movement from the body, for, indeed, it was a human form.

I moved toward it, praying that I was wrong, that it wasn't Trevor Musgrove. But my wishes were not to be answered. The owner of Musgrove Manor was stretched out beneath an apple tree. His skin was a faint shade of blue and his face was contorted in a rictus of pain. In his hand he grasped one perfect apple—missing a single bite.

7

The cats guarded the body, all paying homage to the fallen artist. The scene was completely eerie and it took all of my courage not to run screaming from the orchard. I knelt beside Trevor. No pulse. His body was cool to the touch, but there was no rigor mortis.

Pluto walked up to the corpse and put a paw on Trevor's cheek, some type of feline benediction. The cats queued up again and began the march back to the manor. They had done their duty and informed me of Trevor's death. While I couldn't fully believe that the Harrington sisters had witchy powers, I needed no convincing that the cats had brought me to this place to find Trevor's body.

I snapped a photo and texted it, with a message, to Coleman.

He called immediately. "I'm on the way," he said. "I'll pick up Doc. Are you sure he's dead?"

"He is positively, absolutely, undeniably, and reliably dead." I clapped a hand over my mouth. The words from *The Wizard of Oz* had come unbidden from my lips. "I'm sorry, Coleman."

"Are you ill?" he asked.

"No. And Trevor really is, regrettably, dead." I meant it. Trevor was a talented artist, but he'd also been an intriguing man. I would have liked to know him better—not romantically, but as a friend.

"We're on the way."

"I'll meet you at the manor. I left Tinkie there with the witches, Kitten, and the Anti-Satan League. The protesters were keeping their distance, but I'd better get back before that changes."

The cats were on the move, and the last of the procession disappeared down the trail. I was alone in the apple orchard with a dead man, and possibly something else. I felt in my coat pocket where I'd wisely stashed my gun. In our last case, I'd defended my injured partner as she lay in a field behind her wrecked car. I'd winged the man trying to kill us. I hadn't taken him out, but I'd driven him away. I could—and would—defend myself.

I had the sense that whatever lurked out there, just beyond my vision, was something I couldn't kill with a regular bullet. Though I was reluctant to leave the body, I had to get back to the manor to be sure Tinkie hadn't been overrun by protesters.

The apple orchard, which I remembered as a place of beauty, had become a source of dark enchantment. The gnarled branches of the apple trees reached toward the moon, a skeletal monster grasping at the lunar glow.

Movement to my right made me spin around, gun drawn. When I got my hands on Pluto I was going to have him fitted for a harness and leash. Had I not been chasing after him, I wouldn't be in this predicament.

In the bright moonlight, I didn't see anything but the dark shapes of the tree trunks. Movement to my left made me whirl in that direction. Before I could even react, I heard a voice behind me.

"So he's dead." A black-clad figure lifted both arms and the cape he wore—outlined by the moon—created the vivid silhouette of Count Dracula. It took all of my restraint not to plug him.

"Who are you?" I demanded.

He whipped the cape around him and stepped forward. "I'm—"

"One more step and you'll be full of lead."

He halted, obviously a man who took a woman's threat seriously. "I'm Malvik, the leader of the Harrington coven."

This was going to be news to the sisters. They didn't strike me as women who needed a leader of the male persuasion. "What are you doing out here?"

"Following you. It was quite an interesting procession. The cats, you, now the body."

I motioned for him to get in front of me and start walking. I intended to turn him over to Coleman and let the sheriff sort the facts. I could clearly see that there would be no midnight rendezvous with my pistol-packing lawman tonight. I was beginning to believe the sisters had put some kind of anti-romance curse on me. Maybe I would never get laid again. The thought made me push Malvik faster down the path.

"Who are you, really?" I asked. Malvik couldn't be a real name.

"The warlock of the Harrington coven. Malvik is the name I go by now. My past has been erased. I renounced my birth name and birthright and was reborn a lord of Hecate, the goddess of the moon."

"You'd better can that mumbo jumbo when you talk to the sheriff or you'll end up in the state mental institution, and that isn't a place any person wants to be."

"You dupes of corporate religion don't have a clue."

"Keep walking." I wasn't about to debate religion with a guy who looked strikingly like Bella Lugosi in his signature role.

When we arrived at the manor, I was relieved to see Coleman pulling up to the front of the stone manor house with Doc Sawyer in the front seat. DeWayne Dattilo, his chief and only deputy, followed in a second car. I'd heard rumors Coleman had gotten a budget bump to hire another deputy, but so far no action. He needed about ten more men to adequately patrol the county.

Coleman stepped out of the car and for a moment I thought he was going to sweep me against him and plant one right on my lips. Somehow, we managed not to lurch together like two desperate magnets. "Who is this?" Coleman asked.

"Tell him." I nudged Malvik. It was such a better story coming from the man in the cape.

Malvik went through his whole ruler-of-the-empire speech. Coleman's response was to stuff him in the back of the patrol car. "You were at the scene of a dead body. I'll need to question you at the sheriff's office."

I felt relief once Malvik was confined in the car. I had a moment to speak with Coleman. "Trevor is in the apple orchard. Looks like he was either frightened to death or poisoned by an apple. I didn't see Snow White or any of the dwarves." I had to tell him about what else might be lingering there. "Coleman, I think someone else is there, too. Be careful."

"Will do." He unholstered his gun. "Keep the sisters here. DeWayne, Doc, and I will handle the body."

I approached the sisters and Tinkie. The protesters had scattered the moment Coleman drove up. Surprisingly, there was no sign of Cece yet. I had a few questions for the witches while we waited for Coleman to collect the body. "So, Malvik is your leader?" I could see the outline of the strange man in the back seat of Coleman's car. At least he hadn't turned into a bat and flown away.

"No." Charity spoke up.

"Is he part of your coven?" I couldn't believe I was saying the word *coven*.

"He is, but he isn't the leader."

"Who's the leader?"

"In a matriarchal society, there's no need for a leader," Faith said. "We share responsibilities. We're each an integral part of the whole."

"And yet Malvik is a part of your . . . group."

"He is. A lesser part," Faith said. "He just refuses to accept his place." She laughed and the others, including Tinkie, joined in.

"Women don't need a man, Sarah Booth." Tinkie spoke rebellion. She was the Daddy's Girl, the female raised to please men and skillfully manipulate them so that they met her every desire. Men had been created to cater to the whims of the Daddy's Girl.

"If you want to get pregnant you need a man," I snapped. The witches were brainwashing my friend. "Stop this, Tinkie. We have enough going on without kicking up a gender war in Sunflower County."

"Women are powerful. We need to own our power and stop being pushed around by men." Tinkie had no intention of backing down. It was as if our roles had been magically reversed. She was the rebel, the feminist, the recanter of the sacred doctrine of Big Daddy and the male provider. I was now the defender of a doctrine I didn't believe in.

"Did you know Malvik was on the dairy property?" I switched tactics before I was routed and sent home.

"Yes, he's staying in town but he came out earlier to help us prepare for the moon dance. Which has been pretty much thwarted." Faith was not happy with the turn of events. "Those protesters. Now, Trevor's dead. We haven't been able to finish the ceremony."

"How did you know Trevor was dead?" I hadn't said that out loud to anyone but Coleman.

"We know things," Hope said, looking a little annoyed.

It wasn't a satisfactory answer, but I didn't have the legal power to force her to tell the truth.

"They're psychic," Tinkie said. Her awe was showing.

"Or they're eavesdroppers." I looked around for Pluto. It was time to leave. The protesters were gone and I could take Tinkie home and wait until tomorrow to head over to the sheriff's office to get the final report on Trevor from

Coleman. It was clear no one at the manor was overly concerned about his death.

"What were you three doing this afternoon?" I asked the sisters. The answers came from Hope, Faith, and then Charity.

"Napping."

"Mani-pedi here at home."

"Reading."

"You were all together?" I asked.

"We were in our rooms," Hope said. "That's one reason we can share the manor. There's enough space so that we can each build our own world, enjoy our own privacy. We're sisters, but we don't have to be together every moment of every day."

So they had no alibis. The first thing was to wait for a cause of death. If Trevor had a heart condition, he could have seen Malvik flitting around the orchard and suffered a heart attack. "Coleman will be in touch, I'm sure."

"Where will they take . . . the body?" Hope blinked as if she might cry.

"You can call the sheriff's office and ask. There'll be an autopsy."

Faith stood and stretched. "We'll have a service for him, of course."

"There are no Musgrove relatives?"

"None he told us about," Hope said. "He has a computer and he gave me the password. I'll print out his address book for the sheriff."

"I'm sure Coleman would appreciate that."

"What's the issue between you and the law-man?" Faith asked bluntly.

"What do you mean?"

"Sparks fly but no fire. Erectile dysfunction? Frozen womb? What?"

The Delaney women did have a long history of strange womb disorders, from tilted to spastic, with a few Fallopian tube kinks thrown in. But that wasn't common knowledge. "That's none of your business."

Tinkie came forward with a small beautiful silk cloth bag. "It's a charm, Sarah Booth. The sisters made it just for you at my request. Put it around your neck and wear it. The obstacles in your path will clear. I got it for you and Coleman."

Because it was Tinkie, I took the little sack, which was surprisingly heavy. "What's in here, chicken feet and toad lips?"

"Herbs, a quartz rock, some Apache tears, and magical charms." Hope smiled. "Soon you and the handsome sheriff will form a union."

In that instant, I understood completely the lure the witches held for Tinkie. If only life could be impacted by a charm or a potion or a spell. If only good things could be made manifest out of desire and good intentions. Tinkie wanted a baby, and she would shower one with love. She would raise a human capable of helping mankind. How magnificent it would be if those emotions, desires, and needs could create a pregnancy for her. But that couldn't happen. Wishes and magic couldn't override biology.

"Thank you, Tinkie."

"If you throw it away, I'll know." She took it from me and put it around my neck. "Humor me. Just wear it. And when Coleman comes calling, don't get in your own way. Let him take the lead. Men like that."

"I thought Wiccans had no use for men."

"Oh, we have plenty of use for them, and they all love how we use them," Charity said, her laughing blue eyes a match for Tinkie's. "We don't need men, but we do enjoy them. Or at least a few." There was a wistful tone in her voice that made me wonder if she'd left a true love behind on the path to becoming a witch.

"We have to go." I had to talk to Tinkie. It couldn't wait.

I captured Pluto, who was none the worse for wear for all of his adventures, and navigated past the ambulance and cruisers to get to the road. The only sign of the protesters were a few homemade posters left on the ground. I stopped and picked them up. I hated litterers, and I needed a moment to think how to broach what I had to say to Tinkie. Direct and frontal. She deserved no less.

When we were on the road, I turned away from Zinnia and Hilltop and headed toward the Mississippi River. "Tinkie, we need—"

"No, *we* don't. *I* need to talk. I owe you an apology, Sarah Booth. I've been a terrible partner. I've shut you out and focused on my desire for a child. That's behind me. I'm ready to work on the case, and in fact, I found out a lot of facts about the Harringtons while you were stumbling over poor Trevor's body."

If only all hard talks could be so easy. "Great. What did you find out?"

"Charity and Hope ran the school in Lafayette, but Faith is new on the scene. In fact, she isn't a full sister, but a half sister. Different father. And she was raised in Florida, not Louisiana. Harrington isn't her real last name. She took it as a legal name when she found her sisters."

"So the Harrington mother had a child and what? Put her up for adoption? Gave her away? What?"

Tinkie leaned toward me. "She was abducted! She's the oldest child and Mrs. Harrington, who was Mrs. Marsh at the time, lived in Lake City, Florida. The abduction of Faith, who was then Ophelia, broke up the marriage. The police never found a single suspect in the abduction. Mrs. Marsh moved to Lafayette, where she was a public school teacher, married Ed Harrington, and had two more daughters."

"That's tragic. Why was Faith stolen?"

Tinkie shook her head. "I guess the woman

who took her wanted a baby badly enough to steal one."

Oh, this was a dark path, because Tinkie had almost done the same. "I'm glad she found her sisters."

"And her connection to the Wiccan heritage. The Harrington family has practiced Wicca since the 1700s. Some of their relatives burned in the great witch burnings in Germany and some were hanged in Salem."

Tinkie had obviously taken in the whole history of witchcraft at the Harringtons' knees. "My timeline on witchy doings is a little . . . non-existent. Could you fill me in?"

"In the 1500s and 1600s a lot of people were executed, mostly burned, for practicing witchcraft. In Germany, the death rate was highest, but the witch hysteria spread all across Europe, including the British Isles and France. Lots of people died, including some of the Harrington ancestors."

"But were they witches?"

"Yes, but not bad witches. Not the kind who consort with Satan."

"That's comforting." Sarcasm dripped off every syllable.

Tinkie sighed. "You have a big chip where the Harringtons are concerned. It's getting really tedious."

"I'm sorry." And I was. Tinkie needed to

believe in magic. In so many ways, she was like the fairy-tale princess whose Prince Charming would always come riding over the horizon to save her. That was her life pattern, and it left her free to believe in charms and potions and spells. She'd retained some of the things that made childhood so wonderful. Those cherished beliefs could also make adulthood painful, but that was a train I couldn't stop.

"It's okay. But enough of that. If I'm pregnant, I am. If I'm not, I'm not. Let's find out what the Harringtons are really up to, and who killed Trevor Musgrove. I was hoping to model for him. I would have been a real Botticelli model with my baby bump. But now I need for you to take me home."

I turned the car back toward town and dropped Tinkie at the front door of Hilltop. Oscar's car was nowhere in sight, but Tinkie said she was tired. The day had stretched for at least seventy-two hours, or so it seemed. I was tired myself. It seemed a lifetime ago I was popping corn and watching my favorite movie of all time.

Tinkie waved goodbye from her doorstep and Pluto shifted to the front seat when I started home. The cat intently watched the scenery flash by, and I wondered if it was because he felt guilty for making me give chase earlier or if his thoughts were somewhere else. It was impossible to tell a cat's motive.

When we pulled up to the front steps, Pluto was out of the car like a shot. I went across the porch and stopped at the claw marks on the door. I studied them for a long moment. It could be a prank. Or Gertrude. Or something that had followed me home from the Musgrove woods. I didn't like any of the options.

8

I awoke from a sound sleep when I heard something downstairs in Dahlia House. A noise or sixth sense had awakened me, some self-preservation instinct that brought me rising from a dark slumber like air bubbles in the ocean's trough.

The tread of a heavy boot moved along the polished wood floors of the front parlor, and I slipped from bed and hurried to the upstairs railing. The floorboards were bitterly cold, and when I gripped the banister and looked down, I saw only the broad shoulders and fair hair of my intruder. Instead of Malvik or some dark entity, it was Coleman Peters. He'd stopped by Dahlia House even though he'd told me he wouldn't.

I hurried along the hallway and down the stairs, trying not to laugh out loud with pleasure. At long last, Coleman and I would have some private time.

He heard my approach and turned to me, his arms opening, his eyes serious and hungry. A moment later I was in his embrace. I'd known Coleman's kisses in the past. In fact, I'd sustained myself on the memory of one long kiss on Harold Erkwell's porch, but this time a kiss wouldn't be enough.

His lips seared through me, hot and hungry like we were burning rocket fuel. His thumb grazed the skin beneath my jaw and I thought I would faint from the sensual rush of pleasure. I'd never been so alive, and so hungry for a man's touch.

Coleman gathered me against him and every inch of my body pulsed. I'd waited such a long time for this. We'd waited. Now the deck was cleared and we could be together.

"Take me upstairs," I whispered, my fingers digging into the muscles of his shoulders and upper arms. Coleman was a strong man in peak condition. Virile and sexy.

"Your wish is my command." He swept me into his arms and the journey up the stairs to my bed—which Tinkie had so rudely interrupted several weeks before—was complete. When he put me down on my bed, even Sweetie Pie and Pluto vacated the room, giving us a little privacy.

"Tell me what you'd like," he whispered, his lips tracing down my cleavage.

"I want you to make love to me. Now." I pulled him down on top of me, feeling a deep satisfaction at his weight, the sense of rightness. This is what I'd wanted for weeks. Maybe for years. And now it was happening.

Coleman's fingertips, slightly rough from

his outdoor work, moved over my collarbones, pushing the nightgown down. Then, with a quick, expert movement, he brought it over my head and dropped it on the floor. A cool breeze teased my skin. When I looked up at him, I saw his love and desire. It was everything I'd ever wanted.

He lowered his head, his lips exploring. "Sarah Booth, I love you."

I savored those words. "I love—"

A loud hammering came from downstairs. Coleman drew back. He stepped away from the bed and into the shadows in a corner of the room. "Wait!" But I knew he wouldn't. I sat up, disoriented. The pounding downstairs continued.

And I was alone in my bedroom. Naked, except for the small silk bag Tinkie had placed around my neck. The charm.

The torrid passion I'd felt only seconds before had been dream induced. There was no Coleman in my bed. No Coleman in my room. I was alone in Dahlia House, under the influence of one helluva dream. I clutched the charm, which hung between my breasts. I'd never had such a visceral sex dream. Was the charm responsible? I didn't have time to ponder the possibilities.

I grabbed my nightgown from the floor and threw it over my head as I hurried to the front door, where someone was about to destroy the beveled glass. "Hold your damn horses!" I yelled. "Who is it?"

I peeked out to see DeWayne pacing the front porch. I cracked the door. "What the heck?"

"Coleman sent me to get you. It's urgent."

"Has something happened to Tinkie?"

"No," he said. "It's Cece. She was attacked."

"Where?"

"At Musgrove Manor. She went out to the crime scene."

Damn. Damn. Damn. I'd called Cece to the scene of the protest and Trevor's murder. When she didn't show up, I'd forgotten all about her. She must have come out to the manor after I'd left. "Give me five minutes to dress."

Instead of heading for Musgrove Manor, DeWayne drove me to the hospital, which succeeded in upsetting me more. I didn't hit him with sixty questions, not because I didn't have a bunch of questions to ask, but because he likely didn't have any more answers than I did. We arrived at the ambulance entrance and I ran inside. A head-swaddled Cece sat with her boyfriend, Jaytee. Tinkie and Oscar rushed in only seconds behind me.

Cece gave us all a weak smile. "I'm not dying. I told Coleman not to call you."

"What happened?" I knelt beside her, taking her free hand. "Who hurt you?"

"I don't know."

Coleman came out of the back room, where he'd no doubt been consulting with Doc. He wore a very strange expression, and when I rose to go back to talk to Doc, he blocked my path. "She's going to be fine, except for a really bad headache," Coleman said. "She took a pretty hard knock to the back of the skull, but, lucky for all involved, she's got a head as hard as a brick."

"And plenty of other physical attributes that make my groin sizzle." Jaytee's salty comment drew laughter from everyone, and the tension broke. We were all talking at once, crowding close to Cece and demanding details.

"I couldn't get out to the manor right away because I was tied up at a secret school board meeting. With the controversy over the Wiccan school, suddenly some of the board members are trying to rework the county policies for school vouchers or tax credits or earned school credits or whatever folks are calling them now to hide the fact it's taxpayer money diverted from public schools to private and religious schools."

I wanted to know why she'd even gone if she'd known she was late, but I didn't interrupt, and she filled in the blank without my asking the question.

"I wanted a photograph of that apple orchard. I remember it from when we'd take school tours to the dairy and Trevor's father, who was running the place, would let us all milk a cow. Remember Bessie? She had a lot of patience for a bunch of nine-year-olds pulling on her teats. I remember the time he tried another cow, Suellen. She kicked Rooster Durant clean out of the barn. That boy did have cold, sweaty hands. No wonder Suellen launched him."

Cece was sounding a little slaphappy. Doc must have given her a shot for pain. "How badly is she hurt?" I asked Coleman.

"Four stitches in the scalp. Whoever hit her used something with a sharp edge."

"Like a shovel?"

He tilted his head and lifted a shoulder, non-committal.

Doc arrived just in time to answer the question of the shovel in the affirmative and I took the opportunity to buttonhole Coleman. "Who struck Cece? Was it Malvik?"

"Malvik's in a holding cell. It couldn't have been him, but I'm going to find out who it was."

I didn't get a chance to press him harder because Cece was growing restless. "Can I go home? I don't want to sit here any longer."

Doc thought for a moment. "If Jaytee has to go to the club, you need to stay here. You shouldn't be alone, and you shouldn't fall asleep."

"She can come home with me." I'd love a chance to babysit my friend. She'd done it plenty of times for me.

"Yes, I'll come, too." Tinkie looped her arm through mine.

"Go back to the club and play." Cece kissed Jaytee long and lovingly. "I'm fine."

"Okay." Jaytee checked his watch. "Call me if you need anything."

We nodded in unison, looking like the bobblehead dogs on the dash of an old clunker car.

A moment later we piled into Oscar's car and headed to Dahlia House. DeWayne offered to drop Oscar at Hilltop, and Coleman had a mission, which he was being mighty secretive about. He should know that such covert tactics only drove me to commit unreasonable actions to find out what was going on.

At Dahlia House I made some strong coffee and pulled slices of frozen red velvet cheesecake from the fridge. We needed sugar and caffeine if we were going to stay up the rest of the night. As it turned out, we didn't need the food and beverage stimulation—but we ate it anyway. Cece had plenty to share that kept us wide awake. Her trip to Musgrove Manor had been more about the Harrington sisters than Trevor Musgrove's body, but she was still very pleased at the fact that I'd photographed the crime scene extensively. She had her apple orchard pictures for the paper, and she had crime scene shots—with the body discreetly covered—from me. She sent the photos from my phone to the night editor as we talked.

"What did you find out that sent you to Musgrove Manor at midnight?" I asked.

"The Harringtons aren't who they claim to be."

"What do you mean?" Tinkie sounded a little defensive.

"Remember how they were going on and on about how they're descendants of the Salem witch trial witches?"

"Yes." My memory wasn't that bad.

"Impossible. Every woman identified as a witch was executed, i.e. no descendants."

Even I had to roll my eyes at that. "Some of them were older women. They could have had children before they were hanged."

"Or burned. Or drowned," Tinkie chimed in.

"I have a newspaper friend in Salem. She went to the land records. The women identified as witches were mostly elderly spinsters or widows. No descendants listed. And not a single one of the witches involved was a Harrington."

That still didn't prove the Harrington ancestors weren't part of the Salem scene, but it wasn't a point worth arguing. It was the first chink in the armor that I could use to help pull Tinkie from their spell. If they'd lie about something that happened four hundred years ago, what else might they lie about? Their ability to make a woman fertile, perhaps?

"What else did you find?" Tinkie asked. She

was struggling to be open, and I put my arm around her and gave her a hug.

"Faith used to be a financial planner and stock broker."

Now that was a shock. From broker to witch. It was an interesting career trajectory, but it could also explain how the Harringtons were flush with enough money to buy Musgrove Manor. "That's a high-pressure job."

"Yes, and it seems like Faith simply walked into work one day and quit."

"I heard the Harringtons came into an inheritance of some type. I wonder if it could be the money Faith saved up while working as a broker." Or perhaps a blackmail payment. Hope had been involved in the dissolution of the St. Pe marriage. What else might she have thrown into her black cauldron to cook up?

Cece put her coffee cup on the kitchen table and sat back in her chair. When she had our attention, she grinned. "There was a murder in Lafayette, right around the time the Harringtons moved here. An older man who made a fortune in the wildcat oil business. He was dating Hope, and he was found floating in a bayou. His death was ruled suspicious. Poison was suspected, but never proven."

The air left Tinkie in a little poof, but she didn't react otherwise. I hated all of this. Because of what it would cost Tinkie. "What kind of poison did they suspect?"

"It was never revealed. I weaseled some information out of the Lafayette Parish coroner. Ted LaRue is the dead man's name. The autopsy revealed massive organ failure and his lungs had filled up with fluid. The corpse had a blue tinge. It wasn't a pretty death."

Trevor had looked vaguely blue, but I'd assumed it was the full moon effect. Sometimes the silvery light cast odd hues on things. "Did the coroner have any suspicions about the source of the poison?"

"You're jumping the cart *and* the horse, Sarah Booth. The Louisiana coroner said he could never identify poison in the bloodstream, but he couldn't rule the death as natural because of the unusual circumstances. But he did say if poison was the cause of death, it was likely from a tropical plant, something grown and compounded, not purchased. Since we're subtropical, a lot of jungle plants can be grown here if they're properly protected." Cece was drilling me with her gaze. She knew about the witches' herb garden. Not that the sisters had tried to keep it a secret. In fact, the herbs were key ingredients in their potions, spells, enchantments, bath salts, soaps, and cooking spices. I'd seen the well-tended garden and noticed nothing amiss. No skull-and-crossbones warning signs, at least.

"Did he say what plant *might* have been used?" I asked. It would be easy enough to photograph the herb garden if I knew what to look for.

"He couldn't be specific. I got the sense that not a lot of effort went into searching for a killer. There was no solid proof. He said the sheriff investigated for a week or so, then the case got pushed down beneath other cases."

"Did the coroner give a motive for possible murder?" I asked.

"That was a problem. Everyone got along with LaRue." Cece was restless, which meant her brain was in overdrive. She stood and started to pace. I didn't want her to be agitated. She'd just had a head injury.

"Sit down," I said, pointing to a chair. "Seriously. Or I'll take you back to Doc."

She made a sour face and sat down. "There has to be a link to Trevor's murder," she said. "Doc won't say it specifically, but I think he agrees."

Now that was tying up two murders in a neat little bow—if either man was murdered. It was highly unlikely that Ted LaRue in Lafayette and Trevor Musgrove in Zinnia would both die of a rare poison. The only element in common between the two men was the sisters. Circumstantial, but highly incriminating.

Tinkie had been silent during the exchange, but she pushed back her chair and stood. "I don't think the sisters would hurt anyone."

I'd expected her to defend the Harringtons. "They aren't accused of anything yet. In fact, we're jumping to the conclusion that Trevor was murdered, and we don't know anything solid about this LaRue fellow. Let Coleman investigate. You know he'll do an honest job of it."

"In the morning, I'll find out all the details of the Harringtons' finances." Tinkie was defiant. "I'm sure what I discover will clear their names."

"I hope you're right." And I sincerely did. My friend didn't need another jab in her heart.

"They're good people with special gifts." Tinkie walked over to me and pulled the charm bag out of my sweater. "Did something happen last night?" she asked, almost as if she knew about my hot little dream.

"Coleman didn't come over."

"Didn't he?" she asked, and dropped the charm so that it dangled on the silk cord against my chest.

By morning we were all exhausted and I was starving. I drove them both home and stopped by Millie's Café for some homemade grub and a chat with Millie. If there was gossip afoot, she'd know all about it and fill me in.

While I was sipping coffee and waiting for a three-egg sweet pepper omelet, I read the local *Zinnia Dispatch*. Cece had a front-page story about Trevor's murder, using the photos of the orchard and crime scene I'd given her. She even gave me a photo credit.

"Sarah Booth Delaney," Esmeralda Grimes said as she dropped into a chair at my table. "I know who you are and all about you."

I preferred to eat alone, but I didn't say anything unpleasant. "Yes, Ms. Grimes, and I can say the same about you. Your reputation for . . . a vivid imagination precedes you."

"I always get my story. I'm sure that's what you're talking about." She grinned.

I had to admit, I appreciated her cheekiness. "Never let the facts get in the way of a good story. That's what I was referring to."

"Yes, my rivals are bitter little peahens, aren't they? Nice story there by Ms. Falcon. She's a friend, yes?"

"Yes."

"I could get her a job with my paper. She'd make six times the salary she makes here and travel around the world."

"Tell her, not me."

"My, my, you are the sly fox, aren't you?"

"Do you always ask a question at the end of a statement?"

She laughed out loud, a staccato burst that I found infectious. Now that I had a chance to study her, I saw she was a dark beauty, with a perfect olive complexion, sable hair that likely wouldn't gray until her nineties, and full lips meant to wear the exact shade of tomato she'd chosen. I couldn't help but join in her laugher. "What can I do for you, Esmeralda?"

"Get me an interview with the witches."

"What?"

"They like your partner. I hear they've made a fertility potion for her. Not something that is their normal, run-of-the mill hex or charm. A real spell."

How in the hell had she found out about Tinkie's fertility problems? I knew better than to act like it was any big deal. "Why don't you call them up and ask them for an interview?"

"They won't return my calls. I'm tainted by Kitten Fontana."

I could easily see how that might work. Kitten left her stink on everything she touched. "I'll ask them. No promises." Millie put my omelet in front of me. The café owner was drawn to Esmeralda like a fly to honey. Millie loved tabloid journalism. She thought the *International Report* was the best paper on the planet because it ran stories of Princess Di, alive and happy and living on Tahiti, lotto winners who discovered a cure for ALS, and alien abductions. She didn't believe the stories to be true, but she loved the bizarre creativity of the authors. They captured her fancy and she often asked with great appreciation, "Where do they come up with this stuff?"

There was more to it, too. In her heart of hearts, Millie wanted Elvis and Princess Di to be alive. And Vivien Leigh. And Clark Gable. There was a whole host of dead celebrities Millie would gladly spend time with. The leading men and women of the 1940s and '50s, the glamour queens and chivalrous gentlemen. Millie could have easily lived in the era of *Sunset Boulevard*.

I couldn't disagree. More often than not, her fantasies held tremendous appeal.

"I'll speak to the sisters." Why not pass on a request for an interview? It was no skin off my teeth.

"Better do it fast." Esmeralda put in her order for biscuits and gravy. She wasn't going to continue to fit into her little black dress if she ate like a field hand.

"Why? What's the rush?" I held out my coffee cup for a refill when Millie came over.

"Esmeralda, did you really see the ghost of Elvis?" Millie asked.

"I did. He was as handsome as he was in one of his movies." Esmeralda grinned at Millie.

I wasn't certain, but I had a suspicion that Millie's question referred to some of Esmeralda's so-called journalism. "Did you write a story about the moon dance?" I hadn't had a chance to check the *International Report*.

"The moon dance and Trevor's murder," Millie

said. "The photo of him is perfectly ghoulish. And that dance. Those women were as naked as the day God made them, prancing around in their front yard." Millie was delightfully shocked and eating it with a spoon.

"Where's the story?" I had a really bad feeling.

Millie went behind the counter and got a copy of the *International Report.* She handed it to me with a flourish. BENEFACTOR OF WITCHES MURDERED—THEY DANCED WHILE ZINNIA BURNED. In the front page photo that covered the whole top half of the tabloid, the Harrington sisters danced around their fiery cauldron. They did indeed look completely naked. Below the fold was a photograph of Trevor's body, his face a rictus of either pain or horror. The photo cutline read: DID TREVOR MUSGROVE MEET THE DARK LORD IN THE LAST MOMENTS OF HIS LIFE? POISON OR TERROR?

I put the paper down and stared across the table at Esmeralda, who ate her biscuits with tremendous satisfaction. "None of this is true! Cece would never print something like this."

"My audience loves this shit. They don't care if it's true or not. They just love the titillation. Witches. That alone is guaranteed to boost my readership straight through the roof. Throw in nudity and poison. No one wants to read about good witches."

"You're highly unethical." Right, like that was

a real punch to her gut. I didn't think ethics were at the top of her priority list.

"And very, very wealthy." Esmeralda grinned. "If you can get me an interview, I'll give you two grand. I want to get inside that manor."

"No, thanks. Keep your money. If the sisters want to talk to you, that's their business." I had a few standards. It hurt to walk away from two grand, but not even my inner prostitute could make me take the deal.

As I left the café, I was aware of several tables of diners gawking at copies of Esmeralda's story. Their whispering sounded like angry bees. If Kitten and Esmeralda kept whacking the hive with a stick, soon people were going to get stung.

9

Even though I was exhausted, I drove back to Musgrove Manor with the tabloid on the seat beside me. I felt an obligation to warn the sisters that trouble was bubbling. Esmeralda—no doubt at Kitten's behest—was whipping the town into a frenzy. Mobs were dangerous. Even the normally placid Zinnia mob.

February sunlight in the Mississippi Delta has the tone of a lemon wash—pale, gauzy, and more white than yellow. The sun's rays touched the dew-soaked fields with the possibility of fairy magic. In the distance, faint blue stained the sky. Once the Delta had been dense hardwood forests that stretched across the entire state. Most of the trees had been removed to allow the vast acreage to be planted with a crop grown in the alluvial backwash from the Mississippi and the blood of slaves and convict labor. Cotton. The cash crop that had once ruled the South's economy and created a society of the fabulously wealthy and the tragically poor.

Cotton was still planted in vast tracts, but corn and soybeans were also important money crops now. The land was fallow in February, but soon the combines would crawl over the fields, doing the work that had once been done by hundreds of slaves, tenant farmers, convict laborers, and the wives and children of the poor. The human labor force had toiled on, ignoring the brutal summer sun, mosquitoes that carried diseases, snakes, and predators, both two and four-legged. Man had tamed the landscape, but at a very high price.

Back before my time but still within the memory of plenty of folks, Musgrove Dairy had been the only source of "store bought" milk. For many decades, from the late 1800s until the supermarket chains had come to the area in the 1940s offering national brands, Musgrove milk was delivered fresh daily by mule-drawn wagons and then trucks. Most country people kept their own cows, but as Zinnia grew and developed, the demand for milk delivery within the city limits increased.

Musgrove Dairy had premium milk, butter, and cheese. Musgrove cows had roamed the rich pastures, lining up twice a day to head to the milking shed. It was a routine you could set your clock by.

Now all of that was gone, and Trevor, too.

The death of my parents had been the end of my age of innocence. I'd been raised in such security and safety that I'd never believed tragedy could touch me. How wrong I'd been. So much of that time had slipped away. Atticus Finch lawyers like my father had passed, too. There'd been a time when lawyers were idolized as living embodiments of justice. People would go to my father's office for help with their problems, and later when he was a judge, they respected his decisions because they believed he was impartial and a wise man.

Now it seemed that corruption touched every aspect of government. Even the schools were manipulated for personal gain.

Looking over the fields, which were deepening in color as the sun rose and the angled rays of light changed, I understood Tinkie's desire to believe in magic and witches and an answer to her dreams that was fair and just. She'd been cheated of the ability to have a child. That was a fact. Modern medicine couldn't change that. But perhaps a spell could. It broke my heart how desperately she wanted this, and how unlikely it was that her prayers would be answered.

I didn't wish any hard luck on the Harringtons, but it came to me again that Tinkie's future might be brighter if the Harringtons left Sunflower County. When this pregnancy failed to materialize, I feared they'd suck her into another potion or spell or enchantment. They could keep breaking her heart over and over again.

The manor glowed in the pale light, and for the first time I saw the true beauty of the architecture.

Limestone blocks, like a Celtic castle, glinted with dew. The slate roof reminded me of Europe in times long past, when the great manor houses of the landed gentry were the hearts of their communities. Few builders used slate now.

The house was solid and had been built to weather the generations. The gargoyles on the third-floor balconies, which I'd failed to notice earlier, were adornments I could have done without. I knew their purpose was to divert rainwater away from the wall, but still . . . why not a bird or a faithful dog? Why grotesques? They looked evil.

I parked and got out of the car. The cats were back in their normal perches, and I made a mental note to push hard for the Trap-Neuter-Return program that would neuter them and begin the process of creating a healthy and stable cat colony. They looked well fed and disease free, but rampant breeding would sicken them and make it impossible to give them good care.

The front door opened and Hope came out carrying a wire kindness trap. Charity and Faith were right behind her, each hauling a trap and cans of cat food. "We have to control the cat population and get them vaccinated," Hope said. "Trevor grew up with the belief that the cats didn't need care—they had rats in the barns and plenty of woods to hunt. We've been feeding them, and now that he's gone, we'll get them started in a good veterinary program."

Check that off my list. "Good plan." I followed them to the barn, where they expertly set up the traps and baited them. The cats would enter to eat, the trapdoors would shut, and the cats could be safely transported to the vet for a checkup, vaccinations, and neutering. Then they would be released back at the dairy to live out their lives.

"Are you here about Tinkie or Esmeralda?" Hope asked when the traps were baited.

"Both."

"We saw the story Esmeralda wrote. Ridiculous. Why would we harm Trevor? He was generous and kind to us."

"Was he selling the property to Bob Fontana?"

Charity frowned. "Well, no. We had a deal. Right?" She looked at her sisters.

"We had a solid deal," Hope said. "Trevor supported us. He'd never go back on his word. He didn't want the land turned into a subdivision. He didn't have cows, but he loved this land and didn't want it paved over. We promised to keep it natural, in keeping with the philosophy of our school. He had plenty of money and he loathed Bob Fontana."

"Kitten was one of Trevor's models." Faith's satisfied expression was rather feline.

"Kitten Fontana?" She was pretty enough, but not in a way that I thought of as a painter's model. At least not a painter of Trevor's talent.

She was more Jersey Shore than Italian villa, but this explained how she had known that Trevor wasn't in his third-floor abode. She'd used the back stairs like the other models.

"Sure enough. She was part of the religious icon series. St. Agnes of Bohemia, I believe, was the woman she portrayed. Born of royal blood and betrothed to a future king, she devoted herself to a life of prayers and healing. Trevor was deeply into the whole saints and sinners thing, though his take on a nude saint stirred controversy." Faith was amused by the whole concept. "Fits Kitten to a T, don't you think? Come back to the manor and let's make some coffee."

It was possible some of Kitten's objections to the Harringtons came from jealousy. If she'd had a romantic interest in Trevor . . . maybe she viewed the witches as rivals. I followed the sisters back to the manor house and into the front parlor where we took seats around what looked like an unusual five-sided game table. The legs and surface held strange and intricate carvings.

"We do our spell work here," Faith explained while Charity brewed coffee. "These are markings of Celtic runes. They're charmed. Just like us."

It was going to be hard work to break through to these witches. "Why don't you three lie low for a few days?" I handed the tabloid to Hope. "You're being accused of murder by a newspaper, if not the sheriff. It would be smart to let things calm down if you're serious about opening a school here. Folks might put up with witches, but I doubt they'll send their children to murderers." I thought of the dead man in Louisiana. "And it isn't the first time rumors like that have been attached to you."

"What do you mean?" Charity asked with a huffy attitude.

"Ted LaRue." I said the name.

Hope's eyes widened but it was the only reaction, until she spoke. "I didn't hurt Ted. We dated on and off, but we were friends." She paused a moment, gathering her thoughts. "He taught me a lot about the geological aspects of Louisiana, and how draining oil was causing coastal erosion and sinkage and the decimation of the coastline. He said it was the death of the incubator zone for crustaceans and other seafood. He came to believe that global warming was the biggest danger the world faced. For an ornery old coot, he was a wonderful man."

"He was an oil wildcatter. He made his fortune drilling for oil."

"And he realized the error of his ways," Hope said. "He was planning to build a solar panel factory in Breaux Bridge to give jobs to the local people. He truly wanted to undo some of the damage he'd done. But then he drowned."

"Drowned? Are you certain there was no foul play?"

Hope looked confused. "We were told he fell into the water and struck his head and drowned."

Interesting. "Who inherited?"

"I got a small inheritance. Ted was a huge supporter of our school and the method of teaching we employed. Had he not died, he would have been an investor in our school here," Hope said. "The lion's share of his estate went to his ex-wife and daughter."

Those facts were easy enough to check, and I intended to do so. Time to move on. "Did Trevor have any enemies?"

"Other than a passel of women whom he painted, screwed, and then rejected?" Faith asked. "And maybe a dozen local husbands who wanted to string him up and castrate him?"

She had a point. Trevor had a long list of people who wished him bodily harm. As my aunt Loulane would say, "Hell hath no fury like a woman scorned." Add to that list the cuckolded husbands of those women and it was a violent mix.

"Tell me more about how LaRue died. There are suspicious elements." I wasn't leaving until I had some questions answered. "I've been hired by Kitten to get the goods on you to run you out of town." I raised a hand to quell their objections.

"If it isn't me, it'll be someone else. You're in her crosshairs. So spill the beans. I'll find out one way or another and it would be best to hear your version."

Hope signaled to her sisters with her eyes. They stayed quiet and let her talk. "Ted smoked cigarettes. And he drank hard. He lived hard." Hope actually looked a little sad. "We tried to steer him to a healthier life. Charity and me both. And then Faith when she came to town. He was bullheaded. He wouldn't give up a single vice, and it cost him his life. I think he had a heart attack and fell in the bayou and drowned."

"Heart attack?" That was convenient, but there had been fluid in his lungs. I wished the coroner had been more thorough—water or fluid. It made a huge difference.

"He had a few dizzy spells, some arrhythmia. Weakness. Pain on his left side. I tried to get him to a doctor, but he refused." A single tear slipped down Hope's cheek.

"The coroner's report noted that he was possibly poisoned."

"Really?" They spoke in unison, and if they were acting surprised, they were good actresses.

"Really. And this is going to come back to haunt you."

"We didn't do anything." Faith was angry. "I'm tired of being accused of every crime in the book just because I follow a different religious practice. We don't harm anyone or anything. We don't even eat meat!"

Other than the fact they were leading my partner along, I actually had no beef with the sisters. I liked them. They had great Goth fashion taste and they were trapping the feral cats to make their lives better. It was a big plus in their favor in my book.

"Okay, if you're innocent about LaRue, what about the St. Pe marriage and the accusation that you, Hope, put a spell on the husband."

"If I'd put a spell on Kenny, it would be to grow a pair. That was the most henpecked man I've ever seen. Lurleen ran over him and he was such a milquetoast he just begged her to dig her stilettos in harder."

"Yet you were having an affair with him." I put it out there.

"Don't be a jackass. I wouldn't touch that blob of testosterone-deprived gristle with a ten-foot pole."

"And yet you were named as a codefendant in his divorce?"

"Without any evidence to the fact. That was Lurleen's weird fantasy. She needed someone to blame because she rolled over Kenny so many times he didn't have a vertebra left. He enjoyed talking with me because I didn't belittle him every five seconds."

"So it was all a false accusation?"

"Have you seen the photographs of us flying on broomsticks? Another picture of us raising Elvis from the dead and dancing nude? You were here. Were we naked?"

She made her point. People who were slightly different, especially in a small town, were often targeted with malicious rumors. But being on the right side of the truth was no guarantee that trouble would be kept at bay. I knew that for a fact. My thoughts took me to the sense of something very dark in the woods.

"Have you noticed anything unusual in the woods around the manor?"

"Other than Corey Fontana and his sicko mother? They were out there yesterday evening with binoculars spying on us. Like we wouldn't be aware they were there."

She raised two big issues. "They were truly spying on you?"

"Yes."

"What time?"

"Late afternoon."

"And you knew they were there and didn't call the sheriff?"

Faith rolled her eyes. "Right. Every time some local yokel wants to poke around, we should call the sheriff." She smiled. "Maybe that big handsome lawman should just move in here, to protect us you know."

I ignored her bait. "How did you know they were in the woods?"

Hope stood and went to a window where a strange collection of sticks, ribbon, and wires had been rigged together to make a dangling ornament. In the center was a pentacle. "It's made from rowan wood," Hope explained. "Blessed by a high priestess. Yesterday, we placed these in the trees around the manor. Now we're protected. The parts here are apple wood, from our own trees. When someone trespasses, we sense it."

It was an interesting bundle of twigs, copper wires, and red ribbon, but I didn't see how it could have magical properties. "How does it work?"

Hope was clearly aware of my skepticism. "You only need to know that it does work. When someone comes close to us, we know. In fact, there's someone coming now. Not far away." She touched the gewgaw and returned it to hang in the window.

I was not so easily distracted. "Is there something in the woods that you're afraid of?"

"Afraid?" Charity pondered the word. "Not afraid. Aware of, yes. Cautious of, yes. But it's shown no propensity to harm us. Others may not be so fortunate."

"Is it something you . . . conjured up?"

She shook her head. "We don't do dark. We've told you that."

Their matter-of-fact dismissal of something sinister in the woods was more unnerving than if they'd pretended it wasn't there. "What is it that's out there?"

"Something that was here long before us," Charity said. "We loved Trevor, but he was a troubled soul. Sometimes talent is bought at great cost."

Living in the Mississippi Delta I knew the legend of Robert Johnson and how he'd sold his soul to the devil for musical talent. It was said he'd met the devil at the crossroads of Highways 49 and 61 and sealed the deal—his soul for musical talent. It was a bad bargain for Johnson, who died at the age of twenty-seven, poisoned by a lover's husband. There was no doubt he was a wildly accomplished bluesman, but he didn't live to enjoy his fame. The parallels were undeniable with Trevor. And more than scary.

I'd never bought into stories of soul-selling or magical enchantment outside of the fairy tales I'd loved as a child. But the Harringtons acted as if such things were commonplace. And that possibly Trevor's outrageous artistic talent came from such a bargain. Had he made a deal and finally had to pay up?

The front door flew open and I jumped at least a foot in the air. A lean man in a black suit and turtleneck stepped inside. "Forgive me, I tried to knock but the door opened of its own volition."

"Who are you?" Again, Faith was remarkably composed. As if strangers walking in the front door was an everyday occurrence.

"Marlow Spurlock, at your service." He whipped an envelope from his coat pocket and handed it to me. "Ms. Sarah Booth Delaney, I do believe."

"Yes."

"The instructions are included."

"Wait a minute. What is this about?" I wasn't about to accept candy—or an envelope—from a stranger.

"I represent the Pickingill Society. That's a check to find the true murderer of Trevor Musgrove. We are content the witches are innocent—until proven guilty."

"The Pickingill Society?" I was the only one in the room who didn't know what that was.

"Thank you for coming," Hope said. "We're honored by your support."

"We will be in touch." Spurlock bowed once again and was out the door before I could gather my thoughts. I hurried to the window to watch him get into a limo and drive away. Hope had been correct that someone was arriving. I glanced at the charm that hung in the window with renewed respect. "What the hell was that?"

"Marlow Spurlock would seem to be a practitioner of the craft. George Pickingill was a cunning man from Essex. The society promotes and protects the rights of witches globally." She was full of herself. "We've attracted some big guns to our cause."

"How did they hear about Trevor's murder?"

"It's more than that," Hope explained. "If we win the fight for school vouchers in Mississippi, it will start a movement across the nation to open Wiccan schools in other states. This is just the beginning."

"What's in the envelope?" Faith asked.

I opened it and looked at the check for ten grand. Clearly marked was the word retainer. "They want to hire Delaney Detective Agency." I unfolded the single sheet of paper. "Find the real killer—and the proof to convict him, her, or them—and we'll meet whatever fees you set."

"Wow." Even Faith looked impressed. "That is a big gun."

"But I can't accept it." It killed me to say those words. I needed that money.

"Why not?" Charity asked.

"Kitten has already paid the agency to find out how you're financing the purchase of the Musgrove lands. DDA already has a client."

She shrugged. "So what? Proving our innocence—if we are indeed innocent—can dovetail with finding out our past sins and financial misdeeds." Her wicked grin flitted over her red lips. "Seems to me it wouldn't be a conflict of interest to do both at the same time."

I wanted to buy in to her line of thinking, but my honest skepticism reared its ugly head. "I don't think that would be ethical."

"As long as you find the truth—and tell it—how would it be unethical?"

I'd have to run this by Tinkie and also Coleman. The only thing I really had going for me was a good name and I wouldn't risk it for an easy ten grand—no matter how much it killed me to walk away. It was time to return to the business that had brought me to the manor.

"Look, Doc Sawyer is searching for the poison used to kill Trevor. If you had to point the finger at someone who would want Trevor dead, who would it be?" I asked.

"We don't falsely accuse people." Faith lifted her chin as she spoke, as if the moral high ground belonged only to her.

"Bully for you. I'm trying to help you. If I had a direction to begin my search, it would make the whole thing go faster."

"Bob Fontana," the sisters said at once.

"Why Bob?"

"Kitten had a thing for Trevor. She was over here a lot and Bob knew it. He would sometimes park on the road, waiting for her to leave." Charity looked guilty. "It wasn't any of our business and we tried to stay out of it. But Kitten and Esmeralda were frequent visitors."

"The tabloid reporter?" How had I missed that huge factoid?

"Yes, she and Kitten often arrived in tandem." Faith knew exactly what pot she was stirring. "Those three were cooking up some kind of mischief, and Bob knew it. Of course we never *saw* anything to confirm our suspicions."

Not when such a sight might melt the eyeballs in their heads. The idea of witnessing either woman in bed with Trevor might put me off sex for good. "Good to know. And Bob was aware of this?"

"Some might think he sent his wife here," Hope said. "We suspected that might be the case. Bob wants this land. Kitten has . . . abilities that can bring a man to heel. She just didn't reckon on Trevor. He'd been a libertine since he was thirteen. There's not much he hadn't experienced and tried. She was just more of the same to him."

"That must have bruised her ego."

"Black and blue," Charity chimed in. "By the way, how is Tinkie? Any morning sickness yet?"

"I'm asking you, please don't mislead her and break her heart. This baby obsession is more than just empty-womb syndrome. This goes bone deep for her."

"We would never harm Tinkie," Hope said, and for that split second, staring into her golden-brown eyes, I believed her. "We're helping her. I promise."

"That had better be true." I prepared to leave just as the front door flew open for a second time in less than ten minutes. Another tall, dark-clad stranger walked into the parlor. It was the man I'd seen in the apple orchard when I'd discovered Trevor's body. Malvik. Coleman had obviously released him from jail.

"What are you doing here?" Faith asked him angrily.

"I've come to help."

"Oh, joy. We'll swing for sure now," Faith said. "Sarah Booth, if you'll excuse us, we really need to have a word with our . . . friend."

I had no choice but to depart, but my thoughts remained on the Harringtons, Malvik, and what was really happening at Musgrove Manor.

10

On the way home from the manor I phoned Cece. We conspired to meet at Millie's. Cece would stop by Hilltop and pick up Tinkie. It was time for an intervention.

I captured a table in the quietest part of the busy café and had a moment to confer with Millie before my friends arrived. "We have to snap Tinkie out of this," I said, letting my chin drop into my hand, elbow propped on the table. I felt exhausted. Something about the Harringtons always left me worn out. I wondered if they might be energy vampires.

"Sarah Booth, I'd agree with you except for the fact that Tinkie needs to experience this."

"What are you talking about?" Millie always backed me up. Even when I was wrong.

"She's getting to an age where this dream either has to happen or die. The same can be said for you."

My God, was she channeling Jitty? Speaking of which, my haint had been unusually silent. She was definitely up to something—another brick on my load of worry.

"Time is marching by," Millie said with such compassion that it freaked me out. "Sure, you can have a baby at forty, or maybe even forty-three or four, but—"

"That's ten years away. That's a decade. No rush."

She tilted her head. "The older you are, the harder it is to conceive and the harder it will be to be a good parent for your child. Do you want to be sixty-five when your child graduates from high school?"

"Old men do it all the time."

She scoffed. "And they are not the primary caregivers. The woman is. Think of the memories with your mom. At the swimming hole, learning to dance with her, making Halloween costumes, and chopping down Christmas trees. Do you want your child to have memories of you in the nursing home?"

My mother had been vibrant and alive. She'd been twenty-six when I was born. Only thirty-eight when she died. I was almost there. I would soon be the same age as my mother when she died. That took my breath away. She'd been so . . . grown. I still felt like a child.

"I don't mean to open old wounds," Millie continued, "but the human body is made to reproduce at a young age." She slipped into a chair and covered my hand with one of hers. "Let her have this dream or delusion or hope—whatever you want to call it. Let it play out. If you don't, she'll never forgive you. You cannot interfere."

"I'm only trying to protect her heart."

"And you're a good friend. But you can't—or shouldn't—jump in the middle of this."

I heard the truth in her words, but there was another truth. The one where my friend did irrational things like stealing a baby. Tinkie was emotional to the extreme when it came to having a child. "She could really flip out. And not come back."

I heard it then—my worry for myself, for losing my friend and partner and being left alone. Again.

"You have to trust in her strength, Sarah Booth. You don't have to encourage her in this, but for heaven's sake, don't make this a choice between you and her need for a child."

I nodded. "Point taken."

She stood up. "She won't leave you. Or Oscar. Or Chablis. Or the rest of us. She may flirt with the edge, but she won't jump."

I didn't know how Millie could be so certain. I wished I had her faith. "Okay." I conceded because I knew any other action would only lead to more damage.

The bell on the door jangled and my two best friends walked in. Tinkie looked grumpy and Cece looked victorious. It wasn't necessary to ask if Cece had leaned on Tinkie to get her here. Clearly she had.

"I don't want to hear a word about the baby," Tinkie said as she sat down and picked up a menu, refusing to even look me in the eye.

"Not a word."

That got her attention and she looked up suspiciously. "Really?"

"I swear."

"Then why am I here?"

"The case." I pulled the check from the Pickingill Society from my pocket. "We have two clients who want the same thing, sort of. Can we work for two people?"

Tinkie fingered the check and looked at Cece. "Yes. The truth will answer both clients' questions. I don't see that it's a problem."

If Tinkie said yes, I was good to go. "Okay. So let me fill you in."

By the time we finished, we'd wolfed down three cups of coffee each, bacon, biscuits, grits, and eggs. And Tinkie had inhaled an order of fried pickles. Not something she normally chomped at breakfast, but we all three enjoyed the crispy tart dill chips. I licked my fingers. "I need a nap."

"Why don't you call Coleman and work off some of that food?" Cece winked at Tinkie.

"Maybe I will." Bacon grease made me sassy. "The problem is that every time Coleman and I have a chance to be alone, something happens. Like Tinkie bursts in the door and terrorizes us."

"Maybe take a room at the Prince Albert," Tinkie suggested. "On me. I booked one the other afternoon for me and Oscar and it was wonderfully romantic. We had private massages, champagne, a fabulous crab salad. And the room had a whirlpool big enough for two. I had to be poured into the bed." She laughed. "Oscar and I have found renewed romance lately. We're as hot for each other as we were when we first married. It's almost . . . magical."

"Good for you," Cece said. "That's the secret to a good life—keeping the romance alive."

I nodded. I'd promised not to badger her about the baby issue, so I sure wasn't going to comment on her sex life. At least not right now. Besides, they'd put the idea of a nooner with Coleman in my head and I was eager to act on the suggestion. Cece stood and stretched. "I'm going to work. Esmeralda is trying to steal my thunder. Where in the hell does she come up with the bullshit she's peddling?"

"She's a genius at exaggeration with a salacious twist." Tinkie stood, too. "I need to get home. Oscar's going to be there for lunch."

"The desk in his office is uncomfortable?" The question popped out before I could stop it.

"The bed is better," Tinkie said. "Besides, I picked up some brownies for us. Afternoon delight." She giggled and twenty years fell away, leaving the girl I'd known in high school who flirted with being naughty but had been raised a proper Daddy's Girl. I couldn't even be shocked that Tinkie was indulging in a little weed and romance. Why not? As Millie had pointed out, time was running short. Soon we would be middle-aged.

"I'll take you home if you share your baked goods," I said.

"Deal." Tinkie picked up the checks. "My treat."

The little box of brownies rode silently on the front seat of the Roadster as I left Hilltop. When I was on the county road, I ate one brownie. Then another. I'd given up smoking cigarettes and had no desire to smoke pot again. The brownies, though, were quite tasty. Tinkie hadn't made them herself, thank goodness, because she was Ptomaine Trudy in the kitchen, but had bought them "from a friend."

Coleman would never indulge—he was a law-and-order man all the way. He held himself accountable to the same law he expected others to obey. And since I didn't want to put him in the position of being in the house with an illegal substance, I ate the third and final brownie as I pulled in front of my home. I called Coleman, a call that was easier to make than I'd anticipated.

"Can you come over?" I asked. "I have an indecent proposal." I had stepped right out of my inhibitions and fears and I had Mary Jane to thank for that.

"On the way."

Was it possible we might actually have some time alone, without interruption? I opened the door and was assaulted by a horrid smell. Something had died in Dahlia House. "Sweetie Pie! Pluto!" I called my critters, frantic at what might have occurred in my absence. Had they found something dead in the woods and brought it into the house? I knew they were miffed at the fact I'd left them home, but this was way beyond payback.

No sign of the animals in the parlor or dining room. I hurried to the kitchen, trying not to breathe. I skidded to a halt at the beautiful woman with long curly hair stirring a pot on my stove. The horrible smell came from the pot. "What the he—"

"A potion to bring your lover close."

"The smell of that would drive a dead man down the road. What the hell is it?"

"Magic." The strange woman turned to me and even though she was pale and fair with long red hair, I knew who it was.

"What are you up to, Jitty?" The beautiful woman in the medieval dress was my very own ghost, come to torment me.

"The power of love is in the ability to enchant the soul. You need some help in the enchantment department."

"The stench of whatever you're cooking up would curdle a man's desire—and Coleman is on his way. I don't want his desire curdled. Clean it up and clear it out."

"It isn't wise to order a witch around."

"Witch, snitch. Who are you pretending to be now?" I opened the kitchen window and back door to air out the room. The smell was truly rancid. I wouldn't even consider looking in her pot.

"Bark of rowan, mold of fern, eggs gone bad, and blood that's burned, bring the past to one who's blind, show her magic of her own kind."

The incantation sent a shiver down my spine.

The kitchen window normally gave a view of the back pasture and my horses. What appeared instead was a moment from my past. I was in the car with my mother on a lovely spring day. The top was down and we were flying through the wide-open cotton fields, the new green plants shooting up. My mother reached across the seat and caressed my hair. "No matter how grown you become, you'll always be my little girl."

And then the scene was gone and the horses grazed peacefully in the pasture once again. Had Jitty cast a spell or were the three marijuana brownies I'd gobbled down having an effect?

"How did you do that?" I asked, shaken by the intensity of emotion I'd felt.

"Enchantment. You need a child, Sarah Booth. Someone to hold you to the future, like you did for your mother."

"Do it again?"

"I'm not here to push you into the past. It's only a glimpse of what you should create in the future." She came toward me, the rich brocade of her dress swishing as she moved. Her green eyes glittered in her pale face, and red curls cascaded down her shoulders and back. She was beautiful. I don't think I'd ever seen Jitty more beautiful, and I found myself giggling.

Instead of being perturbed, she only smiled. "I see you've taken steps to relax. That's good. You know the Delaney women suffer from tilted-womb syndrome. Coleman's little swimmers are fighting an uphill battle as it is. The more relaxed you are, the better the chances."

"Who are you?" She was a witch, but I couldn't put my finger on which one.

"Morgan le Fay."

"The witch of Arthurian legend. Good or evil, or both. You loved the king." My thoughts were a little helter-skelter.

"And I betrayed him."

"Not as much as his wife and Lancelot did." The betrayal of King Arthur by Lancelot and Guinevere had ruined my eleventh summer.

I'd wept for weeks with all the horrid angst of a middle schooler. I felt the tears building again behind my eyes. I was an emotional mess. "Why are you here as the sorceress that destroyed Camelot?" That was a bit of an exaggeration, but I had to get her to depart. Coleman was on his way.

"Love is an elixir that brings tremendous good, but also much pain. Be careful, Sarah Booth."

I put my hands on my hips. "Listen to me. You've tortured me for months to get laid. By anyone. And now that I'm trying, you're going to show up and tell me that I might be inviting disaster into my life? You can't have it both ways."

"The only way to truly love is in the moment. Just remember that."

"You bet. Now scram." I heard Coleman's car pulling up in the front.

Jitty did a twirl and disappeared in a little salvo of regal horns. I was alone in the kitchen with a bitter wind blowing in the open window and no sign of my haint or her stinky concoction. Coleman's knock came at the front door and I ran through the house to open it wide. He stood in the opening, and I hurled myself into his arms. I couldn't say if the pot had totally reduced my inhibitions or if I was so afraid that an army of invaders would arrive to destroy the moment that I felt we had no time to waste.

He carried me inside and closed and locked the door. "Tinkie isn't hiding in here, is she?"

"No. We're alone."

"I can't believe it."

My heart was pounding. "Want a drink?"

"No. Do you?"

"Uh, no." I had no intention of confessing why I didn't need a drink. We had a bit of privacy and I wasn't going to squander it. "No." I took his hand and led him up the stairs to my bedroom. Another door was closed and locked.

The midday sun came through the gauzy curtains and the room took on the glow of February sunlight. I'd daydreamed about our first time with champagne and flowers and romantic music, maybe a little dancing. None of that was important. I felt as if I'd stepped into a dream where the only thing that mattered was Coleman.

He kissed me, and all other thoughts fled. The only thing I wanted was his skin against mine, his hands teasing out the secret places that made me moan with pleasure and desire. I kissed his neck and chest and drew him to me.

He captured the small silk bag that hung between my breasts, the one Tinkie had given me. I hadn't taken it off. I stayed his hand. "Leave it."

"What is it?" he asked.

"Tinkie gave it to me." I didn't want to mention that it was charmed—a love spell to bring him to my bed. I didn't want to believe the Harringtons' magic had anything to do with what was happening at this moment. But I also didn't want to risk destroying this intimacy.

"You should wear emeralds," Coleman said. "Your birthstone."

I shook my head. "I'm very happy with this token of friendship. And the fact that you're here with me. Jewels don't capture my interest."

"You should have a diamond here." Coleman kissed the hollow at the base of my throat. "And a sapphire here." He kissed my belly button. "And a ruby here." He moved slowly down my body, planting kisses on every inch and naming precious stones.

At last, we made love. Slowly, careful of each other at first, until the intensity of our passion pushed us to the brink and over.

11

The day had advanced to afternoon when we faced each other, fully aware of where we were. I felt as if I were waking from the best dream ever, but a bit of lethargy still held me. Coleman pushed my hair back from my face. "I've been waiting for this moment for such a long time. And it was well worth the wait."

"No regrets?" We could never go back and undo the step we'd taken.

"None. What about you?"

"I can't imagine living in Sunflower County without your friendship, Coleman. Whatever else happens, we can never become enemies."

"Love is a risk."

He sounded a lot like Jitty. "I'm a little risk-averse right now." I traced his lips with my finger. He was an incredible kisser. Incredible, in fact, with every aspect of lovemaking.

"I promise I'll never intentionally hurt you. I won't betray you or—"

I put my finger on his lips to stop him. "A very wise person told me to love in the moment. We can't predict what the future will hurl at us. Right now is all we can guarantee, and it's enough."

"Your friend is wise. Was it Tinkie?"

"No. An older friend."

"Will I meet her?"

"Maybe." I couldn't tell. Would Jitty show herself to Coleman if he was part of my daily life? It would be interesting to see. Or maybe I was just a bit nuts, and Jitty was a delusion that only I could appreciate. "Coleman, do you believe in magic?"

He drew me close against him. "*This* is magic, Sarah Booth. It's really the only magic that humans are given. To love each other and share such pleasure and this deep bond. How can you not believe?"

"I didn't say I didn't believe." My hand went to the charm around my neck. Did I owe this fabulous episode to the Harringtons and their witchy power? I resisted that. I wanted Coleman in my bed for one reason only—because he loved me and wanted to be there. The idea that he'd been tricked made me want to cringe.

Coleman lifted my chin so he could look into my eyes, blue into green. "I've loved you for such a long time, Sarah Booth. Since high school, though I couldn't see it then. You were so . . . aloof. I know now it was because you'd lost so much so early. You were always there as a friend for me, but any time a guy tried to move closer, you edged backward. I saw it more than once, but I didn't understand. I knew you were destined for a life outside Zinnia. I just assumed you knew it, too and were looking to the future. That you wanted to remain free to pursue acting."

I'd lost too much. Coleman was right about that. In high school, I'd had my share of fun and good times, but there'd been no going steady or dating one guy exclusively. I'd kept everyone at arm's length. Even Coleman. "I never felt more secure than when I was with you. Never. I see that in hindsight. But I did have to leave Mississippi." I'd wrapped myself in the dream of being a Broadway star. I had to try, or I would have regretted it the rest of my life. It hadn't worked, but it had led me to my career as a private investigator. "It was the path I had to travel to get here."

"And God knows I'm glad you're here." Coleman delivered another searing kiss, followed by a wicked grin. "I have to get back to work."

"Me, too." This was the tragedy of a nooner. The rest of the day required adult, responsible conduct. It was going to be very hard to leave the warm bed and Coleman's body. The reality of day-to-day life was like being splashed with cold water. Not pleasant.

Instead of moving to get out of bed, we snuggled closer.

When our cell phones began to ring, we both

sighed. The real world demanded our attention whether we wanted to give it or not.

"DeWayne," Coleman said, looking at his phone.

"Tinkie," I said, looking at mine. But even though her call forced me out of my warm bed and Coleman's arms, I was glad to see my partner participating in life again. "We should get up before they storm the front door. Tinkie's put aside her baby fanaticism to aggravate us."

"By the way," Coleman said as he slipped into his pants, "Esmeralda has invited me to dinner tonight."

My head popped through the sweatshirt I'd chosen to wear. "Dinner? Are you going?"

"Of course," Coleman said with a wicked grin. "I'm working a case."

"What case?"

"Trevor's death."

That calmed me considerably. "You think Esmeralda is involved in the murder?" Having dinner with a murder suspect came under the heading of Job Description for my favorite sheriff. I'd done the same a few times, hoping to elicit leads.

"Esmeralda had sued Trevor over a nude painting. She wanted to buy it and he refused to sell it to her. She took him to court and lost. That's when she and Kitten Fontana became thick as thieves."

"Kitten was a model, too. Any leads on how Trevor died?"

"Doc still believes he had to be poisoned, and he's working to identify the substance used and how it was administered." He turned away to slip into his pants. I'd never imagined Coleman would be so modest.

True to my predictions, I heard a loud pounding on the front door. Sweetie Pie began to howl and Pluto rushed into the bedroom and hurled himself at the bed. Our respite was over.

Still zipping my jeans, I raced down the stairs and to the front door to let Tinkie in. Instead of my partner, Esmeralda Grimes stood in my doorway. She wore five-inch stilettos, what looked to be a tiger-skin coat, and a black miniskirt that almost showed possible, as Aunt Loulane sometimes referred to the female anatomy.

"We have to talk." She tried to push past me.

"Is that real tiger skin?" Her answer would determine her fate. I might have to wring her neck and bury her in the back pasture if she said yes.

"Fake. It's fake. For heaven's sake, you bleeding heart. I can't afford tiger skin."

"You'd wear it if you could afford it?"

Perhaps she heard the edge of mayhem in my voice because she really looked at me. "It's a moot issue. I'm here to talk about those witches. They're dangerous and you need to put a stop to them."

"Me?"

"Is there someone else here that I'm talking to?"

Coleman stepped out of the shadows. He was in full uniform. "Yes, I'm here. Care to explain what you're accusing the Harrington sisters of?"

Esmeralda looked from Coleman to me and back to Coleman. I swear, green shot from her eyes. "The sisters told me they put a spell on the sheriff so he'd view you romantically. They are powerful, aren't they? He certainly wouldn't be here unless someone had cast a big mojo on him. How does it feel to be controlled by outside influences?"

"Oooooh. I love it that you're jealous!" I couldn't stop myself.

Coleman took Esmeralda's arm and walked her out onto the porch. "Close the door, Sarah Booth. I'll be in touch."

I did as he asked, but I peered out from the sidelight to watch the expressions on their faces. If only I could lip-read.

I heard those regal bugles, *ta-da-da-DAAAAAA*. Suddenly, I could understand everything Esmeralda was saying by watching her lips. I'd been given the power to read lips—or else the marijuana was playing with my reality. I couldn't see Coleman's lips, only the back of his head. But his posture told me he was intense.

"Don't tell me you've hooked up with that

Sarah Booth. I've never seen her in a dress. Does she even shave her legs?" Esmeralda asked. "Is she really even a girl?"

My fists clenched on the curtains. I really wanted to show a little girl power and kick her butt down the steps. Whatever Coleman said, she laughed.

"I heard you'd been mooning after her. Too bad. You could do so much better." Esmeralda wore red, red lipstick, which actually made it easier for me to follow what she was saying.

Coleman pointed to her car.

"Are we still on for dinner?" Esmeralda asked. "Give me a chance to show you a romantic alternative."

Coleman gently took her arm and walked her down the steps to her car. At last he turned so I could see his lips—and what lips they were. The thought of what they could do to my body made me flush.

"I'll see you tonight, Esmeralda. At the Prince Albert. At eight."

She stood on tiptoe, which was damn hard to do in five-inch stilettos, and kissed his cheek. "It's a date," she said. In a moment she was gone, tearing down the driveway and sending dead sycamore leaves out behind her in a whirlwind.

Coleman came back to the front door.

"I may have to kill her," I said. "Just on principle."

"I may have to help." He kissed me. "But until we find Trevor's killer, let's just let it all play out. I'll see you when I finish my date with Esmeralda."

"If you find what killed Trevor, let me know. I might have need of it."

He only laughed as he got in the cruiser and drove away.

"How was it, Sarah Booth?" Tinkie asked when I called her back.

"How was what?"

"Oh for crying out loud. Stop acting like a silly virgin. We all know you and Coleman got it on. We're all dying for the details."

She'd accomplished their goal, because blood rushed to my face. And I wasn't even dealing with Tinkie and my friends in person. "I don't kiss and tell."

"Either it was very, very good, or so awful you can't deal with it." Tinkie's charming laugh tinkled like silver bells.

"It was good." I couldn't help it. She was my best friend, and who else would I share the glorious details with? "Actually, it was magnificent."

"Oh, Sarah Booth, I'm so happy for you."

"Me, too. Now let's get to business." I couldn't talk about it anymore. It was just too intensely personal. I'd suffer at the hands of my friends—

because I'd certainly tormented them about their personal lives. But it was all done in love, and I would survive.

"I think we need to dig into Bob Fontana's real estate developments," Tinkie said. "Meet me at the bank."

"Only if you promise not to take Oscar down on his desk."

"I make no promises," Tinkie said with a naughty wink in her voice. "Maybe you could give me some tips. You know, different positions, what do you say when you're excited. 'Oh, cuff me, Coleman. I've been a very bad prisoner.' "

"Goodbye." I hung up before the blush shot out the top of my head and left me a vegetable. Tinkie really knew how to get me going. Before I picked her up, I needed to find a defense mechanism that would keep her from making me blush. Once she got hold of the fact she could do that, I'd be dead.

"Come on, Sweetie Pie, Pluto. Let's hit the road. It's almost time for something to eat." And I had to admit, I'd worked up an appetite with Coleman. Whoever said making love didn't qualify as a high-intensity workout had never made love with Coleman Peters.

Tinkie and I sat across the desk from Harold Erkwell. Tinkie might want to tease me, but she wouldn't risk Harold's feelings. I'd been completely up-front with him about Coleman, but there was no sense rubbing his nose in it. I was safe from her teasing as long as we were working with him.

"I can't violate Bob Fontana's privacy," Harold said with a twinkle in his eye. "But I can give you some leads. It's up to you to follow through." He quickly wrote a list of former partners, contractors who'd worked for Fontana Construction and Development, homeowners, and one woman who had no job description by her name. Lisbet Bradley.

"Who is she?" I asked.

"Best to discover that on your own."

I rolled my eyes. "Thanks." But when I realized how spoiled I sounded, I laughed. "I mean it. Thanks. Nothing like a little mystery to get me going."

Sweetie Pie had fallen asleep in a corner of Harold's elegantly decorated office. Pluto sat on his desk staring at Tinkie as if he knew of her activity in Oscar's nearby office. "Give me a break," Tinkie finally said to the cat. "You can't turn me to stone. Or a pillar of salt. I'm married. What I did was perfectly legal."

"Shame, shame, shame," I muttered.

Harold laughed. "What are the Harringtons up to?"

"Spells, enchantments, strange men in black formal attire."

"I met Malvik. Quite the character. I have to

say, I liked him." Harold leaned back in his chair. "He was asking about Fontana Development, too."

"Really?" Malvik had been in Zinnia the night Trevor was killed. He'd called himself the leader of the Harrington Coven, but perhaps he merely did the sisters' bidding.

"He knows a lot about the Harringtons and their business. And he's very talkative."

"Does he bite?" I asked.

"He didn't try me, but you and Tinkie may be far more tempting. I'd say he's definitely worth checking out."

While we were in town, it was worth a trip to the hotel to see if we could find Malvik when he wasn't with the sister witches. If he had his own agenda, he might be willing to spill a few beans on what Faith, Hope, and Charity saw in their futures. Tinkie and I decided there was no time like the present.

The hotel was only a block or two from the bank and we walked. The day had turned warmer with a bright sun. Walking was exhilarating. I loved the Prince Albert, which had been a storefront and warehouse, but had been remodeled into a boutique hotel. The staff members had the whitest, prettiest teeth I'd ever seen. And they smiled all the time. They made customer service into an art form.

Before we could blink, Tinkie and I were seated

on a plush sofa in the lobby sipping peach iced tea while the staff went to speak with Malvik and tell him he had guests.

"Do you think he'll come talk to us?" Tinkie asked. She was eating the lemon out of her tea—a move that made my mouth pucker in sympathy.

"Why not? We can't force him to talk and I get a sense that he's very competitive with those witches. He might want to cast aspersions on them."

"That's not my motivation." The voice came from behind us and I felt a flush run up my neck. Not my finest moment.

"Good to know," Tinkie said smoothly. "So why are you willing to talk to us?"

He signaled us up and over to the small and quiet bar area. When we were at a table, he ordered for us. "Three pomegranate and blood orange vodka cosmos."

Nothing like a shot of vodka to while away the rest of the afternoon, but I wasn't about to object. Our drinks arrived and I tasted mine, which was excellent and a beautiful bloodred color that was perfectly suited to Malik's vampiric look. He was still wearing his cape.

"Why are you in town?" Tinkie asked him.

"Do you believe the witches have powers?" He countered with a question of his own.

"Yes." Tinkie didn't even hesitate.

He arched his eyebrows and waited for me to answer.

"No." But I was lying. A little. My hand went instinctively to my chest where the silk charm hung beneath my shirt. I did believe. The afternoon of lovemaking with Coleman had been extraordinary.

Malvik grinned. "I see." He sipped his drink and I wondered if he was giving me a chance to come clean. "They are truly witches. Genetic witches. And they have powers. Which they use mostly for good. They are also exceptional teachers, and the world needs the things they want to teach."

"Okay. So how does that involve you?" I asked.

"I'm going to teach the physics, astronomy, and geography courses. Hope is strong in the creative arts and languages. Faith is a genius with math and business. Charity is into agriculture, growing things, caring for the planet and the environment."

"She's the one with the green thumb?" I asked, wondering again what kind of poison had killed Trevor Musgrove and if it could be growing in the Harrington herb garden.

"Yes, she can grow anything, and they plan to produce all of their own organic foods at the school. Imagine the impact. Students will learn to sustain life, provide clean and healthy food for themselves, and also apply themselves to the subject matter that elevates the human soul. Compassion and responsibility. And they'll be disconnected from technology while they garden and farm."

It did sound like something the world needed. Too bad it came with a dollop of murder. "Do you know what happened to Trevor?" I was tired of pussyfooting around.

"I believe he died of fright."

Now that was an unexpected answer. "What could have frightened a grown man to death?" I asked. "After all, he saw Kitten Fontana naked and he didn't die from that." Tinkie and I high-fived each other.

"You've felt something there, at the manor, haven't you?" Malvik stared at me, watching.

The claw marks on my door and on the beautiful old wood of the third floor—Trevor's floor—came back to me. I had sensed something very sinister in the woods. And Tinkie had, too.

"What is it?" Tinkie asked Malvik. "Do you know what it is? Faith warned me that evil was afoot in Sunflower County."

"She did?" I was more concerned about Tinkie than ever. What if they'd given her some kind of hallucinogen to make her believe she was pregnant? "What kind of evil?"

"You've felt it. The oppressive presence. The sense of being watched." Malvik finished his drink, eyed Tinkie's full glass, and signaled the bartender for another. He was going to be toasted by five o'clock. "There is something afoot here in Sunflower County, and it isn't the witches. But it is dark. I believe Trevor was a victim of this darkness."

"That's mumbo jumbo, and I don't scare that easily." I felt it was imperative that I didn't show him that he was succeeding in frightening me. Once Malvik and the sisters realized they had gained the upper hand—the perception that they were powerful, magical people—we would all be their victims.

"It's not made-up, and you know it. Deny it to me, but in your heart you know exactly what I'm talking about."

"There are these huge claw marks on Sarah Booth's door," Tinkie said before I could stop her.

Malvik's gaze was almost mesmerizing. I couldn't look away when he spoke. "You're a target, Ms. Delaney."

"Anyone could have done that to frighten me."

"Yes, that's one possibility. And the other possibility, that something wicked and cruel is roaming the countryside, is the one you run away from. To quote the bard, 'There are more things in heaven and earth.' Shakespeare knew many things."

That was a quote my aunt Loulane used when she wanted to make a point that my worldview was too narrow. Hearing it on Malvik's lips was upsetting. "If there's this evil creature in the woods, what is it? What does it want?" I asked.

"It protects the sisters. And it will do whatever is necessary to make sure no one threatens or harms them. You know about Ted LaRue. He might have had a heart attack, but it wasn't from natural causes. And Kenny St. Pe. Were you aware that shortly after his divorce-court episode his wife Lurleen drove off the road on a perfect, sunny day and into a slough? They said she was alive when the alligators came after her."

He was scaring me, and good.

"Then you're saying the witches are responsible for this evil?" Tinkie asked.

Malvik hesitated. If he was pretending to consider his words, he was doing a fine job of it. "Not responsible. It's not as if they willed this thing into existence. It's part of their heritage."

"All the way from Salem," I said sarcastically.

"The witch trials in Salem and subsequent hangings were only one of the horrific events aimed at females who lived even slightly outside the norm. They were burned at the stake, drowned, crushed, tortured. It was a wholesale war against women of property who didn't have a husband to protect them. The witch hunts were far more economic than religious."

"And they were all innocent? None of them practiced magic?"

Malvik grinned. "I didn't say that. But the practitioners and the cunning men, such as I am, weren't generating plagues and curses on communities as we were depicted. Witches were and often still are healers, those trained in the use of barks and leaves to make potions and poultices. The idea that witches or those who practice Wicca are Satan worshippers is laughable."

"A lot of people aren't laughing," Tinkie said.

"Because they haven't bothered to do a simple Google search of Wiccan beliefs."

"And you're saying there are no witches who call upon the darkness to aid their agenda?" I wanted to pin him down.

"There are people who court the devil in all professions and all religions. Pedophiles who use their religious power to abuse children. Doctors who do the same. CEOs of companies who knowingly leave indigenous populations starving after the land has been raped. Evil is everywhere. Just because three women like to perform modern dance around a cauldron doesn't make them evil."

I couldn't argue with his point, but *my* thoughts on Wicca and witches wouldn't amount to a hill of beans. It was what the public thought. And if the masses were pushed into fear, a mob would result. Then, innocent of any misdeeds or not, the Harrington sisters could be injured. Kitten had already shown success at gathering a group of people upset by the idea of witches. The group had been restrained, but that could change.

"If the Harringtons aren't evil, why is this dark presence following them?"

"They are chosen." Malvik put just the right emphasis on the phrase so that it made the hair on my arms stand on end.

"Chosen for what?" I asked.

"They are true witches, Ms. Delaney. It's their birthright. They have abilities, and you should never forget that."

"The ability to frighten a healthy man to death?" I'd had enough of his attempts to intimidate me.

"I don't think Trevor's death was their intent or ambition. I think he was meeting someone in the apple orchard that he didn't want the sisters to know about. I believe he was getting ready to betray them and sell the land to someone else."

"That would be crappy," Tinkie said. "They're making improvements on the property, and they've done a lot of work to get the school accredited."

"Yes, it would be a bitter disappointment." Malvik let us draw our own conclusions.

"Was Malvik meeting Kitten Fontana in the apple orchard?"

"I don't know. But if I had to guess, she would be at the top of my list."

"What does Esmeralda Grimes have to do with any of this?"

He shook his head. "I pay attention, but I've not been able to determine how Ms. Grimes benefits from this association with Ms. Fontana. Perhaps that's a lead for you."

"Perhaps it is."

"Now I must be off. I've chartered a flight to New Orleans to pick up some herbs for the sisters. They're brewing up a concoction that should draw the roaches into the sunlight. Be ready to smash them with your shoe."

He signed the check for the bar tab and was gone with a flutter of his cape.

12

This was going down in history as the longest day of the year. It wasn't even cocktail hour and I felt like I'd completed the Iron Man Triathlon. I was exhausted. Sex, drugs, and rock 'n' roll. That would teach me to jump Coleman's bones in the middle of the day.

By mutual consent, Tinkie and I walked through town and to the courthouse square. Coleman's cruiser was gone, and I felt a stab of disappointment coupled with relief. How could I possibly greet him in public without fainting or kissing him?

"Thinking of the sheriff?" Tinkie asked.

She was damn perceptive. "Yes."

"I know you're scared."

Did I mention she was perceptive? "I am. What if I blow this up?"

"You didn't blow up Graf. And neither did he. I'm over being mad at him. He didn't know about his daughter. The whole thing was just . . . maybe it was destiny."

"Maybe it was."

"If I'm pregnant, Sarah Booth, I'll continue as your partner."

I hadn't even given that consideration, because I knew she wasn't pregnant. "Of course."

She chuckled. "You say that so easily because you have no belief that I'm with child. But you'll see. I'll be the best pregnant partner ever."

I put my arm around her shoulders and gave her a squeeze. "Now *that* I have complete faith in. And you shared some brownies with a powerful punch to them. I wouldn't have been brave enough to be with Coleman without a little weed to relax me."

Tinkie stopped dead in her tracks, her mouth a little O like Mr. Bill about to be crushed. "Uh, about those brownies. I need to tell you—"

I laughed. How like Tinkie to try to wiggle out of even mild drug use. She was a Daddy's Girl through and through. "They were pretty mild. Just enough to take the edge off my anxiety."

"Really, Sarah Booth. They were double-chocolate walnut brownies. You needed permission to reach for what you wanted, but you had to give it to yourself. The idea of being a little stoned did that for you." She shrugged. "So it worked. Good for us."

"I can't believe—"

She cut me off. "Let's check Esmeralda's lawsuit against Trevor. That could prove interesting. We can use Coleman's computer."

He wouldn't care and we'd share what we found with him. "Sure. And I'll follow up on the lead Harold gave us with Lisbet Bradley."

We found DeWayne sitting at the dispatcher's desk reading a Western. He gave a wry grin and waved me into Coleman's office when I asked to use the computer. Tinkie went down the hall to the chancery clerk's office to see about the civil suit Esmeralda had filed against Trevor. I'd know soon enough if there was serious bad blood between the so-called journalist and the artist.

A Google search of Lisbet Bradley brought up some very interesting facts right off the bat. Lisbet was serving time in the Central Mississippi Correctional Facility in Rankin County for embezzlement and fraud. Lisbet had been a real estate broker who'd sold homes in the Arlington Woods subdivision just north of Jackson, Mississippi.

The subdivision had been built on fill land near the Pearl River. At first it was unstable foundations that cracked and began to sink, but the real trouble came with a record-high flood of the Pearl River. The homes were destroyed, for all practical purposes. And it turned out the subdivision was clearly in a floodplain and Lisbet had known about it all along. She'd gambled that the river would never get that high in her lifetime—and lost.

And Bob Fontana had been the contractor on the houses, yet Bob was not named in the prosecution.

It was a nasty kettle of fish. Lisbet had taken the fall and never implicated Bob Fontana. Tinkie was going to love this. It seemed that Bob and Kitten had their fingers in a lot of pies. Now if we could tie them to Trevor's murder—because I didn't for a minute believe Trevor had died of fright—then we'd be on the road to solving the murder and putting the guilty behind bars.

The one ball I'd dropped was investigating the Harringtons' finances—what I'd actually been hired to do. Digging into the witchy sisters involved Trevor's murder, and possibly a whole lot more nefarious events, including Musgrove Manor and how the witches had come up with the money to pay for it. Somehow, the Fontanas were at the root of a lot of problems. It was puzzling why Kitten would hire a private investigator to look into something that might splash back on her and her husband. She was either not very bright or very delusional—or both.

I made notes on the details of the Arlington subdivision case to share with Tinkie, and just as I was finishing she returned from her quest.

"I ran into DeWayne in the courthouse hallway. He told me Coleman picked up Corey Fontana at the *Zinnia Dispatch*. Corey slashed two of Cece's car tires. He said she was writing lies about his parents."

"That boy needs professional help."

"Unless the court orders it, Kitten won't get

it for him. She thinks he's standing up for her. That's what she told Coleman. Anyway, the Fontana lawyer got him out. Kitten bought Cece four new tires."

"If I had more time, I might pity that boy. He's been raised by wolves. Right now, he seems more like a little punk than someone to be pitied. Why isn't he upset about what Esmeralda writes?"

"Esmeralda is nuts," Tinkie said. "She sued Trevor for selling the nude painting she modeled for, saying she was never paid for modeling."

"Did Trevor pay the models? How much does a model make?" It was a legitimate question. "Who did he sell the painting to?"

Tinkie rolled her eyes. "One question at a time, please. You sound like you're on speed." She stepped close to me and peered into my face. "Trevor normally didn't pay models, as far as I can tell. Who knows what models make, and I have no clue who bought Esmeralda's painting. Your eyes are really red, Sarah Booth. I hadn't noticed before." She grinned. "Maybe there was something illegal in those brownies. I hope Coleman doesn't catch on that he's sleeping with a drug hoochie."

"Stop it. *You* gave me the brownies."

"And *you* ate them." A sly smile slipped over her features. "I can't believe you ate all three of them."

"Speaking of eating, I'm starving."

"I'll just bet."

"Let's go to Millie's and you can tell me all about the nude model lawsuit."

"Time's a-wastin'," Tinkie said, and for yet another time that day, I was reminded of my aunt Loulane.

Tinkie had another order of fried dill pickles and a diet soda, and I had a pulled pork sandwich with Millie's famous coleslaw. Memphis eateries tried to lay claim to the best barbecue title, but I'd give it to Millie any day of the week. "So what about the lawsuit?" I mumbled around a mouthful of tangy sandwich.

"Esmeralda claimed that Trevor agreed to pay her ten grand to model for him, but then he reneged. When she asked for the painting as payment, he said he'd sold it already and refused to tell her who had purchased it."

"And?" I was curious where the painting had ended up.

"The owner of the painting wasn't disclosed in the suit, only listed as Customer X, because that's how Trevor had listed the purchaser. The judge said Trevor didn't have to disclose who had bought it and pretty much said if Esmeralda didn't have a written contract stating the terms of her modeling, she was up the creek without a paddle."

"Disappointing for her." Sarcasm was my friend.

"I wish I knew who bought that painting." Tinkie ate the last dill pickle with a sigh. "These things are addictive. I try not to eat fried, but I can't get enough. Especially with Millie's special sauce."

I'd once gone on a binge of eating chocolate-almond mocha ice cream that lasted five days. My consumption rate was probably worthy of a record, but I was too horrified to tell anyone. I wasn't going to rag on Tinkie about some pickles. Especially not when I'd stuffed down a huge sandwich and what might have been a pint of slaw.

"Why are you so interested in who bought Esmeralda's painting?" I asked.

"Call it a hunch. I think it figures into what's going on with the witches and Trevor. Esmeralda and Kitten both had a thing for Trevor. It smells of a good reason for murder."

"Shush!" I watched Esmeralda come in the door and make a beeline for our table. "Esmeralda is here." I wondered if she was still meeting Coleman for dinner. I had to admit, it didn't sit well with me, case or no case.

"Did she park her broomstick outside?" Tinkie asked.

"Hush!" She was almost at our table. "She can hear you."

"Good. I can ask her myself." And she did just that as soon as Esmeralda plunked down at our table.

"Grow up, Mrs. Richmond," Esmeralda advised. "I don't have a broomstick."

"I've heard there's some interest in who bought Trevor's nude portrait of you." Tinkie smiled. "Did you ever find out who the buyer was?"

"No. There are no records. Someone local is all Trevor ever told me." She tried to show disinterest, but her right eye started twitching.

"Local, like in Zinnia?"

"Somewhere around here. Trevor was gleeful about it. Sometimes he could be so mean. He knew I wanted to own that painting and he took pleasure in selling it to someone else."

"How was that mean?" Tinkie asked. "I've read the stories you write about people. Now that's what I consider mean. I don't even understand why a paper based in Memphis would be interested in anything that goes on in the Mississippi Delta. We're a world removed."

"You don't understand what sells papers," Esmeralda said. "It's my job to create drama, to exaggerate, to stir people up and get them talking. The more they talk, the more the newspapers fly off the shelf."

"I wouldn't call the *International Report* a newspaper. It's more of a . . . tabloid. But sometimes people get hurt. And badly. If you keep getting people incensed about the Harringtons, it could get out of hand."

"And that would be a bad thing?"

"Why do you hate them so?" I asked.

"Before the witches moved here, Trevor and I were . . . well, we had fallen into a convenient relationship. When I was in the area, we were a couple. And I accompanied him on some of his European travels. It wasn't like I wanted to get married, but we'd put the whole painting thing behind us, and I was helping him promote his art. Not that he needed the help. He was selling all over Europe. The rubes around here didn't understand the depth of his vision. In Europe, he is quite celebrated. Since his death, which I reported in my paper, the price of his paintings has tripled."

I started to bring up Kitten's modeling and alleged romance with Trevor, but I held off. It was interesting to see that Esmeralda actually seemed to feel something for the painter.

"We're digging into some background matters on the Harringtons. If we happen across the owner of your painting, would you be interested in knowing?" I asked.

Her eyes widened. "How much would you charge for the information?"

"Charge? I hadn't planned on charging anything, but now that you mention it . . ."

"No charge," Tinkie said. "We'll let you know if we find anything."

"The Harringtons won't let me in the manor. I left some personal items there I'd like to recover."

"We can get them," Tinkie offered. "What?"

"Some jewelry around the bedpost. It looks religious, and it has special significance to me. Some undies and high heels, a camera and a notebook."

"Sure thing." We could pick up those items.

"Weren't you jealous of Kitten's relationship with Trevor?" Tinkie asked. "I mean, she has Bob and she wanted Trevor."

A spark lit Esmeralda's eyes in a split second. "Kitten didn't want him as her own. She's sexually . . . carnivorous. Bob isn't enough for her all the time. But I didn't mind sharing. She kept it interesting for both of us. She didn't want him full-time and neither did I."

Now that was an open attitude. I could never share Coleman. Never. Was the lack of jealousy real or merely an act? I couldn't tell.

My cell phone beeped and I saw Coleman was calling. I excused myself and walked outside. My conversations with the sheriff were suddenly very personal. "What's up?" I asked.

"Harold stopped by and left a hound dog and one pissed-off kitty in the sheriff's office. Pluto has been chasing DeWayne around the office."

"I didn't intend to be gone so long. Sorry." I filled him in on what I'd discovered. "I'm headed there to collect the critters. Tell DeWayne I'm bringing him some apple pie. And you, too. You have to keep up your strength."

"That would be greatly appreciated."

I returned to the table and put in an order for two apple pies and two coffees to-go. Esmeralda stood to take her leave. "The Harrington sisters are dangerous. Not just to the schoolchildren, but to everyone who crosses their paths. Men die around them. I wouldn't cozy up to them or allow them to offer treatments or charms."

A chill rippled through me. "Oh, really?"

"If they have magical abilities, they received them from somewhere. And there is always a price to be paid for magic. Always."

"Good magic doesn't have a price tag," Tinkie said. I thought there was a hint of worry in her voice, but her expression was placid and calm.

"For every bargain, there's a price. Keep that in mind."

Millie put my to-go order on the table as she watched Esmeralda leave. "I don't like her and that's a shame because she writes some great stories for the tabloid."

Tinkie looked like she'd been gaffed. "Don't pay any attention to Esmeralda," I said. "She's just bitter."

"Right." Tinkie shook off the moment and we headed to the sheriff's office.

Coleman was waiting for us when we arrived. Millie had packed a little treat for Sweetie Pie and Pluto, and the critters chowed down while Coleman and DeWayne enjoyed their pie. Tinkie had a go-box for Chablis, but she was in no hurry to head home. She was about to pop with wickedness. At last, she couldn't hold it in.

"So, Coleman, been up to anything interesting lately?" she asked, then gave a big wink that DeWayne saw and burst into laughter.

"Something on your mind, Tinkie?" Coleman asked, cool as a cucumber.

"Yes, I was just curious about your day. Anything of import happen?"

"He was gone from the office until afternoon," DeWayne threw in. "Came in the door looking rode hard and put away wet."

"The horse terminology works well for Sarah Booth, I'd think." Tinkie smiled sweetly at me. "You always lecture me about the importance of brushing or hosing your mount off after a rigorous ride."

"Tinkie—"

"Sarah Booth looks a little . . . exhausted. Notice how red her eyes are."

I was going to kill her. Any minute.

"They are red," DeWayne said, coming over to the counter to scrutinize me more closely. He turned to Coleman. "Do you think Sarah Booth has been up to something?"

Little did he know what all I'd been up to. Tinkie, on the other hand, knew and was determined to make me squirm.

"Whatever she's been up to is none of your business." Coleman was seldom at a loss for a defense tactic, but neither one of us was doing well at stanching the teasing.

"Sarah Booth, what did you do today?" DeWayne asked. He was second on my list to be killed.

"Just working a case," I mumbled. Tinkie and DeWayne had truly gotten my goat. I couldn't think of a snappy comeback to save myself.

"Were you doing some in-depth interviews?" Tinkie asked. "Might I even call it . . . probing?"

I couldn't believe that the first lady of Zinnia and the ruler of the Daddy's Girls society was bantering so fluidly in innuendo.

"I think Coleman was chasing a suspect," DeWayne threw in. "When I called him, he was certainly out of breath."

"I'm going to get you two a job working for Esmeralda Grimes at that tabloid rag," Coleman said and then yawned. "I need a nap. I have a date tonight."

"Where are you going for dinner, Sarah

Booth?" Tinkie asked. "Oscar and I might join you."

"I'm not his date." I grinned. At last I had the upper hand in this conversation. "It's Esmeralda. She's hot for Coleman's body. It's a good thing I drained his energy or I might be worried."

Coleman laughed out loud. "Good shot, partner!" He fist-bumped me.

"I'm worn out. I'm going home. It's already dark outside, the courthouse is closed, and I need to feed horses." I picked up the empty containers that Sweetie Pie and Pluto had cleaned to the point they looked washed.

"I'll walk you ladies to your car," DeWayne offered. "I don't think the sheriff can stagger that far. Besides, I've heard that reporter woman is hot stuff." He licked his finger and held it in the air, making a sizzling sound.

"Trust me, Coleman can handle Esmeralda with one hand tied behind him." I walked up to him and kissed his cheek to applause from the peanut gallery.

13

After the horses were fed and the doors and windows locked and double-checked, I took a long, hot shower and propped up in the den to watch television. I was far behind on my favorite shows, and my brain was too tired to work on the case. Besides, though I trusted Coleman with my life, I couldn't stop wondering how his dinner with Esmeralda was going.

I'd polished off one Jack and water and was thinking of making one more when Sweetie Pie slowly rose to her feet, hackles raised, and began to growl. Inch by inch, she advanced toward the large windows that opened onto the back porch. They were locked, but anyone could crash through them if they were determined to get in.

My gun was in the china cabinet in the dining room. I put my drink on the side table and slowly eased to my feet. Sweetie definitely saw or sensed something outside the windows. Pluto arched his back and hissed at the darkness.

My impulse was to rush to the glass and look out, but I stopped myself. Sidling toward my protective hound, I saw movement outside. The night was still, and I angled closer. Only inches from me, a pale face materialized in the glass. The reflection was contorted, as if the person was in anguish, a pale white mask of suffering. I stifled my scream and stumbled backward, tripping over a hassock.

I went down hard and cracked my head on a coffee table. Sweetie Pie lunged at the window, snarling. Saliva flew over the windows as she barked and growled. She was protecting me with everything she had in her.

Pushing up from the floor, I ran to the dining room and got my pistol. Before I could think, I went out the back door, Sweetie Pie charging past me. We ran around the house to the den window. In the light coming from the room I could see the area was empty. Whoever—or whatever—had been there was gone.

I stepped closer to examine the area. The wood near the window was gouged, as if a creature with large claws had taken a swipe. Just like the marks at my front door and on the third floor of Musgrove Manor. Malvik had said some entity guarded the Harrington bloodline. He'd warned me and I'd scoffed.

I moved back around the house to the kitchen door. Tomorrow, in the daylight, I'd search the area around the window for prints. Tonight, I wanted to get inside in the warmth and light. The sense that something watched me was strong and frightening. I spun around and scanned the backyard, but I didn't see anything.

The horses were in the pasture and came running up to the fence, snorting and bucking. The cold weather made them frisky. I worried that someone meaning to harm me might go after the horses, but they were far safer free in the pasture than shut in stalls in the barn. They were friendly horses, but not inclined to rush up to strangers.

I stroked their noses and sent them off to the far pasture, wheeling and rearing. In a moment there was only the sound of their pounding hooves in the night. Sweetie Pie and Pluto were at my side, edging me back toward the kitchen and shelter.

Standing at the pasture fence wouldn't keep the horses from harm if someone was out there with evil intentions, but I knew who would. I checked my watch. It was after ten. If Coleman hadn't pumped any information out of Esmeralda by now, he'd hit a dry well. I called him.

His phone went to voice mail and I left a message, a dart of concern shifting through my mind. I didn't trust Esmeralda as far as I could throw her. She could have poisoned Coleman. Like someone probably poisoned Trevor. With Trevor out of the way, Musgrove Manor would go on the auction block—to the highest bidder. And it was possible Coleman had discovered too much about what was happening at the old dairy.

I had to consider that Esmeralda was working for Bob Fontana.

It was hard to believe Doc hadn't found the source of the poisoning already. I didn't believe for a minute the artist had been frightened to death. Then again, that face staring in the window at me had done a pretty good number on my heart. The adrenalin rush must have tripled my heart rate. Still, I didn't buy it that a grown man could be scared so badly he'd drop dead. And even though I'd seen something outside the window, I was having a hard time believing it was something conjured up by Harrington witches in the 1600s. Call me a skeptic.

In the parlor I made another drink and returned to the den, closing all the draperies. Whatever had been outside my house was gone, but I didn't want to chance seeing that face again. Had it been a hallucination? Some remnant of my brownie binge? And I'd almost been asleep. Maybe it had been dream induced. But Sweetie and Pluto had sensed something, too.

When eleven o'clock came and there was no response from Coleman, I went upstairs to bed. I wasn't going to be the woman who allowed worry to control her world. Coleman was plenty capable of taking care of himself.

I'd just settled under the covers and felt my body relaxing when my cell phone rang. Coleman.

I answered a bit breathless at the memory of his body in my bed.

"Can you call Tinkie and meet me at Musgrove Manor?" His voice was terse.

"Sure. What's going on?"

"Esmeralda Grimes seems to have fallen from the third-floor balcony outside Trevor's studio."

I was wide awake. I found my jeans and boots and dressed as I held the phone to my shoulder and talked to Coleman.

"Did she jump? Was she pushed? What happened?"

"Doc is on the way. There are a lot of dead bodies, all associated with that old dairy. We're going to get to the bottom of it."

It was now or never. "Coleman, something or someone was at my window earlier. Pale mask like a suffering monster, a grotesque. There are fresh claw marks." It was something of a shock to realize the face at my window had borne a remarkable resemblance to the gargoyles at the manor house.

"You're kidding me, right?" Coleman sounded hopeful I was pulling his leg.

"No."

"Meet me at the manor. Leave now. Call me when you're on the road."

I was dressed and ready to go. I bundled into my coat and gloves and headed for the car with my critters.

Esmeralda had landed in a koi pond just below Trevor's third-floor balcony. At least the body's fall was broken because the water had absorbed a lot of the shock. Tinkie and I hung back, letting Coleman and Doc work the scene. The Harrington sisters were behind us. They didn't cry, but they appeared to be distressed.

"I didn't like her, but I didn't wish her dead," Hope said.

"I wished her gone," Faith said. "I should have been more specific."

"Let's get her out," Doc said after Coleman had thoroughly photographed the scene. It was a bit disconcerting to see the cute goldfish swimming around the body.

Cece arrived and snapped a few photographs. The newspaper wouldn't use a picture of the body, but Cece documented everything. She was a journalist through and through.

Coleman waded into the pond and was as gentle as he could be when he brought Esmeralda out. Her hair fell away from her face and we all gasped. Her expression was pure horror. As if she'd seen the worst possible thing imaginable before she died—and it had threatened her.

The face at my window came back to me. It had been awful, and it was outside my house. This, though, was far worse.

"What was Esmeralda doing here?" Coleman asked the sisters.

"We didn't know she was here," Hope said. "She often visited Trevor and used the back, exterior stairs." She pointed out the staircase that zigzagged up to the third floor. "He liked his privacy and so did his models. If she got inside, I guess she had a key."

I wondered how many other models had keys to the manor. If I were one of the Harringtons I'd be changing locks at first light. And I knew why she was there. The possessions she'd asked Tinkie and me to fetch for her. It would seem she decided to get them on her own. Perhaps because she didn't want us to know what all she'd left in Trevor's rooms.

Doc did a preliminary examination, then signaled the medics to bring a stretcher. "I'll have some answers after the autopsy," he said.

"That look on her face. It's like Trevor's," Tinkie said. She almost staggered and I grabbed her elbow for support. Tinkie, for all of her training as the premiere Zinnia princess, wasn't squeamish. A body wouldn't make her keel over. "I'm fine," she whispered. "I caught my heel."

I let it go but the ground was level and she was wearing boots with only a two-inch heel instead of her normal high-fashion stilettos. Tinkie wasn't a stumbler.

"So none of you knew Esmeralda was in the manor?" Coleman asked the sisters. They all shook their heads.

"We have protection against strangers, but Esmeralda wasn't really a stranger. She was a frequent flyer," Charity said.

"Any idea why she might have snuck in?" he pressed. "She knew Trevor wasn't here."

Another trio of headshaking.

"She said she'd left some personal things in his room." I supplied a possibility. "Tinkie and I saw her at Millie's earlier today. She asked us to retrieve some lingerie and jewelry she'd left here. I guess she decided not to wait on us to do it."

"I'll look for those items later," Coleman said. "For now, I don't want anyone on the third floor. It's part of the crime scene."

"Not a problem," Charity said. "Every time I go up there I just miss Trevor. He was a cool guy. We had some lovely conversations about his ideas for paintings. He saw everything as progressions. The seasons paintings were my favorites, but the religious icons—Faith was magnificent. Fierce and fiery."

"Did anyone see the painting of Esmeralda? She desperately wanted to own it." I kept it conversational.

"She was in the religious-icon series. She was a sultry summer saint. I hate to admit it but she was lush and gorgeous the way he painted her." Charity rolled her eyes. "I wish I'd thought to photograph that painting before Trevor shipped it off to the new owner. Just think, if I'd had a photo, I could have sent it to Esmeralda's paper. I wonder if she would have been so quick to print something she preferred to keep secret. She certainly didn't mind maligning all of us."

The sisters were standing over Esmeralda's dead body and still giving her what for. They'd never heard Aunt Loulane's admonition not to keep beating a dead horse. And Coleman was paying attention, though he did seem somewhat preoccupied.

I stepped closer to the body the medics were getting ready to put on the stretcher and noticed Esmeralda had gone to some trouble to dress and do her makeup a bit more conservatively for her dinner with Coleman. The thought made me a little sad.

"Did you hear anything?" Coleman asked the sisters.

"Not a thing. We were performing an incantation in the front of the house," Hope said. "We were beating drums and chanting. We didn't know a thing until I was going to bed and I heard something out in the yard. I thought it was that vile little Fontana juvenile, so I jerked open the kitchen door. The motion detector light came on and there she was. I checked, but she was dead. Then I called you."

"Have you noticed anyone else around your house?"

"Kitten Fontana and her spawn of Satan." Faith

had no problem calling a spade a spade. "They lurk out in the woods, spying on us. And she and Esmeralda were at each other's throats a day or so ago."

"They were working together," Tinkie said. "Kitten was using Esmeralda to stir up a mob against the Wiccan school."

"Maybe at first they were working together. Not now." Faith yawned. "I'm exhausted. Can I go to bed?"

Coleman shot her a glance, then shrugged. "Sure. I may have more questions later."

"We'll be here. We aren't going anywhere," Faith said before she started toward the house.

Hope and Charity followed her, but I hung back to talk to Doc and Coleman. They were huddled up by the body, acting like linebackers during a play.

"I have to get home," Tinkie said, checking her watch.

"Really?" I frowned.

"I have an appointment with Oscar. It's time for our . . . reunion."

I'd hoped she'd given up the baby-making obsession, but obviously she had not. "Cece might give you a ride. I'll finish up here."

"Oooooh, I'll bet you will," Cece said, winking at Coleman.

"Go." I was happy to be done with them.

And I was glad it was dark. I could feel a blush climbing into my face.

"Where's Pluto?" I realized that while Sweetie Pie was resting on the back porch, there was no sign of my black cat or the dozens of ferals. It was as if they'd disappeared from the property by magic. And that was a troubling thought. Whatever had clawed my door and window, if it was a wild mutant creature it could easily kill cats.

"He was over there." Tinkie pointed to a cluster of small trees. Coleman had set up a series of large lights to allow Doc to examine the body before it was moved, and I could see the outline of the trees at the edge of the illuminated zone. The trees were peculiar—somewhat tropical. Not a normal Delta tree that I was familiar with.

When I went to look for Pluto, I made the mistake of grabbing one of the slender trunks. Dozens of sharp thorns penetrated my palm.

"What the hell?" I quickly drew back.

Hope appeared on the back porch as if she'd been watching through the window. "The trees are devil's walking sticks. We use them in our spells, healing potions—and salads. The plant has unusual properties."

"And it's mean." My palm felt like it had been bitten by a shark.

"Stay out of the thicket," Hope said. It was

an order, not a request. “Those plants can be dangerous, especially in the dark.”

“My cat may be in there.”

“Cats know their business. He’ll be fine. You, on the other hand . . .” She seemed to consider her words and then shrugged. “It’s your skin. Some people have very strange reactions to those plants and we won’t be responsible.” She went back inside.

14

The thicket of trees with their thorny trunks was as effective as a razor-wire fence, but I wasn't about to give up on my cat. "Pluto," I called, because he disdained the "kitty, kitty, kitty" that most felines seemed to enjoy. "Pluto. You'd better come out of there."

Coleman and Doc were helping to load Esmeralda's body into the ambulance to transport to the hospital for an autopsy. It was time to go home—but I couldn't leave Pluto. None of the cats were around. The felines had some unique communication that allowed them to gather and disperse without making a sound.

I felt someone's gaze on me and looked up to the third floor. A dark figure was pressed against the wall on the balcony outside Trevor's rooms. My heart lurched—the figure induced a primal fear in me.

"Coleman?" I spoke softly, my gaze riveted on the figure. "Coleman?"

"Sarah Booth." He looked up and saw the tension in my body. "What is it?"

"There's someone on the third floor."

He shifted gradually, subtly, so he could look up. By the time his gaze was directed at the balcony, the figure had disappeared, almost as if it had been absorbed into the stones of the wall. "What did you see?"

It was a good question. I couldn't be certain. Maybe it had just been a shadow. "It looked like a large man dressed in black." I shook my head. "I'm tired. Maybe it was nothing."

"You go home, or go to the hospital with Doc. I'll check out the upstairs. DeWayne went through Trevor's rooms, but he didn't find anything but a lot of wine bottles and clutter. No evidence that Esmeralda was pushed or had struggled, but we definitely need a more thorough search."

"Let me come with you." I suddenly had a terrible feeling about Coleman entering the manor.

"It's not safe," he said. "I need to check it out and see if someone is up there."

"Make DeWayne stay with you."

Coleman chuckled. "I'll be fine."

"You know, when you ask me to be careful?" I waited until I was certain he understood. "The shoe is on the other foot now. I know how you feel when you think I might be injured."

"It's my job, Sarah Booth."

I nodded. I would not allow myself to argue or hover. Coleman had taken care of himself for a long time and with a lot less physical damage than I'd sustained. When I'd taken him into my bed, I'd opened the door to my fears. It seemed the people I loved the most were always taken from me. I couldn't let that be my reality, though. "Be safe." I kissed my palm and blew the kiss to him. "Call me when you're done."

Coleman's eyebrows shot up in surprise. "I will."

I called Pluto again and was rewarded when he popped out of the thicket of devil's walking sticks and fell into step beside me. We went to the car and got in.

A low, friendly voice made me jam on the brakes. "It's just not suitable to leave that single lawman in a house with three women."

I almost got whiplash swiveling around to the woman who sat in the passenger seat of the Roadster. She wore a blue tam with a big ball, and her swanlike neck was elegant, though she seemed a bit flustered.

"Who are you and why are you in my car?" I asked.

"We have to find the final spell," she said. "Otherwise, it's all for naught. All of the spells and learning and . . . where are the children?"

I knew her then. Angela Lansbury playing Miss Eglantine Price. She'd been one of my mother's favorite characters from her childhood.

Miss Price was an eccentric with a giant heart and a real belief in magic. The woman in my car portrayed her perfectly.

"There are no children and you are no witch in training," I said.

"Filigree, apogee, pedigree, perigee!"

"If you can't make sense, I'm not going to give you a ride back to Dahlia House."

"I have my broomstick."

I would pay good money to see my haint riding a broomstick around Musgrove Manor. Now that would give the Harrington sisters something to really think about. "Fire that baby up and let me see you streak across the moon."

Angela gave me a sour look. "I should have frightened you away from Dahlia House the minute you showed up. I'm more than a little responsible for where you find yourself. Had you moved to Tucson, or say, Seattle, you'd probably be married and popping out the babies."

I ignored her and watched Coleman on the front porch of the manor. He talked with Hope and Charity for a few minutes and then came toward his patrol car. He couldn't catch me talking to an empty car seat—because he couldn't see Jitty. It was time to leave.

"Do you want him to see me?" Jitty asked.

"What?" She took me so by surprise that I hit the gas too hard and lurched forward, almost running Coleman down.

"Do you want your man toy there to be able to see me? I didn't stutter."

"Is it within your power to manifest for other people?" All this time and she'd hidden this ability from me!

"What do you want?"

Coleman was approaching my window. "I want you to go home and wait for me. We're going to have a long, long talk."

And she was gone. I rolled down the window. "I wanted to be sure you were okay. They might have decided to make you their sex slave."

One side of Coleman's very passionate lips curled up. "Go home. I'll call you when I'm done with work."

"Did you find anything upstairs?"

He shook his head. "That house is like a maze, though. Someone could be up there and slip around the different halls and passageways and avoid detection."

"Do you think the sisters are hiding Esmeralda's murderer?"

"I don't know what to think," Coleman said, tired and frustrated. "I have two people dead on the same piece of property. Doc can't find out what killed Trevor and I don't think Esmeralda jumped."

"Could it have been an accident?"

"I don't see Esmeralda as the type to fall off a balcony. And what was she doing up there? The sisters denied any knowledge of her presence."

"I think Esmeralda was looking for that painting that Trevor did of her. The one she sued him about."

"Could be." Coleman reached into the car and brushed his hand over my cheek. "Go home. Please."

I had my cat and dog and no good reason to stay at the manor. And I didn't want to be there, alone, in the dark after Coleman left. "Okay." I started the car and waited for him to get in the cruiser and pull out ahead of me.

While Sweetie Pie wisely slept in the back, Pluto sat on the front seat watching the manor intently. In the high beams of the car, I saw numerous pairs of bright kitty eyes. The feral cats had all lined up on the porch roof and were glaring down at us. I slowed to count them. I'd gotten up to twenty-four when Pluto flew through the window I'd lowered to speak to Coleman and darted toward the manor.

"Pluto!" I tried to grab the cat but he was long gone. And so was Coleman. His tail-lights disappeared down the winding driveway. "Dammit." I had a great reluctance to get out of the warm car to chase the cat, but I knew I had to do it. I couldn't leave Pluto at the manor, though he certainly deserved to be left.

I turned off the car and got out. My cell phone buzzed and I prayed it was Coleman, who'd noticed I wasn't behind him. Instead, it was a number with a 337 area code. The text was from Cherie Sistrunk, the reporter in Lafayette, Louisiana.

Give me a call. Interesting development.

I debated on calling her or knocking on the door of the manor. Pluto had jumped on the front porch and disappeared. He had to be somewhere close. I went for the cat. "Pluto!" I called him even knowing he would ignore me. Cats were so damn anti-authority, and Pluto was very smart.

My boots sounded like a clodhopper to my ear as I walked across the boards of the porch. "Pluto." He darted into the shadow by the front door. I was really going to kill him when I got my hands on him. "Pluto."

The front door creaked open slowly. Very slowly, with the chilling *eeeeeeeeek* of the door in the haunted house. I was sorely tempted to turn tail and run. Instead I froze on the spot. Pluto took that opportunity to leap through the door.

I pushed the door open on complete darkness. Where in the heck had the sisters gone? It was as if the house had eaten them and left no remains behind. Pluto darted to the stairs with the dragon motif and started up them. I knew he was going to the third floor. I recognized that Pluto had something important to show me, but I wasn't certain that I wanted to see it.

I followed him up the stairs. If the sisters

caught me snooping around like this, they could have me arrested—and likely would. I wouldn't blame them. It wouldn't matter that I didn't want to be in their home or that my cat was possessed by a demon.

Pluto led me past the second floor and up to the area that had been Trevor's. The claw marks still marred the beautiful wood floor, and I stepped past them and went to Trevor's studio. When I'd shut the door behind me I hit the light switch. I didn't have a prayer of grabbing my cat and getting out undetected, so I might as well search the place thoroughly. If Coleman got mad at me, I'd have a perfect score—everyone I had contact with today would be pissed off at me.

Pluto never moved far away from me—he stayed just out of reach. Sly devil.

I wondered why none of the other cats made any attempts to enter the house. Cats were notorious for darting in and out of places, just as Pluto had done. But none of the dairy cats ever made an attempt to enter the witches' abode. *Hmmmmm.* I'd always been told cats had a sixth sense about spirits and ghosts and such. That they could sense a specter in a room or know when someone was going to die. I'd considered that foolishness, until right this minute. Pluto gave a low growl. He was focused on something I couldn't see, and it creeped me out. What was he seeing?

A heartrending sob answered my question in a

way that made the hair all over my body lift up and tingle. Someone else was on the third floor. Someone in emotional distress.

And they weren't far from me. Yet no one else had detected their presence.

While my brain told me the sobbing person was female, my gut told me it didn't matter. This could be a trap. A deadly one. Coleman and DeWayne had searched the manor and come up empty-handed. They were not careless in their duties. Which meant whoever was up here had successfully managed to hide from them. How? Oh, I didn't like the answers that flitted around my brain.

Musgrove Manor had been built before the civil war. Like so many of the old homes, there could easily be secret hiding places and passages. The manor itself had been patterned after a vast estate in the lowlands of Scotland. I had a vague memory of some school lesson about the manor house and the limestone that had been quarried from Tishomingo County and hauled south with great effort.

Mule and oxen teams and slave labor had brought the limestone slabs south to erect the formidable house. As schoolchildren we'd toured the dairy and barns, but we'd never been allowed inside the manor. The Musgrove family had a reputation for privacy, and the public schools were simply glad for a chance to show children where milk came from and allow us to touch a cow and try milking. Many of the students came from farming families, but that no longer included owning livestock or poultry. The land was used for money crops now. Cotton, corn, soybeans. An experience with a moo cow was a true bonus education for the lower grades.

My substitute history teacher, Budgie Burton, who took over the eighth-grade class whenever we'd driven Margie McLeod to a weekend bender—her fondness for vodka stingers was well-known but the county paid so little no one else would even consider taking over the class—had been something of a conspiracy nut even back then and was always talking about the big houses of the Delta and how they had been renovated to create survivor's "dens" where the wealthy could endure a nuclear holocaust. Musgrove Manor was a favorite topic of his.

I could still hear his voice as he drew all of us into his world of secret passages, Nazi spies, Russian counterintelligence, and his hero, James Bond. "British intelligence found secret chambers in many of the old British and Scottish estate homes. Musgrove Manor's interior design was patterned on a portion of Finwake's Priory." Budgie was positive that estate had been used to house part of a religious complex that had hidden various books of the Bible actually written by Jesus.

Whatever he was selling, Budgie made it exciting and interesting, but not particularly believable. Now I wondered about the manor and what secret rooms might truly exist. And what might be hiding in a secret room. Budgie did not seem nearly as nuts as he had before the low keening echoed through the third floor. The claw marks on the floor—and at Dahlia House—had burrowed into my subconscious with the stealth of Freddy Krueger. Nightmare images flooded me. For a few seconds, I was literally paralyzed by fear.

Pluto's sharp claws startled me out of my inertia. I wasn't any safer standing in the third-floor studio or in Trevor's rooms. It was time to fish or cut bait, and I decided to fish. If there was anything to be found here, I meant to find it.

I entered Trevor's bedroom, which still contained the empty wine bottles, dirty glasses with a color chart of various lipstick shades on the rims of some, his clothes—all black—and books and papers. Someone had been in the room and pulled his books off the shelves, scattering their contents and the papers they'd found. Coleman had already examined the rooms so I reshelved the books and picked up the papers to take home for further study. But when I removed the first layer of clutter, I was able to see that aside from the wine and libidinous behavior, Trevor had been relatively neat.

The papers had come from a filing cabinet in a corner, and when I checked it, I realized he'd had his affairs organized. There were empty folders for his will, his assets, his holdings. I had no clue what paperwork might have been stolen, but a lot of it was still in the bedroom, along with some crumpled papers I found in a pair of Trevor's riding boots.

Trevor's basic neatness gave me pause. Why would he use his riding boots for a trash can? There were no longer horses at Musgrove Manor, but once upon a time Trevor had been an accomplished rider and had been master of the Sunflower County hunt. I'd never approved of the brutality of fox hunting, but I admired the athleticism of the horses and riders. Trevor had cut a dashing figure in his red jacket, tan breeches, and tall boots. He'd ridden a tall blood bay gelding, Fletcher. I still remembered his horse and how handsome he was astride him. Right out of Jane Austen, to my childish imagination.

The boots were polished and clean.

I unfolded the crumpled paper and realized instantly that I'd made a terrible mistake by touching it at all. I read the words aloud, " 'I am going to cut your gizzard out and serve it to you in a black grape and balsamic sauce.' "

It was unsigned. And it had likely come from one of Trevor's models. I wondered if

Esmeralda or Kitten knew anything about sauces. It wouldn't be hard to find out. But first I had to figure what was in this creation. I called Millie. Though she served Southern fare in her café, she was a fine French chef. She experimented all the time for her personal satisfaction. When she answered, I asked her about the sauce.

"Not difficult if you have some reduced brown stock, a glace. Then it's basically drippings and fat from pork, shallots, some seedless black grapes, the glace, herbs like sage and thyme, and the balsamic vinegar. It's a lovely, lovely sauce. Why are you asking, Sarah Booth?"

"Who in Zinnia would know about or serve this sauce?"

"Plenty of people in the planter class. It isn't something your average housewife would whip up, only because it isn't traditional fare around here. People tend to cook what they grew up eating. Southern style. It's not a lack of sophistication or culture, it's just how humans are designed. The familiar brings comfort."

This wasn't the help I'd hoped it would be. Many of Trevor's models came from the upper crust. It was curious to me that ladies who spent thousands of dollars on their wardrobe were so eager to drop their clothes to pose for a nude painting. Any number of women could have left that note for Trevor—for any number of reasons.

Still, I wished I hadn't touched it. I could only hope that I hadn't ruined any fingerprints that might be on it. Very carefully I put it in the middle of the stack of papers I'd picked up from the floor. It occurred to me that whoever had trashed his room might have been looking for that note. And while I was looking, I didn't find any dainty female undies around that might belong to Esmeralda or any jewelry hanging on the bedpost. There was a rosary on the floor under a chair, sort of a strange object for Trevor, who expressed views more in line with pantheism and harbored Wiccans. Esmeralda's possessions were nowhere in sight. I wondered if someone had beat us both to the punch.

I reached for my phone to call Coleman. I had to alert him to the note and to the possibility that he'd missed whoever was hiding in the manor. He was going to be angry that I'd returned—not even retrieving Pluto would be a good enough excuse.

Just as I started to call, I heard my cat screech as if someone had slammed a door on his tail. Pluto was not a screecher. I pushed the phone in my pocket and went after my cat.

I moved through Trevor's studio, aware that all of the paintings seemed to be watching me. The sensation was really creepy. I kept darting glances at the women captured on canvas, and their gazes seemed to connect with mine—and follow me as I moved down the long room. Outside the windows, a full moon floated high, illuminating the grounds of the manor.

Pluto's angry scream came again from the far end of the studio, and I jogged toward him. Out of nowhere a beautiful Siamese-looking cat shot out of the darkness and almost knocked me down. Pluto was close on his heels.

"Dammit, Pluto." I caught the cat and picked him up. "You can't come in here and chase the cats who live here." I was so relieved I kissed the top of his head. I'd been afraid that Pluto might have met something much meaner than another cat. "Let's get out of here."

My thirst for answers was submerged by my desire to exit the manor. Coleman and DeWayne could come back in the daylight and search. I had Pluto and it was time to get while the getting was good. As I turned to leave, I saw someone on the lawn. With the lights on in the studio, I was highlighted to whoever was out there. It was no point trying to hide now. I went to the window and looked down.

Pluto let out a low growl, his tail flicking, as he gazed down on the slender silhouette. The person was dressed all in black in a hooded cloak. Witch, warlock, or Fontana, I couldn't tell. But the way the figure stood, like something from a horror movie waiting for the right moment to strike, chilled me to the bone. Who the hell was it and what did they want? How were they involved with Esmeralda's and Trevor's deaths?

I had two choices. I could pursue the figure or I could call Coleman. By the time he arrived, the intruder would be gone. So actually, I had one choice.

I went back to Trevor's bedroom and picked up the stack of papers, including the note. I couldn't risk leaving it for fear someone would come back and destroy it. Moving as quickly as I dared with a fifteen-pound cat and a stack of papers in my arms, I hurried down the stairs and out the front door. I put the papers in the car, but Pluto was not so easily managed. He shot out of my arms and took off.

Retrieving the gun from the trunk, I was in hot pursuit. When I rounded the corner of the manor, I saw my cat halfway to the figure—who had not moved an inch! It dared me to come after it. And I was up for the challenge.

Just when I thought the intruder might be a tree trunk or something stationary, it started to run. And it was fast. But not as fast as Pluto. The cat jumped on the fleeing person's back and was rewarded with a yelp of pain. But the figure didn't slow down. It moved faster. I ran as fast as I could, but I had no chance of catching the interloper. Whoever was beneath the black cloak was in good running shape. That left out Kitten Fontana. So who could it be? Malvik? But why would he be standing outside like a scarecrow? Or a murderer?

The lights of the back porch came on and all three witches came tumbling out the back door. "What the hell is going on?" Faith demanded.

"Call the sheriff," I said. "Someone was trying to break in."

"Yeah, you! You're trying to break in." Hope was clearly angry.

"I was trying to retrieve Pluto." My excuse sounded lame even to me. "There was someone on the third floor, and then there was someone in the woods."

The sisters looked up to the third floor with skepticism, as if I'd made up the story. I had the tiniest taste of what it must feel like to Tinkie to have what she believed to be truth ridiculed. Tampering with someone's belief system was dangerous ground, even for a best friend.

"Please call the sheriff," I said.

"Not tonight." Hope put her foot down. "We're exhausted. The state board of higher education is sending an inspector soon to tour the facility. We have lots of work to do, and we haven't had any sleep. The sheriff can come tomorrow and search. Tonight, you are leaving and we're going to bed."

I was tired, too, and I knew Coleman had to be worn out. The truth was, I didn't want to fight them on the matter. I had the papers I'd found.

There wasn't anything left to destroy. And I'd honestly come to believe that the sisters weren't complicit in Trevor's or Esmeralda's deaths. The sisters had been inside the house and I'd clearly seen someone on the grounds. Daylight would give us a much better chance of finding evidence.

I captured Pluto, whistled up Sweetie Pie, and went to my car. When I opened the driver's door, I saw the stack of papers I'd gathered thrown over the floorboard and back seat. The threatening note was gone. If anything else was missing, I couldn't tell. It would be futile to attempt to gain entry into the house. If the sisters had the note, I'd be willing to bet it was now a heap of ash. I'd really screwed up.

15

I awoke to the tantalizing smell of bacon sizzling. I had no memory of the drive home from the manor or of falling into bed. I was wearing a nightgown and my clothes were puddled on the floor beside Sweetie Pie, who also snoozed soundly. Pluto was nowhere in evidence.

The bacon obviously had to be a Jitty illusion. She was down in the kitchen doing everything in her power to wake me up at the crack of dawn. I would kill her if she wasn't already dead. Yawning, I rolled out of bed and headed downstairs to make coffee and see if there was anything in the refrigerator that wasn't pulsing in a Tupperware container. I'd seen some of my recipes take on life forms—nothing I wanted to witness on this bright winter morning. I needed sustenance before I confessed my sins to Coleman.

As I crossed the dining room, the wonderful smells of breakfast cooking grew stronger, including freshly brewed coffee. Cutlery scraped pots or plates. Jitty was going whole hog with the smells and sound effects. I pushed through the door and stopped in my tracks.

Scott Hampton, the best blues player on the planet, stood at my stove with a cast-iron skillet going and a spatula in his hand.

"Good morning, Sarah Booth."

Scott and I had been lovers, and he was a man I cared greatly for. And I owed him some details of the recent decision I'd made. Scott had been in Chicago negotiating with some blues clubs to form an alliance that would bring national talent to Zinnia on a regular basis. Scott had the European blues market sewn tight, but a new crop of young blues players was coming up and many found Chicago a great place to start.

"I didn't know you were home."

"Got in late last night."

"I'm glad you're here. I need to tell you something."

"I know about Coleman. Jaytee told me. I'm happy for you." He expertly flipped the bacon onto a plate lined with paper towels.

I'd chosen Coleman over Scott and Harold. At least I'd had a chance to tell Harold in person. "I wish Jaytee had given me a chance to tell you myself."

Scott put down the spatula and came over to give me a hug. "I could see it coming, girl. Everyone could see it but you and that lug-headed lawman."

"I—"

He didn't let me finish but tightened his hug.

"I don't know that I'll ever love anyone the way I do you, but I wouldn't stand in the way of your happiness for anything. And I wouldn't want to lose our friendship."

"That won't ever happen. I do have guilt that maybe you moved here thinking this would have a different outcome."

"I did." He grinned and pushed his beautiful white-blond hair out of his eye. "But coming to Zinnia was the smartest business decision I've ever made. Morgan Freeman knew it—the Delta is ground zero for the blues. I'm living and playing on the very land where the blues were created. It's given me inspiration for new songs, the club is making more money than I can spend. It was simply the smartest thing I've ever done."

Women threw themselves at Scott every single time he performed. He could have his pick of anyone. I knew that, but I also remembered vividly what it felt like to be the one left behind. I'd never wanted to hurt him or Harold.

"Are you marrying Coleman?" he asked.

The question caught me off guard. "We haven't discussed such a thing. We're not even sure how this is going to work." We'd had our differences in the past. We both had dangerous jobs and Coleman had been overprotective. "We're feeling our way forward."

"Smart. Now how about some French toast? I

made it just the way your aunt Loulane used to make it. Like you taught me."

I didn't know what to say. Except, "Thank you, Scott."

He dipped some slices of French bread in the batter he'd already prepared. "I'm not giving up. At least not yet. I hope you and Coleman are happy. But if you aren't . . ." He didn't finish, he didn't have to.

"I don't want that for you. Find the woman who completes you. She's out there. You just have to be willing to see her."

His smile was as sensuous as his guitar playing. "That sounds awfully like wisdom, Sarah Booth."

"I wouldn't go that far. But I love you and I want you to be happy, too."

"Then let's make it so. We'll take each day as it comes at us."

I nodded and sat down in the chair he pulled out for me as the French toast sizzled in the skillet. It surely wasn't the way I'd intended to start my morning, but I was happy to take it. I sipped the coffee he put in front of me and watched him cook. I couldn't help but think that while my heart had suffered more than one break, I'd been incredibly fortunate in the men who populated my world. None were mean or malicious. All of them wanted only the best for me. And me for them. I'd tried hard to act with integrity, and they'd more than matched me.

When the front door blasted open and I heard the *tap-tap-tap* of Tinkie's stilettos crossing the old floor boards of my home, I couldn't stop my smile. This was going to blow her mind.

"I smell something good," she said as she pushed open the swinging door. And stopped dead in her tracks. "Scott!" She turned to me. "Well, don't you look like the cat that swallowed the canary."

"And he was delicious," I said.

Scott picked up instantly on my mischief and said, "We've really worked up an appetite, Tinkie. Care to join us for some French toast?"

Tinkie took a seat, glaring at me. "How could you?"

"I finally did what you've been pushing me to do."

"I did not push you to be a hoochie-coochie mama."

Scott barked out a laugh and covered it with a cough. I only grinned wider. "Why buy a cow if you can get the milk free from a herd?" I quoted Aunt Loulane in a way she would have been horrified to hear.

Tinkie reached over and pulled the charm bag from beneath my nightgown. "Take this off right away. It's affecting your . . . common sense."

I'd almost forgotten about the love charm that Tinkie had given me. Now I was really going to have some fun.

Just as Scott put a stack of French toast in front of both of us, I said, "I just can't get enough, Tinkie. It's like I don't have any restraint. My body actually twitches with uncontrollable desire. In fact, right now, I feel another powerful urge coming over me." I glanced at Scott and winked before I had a mini-seizure, grabbing the table to hold myself upright.

"Call an ambulance!" Tinkie commanded. "She's having a fit. What have I done? What have I done?"

"I must have sex," I moaned. "I'll die if I don't."

"She's been like that since I got here," Scott said. "Let me take her upstairs."

"No!" Tinkie said, stepping between us.

"Okay, you can watch," Scott said.

I almost choked but I started to slowly come around. When I quit twitching, I continued, "Tinkie bought a charm because I was too inhibited. By god, it worked. I just can't stop myself sometimes."

"I'll say," Scott threw in. "Wanton! Hyper-sexed. That's what I'd call it. I didn't know if I'd live to get out of that bed."

"This is my fault." Tinkie's eyes filled with tears. "What have I done?"

I couldn't take it any further. Teasing was one thing, but this had gone far enough. "It's a joke, Tinkie. Scott and I didn't do the deed."

She blinked, and then a laser-sharp blue gaze filled her eyes. "I am going to get you, Sarah Booth Delaney. You had me worried sick. I thought you might have turned into a deviant because of that charm."

"Now you know how I feel," I said, dropping the charm beneath my nightgown. For some strange reason, I didn't want to take it off. Sue me, I was superstitious. It had finally brought Coleman to my bed and I'd managed to stay friends with the other men in my life. I couldn't say positively that the charm had played a role, but I saw no reason to risk success.

Tinkie's brow furrowed, and then it cleared. "I came over here to tell you that Kitten Fontana was shot at last night."

"I don't believe that for a second, unless Bob was trying to kill her so he didn't have to pay alimony."

"Possibly true, but she called me at the crack of dawn this morning when she couldn't reach you."

"She didn't call me." But the first thought was that I had no clue where I'd left my phone. It could be dead or it could be in the car or at the manor. Or dropped somewhere along the way. I hadn't even looked for it when I got home last night. I'd dropped into bed and then this morning Scott had distracted me.

"Oh, she said she called at least twenty times.

She was upset that you 'ignored her summons.' "

"Oh, that really makes me want to respond to her. Right. Let's finish breakfast and then pay her a call," I suggested. If I got a chance to search her cabinets, I wondered if I'd find the ingredients for a special sauce.

"I'll clean up the kitchen," Scott offered. "I have some time to kill before I have to go to the club. Mind if I use your computer and printer?"

"Help yourself."

The minute we were in Tinkie's fine new car—full as ticks on an old hound—she turned to me. "I didn't want to say anything in front of Scott, but I think someone dangerous is in Sunflower County. Someone with an agenda that we don't understand at all. Someone who took a shot at Kitten."

As if witches, warlocks, cunning men, spells, charms, dead bodies, and viable sperm weren't enough to worry about. "Why do you believe this?"

"Because . . ." She pulled the car over at the end of the driveway and reached into the back seat to retrieve a piece of paper.

She handed it to me, and I read the words aloud. " 'The wages of sin are death.' That sounds like something Aunt Loulane would say." And it did. But my wonderful aunt had seldom been sinister, only religious. Her point was that people earned their place in Heaven by their actions on earth. Bad people were sent to smoking rooms, reservations determined by St. Peter.

I studied the block printing of the note. Some of the letters looked similar to the note I'd found in Trevor's bedroom, but I couldn't be certain because that note was now missing. But we had this one. Coleman could get someone to analyze the handwriting. Or perhaps that was something he'd learned during his stint at Quantico.

Tinkie returned the note to the back seat where it should be safe. Before I lost my nerve, I confessed the loss of the first note to her. "Coleman is going to be mad for several good reasons."

"Hold off on telling him." Tinkie patted my shoulder. "Really. We may be able to figure this out."

Sweet relief and guilt flooded me. "A lie of omission . . ."

"I didn't say never tell him. Just hold off until we can study this note a little. You were foolish to go in that house without backup. Why get Coleman all stirred up unless we have to?"

I liked her thinking, even if it made my conscience prickle. "Where did this note come from?"

"Kitten's mailbox, or so she said. She had it in the house and I picked it up when I talked with her." Tinkie got back on the road and headed toward Bob and Kitten Fontana's McMansion on the east side of town. "We'll get the truth out of her."

"Can you confirm the gunshot was directed at Kitten?" I asked.

"No. I've thought about that. She could be making it up. She and the truth seldom walk hand in hand. I'm partially convinced she wrote the note herself, but she did seem to be upset."

"What time did you make it over to Kitten's last night?" I was thinking about the intruder at the manor. I'd given serious consideration to the idea that the person tormenting me was Kitten. The figure had been smaller than Bob Fontana.

"I talked to her for a while. Maybe from eleven until one in the morning. She was upset and Bob was drunk."

Which meant that it couldn't have been Kitten roaming around the manor. And Bob was drunk, so it wasn't him. The person I'd seen was in full control of their faculties. "Where was the kid?"

"I do have some questions about Corey's whereabouts. Kitten said he was spending the night with a friend. I didn't hear a peep out of him, which doesn't really mean anything." She frowned. "The house is huge. Maybe eight thousand square feet. Who needs that much space?"

"People who hate each other?" It was no secret Bob and Kitten fought like cats and dogs. They got into it at parties, board meetings, church, on the street. Yet they seemed to pull in tandem when the chips were down in the business.

"You know, one area we really haven't looked into is Bob's development deals." I was thinking out loud. "What if all of this—the strange deaths, the thing in the woods, the fear that's building in town—what if this is about him and not the witches?"

Tinkie actually slapped her forehead. "Genius, Sarah Booth. The witches could be a diversion. I'd heard rumors that Trevor and Bob Fontana had been seen arguing back during the holidays, and everyone knows Bob has lusted after the Musgrove property for several years. What if Trevor brought in the witches just to mess with Bob and that's what they were arguing about. I just assumed it was because of Kitten and her crush on Trevor. But knowing Bob, he'd be a lot more upset at losing the property than his wife cheating on him."

"But why kill Esmeralda?" She was a real pain in the patoot, but that didn't warrant a death sentence. If I bumped off everyone who annoyed me, there would be no traffic jams in the Southeast.

"What if Esmeralda was onto the development thing? She mostly wrote made-up gossip, but she had good reporter instincts. Cece told me that when she first started out in journalism, she was offered a job at the *Charlotte Observer*, which was one of the nation's top papers at the time. She went with the *International Report* because the salary was six times higher. But she had the chops to be a great investigative reporter. Or that was Cece's assessment."

I hadn't seen that side of Esmeralda, but Cece would know. Before I could pursue my thoughts on calling the *International Report*, Tinkie stopped at the turn to the driveway of the Fontana's huge home. All eight thousand square feet of it. Though we were still a hundred-plus yards away, I could see the full scope of the house. Truly I could murder someone on one end and people at the other end would never know. What a waste of space and air-conditioning. The house had none of the graciousness of the old Southern homes. It was a federalist box of a house with blunt, square wings on either side. It was hard for me to picture Kitten Fontana being happy here. I always envisioned the Fontana McMansion as something with a large front porch, rocking chairs, pots of geraniums, and a bit of old Southern charm. This house was cold and sterile.

"Talk to Kitten about the gunshot," Tinkie said. "I'm going to do some snooping around."

"Snooping where?" Tinkie's sudden shift back into a kick-ass private eye was a bit alarming.

"Bob has an office up on the second floor.

I need to get in there and see if I can find his contracts for developments."

"You don't think Bob has some alarms and safeguards?" I didn't like the idea of Tinkie trying to break into Bob's office like this. Oscar would kill me if she got caught—it might impact the bank's role in financing future Fontana developments. I knew almost nothing about such things, but I did know enough that I should be the one poking around. Then I had an even better idea. "They'll have to let Coleman in to search for the bullet since someone fired at Kitten." I had another thought. "And why didn't Kitten call Coleman instead of you and me?"

"She said she'd already paid us, and the 'bumbling sheriff and his deputy' might destroy evidence. She said it was our job to investigate. She has a point. She has paid us."

"Okay, you talk to Kitten. I'll search. That way the resulting crap won't fly back on the bank and Oscar if I'm caught doing something illegal."

Tinkie's expression shifted rapidly to sly. "If there is anything, she's smart enough to destroy it. What if she wrote both notes *and* killed Esmeralda. Maybe there's evidence."

"Keep Kitten distracted. If there's anything to find, I'll get it." I nudged her shoulder. "Entertain her. She likes you a lot better than me."

"You have twenty minutes. I can handle her for that long. Then you'd better show."

"I'll do my best." Tinkie was really getting bossy. Normally we didn't bicker about division of duties. We each had our strengths, and Tinkie was by far the superior handler of rich bitches with an attitude.

She let me out of the car and I walked around the corner of the house to a backyard that included swim cabanas, a pool and whirlpool, tropical gardens, and what looked like a butterfly garden. Who knew Kitten could make plants grow. A beautiful orange and purple flower caught my attention, but I didn't dillydally in the garden. I made haste for the back door. I could only hope I didn't run into a maid or butler or some other servant. Tinkie would keep Kitten occupied but it was up to me to dodge the staff.

The back door wasn't locked—not unusual in Sunflower County even in this day and time. A world where dead bolts and barred windows was de rigueur for most of the country didn't apply in Zinnia. We still lived in the haze of days when the county was a community. People looked out for one another. The home invasions, brutal robberies, killings for no reason, they weren't part of Sunflower County. Not yet. It was coming, but not yet.

I heard conversation in the laundry room, and I slipped past and made it to the kitchen. I found the pantry, and right on the top shelf was a box of dried black grapes. Not evidence, but enough to make me believe Kitten had authored my missing note.

The sound of someone coming sent me darting up the servants' back stairs to the second floor. The clock was ticking and I didn't waste time looking at the portraits hanging on the walls, though I really wanted to inspect them. I'd heard of a service that painted "royal ancestors" for wealthy people with no bloodline. A cursory glance as I passed showed me portraits of men and women in rich brocades, velvets, and ruffs—no doubt to hide double chins. The people depicted should have come from the seventeenth and eighteenth centuries. I had no evidence, but Kitten and Bob seemed to be the kind of people who worked hard to create a family heritage that didn't exist. Some people had to have a pedigree, even when it was fabricated. These were the same people who thought an American Kennel Club pet had more value than a pound pup.

As much as I wanted to photograph the paintings for later study, I hurried past, checking doorknobs until I found Bob's office. I entered quietly and froze. Bob Fontana was sprawled on the floor, unmoving.

"Oh, crap." I closed the door behind me and leaned against it. Kitten had called Tinkie about a gunshot. Maybe Kitten really had heard something. She'd called us—and failed to check to make sure Bob wasn't hit. Heck, maybe she'd pulled the trigger herself. It wouldn't be the first time a spouse killed a spouse and tried to blame it on a stranger. Tinkie was her alibi. That's why she'd called Delaney Detective Agency and not the police. Damn! She was smarter than I'd given her credit for.

I inched toward the body. I needed to see how he'd died. I reached into my pocket for my cell phone only to realize I'd never found it. I couldn't photograph the body, but I still had to look. And I had to call Coleman. People were dropping dead all over the county.

I knelt beside Bob. He lay on his stomach, sort of. One leg was curled beneath his body and his arms were flung wide, the right side of his face smushed into an expensive Turkish carpet. Some vile effluvium leaked from his mouth.

I reached to his neck to feel for a pulse, and to my surprise, the body was still warm. I was about to withdraw when Bob snorted and flung an arm over, whacking me in the face. He rolled with great force and his hand hit me so hard I fell backward on my butt.

Bob snorted another big snore, then cut loose a fart that shook the window panes.

And I held my breath, hoping he didn't wake up. Kitten hadn't been lying about one thing last night. Bob had been on a terrible bender, or else he was a narcoleptic. The vodka bottle beside him seemed to support Kitten's contention that he was drunk. But at least he wasn't dead.

As I crab-crawled away from his body, I finally realized the room had also been trashed. Maybe Bob had been hit on the head when he surprised someone searching his office. Someone with the same idea I had.

He ripped another simultaneous snort-and-fart, flopped over again, chewed a little bit, and sank into a deep sleep. The good news was that I could now search the office and no one would be any the wiser if I dumped over a few drawers. Bob wouldn't hear me, and with the mayhem already around, no one would be able to tell I'd been there.

Bob had a bank of filing cabinets in the far corner and some of the drawers were open, folders spilled over the carpet. The disarray was much like the state I'd found in Trevor's rooms. Someone had also gone through his files. That was too coincidental not to have meaning.

Blueprints of houses, illustrations of buildings, and maps of subdivisions were everywhere. Some were schematics for plumbing and wiring, others showed the layouts of the houses. I was tempted to just grab up everything I could and dash out of the house. That wouldn't work, though. I needed to search more thoroughly, and I only had ten minutes left on Tinkie's clock. Not to mention the snoring beast on the floor might surface to consciousness at any moment.

Aunt Loulane had always told me that death was the great equalizer—that we were all reduced to dust and bone. Alcohol had the same effect. Too much of it brought even the most dapper men and beautiful women to sordid heaps of flesh and flatulence.

While the blueprints were interesting and probably contained a lot of cost information that clients would love to know, I didn't see anything that tied Trevor, the witches, or Musgrove Manor together. Maybe I was barking up the wrong tree.

I hit a file filled with receipts. My fingers fumbled because I was stressed by the ticking clock. I pilfered through them as fast as I could, stopping at one from Lisbet Bradley, the broker for Arlington Woods subdivision who was now in prison, dating back two years. If I recalled, she would have been in prison on the date of the invoice. I reached for my phone to snap a photo of the receipt only to be reminded I'd lost the dang thing. I'd truly come to rely on technology, something I'd vowed to avoid. There was no other way than theft. I folded the receipt and put it in my pocket. I'd figure a way to return it later.

I swallowed my impatience and anxiety. Bob had files on top of files. It would take a forensic accountant six months to slog through all of this. And I had about six minutes. I found another folder marked *Art.* Curious, I opened it and saw only a list of names. I took it, too. What the heck. None of it looked promising, though.

I was about to give up when Bob rolled over again. “Stay away,” he mumbled angrily. “Don’t touch it.”

I looked around to see what he might have been defending in his stupor. This room contained none of the vintage family portraits. This office was modern and new, clean lines on the desk and other furnishings. The only thing out of place was a gorgeous oil painting of a tree. The morning sun cast a strange glare on the painting and I had to move to another location before I could clearly see it.

It took me a moment to discern Kitten Fontana in the beautifully contoured limbs and trunk of the old cedar, but she was there. The painting was a masterpiece. And Kitten had shaped herself into a beautiful swirl of trunk. This was one of the series that the witches had been talking about. The nature series where each nude woman assumed the posturing of a particular tree.

“Stay back!” Bob abruptly tried to sit up. He shook his head to focus his eyes, and I knew I had to leave. It wasn’t worth the risk of getting caught and having to explain why I was upstairs in his office. As much as I hated leaving mostly empty-handed, I did. While Bob fought gravity and gas, I eased out the door and down the hall.

Five minutes later I knocked on the front door

and waited for Kitten to properly let me inside. "Where have you been?" Kitten asked, looking out the door as if I might have a legion of demons with me.

"Tinkie got mad at me and put me out of the car about a mile down the road. I had to walk. She's going to pay for that."

Kitten laughed. She really liked that answer. "I didn't realize Tinkie had such good taste."

"Funny har har," I said. "Where's my partner?"

"Morning room."

"Lead the way."

16

I endured Kitten's obnoxiousness for about ten minutes before I was ready to lock and load—or leave, which seemed the better option. I really didn't want to shoot her. Well, I really did, but leaving was less messy and wouldn't require a call to Coleman. Tinkie was ready to go, too. We only had a few questions left to ask. Since I knew Bob hadn't been shot, we still hadn't found any evidence of the gunshot that had set our entire adventure with Kitten in motion.

"Where did the bullet enter the room?" I asked. I didn't see any broken windows, no sign that someone had violated the Fontana castle with a lead slug.

"Oh, it didn't come in the house." Kitten shrugged. She rang a little silver bell on the table beside her chair. When a maid silently appeared, she ordered a mimosa. When the maid left, she looked at us. "Oh, would you like one, too?"

"No, thanks." Tinkie and I spoke in unison as we often did. "We're working," Tinkie added. "We wouldn't want to take your money and your alcohol."

"So where were you shot at?" I pursued my goal like a dog with a bone. "If you want us to investigate, we have to examine the scene."

"I didn't say I was shot *at.* I said I heard a shot. The bullet was outside. I *heard* the shot." She pointed at her ear as if I needed sign language for clarity.

"So how did you know it was directed at you?" I wasn't confused, she was nuts.

"No one else lives around here for miles. The shot had to be directed at me or Bob and Bob was binge drinking. I'd been out in the gardens. Most people love Bob, but they have no idea what a sloppy drunk he can be. Anyway, I figured the bullet was meant for me."

Between the two I had no doubt Kitten was the target. Suddenly I wondered if she knew about Esmeralda's death. I didn't think Tinkie had told her. Coleman hadn't released the story to the news media yet. No one really knew but the paramedics, Doc, the witches, and DeWayne. It would be interesting to witness Kitten's reaction. She and Esmeralda were frenemies.

"What do you make of Esmeralda's death?" I asked.

Kitten's superior smile slipped only a fraction. "What are you talking about?" Her gaze darted to Tinkie and back to me. She was either very good or very innocent.

"I'm sorry. I thought you knew. She was

murdered last night. Thrown from the third floor of Musgrove Manor." I was stretching the few facts I had into a story that Coleman might not recognize.

Kitten started to rise but fell back, as if her legs wouldn't hold her. "She went for that damn painting." She spoke before she could govern her tongue. She all but clapped her hand over her mouth.

"What painting?" I asked.

"Oh, the one she and Trevor bickered endlessly over." She waved a hand in dismissal. "It was the same old, same old all the time. He'd say he sold it, then tell her he had it back. She'd go to get it, and he wouldn't have it anymore. He toyed with her. Boring, actually."

The maid entered with a tray and her drink. Kitten took the champagne flute and speared the maid with a glare. "Get two more for my guests."

She intended to loosen our tongues with alcohol. Even so, I wouldn't object. But only one. I had a long day ahead of me.

"So Esmeralda died of a fall?" Kitten asked, swirling her drink. "I'll bet she didn't see that one coming."

"Maybe it was a fall." I shrugged innocently when her gaze snapped up at me. Two could play at nonchalance.

"She did or she didn't die from falling. Or maybe you just don't know."

"Maybe." It was like poking a snake with a broom. Not really smart but fun. How far could Kitten lunge when her fangs snapped down?

"I am paying you good money and I am getting nothing for my investment. How did Esmeralda die?"

"Grow up," Tinkie finally said. "You hired us for our detective skills, not to brown nose you into a good mood. Doc isn't sure how Esmeralda died, but he's going to find out. She had that same look of horror on her face as Trevor. There is definitely something going on at the manor, but we can't say yet it if originates with the witches or someone"—she paused and stared at Kitten for a pregnant moment—"who is trying to frame the Harringtons. Say, someone who might kill a friend just to hang that death around the pretty Harrington necks."

"I didn't hurt Esmeralda. Maybe it was that sheriff she was all atwitter about. They had dinner and she was beside herself with his charms." She leveled her gaze at me, twisting the knife. "She said it was a very intimate . . . meal."

"So you talked to her *after* the dinner?" I was on top of my game.

"What if I did?"

"Then you may have been the last person to see her alive." I loved it when I got to say that to a suspect I really disliked.

“Bite me.” Kitten was reduced to eighth-grade replies.

“No, thanks. I don’t eat aged and marbled beef.”

Tinkie had taken a dainty sip of her orange juice, which caused her to splutter. I slapped her on the back to help her catch her breath. “That was a good one, Sarah Booth,” she whispered. “Let’s ditch this joint. I don’t think she was involved in Esmeralda’s death.”

“I agree.” I turned to Kitten. “Coleman will be by, I’m sure. You can ask him yourself about his dinner with Esmeralda since you’re so consumed with curiosity. I’m sure he’ll have some questions for you.”

“You two are fired.” Kitten stood up to her full five foot three height. “Leave my home.”

“No refunds,” I said.

“Of course you wouldn’t refund my money.” She pointed toward the entrance hall. “Just get out.”

I drained the mimosa. Why waste good liquor? And Tinkie and I headed west.

Not five minutes on the way home, I felt my world slip out of control. “Something is wrong. Everything is spinning.”

Tinkie pulled to the side of the road and looked at me. “One mimosa wouldn’t hit this hard. You’ve been drugged.”

"You didn't drink much of your drink?"

"Only a sip. Because . . . Lean back. We're going to the hospital."

Since I couldn't do anything but lean and slump, I didn't argue. Five minutes later we pulled into the ambulance bay and Tinkie sent for an orderly with a wheelchair. He pushed me straight into the emergency room, where Doc Sawyer tut-tutted when he saw me. "Kitten Fontana spiked your drink, eh?"

"It had to be her," Tinkie said. "Maybe she drugged Esmeralda and pushed her over the railing."

Doc didn't reply as he shined a penlight in my eyes that made me yelp in pain. "Photo sensitivity, dizziness, loss of coordination. Sarah Booth, can you think straight? Don't answer that."

"I can think, dammit. I can't walk. And I am not a vegetable sitting here to be discussed. I'm not a squash. Or a rutabaga. Or a turnip."

"Stop with the produce. I can fix this." He went to his cabinets and came back with a horse needle and syringe. It looked like he was going to spike an artery and put in a spigot.

Before I could get my tongue unwrapped to scream, it was over. And sure enough, the wooziness started to pass and my clarity returned. Even my feet would tap when I asked them to. "Thanks, Doc. That's a lot better."

He leaned over and whispered in my ear. "You need a better group of drinking buddies. You were drugged."

"With what?"

"Some form of Klonopin or a similar drug."

"And that would be?"

"You were given an antianxiety drug." He checked my eyes again. "You're fine. You could have slept it off, but since you were here . . ."

I looked at Tinkie. "Why didn't you drink your mimosa?"

Tinkie paced the exam room. "Kitten was just way too sly about finally offering us a drink. I knew she was up to something."

"And I fell for it."

"No, but you were so determined to stick it to her that you swigged it down without thinking."

A lesson on being a greedy girl I needed to think about—at a later date.

"So why was Kitten drugging you?" Doc asked.

"Because she's mean?" I asked.

"I think that covers most of it. Sarah Booth had been tweaking her pretty good since we got there. Kitten finally had enough and reverted back to the days when she used to drug and roll her bordello clients."

"Whoa, there." I nodded my approval.

"You're okay, Sarah Booth. Grow up. Stop drinking with your enemies. Now get out of here."

"Anything on Esmeralda's cause of death?" I was really right as rain.

"If she fell from the third floor into the koi pond, she was mighty lucky. She didn't have a single broken bone."

"But how did she die?"

"I can't say just yet. Still running some tests. I will say her death doesn't make sense. Esmeralda was otherwise in fine health. I've checked her records, and there's no history of heart issues or any reason to believe she might suffer from such." He sighed. "I'm still looking."

"Do you think the witches cursed her?" Tinkie asked.

I held my breath. I didn't want to admit it, but the same thought had run through my mind. Bit by bit, I was beginning to see the witches as a force or power. Good or bad, I couldn't say. But the charm that hung between my breasts had moved me from a skeptic to a reluctant believer. And that opened the door to some wild possibilities. What were those sisters capable of?

Doc studied Tinkie. "I'm a man of science. Hexes, charms, curses—they're only effective if the person believes in them. It's psychological, not magical. I don't believe in curses, Tinkie. You know that."

"I do. But there isn't another logical explanation."

"There is. I just haven't found it."

• • •

"Do you think Kitten ordered the maid to drug me?" I'd pondered this silently for most of the ride to the DDA offices at Dahlia House.

Tinkie turned down the driveway. "I don't know. How did she communicate that message to the maid? Do you think maybe the drug was meant for Kitten?"

"Why would the maid drug Kitten? Why would the maid drug any of us? That whole episode doesn't make sense. The gunshot that didn't really happen, obviously. Her getting us over there to do what? It's just . . . nonsensical."

Tinkie's mind was more orderly than mine. She hated illogical things.

"I'm just glad I didn't fall over and crack my skull open. I couldn't make my arms and legs respond." I didn't say it out loud, but I wondered if Bob Fontana had been suffering from a little dose of an antianxiety drug. His body had been almost boneless in its relaxation. I quickly filled Tinkie in on the details of Bob's intoxication.

"Why was it so important for us to be at Kitten's house? Who benefits from us being there?"

Tinkie was at least asking the right questions as we coasted to a stop near the front steps. Moments later she headed to the office and I was in the kitchen putting on a pot of coffee. Sweetie Pie, Pluto, and Chablis were glad to see me, especially when they realized I had some delicious catfish leftovers in the refrigerator for them. I understood the ways of my critters. If only humans were as easy to interpret.

"Sarah Booth! Come quick!"

I put the box of fish in the sink and ran toward Tinkie's voice. She never panicked unless there was a good reason—or a cockroach. "What?"

But she didn't have to answer. I saw it. Someone had been through our agency office like a tornado on an April day. Papers were scattered everywhere. Files had been pulled from drawers and filing cabinets turned over. Whoever did this might have been hunting for something, but they'd also done the maximum damage they could. "Well, damn."

Tinkie leveled a gaze at me. "You asked who benefitted from us being at Kitten's. Now we know. Whoever did this. It got us out of the way for certain so they could get in here and tear through our files."

I examined the big window and saw how they'd entered Dahlia House, breaking the old lock that had never been designed to forestall a modern intruder. "I need new locks on the windows. I'm glad there aren't any more of those claw marks."

"Find the sunshine, little miss," Tinkie said. "I'm aggravated." She kicked off her heels and knelt on the floor as she began picking up papers and files.

I sat at one of the computers and went through our case files. It didn't seem that anything had been taken or deleted. I had no way of knowing if a file had been copied.

"We don't keep that much stuff on the computer," Tinkie said.

"Right. It looks okay." I put in a call to the local hardware store and got the name of someone who could change out the window locks. I made an appointment and slid to the floor to help pick up the debris.

"Did you find anything in Bob's office?" Tinkie asked.

I removed the pages I'd taken from my back pocket and unfolded them as I talked. "There was a receipt from Lisbet Bailey sent to Bob."

"For what?"

I looked at the page. "It doesn't say. It's just a receipt for two grand."

"Wasn't Lisbet in jail for that embezzlement and fraud scam at Arlington Woods? She's *still* in jail. Why is she paying Bob anything?"

"We need to make some calls. Too bad we don't have any personal connections to the correctional officers at the Central Mississippi lockup."

"Keep on the path you're going, Sarah Booth, and I'm sure we'll have some close prison contacts before too long."

17

The day was still young when Tinkie and I decided to head south on Highway 49 to pay Lisbet Bailey a surprise visit at the prison. Before we went anywhere, I had to find my phone and I hoped I'd dropped it in my car. To that end, we went out and began a thorough search.

Knowing my propensity to let items slide out of my lap as I drove, I immediately began a search of the floorboard under the driver's seat. Once I'd had a billfold slide off my lap and wedge under the brake pedal. Not a good move, trust me. At least the thin phone wouldn't prevent me from stopping the car, but shifting around under my feet would not prove healthy for the device.

"How can things hide in such a small area?" I asked as I wallowed around in the tight space.

"Sarah Booth, it's right in the back seat," Tinkie said.

"You've got to be kidding." I unscrewed myself from beneath the steering column and looked at the back seat. Tinkie wasn't hallucinating. "I just don't remember putting it there." But I was glad to have it back and plugged it into the charger as we piled in for the drive downstate.

In our work as PIs, we'd learned that long prison sentences sometimes made people more talkative. Especially if they were stewing in the juices of revenge. Lisbet might be willing to dish some dirt on Bob Fontana, Kitten, and the real estate developments that had gone sour and ended up with her spending her reproductive years in jail.

"Why would she take the heat for Bob?" Tinkie asked the question that troubled me. "Why would she take all the blame and let him off scot-free?"

"Maybe she'll tell us."

The clarity of the air made driving a pleasure, and though we took the convertible, we left the critters at Dahlia House. Waiting in a prison parking lot in a car wasn't a productive way for them to spend the day, and I didn't know how long, or if, we'd be allowed to talk to Lisbet. As a personal favor to me—and without asking too many questions—Coleman had called ahead for us and opened the door for the interview, but institutions such as prisons moved at a crawl, even with the best prompting.

"I did a little internet research on Lisbet Bailey," Tinkie said. "I couldn't find much. The case against her was pretty damning. They found documentation in her files that she knew the land they built on was in a floodplain, that the area was unstable, that foundations were liable to crack, yada yada. Lisbet simply never disclosed that information to the construction crews, or so the paperwork indicates. I don't believe that, though. She and Bob were partners, but it seems she deceived Bob and everyone else. She went straight for the finish line and the payoff and so she paid the ultimate price."

"People build on bad land all the time when they rush to throw up developments. The problem is, they just don't get caught until fifty years later when the foundation issues start to show up. Then the developer is out of business and the homeowners are up shit creek."

"How eloquent you are, Sarah Booth."

"It might apply, literally, in this case. When the Pearl River floods, there's a lot of toxic sh . . . stuff floating around."

Tinkie slugged my arm with a lot of force. "You are too gross."

"Stop it. I'm driving."

"She's touching me. She's touching me." Tinkie mocked me.

I didn't bother replying as we pulled into the check-in booth at the prison. Coleman had done his work and we drove down to the admin building. They would bring Lisbet to the visitor area. As I got out and looked around at the prison grounds, I could only hope Lisbet would view us as a distraction in an otherwise long and bland day and actually agree to meet with us. No one could force her to do so.

Because Coleman had removed the hurdles, we entered the prison and were told Lisbet was waiting for us in an interview area. A guard would stay with us. I would have preferred to be alone with her, but I was glad she'd agreed to speak to us.

When I opened the door, I saw the guard in the corner and a woman in her early forties with blond hair and dark roots dressed in an orange jumpsuit. Her eyes were a little wild, as if she'd been netted and brought to civilization against her will.

Tinkie took the initiative and introduced herself. The woman eyed the guard and leaned forward to speak privately to us. "If Lisbet Bailey sent you, you can tell that bitch when I get out of here I'm going to skin her alive."

It wasn't exactly the opening salvo I'd anticipated. I approached the topic with caution. "Aren't you Lisbet Bailey?" I asked.

"No." She looked over at the guard. "I've been trying to tell these pinheads I am not Lisbet Bailey for a while now. This is a big mistake. I took a payoff to show up at those development homes *pretending* to be Lisbet Bailey. It was a simple scam. I just put out the paperwork, made a few bank calls for financing, got their signatures on the line. You know, closed the deal."

"And you did this why?" I asked.

"For each deal I closed as Lisbet Bailey, I got a nice payoff. Imagine my surprise when a swat team of po-pos crashed through the door at this brick five/four I was showing. You would have thought I was Charles Manson. They hurled me to the ground and cuffed me. I was arrested and charged with a list of crimes as long as my arm. Now no one will believe that I'm not this Lisbet Bailey who cheated all of those homeowners. I don't know a damn thing about bad foundations or floodplains. I was the front woman to close the deals that Bob Fontana had already set in motion."

"Who are you?" I asked.

"Claudell Myers." Tears welled in her eyes. "I'm Claudell Myers. Sometimes I think that I've lost my mind and made up Claudell. But that's me. Even though they've pretty much erased me." She grabbed my hand. "You have to get me out of here before I disappear completely."

"Do you know Lisbet Bailey?" I asked.

"Never met her face-to-face. Like I said, I was hired to pretend to be her. All I had to do was show up and get the signatures on the house contracts. I'm a small-time con. I impersonate people and steal identities. When I got a call asking me to pretend to be this Lisbet person, the pay was too much to turn down. I should have known it was too good to be true."

"How much pay?" The question popped out and I wished I hadn't spoken. She was on a roll and I'd thrown up a roadblock.

"Not enough. I think about that a lot, lying on the two-inch cardboard mattress staring at cinder blocks. I sold my life for a song."

"You were tried for these crimes," Tinkie said, pacing on our side of the table. "How could you go through the trial and be convicted and not be able to prove your true identity?"

The woman sighed. "Because I am as stupid as I look. They convinced me to keep up the pretense of being Lisbet during the trial. They said they'd set it all straight eventually, when the real Lisbet Bailey had a chance to get out of the country. They promised they'd come back and make this right and in the meantime, they were putting deposits into my bank account. Right. Of course they didn't. When that prison door slammed shut behind me, I never saw them again. I was a fool." The last was said with such bitterness that I almost felt sorry for her. Almost. But she was still a conned con who'd lost her freedom in a scam that had gotten a lot bigger than she was.

"I can't believe this," Tinkie said. As the more logical partner, she was going on facts, not emotions. "Surely you could prove who you are."

"My entire life had been erased. Just erased. Oh, they did their job well. I don't have family, and they knew that. High school dropout. I'd drifted around the country running scams, making sure not to leave any tracks behind. They knew everything about me that made me the perfect patsy to carry the weight on this. And I played right into their hands. I never dreamed anyone could be so deceptive."

Pot, kettle, both black. I didn't say it. There was no point.

"But the people who bought houses—surely they could testify that you weren't Lisbet."

"Oh, really? They'd only talked to Lisbet on the phone. Since I met them for the closings and the document signings and the dealings with financing and the banks and said I was Lisbet"—she held out her hands palms up—"and as a con artist, I'd learned enough about financial matters that I could sell it, with some coaching from that bastard Bob Fontana and that bit—" She closed her eyes and rubbed her forehead. "I've developed high blood pressure in here. I can't get worked up. It doesn't do any good and just damages my health."

"Well, I'd get worked up. If I'd spent my savings on one of those houses, I'd be really worked up." Tinkie wasn't sympathetic at all. "If what you say is true, the real Lisbet Bailey is running around living her life while you're serving time for her crimes. I think you both need to be in jail."

I nudged Tinkie in the ribs. She wasn't meaning

to be a bruise masher, but she was doing a damn good job of it. "Ease off, how about it?"

"Sorry," Tinkie said. "The wages of sin . . ." The strangest look crossed her face as we both thought of the note left in Kitten's mailbox. It was like a little comment bubble with a lightbulb had been shared between us. The light clicked on.

"What does Lisbet Bailey look like?" I asked.

"Like some Jersey Shore meatball."

I wasn't sure I understood what that meant, but a very ugly picture was starting to become clear in my head. "Does she look like the TV show person Snooki?"

Claudell nodded. "I think Snooki is her hero. She wore short, tight dresses, stacked sandals, lots of ugly print and bling, huge earrings, and that stupid hair poof. I have to say, when I was playing the part, I put a little class in it." Her hand went to her hair. "Now look at me. I haven't had my hair done in forever."

She certainly wasn't ready for her glamour shots, but I also wasn't sympathetic. I was on a hot lead. "If I showed you a picture, could you identify Lisbet?"

"Maybe. What's in it for me?"

"Maybe your freedom," Tinkie snapped. "We don't have to help you and I'm pretty much ready to walk out the door."

"No one helps me out of the goodness of her

heart. That's one lesson I've learned the hard way. What are you two up to?"

"We're private investigators and we're working on a case." I scrolled through my phone until I found the photos from the school board meeting. There was Kitten Fontana, big as life and twice as tawdry. "Is this Lisbet?"

Claudell looked at the tiny screen for a long time. "That's her. I'd begun to believe I made up how cheap she looks. But there she is, in all her glory."

"You're sure that's Lisbet Bailey?"

"Positive. She looks like she's in a fight at some meeting. What's she doing in that picture?"

I ignored her question. "Bob Fontana had an invoice for two grand. It was nine months ago."

Her answer was a blank stare. "I didn't do that."

"Why would he have that payment in his books?"

She slowly shook her head. "If I'd somehow gotten someone to listen to me, a reporter or someone, maybe they put in payments to make me look guilty. Or maybe there really is a Lisbet Bailey who's paying them off. All I know is that I don't have two hundred dollars to pay anyone."

"How much longer is your sentence?" Tinkie asked.

"Ten years."

"We'll do what we can." It was time to hit

the road. Kitten Fontana had some questions to answer and I couldn't wait to get Coleman to ask them. I just couldn't believe she and Bob had successfully pulled off such a huge scam and not one single person had caught on to it. Claudell Myers had lost everything, including her past. The wages of sin, indeed.

There was still daylight left when Tinkie and I got back to Zinnia. We picked up the critters—it was either that or risk being eaten alive in the middle of the night—and drove toward one place I'd never in a million years thought I might go. Budgie Burton's house.

The former substitute history teacher lived in a small, older subdivision on the south side of Zinnia. The houses had been built during World War II, and some were in not great repair. The entire place would look better in the spring when the trees were leafed out, but it was pretty barren-looking now. Budgie's house was neatly maintained with painted shutters and an edged sidewalk. The flower beds had been turned with the promise of some bright color in the future.

Budgie Burton had left the teaching profession and taken a job at the state prison in Parchman. It was a position that Sunflower County High School had prepared him well for since a lot of my classmates'd had criminal tendencies.

Budgie had agreed to meet with us and talk

about Musgrove Manor and the architecture of the houses he considered part of "the spy network."

Budgie's concession to the passing years was less hair, a tad more stomach, and a much calmer expression. He still wore khakis and long-sleeved dress shirts with sweater vests. His wardrobe had earned him a lot of torment from the students, but he'd never changed. He was clean-shaven and neat, and he ushered us into his living room, which was also orderly. Looking at him now, I realized he was probably only in his early forties. He'd seemed so old when he taught me.

"So you actually ended up in an honest profession, Sarah Booth," he said. "I had some sincere conversations with your aunt about your future."

That was a startling bit of information. "Aunt Loulane thought I'd grow up to be a criminal?" She'd never uttered a word.

"Not a criminal. She was afraid you'd never be happy. That you'd never trust another person enough again to be happy. You absorbed that terrible shock and loss and you went on. You wouldn't let anyone help you."

I swallowed a sudden lump in my throat. I'd had a difficult time after my parents' deaths. That was true. But I didn't recall rebuffing any offers of help. Then again, I'd been a shy and silent young girl who grew into a physically active teenager. I'd hurled myself into acting and sports and big dreams in New York. If anyone tried to talk to me about my feelings, I shut them down. I did remember that much.

"Lots of people reached out to you, Sarah Booth. You just weren't in a place where you could take a hand. You had to struggle through those emotions on your own."

Funny how my perception of Budgie Burton had missed so much of his depth and kindness. But I didn't want to talk about me. "We're here about Musgrove Manor and what you might know about secret passages or hidden rooms in the manor." I had to move the topic off my personal past. The swell of emotion I felt was genuinely uncomfortable.

"Based on the year the manor house was built and that it was patterned after a famous priory that did contain hidden passages, I'd say there's a better than average chance you'll find something. The border wars between Scotland and England resulted in a lot of tunnels and passages where those trapped in one of the large estate houses could either hide until it was safe to come out, or escape. Those passages were also employed in World War Two."

"Where should I look for rooms or passages?" I asked.

"At Musgrove Manor, I'd look for hidden staircases that led to tunnels that go out into the barns and tractor sheds. That would make the most sense. From the barns, someone could easily move into the woods." He took a breath. "I heard some witches had taken over the house."

I didn't feel like getting into a debate over the merits of Wicca, so I changed the subject. "You know Trevor is dead?"

"Yeah, it's all over town he was frightened to death by those witches."

And we were back to the witches. "Would you like to meet them, Budgie?" It felt only a little weird calling him by his first name, but I thought I'd found the bait that would lure him into helping us.

"Yes." He had no hesitation. "I'm open to all kinds of spirituality and I must admit a real curiosity about those Harrington sisters. Who would come to an ultra-religious community like Zinnia and proclaim themselves pagans? I'm fascinated by either their courage or their ignorance."

"They aren't so different from us," I told him. "But if you want to meet them, I can make that happen. Will you help me search for a secret passage?"

"Sure." He looked around. "I'm off tomorrow. How would that be?"

"I'll arrange it," I said.

Tinkie had been strangely silent during the exchange, but she rejoined the conversation.

"Budgie, were we bad kids when you had to deal with us?"

"A lot of the time you were bored. Sarah Booth, too. It's hard to be well-behaved when you're held captive somewhere and left without a challenge."

"If you had a child, would you support the public schools or go with a charter school?"

My stomach flipped as I realized that Tinkie had spent the last fifteen minutes not furthering our investigation or even day-tripping to the past, but spinning out the future of her would-be child and his/her education. This wasn't a theoretical question. She was making plans.

"Public education has been the backbone of America's superiority across the globe. In past generations, every citizen had an opportunity for a basic education, and that's been our greatest strength. That's not true anymore, though. Rural children, those growing up in inner cities, and those from poor backgrounds are being left behind. If parents are allowed to take the tax money meant for public education and spend it at charter schools, it will wreck the public school system. Then the divide between the haves and the have-nots will only grow wider."

I had a sudden memory of Budgie Burton standing in front of our raucous eighth grade class. We were little more than hormonal thugs, squirming and sweating and all too aware of the romantic intrigues that swirled over us. I wondered how he'd restrained himself from bonking us on the head simply to get our estrogen- and testosterone-addled attention.

"Why did you even want to teach us?" I asked him.

"I like kids. There was so much potential in every classroom I ever walked into. I'm not the brightest lamp on the street, but I know that if we don't teach our youngsters history—the true history of this country—the good, bad, and ugly, we'll forever be caught in a loop of repetition. Sanitized history books are useless and that's what's being taught now. America never made a mistake. The Native Americans wanted us to take their land. Slavery is just another form of migration. Bull crap like that."

I was smote by a memory of Budgie handing out excerpts from a book called *Black Like Me*. He'd been talking about the black experience in America, from slavery to the racial conflict of the 1960s. He'd created a stir and some parents had complained to the school board. Budgie had defended his choice of material with much the same speech he'd just given. I remembered Aunt Loulane had gone to the school board meeting to stand with him. At thirteen, I'd found the whole business tedious and silly. The thought of trying to see life from the perspective of another person had seemed simply unnecessary. Budgie had been the first person to point out to me how such an attitude was a rare privilege awarded to only one segment of our society. For his trouble, he'd been sued.

"And now you work at a prison." Guilt at my own complicity knotted my stomach. I should have fought for him, too.

"That lawsuit didn't go anywhere, Sarah Booth. I left teaching because the pay at the prison is better and to be honest, the work is less stressful these days. Also I'm teaching some GED classes and the inmates I work with want to learn." He shook his head. "That's a helpful attitude."

"Glad you have a sense of humor," Tinkie said.

"You two were good kids." He smiled and years fell away. "Tinkie, you were destined to be the social leader of the Delta. Sarah Booth, you could have gone either way, criminal or force for justice. You picked the latter. Your aunt would be so relieved. At any rate, I'm glad you came back to the Delta, Sarah Booth. I know it must not have been easy."

I nodded. "In some ways, very easy. In other ways, difficult." Expectations were always the worst thing I had to overcome. I'd returned home because I had nowhere else to go. But the home I'd known was forever gone. What I'd found was a house in need of repair work and a snarky ghost who tried to get me wed and bred before I'd unpacked my suitcase. No loving aunt or parents met me. No network of high school routines to instill some order in my life. Still, it could have been a lot worse.

"We find our path, don't we?" Budgie asked. "While I've been working at the prison I've had the time and energy to write my book about the feudal system in the old South. I've gotten a nibble from a publisher."

"That's terrific." I was pleased for my old substitute teacher. "We'll pick you up in the morning for a jaunt over to Musgrove Manor."

"See you then."

He showed us out and stood in the doorway as we drove away. Because I had no food in the house or any intention of cooking, we swung by Millie's on the way home and took to-go plates for us and the critters.

Cooking wasn't on Tinkie's agenda either, but Oscar definitely needed sustenance for what she had in mind.

18

When I pulled up at Dahlia House after dropping off Tinkie and Chablis, I wanted only to slog into the house and spend a few quiet minutes talking to Coleman on the phone. What I really wanted was for him to call me, to tease me gently about the intimacy we'd shared, to show that it had meant something to him. Radio silence after sex is one thing that can drive a woman to mayhem. And I hadn't really talked with Coleman since we'd made love. Not really. Sure I'd seen him at a crime scene, exchanged facts, all conversation he could have had with DeWayne. My insecurities had begun to circle their wagons and draw closer to me. I hated that my brain even went to that place of doubt—was it just something he preferred not to pursue? Had he had second thoughts?

If I'd been a cuticle chewer, my digits would be bleeding. As it was, only my poor, doubting heart was leaking fluids all over the cold front porch.

I unlocked the door and stepped into the perfume of roses and a roomful of flowers. Vases of red roses, stargazer lilies, and of course, dahlias and zinnias, had been set in the foyer and by the wet bar where I would be sure to see them. The delicious rose perfume made me stop, close my eyes, and simply inhale.

Coleman!

I had no doubt who'd delivered them, and the shadow fell away from my heart and I felt as if a belt that had tightened across my lungs was suddenly released. Coleman was thinking of me—good thoughts. Good enough to raid the entire stock of flowers at Blooming Things, Zinnia's florist.

I snapped a few photos and sent a quick thank-you text. I kept it short and fun. He would call when he had time. Reassured that if Coleman didn't respect me, at least he still liked me, I basked in the beauty of the flowers. What a relief it was to drop the burden of self-doubt. And I wondered, not for the first time, why I was prone to doubt myself.

"Jitty!" I called for my haint. I wanted someone to share the flowers with and to gloat a little. Jitty was always deviling me about my man skills. I wasn't about to send photos to Tinkie or Cece. That was a waste of a proper impact. I would invite them over for coffee in the morning and they could discover the garden of delights Coleman had created for me. They would be suitably impressed.

It occurred to me that Tinkie had to know what

my lawman was up to—she must have given Coleman her key to Dahlia House, after all. Those two! She hadn't even hinted. I would pay her back in kind at the first opportunity.

"Jitty!" That she gave no response didn't bode well. She was either engaged in business of the Great Beyond, or she was plotting something tragic for me.

The emptiness of the house stopped me for a moment. This is what it would be like if Jitty ever disappeared. It nagged at me that, somehow, I would violate the rules of the Great Beyond and Jitty, too, would be taken from me. But so far, it seemed that Jitty was my companion, boss, protector, and albatross to carry. And right now she was absent from my life, which left me a little sad.

I gave myself a pep talk. "Grow up, Sarah Booth. You're insecure about Coleman; you're missing Jitty. Take it upstairs and get in bed. Tomorrow is another day."

I sniffed the beautiful roses and the stargazers, then took my own good advice, hustled up the stairs with the dog, cat, and our takeout, and jumped into bed. Nothing like a midnight snack and warm critters to snuggle with. Tomorrow I'd figure out what was what with Jitty and what I needed to do next with Coleman.

Five minutes after I stretched out, I was gone.

I awoke to the sound of huge waves crashing

against a high bluff. Snuggled deep under quilts, I looked toward the bedroom window where flimsy curtains danced in a chill wind. Who'd opened the damn windows? What was going on?

The sound of a wild and raging sea was even more confusing. I was smack-dab in the middle of the world's most fertile alluvial soil. There was no salt water near. No waves to crash or rocks to break over. The Delta was flat! But no matter—the sea ran wild outside my bedroom.

When the first, chilling strains of the theme music vibrated throughout the room, I knew instinctively that I was in big trouble. I recognized the soundtrack from the old daytime soap, *Dark Shadows*. Reruns of the show had terrorized me as a child and pushed Aunt Loulane into forbidding me to watch them. Of course, forbidding me anything was the surest way to make certain I'd do it. I'd watched the *Dark Shadows* tapes over at a girlfriend's house, unable to steer clear of the compelling chill of Barnabas Collins and his star-crossed love.

I knew the dark and twisted secrets of the cast like an old forgotten song. The wavering music compelled me, but it also meant that Barnabas Collins was somewhere in the near vicinity, waiting to drink my blood.

I sat up slowly in bed, aware that Sweetie Pie slumbered on the floor and Pluto snored lightly on the pillow beside mine. The animals hadn't heard the music and sea—or if they had, they weren't disturbed by it. Perhaps because they'd never watched the television show.

Slight movement in a corner of the room made the hair on my neck tingle. A slender blond woman, her hair piled in ringlets, wore an aqua peignoir that fluttered in the wind from the open window. She held something in her hand. I couldn't discern what it was and I was literally too scared to move.

"You'll never leave here," she said, stepping into a shaft of moonlight so that I could see the doll in her left hand. In her right was a long, sharp needle. "I'll control him by keeping the child sick." She slid the needle into the doll's shoulder. "And another here."

"Hey! Stop that." I made a move toward her but she whirled away.

She was a beautiful woman, but the glare she gave me could have curdled milk. "You will not interfere. The future is predetermined, and Barnabas is mine. I will curse him so that he never finds true love."

I recognized the witch, Angelique, and her willingness to do whatever was necessary to keep Barnabas with her. "Stop this, Angelique. No good will come of voodoo dolls and curses."

"He will always be mine!" She came toward me, needle ready to stab the doll again.

Adrenalin shot through me and I drew in

breath, ready for battle or at least to tackle her. Something about the curve of her jaw stopped me.

"What the hell are you doing?" I threw back the covers. My bare feet hit the floor and Sweetie Pie jumped to attention. She looked over at the blonde, yawned, and flopped back down.

"Jitty!" I knew then it was my haint doing another of her insidious witch impersonations. But why a witch from a soap opera? Angelique had been obsessed by a love she could never have, a love never returned. Her desperation only brought misery to herself and the people she cared about. What did Angelique have to do with my world of Zinnia, Mississippi?

Angelique's milky skin took on the soft mocha coloring of my haint.

I could not believe this. Jitty was determined to torment me to madness. "I know what happened," I said. "I died in my sleep last night, and I have been sentenced to hell, haven't I? I'm going to have to spend eternity with a ghost pretending to be a television star pretending to be a witch. It boggles the mind!"

"I could make a little doll to look just like you," Jitty said in her sultry Southern accent. "Keep harpin' on like an old magpie and see if I don't. It'll have pins poking out of every inch of it."

"Why are you doing this? I'm desperate for sleep. Don't you want me to be refreshed and ready for some action when Coleman has time for me?"

"If you worked that moneymaker properly, he'd be beatin' down the door right this minute."

I couldn't believe it. A roomful of flowers wasn't enough. Now Jitty was going to give me guidance in the art of lovemaking? This was beyond the pale, even for my bossy, pushy ghost.

"Get out of here. And get out of that cotton candy nightgown. The only thing it's good for is mosquito netting. If you think that's sexy, you are about seventy years behind the times."

"Where is that big hunk of man? Why are you up here sleepin' all by your lonesome?"

"We don't have to spend every freaking second with each other. I need some sleep. I can do that by myself. So can he."

"I'll bet Tinkie's working on her situation. You're never gonna catch that lawman unless you put some effort into it."

Not even two hands would give me enough fingers to count the ways Jitty's behavior was wrong. She had to get over the idea that a single female wasn't enough—at life, a job, a household, or whatever she wanted to do. I wouldn't become one of those codependent women who couldn't take out the trash without her boyfriend or husband to tell her how or to hold her hand while she did it.

"I don't aim to *catch* Coleman. I aim to enjoy

him," I said. "If it turns into a permanent thing, all the better. You can't hurry love, Jitty." I threw the line from one of her favorite songs at her.

"You better put a spell on that man while you can. Bond him to you with love and laughter and some bone-melting sex."

The aqua peignoir disappeared and there was Jitty, wearing my best black jeans and favorite sweatshirt, looking as modern as you please, and holding a microphone. She broke into a rendition of "I Put a Spell on You" that had me transfixed. I even forgot that I was mad at her. Of all my girlfriends, Cece could really belt the blues, but Jitty would give her a run for her money. She was that good.

"Stop it, Jitty. Just stop it. Leave me alone."

The guitars and harmonica ceased, and the room was silent. Jitty sat on the foot of my bed. "You don't need a spell or a curse to hold that man to you, Sarah Booth. But you do need to let him see your heart."

The torment was over. This was Jitty honestly trying to be helpful. And her concern deflated my anger. "I'm not so good at that." Even Budgie Burton knew my biggest weakness. I couldn't allow myself to be vulnerable. I simply couldn't. If someone else saw that, I might be forced to own it. And my carefully constructed fortress might crack and shatter.

Jitty was suddenly moon-glow pale and wearing that damn peignoir again, and she held a little doll that bore a remarkable resemblance to me. "I'm going to curse you with the gift of allowing your heart to open to love, Sarah Booth."

I wanted to hug her. She was trying to help. "Thank you, Jitty."

"Be careful. If you never love fully, you can never lose fully."

Far in the distance were the strange tones of the theme music to *Dark Shadows*, a story about a man who could never truly love. "Don't do this, Jitty." I was suddenly terrified. Loving another person was the most dangerous thing in the world. I thought of Tinkie—she was so willing to give her whole heart, her whole self to a child. Would I ever be that courageous?

"You will love. You owe it to yourself." Angelique stabbed a huge pin into the heart of the doll that resembled me.

I sat up in bed gasping for air, rising from the dream like a fish gulping the useless oxygen on a riverbank. Cold sweat slid from my hairline down my face. I looked around the room. No Jitty. No Angelique. No open window. No raging sea. It had all been a terrible nightmare. But I had been cautioned. Like all lovers before me, I knew that the only thing worth risking was my own heart. I just didn't know if I was brave enough to do it.

• • •

My reception at Musgrove Manor left something to be desired, from the snub Budgie and I got from the feral cats to the three sisters sitting on the front porch drinking coffee and ignoring us. Tinkie had been a no-show, but she finally called saying she was on a lead involving the Arlington Woods subdivision and the Fontanas. I was glad to keep her away from the witches and the influence they had over her.

The three sisters sipped coffee and eyed Budgie as if he might be the next human sacrifice. "I know you're here for something," Faith said in a slow drawl. "Care to tell us what it is?"

"We need to explore the third floor," I told them, after introducing Budgie.

"Go right ahead," Charity said, waving a hand absently. "The sheriff has been here and searched the place up and down."

"Thanks." I motioned Budgie inside before they changed their minds. He was so busy ogling them that I had to snatch him by the arm. "They will put a spell on you," I warned him.

"They're gorgeous. I thought witches were old and warty."

"Only in fiction," I said. "The Harringtons are modern witches."

"That brunette looks like a model. All of them do. Those miniskirts are hot." Budgie was loosening the collar of his shirt with a finger.

"You've been working at the prison too long," I told him as we trudged up the stairs to the third floor. He stopped at the claw marks in the beautiful wood. "What do you make of that?" I asked.

"I've never seen a Delta creature with that wide of a paw. We still have a few little black bears, but that must be eight inches across."

"So what is it?" If I could identify the mark at the manor, I'd also know what had been hanging out at Dahlia House.

"I don't know." He snapped a photo with his phone. "But I'll bet I can find out."

Some detective I was. I hadn't even thought of snapping a photo and contacting some of the university biology departments. We moved into the studio and I gave Budgie a few moments to gawk at the beautiful paintings. "My goodness, Trevor was talented," he said. "I never appreciated him for what he could do."

"Trevor never tried very hard to build a local audience. I think it goes without saying that most local talent is never appreciated at home. He's supposed to be very popular in Europe, especially Italy. And also in South America."

Budgie nodded. "I remember when the school groups used to come out to the manor. We had no clue he was up here painting naked women."

"No, we didn't." I maneuvered him into the hallway near Trevor's bedroom. "Let's look for those passages."

Together we tapped and sounded on the walls and floor, seeking anything that echoed hollowly or indicated it was a false front. We moved along companionably, not really talking, just working. When we came to the fireplace in the little parlor off Trevor's bedroom, Budgie hit pay dirt.

"Here it is," he said. He tapped the wall beside the mantle. "It's back there. I just don't know how to access it."

"It's always the mantle in the movies," I said, pulling down hard. Nothing happened.

"Or a book in the shelf." Budgie tried that approach with a collection of leather-bound volumes to the side of the mantle.

"Or a brick in the fireplace." I reached into the chimney and pressed and pushed. For my effort I got sooty hands. And nothing else.

"It has to be here." Budgie touched the beautiful scrolled column of the fireplace. "This is quite elegant."

And it was the lever that shifted the paneled wall toward us just enough to reveal a recessed room. We hadn't brought flashlights, but there were numerous candles stuck in wine bottles. I grabbed two and lit them with one of the many lighters scattered on all flat surfaces. With Budgie right behind me, I stepped into the darkness.

19

The thick dust in the narrow room made me want to sneeze, and the candles gave poor illumination. Still, I trudged forward across the rough-planked floor toward the darkness at the end of what looked to be an ever-narrowing corridor.

"There has to be stairs or a passage to another part of the house," Budgie whispered. "Otherwise this is just a hidey room and could easily become a death trap. If someone decided to burn the manor during an attack, any person hiding here would be roasted alive."

"Great image, Budgie," I said. "I don't remember you being so macabre in history class."

"That's because you hardly ever paid attention in class. You were always reading. I don't think there was a book in the library you didn't go through. You loved Beth Henley's plays most of all, though. You'd sit in the back row with a play tucked into your history book and this faraway look would come over you. I knew you were dreaming big then. I thought for sure you'd get the lead in *Crimes of the Heart* on Broadway."

Even if it was empty flattery, it was kind of

Budgie to say it. His words were a salve to the raw wound of my failed Broadway career. I had wanted that part—really wanted it. He was correct. I'd dreamed about Margaret Magrath. I'd crawled inside her skin and prepared for my Broadway debut. I grieved when I wasn't cast. Older and wiser, I understood that a known actress with a big name was a smarter, better choice than an unknown. But at the time, the rejection had been brutal. The role of Margaret Magrath had been written for me, or so I'd thought. Water under the bridge.

"Budgie, I did pay attention. At least some. I mean, I remembered about the hidden rooms in the old manor houses."

"And I'm shocked," he said without meaning to be sarcastic. "Hush a minute. Listen. I hear a cat."

I kept my lip zipped and focused on the silence. Far away, I heard the cry of what sounded like an adult kitty. Pluto and Sweetie Pie had come with me, but I'd left them in the car. Which meant they could be anywhere. Pluto was like a rat. He could crawl through the smallest openings, balance on the thinnest ledges, and hide in shadows undetected. He and Sweetie Pie were capable of conning the Harrington sisters into opening the car door and letting them out. If Pluto was in this secret passage, I had to get him before I left. That might not be an easy chore.

"Me-ow!" The call came to me muffled by the thick walls and layers of dust.

"Pluto!" I had no doubt now it was my kitty. How he'd gotten inside the passage I had no idea. "Pluto! Where are you?"

"Are you sure it's your cat?" Budgie asked. "There are dozens hanging around here."

"It's Pluto." I recognized his distinctive voice. "He's down this way."

There was barely room to edge down the passage, and I worried that if there was no outlet and Budgie got stuck, since he was following me, I'd be trapped in the walls forever. The sisters wouldn't find us until we started to stink. Damn. I was as macabre as Budgie.

"Pluto, you'd better come here right now," I called softly as I crab-walked down the passage. This had sounded like it might be fun to explore the old manor and maybe find leads to evidence of who—or what—might be lurking around Musgrove Manor scaring people to death. I thought of Trevor's and Esmeralda's faces and realized that if I did run into something in the passage, I would likely die of terror, too.

"Keep moving," Budgie huffed. "I'm getting claustrophobic. It's like the passage is getting narrower and narrower."

Sadly, he wasn't hallucinating. I'd noticed the walls closing in, too. "There's a bigger space ahead." The darkness sucked at the light of my candle and gave nothing back. It was either a room or a black hole to another universe.

"Sarah Booth, don't stop." Budgie nudged me. I'd become paralyzed by my own stupid imagination. The tightness of the passage had to be even more uncomfortable for Budgie because he was taller and stouter.

I inched forward, holding the candle in front of my sideways progress. People really were smaller back in the day. I'd laughed at the little short beds in tours of antebellum homes. Now I understood that stature was no laughing matter. Tinkie would have been much better at this assignment because she was a petite keg of dynamite. Budgie wasn't fat, but he was struggling.

"Just a little more." My candlelight was absorbed by the total darkness. No wall blocked it, so I could only assume we were nearing an opening. I exhaled, making my rib cage as small as possible, and pushed on. Something scuttled across the floor not ten feet from me.

"What was that?" Budgie asked.

My heart pounded so loudly, I didn't know if I could speak over it. "I don't know," I whispered. And the truth was, I didn't really want to know. Whatever was creeping around in the dark—I didn't want to lay eyes on it. "Maybe it was Pluto." I clung to that hope. Maybe it was just my very own black cat. In my dark imagination, though, I saw the claw marks that had marred my front door and window, and the third floor of the manor. Something deadly could be lurking, waiting.

We couldn't remain in that horribly cramped corridor. I pushed forward, holding the candle with my right hand. A draft of cold air blew against me, making the candle gutter. Almost as if someone had opened a door up ahead and allowed the outside air to intrude.

The right side of my body was suddenly freed of the compression of the passage and I wiggled fully into an open space. Budgie squeezed out behind me and inhaled.

"Man, I thought I would suffocate," he said. "Wherever we are, I'm not going back through that passage even if you have to get those witches to take out a wall."

I had similar sentiments, but I was focused on the sense that someone shared the space with us. I reached to find Budgie's hand and pressed it. We pushed together, back to back, illuminating the space around us with the candles as best we could.

The old bricks of the enclosure, which wasn't large by any means, told me the room had played a role in the history of the house. In the corner was an old trunk and a cheval mirror. Our images, cast back at us in the weak candlelight, showed two very stressed individuals.

As I advanced into the room, I saw a narrow

cot against another wall. This had been someone's room. Someone who was hiding here? Or someone who had been a prisoner? The latter thought was chilling. All the old stories of crazy relatives held captive in attics because they were a danger to themselves and others and the family was too ashamed to put them in an institution smacked into my brain with the force of a hammer. Had this been the "ward" of such a mentally unstable person? One capable of killing Trevor and Esmeralda? I had to get out of that room and research the old Musgrove line. Had there been crazy aunts or uncles that disappeared into the dust of time and the hidden room? And what of the Harringtons? Had they brought someone dangerous out of the Louisiana bayous and into Sunflower County?

So much had gone wrong since they'd come to town.

"Do you smell that?" Budgie asked.

A whiff of something burnt and a bit sulfuric drifted to me. My body reacted before my brain. Lizard impulses for survival aren't rational, but they are strong. I ducked, pulling Budgie down with me just as both of our candles extinguished in a blast of frigid air and a large knife slammed into the wall, reverberating, where my head had once been.

Some material brushed against my face.

"Aaaaaaaaaarrrrgh!" Budgie hurled himself

into the darkness. He landed on the floor with a woof as the air rushed out of his lungs.

Torn between helping Budgie or trying to pursue the knife thrower, I went to Budgie. I couldn't see a damn thing in the dark, and chasing after someone who might be armed was too dangerous. I found Budgie and helped him sit up until he caught his breath. He'd been flattened and had the air knocked from his lungs, but he wasn't hurt.

"Who was that?" Budgie wheezed.

"I don't know." I felt around on the floor until I found one of the candles. I'd put the lighter in my pocket and soon had illumination. I swallowed dryly. Budgie was sitting in the middle of a pentagram drawn with a series of symbols and signs. He looked around at the floor and jumped to his feet.

"What the hell is going on here?" he asked.

The cheval mirror gave us the reflection of two unhappy people staring at what could only be described as a Satanic symbol on the floor. I didn't have an answer, so I said nothing.

"Let's get out of here," Budgie said. "There has to be a way out. Someone was here and now they aren't. They didn't just vaporize."

I couldn't argue with his logic and I also wanted out of that stale, dark room. The sound of a cat calling made me put a hand on Budgie's arm to hold him still.

"Kitty? Kitty?" I called. Pluto disdained any form of address except the sound of a can opener, but I hoped if he was in the labyrinth of secret rooms and passages we'd traversed that he would come out and go home with me. Whether Pluto came or not, I had to get Budgie out of there.

"The door has to be here." Budgie took the candle and went across the space and began pressing on what looked to be a solid wall. His instincts were good and the wall gave, revealing another doorway designed for someone under five foot five and no more than a hundred pounds. Budgie went for it, but he hesitated, turning back to be sure I was following.

"Let me check the trunk," I said, taking the candle and using it to find the one we'd dropped. "Go on out. Just don't let that door shut."

Budgie didn't need urging. He pressed through and was gone. I went to the trunk and knelt in front of it. Opening it slowly, I once again caught the sulfuric scent of something that had burned. On top of a pile of clothes were what looked like gloves, except they had blades attached to the fingers. And they were big. Bigger than any normal hand I'd ever seen. When I picked one up and slid my hand inside, I understood. The glove had been padded to fit a smaller hand, but it looked like a huge paw.

It didn't take a three-digit IQ to figure out what

had made the marks on the door and window of Dahlia House. But who had been wearing the gloves?

"Sarah Booth! Someone is coming!" Budgie whispered through the opening. "Hurry."

I grabbed the gloves and closed the trunk lid. Coleman could explore later and the gloves would give him the grounds to execute a warrant. Just as I rose to my feet, I saw something in the mirror.

Black material billowed and then disappeared.

Malvik! Now I knew who'd been in the secret room. Who was *still* in the room. Malvik! With his black cape and soundless footsteps, he could have been a damn bat.

"Sarah Booth!" Budgie sounded like he was about to bust a gut. "Get out of there. Someone is coming."

His voice galvanized me into action and I hurried to the slit of light, even stepping into the pentagram drawn on the floor, though it gave me the creeps to do so. Once at the opening, I edged into what looked like a guest bedroom. I was disoriented until I realized this room had an exit door to the exterior staircase on the back of the house. This was perfect for Malvik to come and go at will.

Footsteps came toward us and I was torn between staying and rushing out the back exit. "Hold your ground," I said to Budgie. "We have permission to be here." Nonetheless, I tucked the bladed gloves behind me, just in case.

The footsteps stopped outside the hallway door of the bedroom. Slowly the crystal knob turned and the door creaked open. Tinkie stepped into the room, a frown on her face.

"I've been hunting everywhere for you," she said. "Why didn't you answer me?"

I truly hadn't heard her calling. "Sorry, how long have you been here?"

"Forty-two minutes, give or take a minute. I was getting worried. Did you find anything?"

Boy howdy, had we found things. I eased the bladed gloves from behind my back and held them out to her. "Hidden passages, secret rooms, gloves with blades on the fingers, and Malvik hiding in the dark."

20

Tinkie hadn't spent her morning unproductive. She, too, had plenty to share. Budgie continued to explore the rooms of the manor while Tinkie and I huddled on the exterior staircase to talk. It was best to keep our discoveries completely to ourselves. "What did you find out about the Fontanas' involvement in the Arlington Woods subdivision case?"

"I don't have the paperwork in my hand, but the subdivision deal originated with the Fontanas. I talked to one of Fontana Construction and Development's competitors, Paul Bousquet. He runs another construction company and said Bob Fontana had tried to lure him into a partnership. Paul took a look at the land and passed. He said a fool could see it was a hinky project. So Bob had to know from the get-go that the riverfront land shouldn't be developed, but they did it anyway because they had a patsy, Claudell Myers, to take the fall. The whole scheme was well thought out. Fontana Construction and Development made a killing off selling that land and those homes. The owners and the bank that financed the development took the consequences. And Claudell Myers, of course. She's still paying."

I believed Tinkie was correct, but without evidence, we were up the creek without a paddle. "We need evidence. And how does this involve the Harringtons?" That was where we had to focus.

"Working on it. It's tricky. Harold can't really help me. Magnolia Land Bank financed the deal, and they refused to talk to me. But I did find one little thing that was interesting."

Tinkie was such a tease. And a holdout. "What?"

"An elderly man in Florida, Florian Keel, was the seller. Sell price was three thousand an acre because the land was considered to be usable only for timber. The buyer was an off-shore business that I believe will trace back to the Harringtons."

"Okay."

"This Florian Keel is from Lake City, Florida. The sell was managed several years back by his stock broker-slash-financial advisor. A young woman."

I caught the scent of a great lead. "Wasn't Faith Harrington a broker? In Florida?" And Cheri Sistrunk had told me the sisters left Louisiana after some type of inheritance.

Tinkie nodded. "It's too early to point the finger, but this may be the link between the Harringtons and the Fontanas."

"Excellent detective work, Tinkie." My partner was worth her weight in gold.

"This is cheap talk and speculation, Sarah Booth. I don't have any proof yet." She pointed to the thicket of devil's walking sticks. "Pluto just went in there. We'd better get him before he's hurt."

"Check on Budgie, please. I'll grab my dang cat." From now on, it didn't matter how mad Pluto got, he was staying at Dahlia House. Whenever he got to the manor, he became wild and unresponsive, like he was possessed by the spirits of his panther ancestors. I'd simply had enough of it.

Tinkie went back inside and I hurried down the exterior stairs and into the backyard. I was eager to let Coleman know about the financial connections and the bladed gloves. The first order of business, though, was grabbing Pluto and getting him into the car. Sweetie Pie was sprawled out under a big, leafless maple tree. For a split second I thought she might be injured, but she sat up and looked at me as if I'd transmitted some psychic message. She yawned and flopped back to the ground.

"Pluto." I approached the thicket of thorny plants. In the daylight, I could see how wicked they were. Thorns ridged the entire trunk. There wasn't a place to grasp the tree without suffering a painful wound. Even the leaves had pointed, razor-like protrusions. I'd grown up in the Delta and had wandered the fields, woods, and brakes in all kinds of weather. I'd never seen those walking sticks before now. I had a sneaking suspicion they weren't native to Sunflower County at all.

The trunks of the slender trees grew close together, and I knelt and leaned forward to peer into the dense growth. A black ball of energy hurtled out of the foliage and struck me square in the chest, knocking me over into the grass. "Pluto! Dammit! I'm going to get you for that." My very own cat had rolled me over. I regained my knees and was brushing the dead grass and leaves off my sweater when a large black snake slithered toward me.

I rolled away from the snake, aware that February was not a month when snakes would normally be crawling. They were "cold-blooded" and slept the winter months away, waiting for the hot spring sun to warm the ground and bring them out. Something had chased the snake out of its nest. Even though it was harmless, I didn't want a personal relationship with the reptile. I stayed clear as it slowly moved through the dead grass and leaves. What else could be lurking in that thicket of thorny trees?

I heard something, but the growth was so dense that sunlight barely penetrated. I thought I saw movement, almost like a shadow. What could glide through those thorny trees so effortlessly? The chill that touched my body told me what my brain didn't want to register. Something supernatural was in the woods. Malvik might be the owner of the claw gloves, but that didn't mean there wasn't something else about the grounds of Musgrove Manor. Corey Fontana, Tinkie, and I had experienced the sense of being pursued by something swift and dangerous in the woods. No creature that I knew of could move so fast.

Even as I peered into the trees, a pair of glowing red eyes stared back at me.

I cried out and stumbled backward. Pluto came to my defense, arching his back and dancing sideways. He hissed at whatever was in the thicket. Sweetie Pie ambled over and growled deep in her throat, a warning to whatever she sensed was a danger. As I gained my feet and backed away, I realized that the clowder of feral cats had formed a semicircle around me. They were all sitting, gazes on the thicket and tails twitching. I'd never seen anything like it. It was almost as if Pluto commanded their allegiance and they had come to his call. I wasn't certain if it was to protect me or maybe to eat me—cats could be so unpredictable. Still, I was glad for their presence.

"Sarah Booth!" Tinkie called to me from the landing of the exterior staircase. "Are you okay?"

I nodded. "Fine."

"Grab Pluto and let's get out of here."

I bent down and captured my black feline. He wasn't going to get away from me now. Tinkie was correct, we had an investigation to run. It was time to move on.

Budgie and Tinkie met me at the front porch, along with Hope. Budgie wandered out into the yard, giving us a final chance to talk. Hope assessed me with a critical eye. "What did you find up there in Trevor's rooms?" she asked.

"These." I held out the gloves for her to look at.

"What in the world?" She reached for them but I withdrew them. "Coleman needs to test these for DNA. You don't want yours on them." My DNA wouldn't be an issue, since I wasn't a suspect in two murders and I would readily admit to handling the gloves.

"What kind of gardening gloves are those and why would the sheriff be interested?" Hope asked.

Faith came to the front door and slipped out to join us. "Looks like something Freddy Krueger would wear."

Tinkie frowned. She didn't get the reference.

"*A Nightmare on Elm Street.* Great horror movie," Faith explained. "He appeared in the dreams of teenagers and killed them. He wore gloves like that."

"Any idea who would have these up on the third floor?" I asked.

“Everything there belonged to Trevor. If they were on that floor, either he or someone he knew had them there.” Hope was matter-of-fact. “We’ve never seen those things.”

“Was Trevor involved with the Fontanas in any of their land-development projects?” Tinkie asked. “I mean, did he ever talk about it? I know the Fontanas wanted to buy this property.” We both watched Faith to see if she reacted. Her expression remained blandly interested.

“Trevor never mentioned any deals with the Fontanas to us,” Hope said.

“Faith, when you were in Florida did you work with any real estate?” I asked.

“A few clients liquidated property and invested.” She yawned. “That was a tedious job.”

“Has Malvik been around lately?” I followed up.

“As far as I know, he’s at the Prince Albert?” Charity answered as if she wasn’t sure. “Why?”

“He’s in the manor. I know it, and you know it. Now, where is he?”

Faith came to stand right at the edge of my personal space. “I don’t care for your tone. What are you accusing us of?”

“There’s something going on here at the manor. Two people were found dead on these grounds. This is all tied in with the Fontanas and their land-development schemes. I’m going to put it all together.” I hoped to provoke her into revealing what she knew about the Fontanas and any deals regarding the dairy.

"I hope you do," Charity said. "But you're going to be disappointed when you realize we don't have anything to do with the Fontanas. Now what Trevor might have been into, I can't say. You'd best realize that Trevor promised a lot of people a lot of things. He enjoyed messing folks around. He would laugh with us about some of the women who came to model for him and how easy they were to manipulate."

"What do you know about the hidden room and corridors on the third floor? The one with the pentagram drawn on the floor." I hadn't meant to blurt out my find, but I wanted to rattle the sisters out of their bored denials.

"What are you talking about?" Hope looked shocked.

Tinkie might like the Harringtons, but I was her partner. She came to stand beside me. "There's something going on here, ladies. You know I support you, but events have to be explained. Who's been hiding in those secret rooms?"

Hope shook her head, and Charity simply said, "I have no idea."

"We never explored the third floor. That was Trevor's domain."

"You were going to buy the property," I said, not bothering to hide my incredulous tone.

"Trevor would remain living on the third

floor," Hope reminded us. "We had every reason to believe he'd live for a long, long time and we didn't want to intrude on his living space. We had plenty of room without the third floor."

"You're saying you never went up there?" I asked.

"I did." Faith lifted her chin. "I modeled for him and I slept with him. We got drunk together. But I didn't poke around his possessions or his rooms."

"You're smart women. You aren't oblivious to what goes on around you. Who's been hiding out in that room? Is it Malvik?" I followed up.

"Malvik isn't staying here," Faith answered. "As to secret rooms, we haven't been on the third floor—I don't know how to make that more clear. Whatever is up there has to do with Trevor or his friends, not us."

"You didn't paint the pentagram on the floor? There are symbols in each corner of the star."

"Let's take a look." Hope was ready for action.

"Yes, let's." I was, too.

We were walking in the front door when a scream stopped us all in our tracks.

Budgie! He'd wandered off into the yard and disappeared.

"Budgie!" Tinkie raced across the porch and down the steps. "Budgie!"

We scattered across the yard and grounds

calling his name, but Budgie had disappeared as completely as if he'd been snatched from the surface of the planet by aliens. It was difficult to tell for certain, but Budgie's yell seemed to have come from the back of the house, and I hurried there. The only sign of the missing man was one of his fur-lined leather gloves. I'd noticed them because he'd taken them off in the house and tucked them into the pocket of his khakis. The glove was lying on the ground near the thicket of devil's walking sticks. When I examined the area more closely, I found droplets of blood on the grass and on some of the thorny tree trunks. But the thicket was too dense for Budgie to enter. It would take a magician to get a man Budgie's size through that thorny jungle without leaving bits and pieces of him all over the place. There was no sign of anyone trampling the plants. Nothing was disturbed.

"Where is he?" Tinkie asked. She brushed her hair out of her face. "Sarah Booth, I fear something terrible has happened to him, and it's our fault. We brought him here."

I dialed Coleman. We needed help, and we needed it right away. Coleman wasn't a deer or game hunter—he'd never taken pleasure in killing animals for sport. But he was an exceptional tracker. When we were in high school, he'd track turkeys, wild hogs, deer, and a host of other creatures for me to photograph. We'd both enjoyed being outdoors in nature, and tracking animals for my photographs had been great fun. Now I needed his skills.

"Coleman is on the way," I told Tinkie. Neither of us had attempted to touch the glove or the blood. "This is way out of hand."

Two murders and a disappearance, all on property that was meant to be a place of learning and safety for schoolchildren. I didn't know whether to blame the Harrington sisters for the turmoil or to feel sorry for them because they'd put all of their eggs in the basket of the Harrington School. If they lost the property—or the public's trust—they would lose all the grubstake and elbow grease they'd put into the manor and grounds. That was the one consideration that made me believe they weren't involved.

But the Fontanas surely were.

The sisters moved away from the thicket of thorny plants and began working toward the dairy, calling out for Budgie. Tinkie went with them, and I waited for Coleman. While everyone else was out of the way, I made sure Pluto and Sweetie were safely in my car and I grabbed my pistol and a flashlight from the trunk and hurried to the third floor. I wanted to photograph the pentagram on the floor of the secret room. And I wanted to finish searching the old trunk. Coleman would be there any minute, but I didn't want to wait. My gut told me there was something important in that room.

The secret doorway had almost closed of its own volition, but I forced it wider, found several hefty books, and used them to block it open. I didn't want to get sealed up in there like a character in some kind of Edgar Allan Poe story. Grasping the flashlight in one hand and the gun in the other, I was ready. I stepped into the airless room and stopped.

The pentagram was gone. It had been brushed away. I knelt and swept my fingers over the floor to discover a reddish dust. The pentagram had been drawn in red chalk and someone had eradicated it. Which meant someone could still be in the room and passages.

I eased toward the trunk. I hadn't had much chance to explore, and I felt badly that I wasn't out hunting for Budgie, but I believed I'd find answers to Budgie's whereabouts here, in this little room. I opened the trunk and knelt in front of it. I removed layers of tulle that shook out to be a fancy ball gown from the 1920s, ladies' white gloves, items that might be packed in a bride's trousseau back in the day when brides had such things. The items would provide a fascinating history, but nothing criminal. I was about to give up when I found the papers at the very bottom of the trunk. I pulled them out and put my gun down so I could hold the flashlight and read. It took me a moment to realize the papers were a land description, a deed for Musgrove Manor. A deed anchored with Trevor's distinctive signature. And with a current date. But who had he signed the property over to?

A shadow fell across me before I heard anything. When I turned to see who'd so silently entered the room, I didn't have time to register anything before I was struck in the head. I was unconscious before I hit the floor.

21

I awoke to find myself in perfect darkness. Whoever had knocked me out had shut the exit and left me without my gun or flashlight. It was possible those items were still in the room, but I had no way of finding them, except crawling around on the floor on my hands and knees, which is exactly what I did.

The pentagram had already been destroyed so there was little damage I could do. At last I found the flashlight in a corner and clicked it on. My gun had been kicked beside the old chest, and I put it in the back of my pants. My head was pounding, but otherwise I was okay. I made my way to the sliding panel and forced it open enough to get out just as I heard the cavalry coming up the stairs and calling my name. Sharp little kitty claws also dug at the secret panel.

"Meow!" Pluto was crying as loudly as he could. He gave another yowl.

"We're coming, Pluto!" Coleman's voice came to me as I pressed and pressed on the panel to no avail. I couldn't get it open. Panic rose inside my lungs, making it difficult to breathe. I had to get out. Immediately. I couldn't stay in the dark another second.

"Sarah Booth!" The panel cracked open and Coleman reached in and pulled me out. He took one look at me and wrapped his arms around me. "Are you okay?" His lips brushed my cheek and ear. "Are you hurt?"

I could have stayed in his arms for a long time, but Budgie was still missing. People were dead. Evil roamed Musgrove Manor. I eased back from him. Close contact made us both susceptible to longings that had no place in our lives at that particular moment. "Someone knocked me out."

"What is that red dust all over you?" he asked.

"Chalk, I think."

Tinkie entered the bedroom, then stepped back into the hallway, giving us a moment of privacy. "We haven't found Budgie," she called out. "He's completely disappeared."

"That can't be." What had I gotten my former teacher into? "He was in the front yard, and then he walked around back, and then he was gone. He couldn't be more than two hundred yards away."

Coleman's hand brushed against the muscles of my tense back. "I've called DeWayne to come out with some volunteers. You're right, Sarah Booth. Budgie can't be far from here. No vehicles were near the manor, so he has to be on foot."

"Maybe he took one of our broomsticks." Faith

had come into the room. "I'm sure somehow we'll be blamed for whatever has happened. It's always our fault."

"But you were with me and Sarah Booth," Tinkie said. She was loyal to her friends, and she considered the sisters her friends, even though we might have doubts about Faith's financial entanglements. "No one can accuse you because you have a solid alibi."

"Where's this pentagram you were so upset about?" Faith asked. "And the secret room?" She looked around as if she expected to see a sign that read secret room this way.

"Right in there, but the pentagram is gone. It was only in chalk and someone erased it." I couldn't tell if she was playing innocent or if she truly didn't know about the secret room.

"I'll bet someone named Sarah Booth erased the wicked pentagram," Faith said. "You have chalk dust all over you. What did you do, get down on your belly and do the gator crawl across the room?"

"I was struck in the head and knocked out. The pentagram had been erased before I hit the floor."

She did look surprised, but she covered it quickly. "Maybe it was a ghost, or Malvik, or some dark creature that we've conjured up."

"Or maybe it's someone you're hiding here." I stepped right into her personal space. I was tired of it and my head hurt. "What's going on in this house? Where is Budgie? He's a harmless soul and he better not be hurt."

Coleman put his arm around my waist and drew me closer to him. "Calm down, pit bull. We'll get the answers we need. No one is leaving the premises until we've investigated the hidden room and found Budgie."

"There were some documents in the trunk. One was a land deed for Musgrove Manor."

Faith inhaled sharply. "Land deed? Where?"

"In the old trunk. Along with some items from a wedding trousseau."

"I'll take a look." Faith sidled toward the secret room. "We've misplaced some paperwork regarding the dairy. Maybe Trevor stuck it in there for safekeeping."

"Not so fast," Coleman said, grasping her wrist. "No one goes in that room or touches anything. It's now evidence in an assault. What you can do is drive Sarah Booth to the hospital and let Doc Sawyer check her out."

"That old sawbones can't even determine the cause of death," Faith said. "You sure you want him checking over your honey?"

I wasn't going anywhere. "Get a chain saw," I said, staring right into Faith's green eyes. "I'm going to cut down that thicket of thorn trees. There's something in there. Pluto and the other cats have been trying to get us to look. Now we're going to see what's what."

"You can't damage our property," Faith said. "I don't care about that patch of walking sticks, but you have to ask permission."

"May I cut them down?" I asked. If she said no, Coleman would simply get a warrant.

"Sure." She shrugged her shoulders. "I need to harvest some leaves and bits of trunk but I can do that after you cut them."

I was surprised by her cooperation, but I wasn't going to look a gift horse in the mouth. "Coleman, do you have a chain saw? We'll find Budgie in that thicket. I don't know how he got in there, but I'm telling you, that's where he is. And we need to find him now. He could be injured."

"Show me the thicket. I'll get some help to cut it down."

"We should explore that trunk." Faith tried to dodge around Coleman, but he grabbed her.

"Finding Budgie is our first priority. That room isn't going anywhere." He shooed everyone into the hall but grabbed my wrist and held me back. Tinkie discreetly closed the door. He lifted my face so he could stare into my eyes. "Are you really okay?"

"I am."

His calloused finger brushed across my lips and cheek. "Are you sure?"

"Very." I put a hand on his face. "I'm fine. It's Budgie I'm worried about. He came here to help me and Tinkie." I had to believe Budgie wouldn't be found dead with a look of horror on his face.

"Something is going on here. I'm not sure what, and I don't know the underlying motives, but we'll find out. That's a promise."

Motive was the key. I'd assumed Trevor was murdered for the manor lands. And Esmeralda? That threw a monkey wrench into the whole real estate plot. She had no legal claim to Musgrove Manor and no ties to any development schemes. Her death benefited no one that I could see. And now Budgie. Who would take a harmless former substitute teacher and current prison employee? And why? Budgie could have stumbled around the manor grounds for the next two years and discovered nothing of substance. Now, a full-scaled search would ensue, with trained law officers looking. This was not a smart move if someone wanted to keep something hidden.

And that was the ultimate question. What was hidden at Musgrove Manor? Satan worship? Witches conjuring dark spells? Real estate deals gone bad? Paintings stolen? What was worth the lives of two people? It was my job to answer that question.

"You ready to go down?" Coleman asked, his large hand spanning my back and applying reassuring pressure.

"Let's get this dog and pony show on the road. I want that thicket removed."

• • •

An hour later I was half deaf from the roar of six chain saws. Devil's walking sticks littered the ground. Coleman had removed the thicket as an audience of feral cats sat on the roof of the back porch watching. Pluto and Sweetie Pie were right at my side, as was Tinkie. The Harrington sisters drank iced tea on the back porch. They offered Coleman and the volunteers refreshments, and Charity went inside to make the drinks.

"Is there any sign of Budgie? A track or anything?" I asked Coleman, who brushed sawdust from his jacket and jeans.

"Nothing."

"What will you do?" I asked.

"Organize the search crews to move farther afield. I've called the highway patrol to put up roadblocks. Somehow the person who took Budgie must have gotten him into a vehicle and driven him off the property. What made you think we'd find a clue in that thicket?"

"It was the only place he could have gone so quickly." I remembered the red, glaring eyes. Something was in there, but whatever it was hadn't left a clue. "What good is Budgie to them?" I asked.

"Nothing about the series of events that have happened at the dairy makes any sense. All I know is that whatever has been lurking in that thicket is gone."

"I'm surprised the sisters let you cut it down."

"You and me both. Maybe they were unnerved by whatever was in there."

Coleman's offhand remark struck a nerve. As the men were clearing the debris and searching the area for anything that could lead them to Budgie, I went on the porch. Charity was in the kitchen. Faith and Tinkie went to help her with a tray of drinks for the workers. Hope was the only sister left. Budgie's absence hung over us all, leading everyone to speak softly.

"You didn't care about that thicket?" I asked Hope.

She never looked at me but watched the men working. "I never liked it. There was always something about it that made me ill at ease."

"What?"

She shook her head. "It's hard to put my finger on. I always felt something was there. We did use the leaves and trunks in our potions, but I can order those tinctures and powders online. I'm glad to have that patch gone. It didn't belong here."

I took a seat beside Hope. I'd never felt as if I'd connected with any of the sisters until this moment. Hope seemed . . . normal. Not witchy or pretending to be witchy. Just like a normal person.

"What do you think happened to Trevor and Esmeralda?"

"No one believes that we were fond of Trevor, but we were. He was a character. Faith was sleeping with him, like all of his models. But it was that artist-model sex thing that doesn't translate into jealousy. It was an ego trip for Faith and a conquest for Trevor. I guess that's the thing I liked best. He was always after the conquest and never pretended otherwise. But if a relationship didn't go his way, no problem. There were plenty of other fish in the sea."

"That might upset some women."

"Not with Trevor. He loved women's bodies. All shapes and sizes. It's hard to find a man who truly loves the feminine form in all its variations. His next project was going to be pregnant women. He had some ideas for natural backdrops that spoke of the lushness of new life. He was truly inspired by the fairer gender."

"Did you ever see the painting of Esmeralda? The one she sued to try to buy?"

"Faith saw it, but I didn't."

"Did she say where she saw it?"

"Up in his studio, I presume. I didn't really ask. She said it was beautiful." Hope hesitated. "But there was something that really got under Esmeralda's skin."

"She was painted as a religious icon. A saint, as I recall."

"That's right, though Esmeralda Grimes was

about as far from a saint as a football is from a pig."

"And what was Trevor's relationship with Kitten Fontana?"

Hope laughed. "He painted her. He said she had a petite, stocky body type that intrigued him. He said she was a real gymnast in the sack. And she amused him. Sometimes I'd hear them drinking and arguing. She liked to break things."

I wondered why Trevor would put up with such bratty behavior. "What did they argue about?"

"Gallery showings, a shade of green, the outbuildings here on the property, you name—"

"What about the outbuildings?"

"Kitten was trying to talk Trevor into razing the old hay barn, the tannery, and the silos. She wanted those buildings destroyed. She said the ground was permeated with death."

"Cow death?" Kitten's concerns over dead cows had to do with . . . money. It was always about money with Kitten. Getting rid of the outbuildings would hamstring the witches and their school plans and make it easier to develop the property.

Hope shrugged. "That's how I took it."

"I doubt Kitten ever walked away from a steak. That's an odd sentiment for a carnivore if not an outright cannibal." I did believe Kitten would eat her young if she saw a benefit to it.

"Now that you point it out, you're right." Hope

frowned. “Kitten was in and out of here all the time. And that spawn of evil of hers, the boy, still hides out and watches us with binoculars.”

“Because he’s a Peeping Tom?” The witches were sexy and perhaps the boy wasn’t just a spoiled brat but had some psychological issues. With Kitten for a mother, that was not improbable.

“You’d have to ask him what he’s watching for, but I honestly don’t think it’s us. He seems to be waiting for something.”

“Do you think Corey Fontana could be involved in Trevor’s and Esmeralda’s murders?”

Hope considered. “Why? How would their deaths benefit Corey? I mean he’s a brat, but he is just a kid.”

A good question. “How do their deaths benefit anyone?”

Tinkie came out the back door, her brow furrowed, her phone to her ear. “Are you certain?” she asked.

The tone of her voice had me leaning forward in my chair, but I didn’t interrupt.

“Thanks for calling, Harold.” She hung up. “Bob Fontana is filing papers claiming that Trevor had agreed to sell the dairy to him. He’s in the courthouse right now with signed documents showing an agreed-upon price and Trevor’s signature for the sale of the property.”

“That’s not possible.” Hope rose swiftly to her

feet. "Trevor would never do that. He'd agreed to partner with us, and then if anything came up, to sell to us."

Tinkie tapped her cell phone against her palm. "Harold got a call at the bank from the chancery clerk, so we know Bob Fontana is truly filing the papers. Bob is claiming that he has a signed sell agreement executed the day Trevor died. He's initiating legal proceedings to have you removed."

"This can't be true." Hope's color drained. "Trevor liked to tease Bob with the property—to offer it and pretend he'd consider selling just to get Bob worked up—but he never would sell it to him. He'd committed to us. We had an agreement."

"What kind of agreement?" Tinkie asked. She nodded enthusiastically. "Show us the document. If you have a signed seller's agreement, then that will be honored."

"A gentleman's agreement," Hope said. "Trevor said since he was involved with the school, we didn't need to hire a lawyer." Even she realized how unsubstantial her claim would be in court.

"You said you had it in writing." Tinkie wasn't chastising her, she was stunned. "That was one of the first things I asked you and you said you had it in writing."

Hope just looked miserable.

"How much have you paid Trevor?" I asked.

"We haven't exactly made a payment. We put in sweat equity. Trevor had fifty percent of the school," Hope said. "We didn't pay cash. We offered him a percentage of the business. He was good with that."

In a gentleman's agreement, a handshake was considered legally binding. Such things no longer existed in today's business world. The sisters had zero legal papers, nada notarized documents. In other words, the sisters had no legal leg to stand on in their claim that Trevor had agreed to sell them the property. Despite the fact they'd assured me and Tinkie that they had a formal buyer's agreement. I didn't believe that Bob Fontana's documents were real. He'd forged them; I had no doubt of that. But now the burden of proof was on the sisters to show that Trevor had intended the property to be sold to them. And Fontana Construction and Development had all of the firepower.

"Sarah Booth! Bring flashlights! Hurry!" Coleman called from the backyard.

Hope and I sprang into action. She got flashlights from the house and I got my big Q-beam from the steps where I'd left it, along with my pistol. If we were going exploring in the dark, I was going to be armed. Coleman must have agreed because he only waved me behind him, and Tinkie came springing down the back steps and fell in behind me.

We scrambled over the felled thicket until we reached one of the volunteers who was working to clear a space. "There's a trapdoor here," the volunteer said. "I heard someone yelling. Either it's a grave and the person isn't dead, or there's an underground chamber and your missing person is in it."

"Budgie!" The relief was remarkably sweet. It had to be him, and if he was making noise, at least he was alive.

"I hope he isn't injured," Tinkie said.

In no time Coleman and his workers had the heavy wooden door free of debris. The wood was weathered and not in the best shape, but the men were able to lift the door. A burst of stale, unpleasant air wafted up. A man's voice called out for help.

"We're coming, Budgie," I yelled into the opening. "We need a ladder." My heavy-duty flashlight revealed an opening that was at least ten feet into the ground. There were no stairs or any way to get out. Or get in. Budgie had not come into the space through the door Coleman had found. There had to be another entrance.

"Wait a minute," Coleman said, taking the flashlight from my hand. "There's a ladder in there. It's pushed back against the wall. And it looks like a series of tunnels."

Once Budgie was safe and we knew he was uninjured, he'd be thrilled senseless by the discovery of tunnels and hidey-holes. "I'll get a rope."

"Don't bother." Coleman jumped into the hole as if it were only a two-foot drop. He landed and stood up. He swung the flashlight around and let out a sigh. "There he is." And he and the light disappeared as he took off down the tunnel. In a moment, I heard conversation between Coleman and Budgie.

"He's okay," Coleman called back. "Someone tied him up and left him here."

In a few minutes, I heard Budgie clearly. "Thank goodness you came to find me. I don't think my attacker is coming back. I could have died in here in the dark, and I would never have gotten to explore. There are tunnels that go everywhere. It's a network. I believe Musgrove Manor might have been a stop on the Underground Railroad to help slaves escape to the North. Or Confederate soldiers might have hidden in these tunnels, sneaking out to attack the Union forces when they came through."

"We're going to follow the tunnel," Coleman called back to me.

Tinkie and I paced the backyard as we waited for Coleman and Budgie to reappear. The problem was, we had no idea where the other end of the tunnel might be. Twenty minutes later, the two men came out of the dairy barn.

Budgie was dirty and his wrists were bruised

and bleeding where he'd been tied, but otherwise he looked okay. "What an adventure," he said. "I just went poking around the old dairy and someone smacked me on the head. I wasn't all the way out, but I couldn't fight back. They dragged me into the dairy and through a trapdoor. It was . . . exciting!"

Thank goodness Budgie had a great sense of adventure. "You're not hurt?"

"On the contrary. I'm fine," Budgie insisted. "I can't wait to write about this incredible find. I'm going to send it to the *Journal of American History*. This is quite an extraordinary thing! Those tunnels were dug by hand and reinforced with baked clay bricks in places. This is a goldmine of historical information.

"There was a lot of resistance to secession, even in Mississippi. Jones County refused to secede or claim either side. If the Musgroves who first built the manor were antisecessionists, they might have felt the need for an escape route should their Union sentiments be discovered."

"Or the tunnels could have been built later," Tinkie said. "I'd heard rumors that Trevor's grandfather was a gambler and a bootlegger. This could be where he stored his whiskey. The tunnels are wide enough for barrels to be rolled down them."

That, too, was a good point.

"Did you see who knocked you out?" I asked

Budgie. I hadn't even caught a glimpse of the person who'd whacked me.

"He came at me from behind. I'm assuming it was a he. It could have been female. Or a team of a man and a woman."

A team! Budgie was brilliant! That would explain how one person could move around so quickly. There were two of them working in concert!

The same bell *ding, ding, ding*ed in Tinkie's head. She looked at me, lifting one eyebrow. "We should have thought of two people working in concert."

"Kitten and Bob?" They wanted to buy the manor and land. We knew they were dishonest and capable of leaving an innocent woman in jail to further their own goals. Murder wasn't such a big step from that.

"At least this case is coming together," Tinkie said. "I haven't been able to fit the pieces into place no matter how I tried."

She was right about that. Land deals, witches, bad publicity, murder. It was all beginning to make a certain kind of crazy sense.

22

My goal was to search the chest in the hidden room, but Coleman was having none of that. DeWayne had brought an evidence collection kit, and Coleman put Budgie in the back of my car, along with Sweetie Pie and Pluto, and sent us off with Tinkie riding shotgun. Her charge—which she fulfilled—was to make sure Budgie and I both saw Doc Sawyer.

"Good thing that noggin of yours is as hard as a brick wall," Doc said when he proclaimed me perfectly fine. "Budgie, too. You're both lucky. Again. I'm just going to keep Budgie here in the ER for observation. Just to be on the safe side." He patted my shoulder. "I hope Coleman finds whoever is running around hitting people on the head."

"Me, too. And scaring people to death." I arched an eyebrow at Doc. "Were Esmeralda and Trevor really frightened to death?"

Doc's lips tightened. He hated it when he couldn't figure something out. He had a sharp mind and years of experience with healing and the reverse—murder. There were times his medical expertise was sought by other jurisdictions. He'd become something of a forensic celebrity. Few things flummoxed him for long, but I could see he had no answers about Trevor or Esmeralda.

Doc had been captivated by the idea of secret rooms, tunnels—everything that appeals to the young boy hiding in all grown men. As Tinkie was giving a rundown on how we'd found the trapdoor and the tunnels, my cell phone rang.

"What's the verdict on your head?" Coleman asked. He kept his tone light, but the very fact he called told me he'd been worried.

"Budgie and I both are fine. No long-term effects, other than a headache." Mine was dull and throbbing. It wouldn't kill me but some aspirin, water, and a warm bed would certainly be appreciated.

"I'll stop by Dahlia House as soon as I can. You might consider sending Tinkie home."

The promise lingered between us, sweet and tempting. "I'm sure she has business with Oscar. The two of them have been going at it like monkeys on a hot-wired fence."

"Sarah Booth, I swear you have a knack for creating the most unromantic visuals."

I had to laugh. "I'm not easy," I said with pride. "If you want me, I'll have to be wooed and won."

"Oh, I am always up for a challenge," Coleman said, his baritone deep and sexy. A flush rose up my cheeks, and I realized Tinkie and Doc were watching me with amusement.

"Stop the phone sex," Tinkie said knowingly. "We have work to do. I swear you two are like randy teenagers. Doc, did I ever tell you about the time I blew in the front door of Dahlia House and Coleman and Sarah Booth were right on the stairs bu—"

"Enough!" Doc didn't need that image of me and Coleman naked on the stairs in his brain. "Tinkie, I promise you. There will be payback. And it will be like Jupiter's bolts of lightning."

Doc and Tinkie looked at each other. "Sarah Booth, you can sure hurl a threat," Doc said. "Tinkie, we'll talk later. Now you two scoot. I have work to do."

I was still formulating payback when we pulled up at Dahlia House. The critters were delighted to escape the car and head into the warm kitchen. I was pretty happy, too. Spring wasn't far away, but looking out at the landscape, I didn't see a trace of it yet. That was the way of spring in the Mississippi Delta. One morning, I'd look out the window and the first trace of green would be poking through the soil. Within two weeks, the landscape would completely shift from brown and dead to green and vibrantly alive. It was the miracle of new life.

"Let's get to work on Florian Keel," Tinkie

said. "While Doc was tapping on your skull, I did a little research. I have his phone number. I say we call."

"He sold the land Arlington Woods was built on. Maybe he knew the land wasn't good to develop."

"He's not legally accountable," Tinkie pointed out. "But if he didn't tell the developer, there's possible grounds for liability."

"He said, she said." Unless it was written in the contract, and no seller would be foolish enough to put in writing that a parcel of land was virtually unusable.

"Call him," Tinkie said. "I'll make some tea. I need a tonic to boost me."

Tonic my butt. Tinkie's nerves were as frazzled as my own. "Make me a Bloody Mary instead, please," I called to her as I dialed Florian Keel's number. On the fourth ring, he picked up.

"Who is this?" he asked.

I told him the truth.

"Private investigators." He laughed and his voice sounded rusty. "I wondered how long it would be before someone came sniffing around."

Tinkie returned with our beverages, and I sat up straight and put the phone on speaker so she could listen. "Why did you think someone would investigate?"

"I told the truth when I sold the land. I'm too old to manage timber cutting all over the South, and I had a lot of holdings. That river land is fertile, good soil. But you can't plant anything but timber because of the flooding. Trees can take rising water. I told Simon Caldwell that. He knew going into the deal that a development on that property would be a fiasco. And he did it anyway."

"Simon Caldwell?" This was a new name. It seems my case was like a cancer. It grew in a thousand directions all at once.

"That's who handled the paperwork on the sale for the investment company."

"What did he look like?"

"Slender man. Elegant. Very well turned out and old-school manners. Like he'd watched a lot of proper British movies."

"Would you recognize him?"

"I think I would."

"Is there anything distinctive you can remember?"

"Like I said, he seemed to come from a different time. Old-worldly, mannered. A few speech quirks."

"Like?"

"He made a reference to a cunning man. I had to look it up. It's a healer or a person who uses magic to heal. He said an ancestor had been pressed to death in old Salem for being a conjurer. It was just a curious turn the conversation took."

"And you handled the sale of the land yourself?" I pushed a little.

"My broker. Miss Marsh. She handled the sale and reinvested the proceeds."

"Thanks, Mr. Keel."

I hung up and faced Tinkie. "I know who Simon Caldwell is."

"Who?"

"It's the man who brought us a check from the Pickingill Society. It's Marlow Spurlock, if that's his real name."

"Why in the world would someone involved in rotten real estate deals pretend to be part of a coven or support witches?"

"It all has to do with the Musgrove Dairy property." I couldn't connect the dots, but I knew they did, somehow, connect. "Esmeralda, Trevor, Kitten and Bob, Malvik, Spurlock. They're all somehow involved with the Harrington sisters and that property." And it was looking like the Harrington sisters, whatever their involvement, might end up being pushed off the property they'd worked to improve.

"At last we have a lead we can follow." Tinkie finished her tea. "And we need to get busy. Where shall we start?"

"I know just who to ask about Marlow Spurlock."

"Malvik." Tinkie's blue eyes held determination.

"Exactly. He's in this up to his ears. Maybe the sisters are innocent, but Malvik is not."

"How are we going to force him to talk?" Tinkie wasn't fool enough to believe Malvik would just spill his guts.

"We're going to trick him." A dark plan had begun to form in my brain. Malvik and Spurlock had shown up on the same day; two men dressed in black and connected to witches and a witch society. They had to be working together. And I had begun to see what their end might be. Land development. A really big deal that could make all involved über wealthy.

Before we left Delaney Detective Agency, I looked up the Pickingill Society. A brief phone conversation led me to the truth. Spurlock had gone rogue. The organization had not voted to send a check in defense of the Harrington sisters. Spurlock, a member of the board, had taken it upon himself to write the check and defend the sister witches.

"We've had our doubts about Marlow," the president of the society said. "His frequent trips to Florida in the past few years. Rumors of land-development schemes that had collapsed. We hear things, though our focus is always of a spiritual nature, not with the physical world. Sadly, Spurlock has betrayed us."

"We'll refund your money." It killed me to say that.

"No need. The Harringtons are genetic witches. They have a heritage and deserve our support. Just tell Spurlock that he will face the consequences of his actions upon his return."

"Why is Spurlock so invested in the Harringtons?" This was a key question.

"He comes from a long line of witches and cunning men. He views the Harringtons as his peers, those whose destinies were chosen for them. They must live with their gifts and abilities, just as Spurlock does. They've captured his sympathy. But there is something else that would prompt him to steal from us. Greed. So now it's up to you. Please, help those young women. Find the truth. And if you discover Spurlock's deeds, our money will be well spent."

"That we will do," I assured him. Dahlia House would get some necessary repairs! I hung up looking like the Cheshire cat.

Now it was time to corner Malvik. Tinkie and I agreed on that point. "We're going to need the sisters to help us."

"Really?" Tinkie was all-in. "Help us do what?"

"We're going to cast a spell on you. And under the influence of magic, you're going to reveal the truth about who killed Esmeralda and Trevor. Look, the Fontanas and Spurlock have some-one on the inside. It has to be Malvik, running around the manor in those secret rooms. He's the one who did in Trevor and Esmeralda. Possibly because Trevor insisted on selling the property to the witches. God knows what Esmeralda unearthed snooping around. She always went for the sensational story, but she was pretty good at digging things up. I believe Esmeralda and Trevor are dead as damage control."

"We're going to make Malvik believe in revenge magic," Tinkie said.

"Yes we are. We're going to catch him at his own game."

23

Of the three sisters, Tinkie felt Hope would be more inclined to help us. The fewer people who knew about our plan, the more successful I felt it would be. We needed one of the sisters to work with us, but the other two would remain in the dark. "Loose lips sink ships" was another of Aunt Loulane's favorite sayings. She had never been one for gossip, and she disapproved of tongue-wagging about other people's business.

We were about to leave for the manor when Coleman pulled up at Dahlia House. Watching him stride up the steps toward me, I felt my heart stutter. After my engagement to Graf Milieu had fallen apart, I'd never anticipated such intensity again. I'd convinced myself that my heart couldn't be tricked into feeling so . . . deeply. And yet watching Coleman walk toward me sent me into a spiral of anticipation and anxiety. The human heart was a strange and wonderful organ.

I saw no reason to hide my true feelings from Tinkie. She might tease me later, but in her own way, she was my biggest supporter in the quest for true love. She was a believer, a person who wanted everyone in her life to share in the joy of a committed relationship. She and Oscar had worked through some hard times and faced a continuing challenge with her whole baby obsession. They'd stuck it out together and grown stronger. I'd thought after Graf that such a thing wasn't possible for me, but the handsome lawman staring at me gave me new hope.

Coleman swept me into his arms and kissed me with a fierce passion that left Tinkie applauding. "I'm leaving right now," Tinkie said. "Don't worry, Sarah Booth, I'll take care of getting Hope in line. You take care of . . . business."

Coleman finally released me and I stepped back, light-headed and buzzing. Coleman's grin told me he knew exactly how he affected me. He turned to my partner. "Wait up, Tinkie. I have news."

"Did you find the legal documents in the old trunk?" I asked.

Shifting his weight from foot to foot, Coleman frowned. "There wasn't anything in the chest but female clothing. And there wasn't any trace evidence inside the claw gloves. Whoever wore them took forensic precautions not to leave any evidence behind. As to the pentagram you drew out, the sisters said the icons represent the five elements of the wise. They said the pentagram wasn't satanic and the elements are fire, water, earth, wind, and spirit at the top. It's common in pagan religion but doesn't have a negative meaning."

"Who drew it and who erased it?"

"The sisters denied even knowing about that little room."

"And those documents are gone?" I'd seen them. "How could they simply disappear?"

"The same way the pentagram was wiped away and you were hit in the head. Trevor's rooms were ransacked, obviously for those papers. Whoever had them stashed them in the trunk until he, or she, could get out of the house with them without being seen. That's why they knocked you out. With the Harringtons' permission, we'll search all of the passageways and tunnels. I followed one tunnel to the apple orchard. I'm pretty sure that was how the murderer traveled the night Trevor was killed."

"Any idea how old those tunnels are?" I asked.

"Budgie seemed to think they date back to the 1840s when the manor was originally built. Once Doc cuts him loose, he's going to look up some priory building in the Scottish borderlands. He says Musgrove Manor was patterned on that house, and perhaps the tunnel system will also reflect the same."

"Thank goodness Budgie wasn't hurt." I still carried guilt at involving him.

"He's thrilled to be part of this, Sarah Booth. In fact, he's going to apply for the deputy opening

I have. And I'm going to give him serious consideration."

"He works in the administrative offices at the prison. He doesn't have any law enforcement background," I said.

"He doesn't need enforcement experience. He can learn that easily enough. He's educated and a lot more in touch with computers. He knows how to research in ways that DeWayne and I don't. And he knows history. You know the old saying that history repeats itself. If that's the case, Budgie could be very useful."

"True." Budgie would love wearing a uniform. His sweater vest and long-sleeve shirts were something of a uniform already. "He's plenty smart."

Tinkie checked her watch, a gentle nudge that time was slipping past. "Tell Coleman about Spurlock and Malvik and our plan."

And so I did, as quickly as I could. I needed his help, too, if I was going to set up a "sting."

Twenty minutes later, Tinkie left for Musgrove Manor. Coleman headed to Bob Fontana's office, and I hurried upstairs to book an appointment at the Mane Attraction, a salon and day spa. Kitten had a standing appointment each week at the salon. That would be the easiest place to catch her off guard. And, as Tinkie pointed out, I really could use a professional haircut.

I'd hoped to find something sparkly and stretchy to wear—in an attempt to fit into Kitten's world—but no luck. My closet was bare of glitz. I found a blue striped sweater and pulled it over my head.

Right behind me I heard Pluto hiss and yowl like his tail had been caught under a rocking chair. I whirled around and stopped. Standing in the doorway was a woman with the most amazing buck teeth I'd ever seen. And her red hair had been fashioned into what looked like ram horns on each side of her head.

She threw her arms wide and advanced, her green floor-length gown billowing as she danced. "I put a spell on you," she sang with gusto. "And there's hell to pay!" This was Bette Midler at her wildest, wackiest best.

I backed up until I hit a wall. I recognized the actress—and the haint who'd taken on her image. Jitty was playing a role, and at last it came to me. Winnie Sanderson from *Hocus Pocus*. And *my* black cat danced and cavorted with the singing creature.

"Pluto!" I finally snapped out of it and lunged for my cat. My hands grasped only empty air. Of course, it was Jitty having the time of her life. Not only had she conjured a movie witch, she'd put a spell on my cat. "Dammit, Jitty." I stood up. "You have to stop this. I'm not in the mood for your shenanigans."

"I'll make you believe in magic," Jitty/Winifred said with a wicked glint in her eyes. "Oh, I'll make a believer out of you. Because it's vital that you believe."

"I don't want to believe. I want things to go back to normal. I want the witches not to be witches, and I want my haint to be the person who protects me, not torments me. This magic foolishness is just a crock."

"Are you still wearing that charm Tinkie gave you?" Winnie edged closer to me.

My hand went instinctively to the little silk bag that hung between my breasts. I hadn't taken it off. Even when I thought about removing it, I'd left it beneath my shirt. It was my good luck charm that had finally delivered Coleman into my bed.

"Give it to me," Winnie said in that grating tone she'd used throughout the movie *Hocus Pocus*.

"I will not."

"Oh, yes you will." She came toward me, her hands extended like claws. Her fingernails were at least two inches long and curved.

"Oh, no I won't." I scurried around the bed like a trapped rat, only to be faced down by a puffed-up cat. "Pluto! You traitor!"

He high-stepped toward me, then do-si-doed back, darting under Winnie's skirt when I grabbed for him. I might not want to believe that a magical charm had lured Coleman into my arms, but my cat was certainly under a spell.

"Bring that lawman in here," Winnie said, sounding more like Jitty than the villainous witch of the movie. "I need to suck the juices from him so I can stay young."

As I recalled the movie, the three sister witches—who were also blond, brunette, and redhead, a perfect parallel to the Harringtons—needed to feed on innocents to stay young. "Coleman is far from innocent." I couldn't help a little preen. "I can attest to that!"

"I'll have my way with him." Jitty snapped her fingers and a high wind howled through Dahlia House. "Bring him to me or suffer the consequences."

"Ab-so-lute-ly not!" The very idea of it was distressing. "Stop it, Jitty. You've taken this far enough." She really was getting under my skin.

"You don't want me to shrivel up and die, do you?"

I'd come to count on Jitty in my life, as infuriating as she could be. "Leave Coleman out of this. And give me back my Jitty. And my cat. You have no power here in Sunflower County, Winnifred Sanderson. Go back to your wicked sisters and leave us alone."

The wind settled down and a glint of Jitty began to show through Winnie. Her eyebrows arched. "I hear you have an appointment to be pummeled, pumiced, and pomaded at that salon place. You need to do something about that straggly mess. Hair is a woman's crowning glory." She patted her curls. "Women reveal so much when they're being beautified. And you could stand a little of that."

I'd lost my curls in an accident—and I was a tad sensitive. "It's growing out. If you're such a great witch, make it grow faster."

"Maybe I can help your hair catch up with your nose!"

Oh, snap! Jitty as Winnie was quick and razor sharp. "I'm the only human you have to haunt, and you keep this up and I'll move to town! I'll leave you out here by yourself."

She smiled. "Never happening. Never. I see your future, Sarah Booth. Critters and clutter. Right here at Dahlia House. You had your Broadway fling. Your future is cast in the rich Delta soil."

I wanted to ask, "And children?" But I didn't dare. Jitty never revealed the future. Never. And in her most recent incarnation as Winifred Sanderson, she was mean as a coiled pit viper. "I can move away. Just keep that in mind. Change your address, change your life." I quoted some inane advertisement I'd heard recently.

"Defy me and I'll turn you to stone." Winnie/Bette/Jitty leaned toward me, those buck teeth protruding.

"Fie on you!" I bolted around her and down the

stairs. I had an appointment to keep and I didn't have time for mean witches or tormenting ghosts. But as surely as this case was over, I would have some payback for Jitty. I would figure out an appropriate revenge. She wouldn't run me out of Dahlia House again—without some big consequences!

As the front door slammed behind me, I heard her cackling. She had that part of being a witch down pat.

I felt no guilt at leaving the two-faced Pluto behind, but I did give a whispered promise to Sweetie Pie that I would bring her something from Millie's Café to make up for not taking her with me. The afternoon was bright and cold, and it wasn't right to leave Sweetie in the car for the length of my hair appointment. I had to focus on the setup of my sting, and I needed all of my brain power.

I parked at the Mane Attraction and sauntered in the door. I was an actress. I could do "casual." The salon was the ritziest day spa in my region of the Delta. A woman had to go to Memphis if she wanted anything fancier. Marcel, the stylist I'd booked, came over and walked around me, fluffing my hair.

"And what is it you think I can do with this?" she asked with a faux French accent filled with elegant contempt.

Perfect. Snooty was the sign of a high-end

salon, and Marcel, with her hollowed cheeks and straight black hair, projected hair haute couture.

Kitten was sitting in the chair beside Marcel's station. She eyed me with merry malice. "I came here because Kitten told Tinkie you could work wonders. I had a hair accident. I need a new style." All of that was true.

Kitten grinned. "Oh, Sarah Booth, I wondered if you'd ever take steps to shape that mop into a style."

"And here I am," I said. "I really was inspired by you, Kitten. You're always so camera-ready. I'm so glad to see you found a stylist who remembered the sixties and how to tease hair." Okay, so it was a mild tweak that went right over her head. I had to control the impulse to snipe. I had a mission, which was winning Kitten over. My assessment was that flattery, not sarcasm, was the perfect ticket.

"Take a seat," Marcel said, pointing at a chair that tilted back into a sink. "I'll have to charge you double for this . . . this *affreux désordre*. We have work to do."

I had no clue what she'd called my hair, but I knew it was an insult. I almost wished her luck, because she didn't have a lot to work with. My hair was growing out, but it wasn't my normal head of chestnut curls. I leaned back and let the shampoo girl's strong fingers massage my scalp as she washed my hair. This was indeed heaven.

When I was seated beside Kitten in the styling chair, I indulged in a little celebrity gossip. Millie knew everything about Hollywood and she kept me up to date. It was easy enough to engage Kitten in a discussion of the cult of Kardashians and other reality stars. I mentioned that I had friends in the movie business and they might be interested in a Mississippi Delta reality TV show. It was a fib, but an effective one.

As I name-dropped director and cinematographer's names—Marco and Lorraine St. John, respectively—and babbled on about dancing with Marco and working for the two film icons, I turned to Kitten. "You know, you would be perfect to host a reality TV show. You and Bob are self-made millionaires. You have a . . . definite fashion sense. The camera would love you. You're part of this community, involved in a lot of different things." None of them savory or of benefit to anyone but her elite buddies and stirring up trouble against people she didn't like, but I didn't say that part.

As Marcel combed and snipped, her expression a permanent sneer, I kept up a lively conversation, talking about how Tinkie had been hired as a consultant on future reality shows by Black Tar Productions. "In fact, Tinkie was supposed to meet with some potential investors today," I said. "Maybe Bob would be interested? You know if we could get some filming going in the Delta it would be good for everyone." When the stylist was almost done, my phone dinged right on time. I checked it. "Oh, dear!" I played it to the hilt. "This is not good."

"What is it?" Kitten didn't really like me, but she epitomized the old saying that curiosity killed the cat. Or the Kitten, if I played my cards right.

"It's Tinkie. She's over at the Prince Albert. Something is going on with her investors and she needs me there right now." I stood up, paid, and thanked Marcel, who'd actually given me a great cut. "Sorry to rush out, but this is an emergency."

I was almost out the door, fearing I'd over-played my hand, when Kitten popped out of her chair and followed me. "Who are the investors?" she asked, catching up to me. She was short and had to take two steps for each of mine, but she hustled and kept abreast of me.

"I don't know," I told her. "I don't run in the same financial circles that Oscar and Tinkie do. Or you and Bob, for that matter." I tossed her another ego bone.

"What's the reality show about?" she asked.

"The glamour of Delta women and how the blending of the past and present have created a woman who is uniquely strong, but also feminine. The iron magnolia, as it were, but with modern women." I was making it up as I went along. "You know, I think there were some real estate people interested in funding this show.

Folks from Bolivar County. They want to film on the Mississippi River, which is of course a huge tourist attraction. And casino gambling. There's some big money interest from that area in seeing a television production come to town."

"You can't let Bolivar County steal this away from us," Kitten said. "We have everything you need right here in Sunflower County. And we have the business expertise." She'd already cast herself in the starring role *and* as head of production. I could see the dollar signs flashing in her eyes like some cartoon character.

"Come with me to meet Tinkie," I said. "You can offer some advice, and if Bob is interested . . ."

"Bob is very interested."

Whether he was or not, he soon would be or he'd have hell to pay. We were at the door of the Prince Albert. A few tourists cluttered the lobby, but it was relatively quiet. Tinkie was supposed to be in the bar.

I pushed through the revolving front door and walked into the central lobby. To the left was a lounge with a baby grand piano. Another more traditional bar and restaurant were to the right, elevators directly in front of me. As if on cue, the elevator doors began to open and Malvik stepped into the lobby. Coleman had done his part. I wondered if he'd also wrangled Bob Fontana.

Malvik and Kitten both did a double take. I

knew then that they were involved with each other. Perhaps not romantically, but financially. The same expression crossed their faces as they eased away from each other. "Run, Forrest, run," was written all over them.

Tinkie stepped out from behind a column near the piano lounge. "Do you two know each other?" she asked.

"Of course not. I mean, we don't *know* know each other," Kitten said. She waved a hand at Malvik. "He's one of those witchy creatures. He hangs out with the Harringtons. I heard from Esmeralda that he's going to teach at their school. If the school ever opens, which I seriously don't see happening."

"I've got friends in low places, but not as low as Kitten Fontana's level." Malvik whipped around so the red lining of his cape fluttered. He was a drama queen of the highest order.

"Not so fast, Malvik." The challenge came from the other side of the lobby, where Deputy DeWayne Dattilo stepped into the room. "I have a warrant to search your room."

"For what?" Malvik asked.

"For papers stolen from Musgrove Manor." DeWayne's timing was spot-on.

Kitten inhaled sharply and her mouth opened wide. She snapped it shut with an audible click.

DeWayne handed Malvik the search warrant.

"You have no evidence I was at the manor. I

categorically deny I was there, and you can't prove that I was."

"That's not true," I said, reaching up to rub the knot on my head. "I saw you. After you hit me and I fell to the floor." It was a bluff, but what the hell. We were playing fast and loose with the truth. All for the greater good. But the biggest part of the bluff was yet to come.

"Where are the investors you were meeting with?" Kitten asked Tinkie. She'd bought into the idea of a reality show so deeply she no longer questioned it. To her, because she wanted it, the show was a concrete fact, and she wanted a piece of the action.

"In the bar." Tinkie nodded toward the bar.

Kitten pivoted and headed that way, but Tinkie blocked her. "Cool your hot britches," Tinkie said. "You're not messing up my deal."

As expected, Kitten rose to the challenge. "Get out of my way." She was about Tinkie's size, and they met eye to eye, both glaring.

"Make me." Tinkie threw down the gauntlet.

Kitten lifted her arm and whammed Tinkie in the chest with her elbow. My partner stumbled back and almost lost her balance. She caught herself, and for one moment, I thought Tinkie might deck Kitten. I probably would have. But Tinkie gasped and stepped out of the way, letting Kitten pass into the bar. The look Tinkie shot me was victorious. Kitten had taken the bait.

She went directly to a table where two men dressed in tailor-made suits sat talking softly. "Are you gentlemen interested in investing in a reality TV show?"

They looked up. "Who are you?"

She sat down and almost purred. "I'm your new star."

I didn't recognize the men at the table, but I had to give Tinkie credit for turning up two guys who looked posh and polished. Tinkie leaned over to whisper, "Harold's cousins. They're brothers and just happened to be visiting. He called them into action."

"And where is Coleman?" I asked.

"Right here." Coleman stepped through the door and caught Malvik by the cape, just as he was trying for the exit. "You'll be coming with me, Mr. Malvik. I have some questions for you. DeWayne, call me when you finish with his rooms."

"Will do." DeWayne's face was impassive, but when I was about to turn away, he gave me a wink. He was in on the sting, too.

So far, so good. Malvik had been roped into the loop. Now it was up to Tinkie. She signaled the two men in the bar who joined us in the lobby. Kitten was right behind them. "Have you considered my proposal on the production?" Tinkie asked them.

"We'd like to see the location. What is the

name? Musgrove Manor?" the tallest man said.

"Musgrove Manor?" Kitten blanched. "You didn't say the show would be filmed there."

"It's the only place in Sunflower County I would consider," Tinkie said. "The sister witches would be a great supporting cast, don't you think?"

"No. I don't think." Kitten balked. If she failed to come with us, the plan would fall apart. "That's a terrible idea. There are a hundred better places."

"We'd like to explore our options." The taller investor held his ground. "Could we make that visit now? Our time is at a premium. We're meeting with others who offer investment opportunities."

"I'll call the manor and make sure it's okay if we stop by. I'm thinking we could film in one of the outbuildings." I pretended to make the call and gain permission from the witches.

Before there were any more complaints, Kitten and Malvik were swept away into Tinkie's and Coleman's vehicles, respectively, and I had the fake investors with me. DeWayne had unfettered access to Malvik's hotel room. So far, things were going according to plan. Now the really tricky part was on us. So much depended on the legwork Tinkie had accomplished with Hope. And how the other sisters reacted.

The winter days were short, and the light was

fading from the sky as I drove along the highway with two strange men in my car. They introduced themselves as Tad and Thomas Erkwell, two of Harold's Memphis cousins who'd come for a dinner party.

"Harold asked us to do a favor and we'd do anything for him," Tad, the taller one, said. "It's easy enough to pretend to be interested in the movies. We'd both like to be actors, but that isn't an option for an Erkwell. We're sensible businessmen."

I glanced at Tad, who was riding shotgun, and he made a sad face. He certainly had the looks and expressiveness, and so did Thomas. "Thanks for helping us out. You guys did a great job. I can drop you off at Harold's house on my way to the manor."

"Could we come?" Tad asked.

"Witches!" Thomas said enthusiastically. "Man, and we thought Zinnia would be a series of porch libations, gourmet meals, and catching up with Harold. This is much more fun. And Harold said those Harrington sisters are hot."

What could it possibly hurt to bring them with me? "Sure. Just play along with whatever Tinkie does."

"You got it."

My car shot through the small town where the store lights had gone dark and the streetlights were coming on one by one. The blue hour had arrived. Some called it the gloaming, but I favored the term that better described my feelings. This was a melancholy time of day for me.

When we passed Millie's Café, I remembered my promise to bring Sweetie Pie something good to eat. Too late. I'd have to hope the Sweetheart drive-thru was still open when I was done and beg forgiveness that I hadn't brought some of Millie's chicken pot pie. That or make it up to her tomorrow.

The diner's interior glowed with light, but even Millie's was slow on a cold February evening. A dinner crowd was there, but not the normal bustle. I saw my friend sitting at a window table sipping a cup of coffee and reading a tabloid. She looked a little sad, and I knew she missed Esmeralda's far-fetched stories. Millie did love the ludicrous and the bizarre. And Esmeralda had been good at her job.

For a moment I was struck with an acute sense of loss. I hadn't known Trevor, and I hadn't really liked Esmeralda, but they were dead. And they had died in a terrible manner if the expression on their faces told the true story. Someone had taken the most valuable thing they had—their life. And it had been taken in a manner that left their expressions twisted in horror.

And none of it made a damn bit of sense.

I'd been swept up in a case that seemed to

have no central organizing motive. Was it a real-estate deal gone bad, an attack on the idea of a Wiccan boarding school, or two murders stemming from jealousy? I'd decided on money as the motivation. Money in the form of real estate. The Musgrove property was extremely valuable. If the sisters prevailed and created the school, then the land would remain undeveloped and natural. Kitten and Bob Fontana would lose an opportunity to make millions.

Thomas interrupted my musings. "Harold told us that the two murder victims met an unusual fate. They appear to have been frightened to death. Is that true?"

We were almost to the manor, and it would be best to fill them in on some details so they wouldn't be caught up short. "Doc Sawyer hasn't formally settled on the cause of death. The look on their faces makes us think they were frightened to death." I thought of the old stories of people whose hair had turned white from fear. Old wives' tales, I'd assumed.

"Ms. Delaney," Tad asked, "do you believe the witches have any powers?"

"What did Harold say?" I was curious.

"He said that magic can be found in the most unlikely places. A dairy would seem rather unlikely."

"I don't know if they have powers or not. I do know that unusual things have happened in

Sunflower County since they arrived. And I do believe the sisters enjoy a certain . . . notoriety. They seek it."

"Harold said they were really hot." Tad repeated Thomas's earlier assessment. When he grinned, he looked a lot like Harold.

"They're pretty," I agreed. "And smart. Be careful."

I turned into the manor drive and watched Tad's reaction. The house was imposing, all limestone blocks with the balconies and gargoyles outlined in the dying light. It was a setting right out of Edgar Allan Poe's Gothic world.

"In for a penny, in for a pound," Thomas said as I stopped the car and he got out of the back seat. "What an adventure!"

"Keep your eyes and ears open," I warned them. "There's a killer on the premises. He, or she, has killed twice. There's nothing to stop them from killing again."

"Do you know who the killer is?" Tad asked.

"I have my suspicions, but it's best that you don't know. That way you can play your part properly."

The two men nodded. "Then let's get on with it."

The front door of the manor was standing open, and I walked into the gloom with Tad and Thomas right behind me. Truth be told, I was happy for their company. Shadows had settled into every corner of the foyer and the parlors to either side. No light was turned on, and I couldn't detect any living presence, even though Tinkie's and Coleman's vehicles were parked in the driveway.

"Where is Vincent Price when you need him?" Tad quipped.

"This is more of a Boris Karloff moment," Thomas responded.

I was impressed with their knowledge of old horror movie icons—and Millie would be, too. These two men would fit right into our Zinnia world. And they were very handsome, like Harold. When we were done with this case, I'd enjoy finding out more about both men.

We advanced through the foyer and into the front parlor that had once been considered the man's parlor. From there we continued to a library, a large study, a gun and smoking room—all dark paneled with the masculine preference in mind. I badly wanted to call out to Coleman and Tinkie, or even to the sister witches, but I didn't. My gut warned me to stay quiet.

"Where is everyone?" Tad asked.

"Good question." This hadn't been part of the plan. We were supposed to meet in the parlor, Hope ready to play her role.

"They couldn't have vanished into thin air," Thomas said.

That was the wrong thing to say. In the land

of Musgrove Manor, strange things could and did happen. "I think we should go up to the third floor," I said. Since they weren't in the parlor, where we'd agreed to meet, Trevor's rooms seemed the logical place everyone might have gathered.

I'd been in the house enough to know that if I exited the gun and smoking room through the western door, I would end up in the formal dining room and finally back to the foyer, where the dragon-laden staircase would take us to Trevor's old rooms. The house was so quiet I could hear the wooden floors creaking softly.

"The detail here is exquisite," Tad said close behind me. "Look at the way snakes have been crafted into the crown molding. And the door lintels have the symbols for Quetzalcoatl, the feathered serpent god."

"How do you know so much about this?" I asked.

"I spent three years in Guatemala and Spanish was my second master's. I like to study. International business was my main focus. I'm the opposite of my brother, Thomas. Tell her what you like, Thomas?"

His request was met with silence. We both turned around. In the semidarkness, there was only emptiness. Thomas was gone.

"What the hell?" Tad started back the way we'd come until I grabbed him.

I hadn't heard a sound that would indicate Thomas was gone, and yet he was. "Stay close," I said. "We'll find him and the others. I promise. But we have to stay together." I didn't want to be snatched by something and I sure didn't want to be the only one left behind.

Tugging Tad behind me, I entered the dining room and stopped. It was an extraordinary room with painted frescoes on the ceiling in the style of the Sistine Chapel. I could tell that because the room was aglow with burning candles. They were on every flat surface, dozens of them in all shapes and sizes. Their flames were reflected in the large mirrors above two hunt boards and over the mantle. The mirrors gave the room the sensation of endless depth. The words to an old Eagles' song, "Hotel California," came to me. We'd checked in, but would we be able to check out?

"Are you *sure* those women aren't witches?" Tad asked.

"I'm not sure of anything at this point." How could I be? A grown man had simply disappeared—without a sound—when he was only five steps behind me.

"We should get out of here. Let's go outside and we can call Harold and some help. I don't have any cell reception in this house."

I had the same problem with my phone. Suddenly there was no service. "Yeah." I edged deeper into the dining room and stopped. The candles on the large old tiger oak table had been placed around a pentagram just like the one I'd seen on the floor of the secret room. Had the sisters drawn this? I wondered if the witches had played me and Tinkie all along. "Let's head for the front door. You call Harold, I'll call DeWayne."

"And I'll turn on the damn lights." Anger was replacing Tad's worry and surprise. He walked to the wall and hit the switch. Nothing. "Whoever is responsible for this has flipped the breakers." He was even angrier. "Someone is messing with us, and I don't like it. I'm going to find my brother."

"Hold on, Tad." I grabbed the sleeve of his jacket. "We have to stay together."

"This isn't funny. Who's behind this?"

"I don't know. And you're right. This isn't funny. It's deadly serious. Now let's just step outside. We can figure out what to do when we're out of this house." I left the dining room and found the short hallway that would give us access to the foyer. Tad was right behind me.

I'd never been in this hallway before and I stopped to get my bearings. Every inch of available wall space in the hall was covered with paintings of nude women. Some of the women looked familiar, and in better light I might have been able to name them. One painting stopped me dead in my tracks. Jane Cunningham, the paragon of virtue and keeper of the societal rules, leaned against the trunk of a huge banyan tree. It was almost as if she was a part of the tree. The aerial prop roots of the banyan had become a forest of trunks surrounding the original tree. In the center, with a cluster of the large, dark green leaves in her hand, was the first lady of anal retentiveness in Zinnia. "Damn," I said, wishing I had more light so I could really examine the painting. "This is going to be big news." I snapped a photo with my phone and was reminded that I could use it as a flashlight. Sometimes my brain didn't engage properly.

"This is the town's keeper of virtue," I said to Tad. "She's the most prim and proper person in town and she's always dragging others over the coals for their inappropriate conduct. Now, look. She's naked as a jaybird." When Tad didn't answer, I turned my phone light toward him. Except there was no one else in the hallway. Tad had vanished. I was completely alone.

24

The door to the dining room slammed shut with such force I jumped at least two feet. The light from my cell phone died, and I found myself in total darkness. A bit of fumbling and I lit up the phone again, but it revealed only what I already knew. The short hallway was empty. Jane Cunningham's naked disapproval raked my nerves like a gun barrel against my spine.

"Bite me," I said to her portrait. As soon as I spoke, I wished I'd come up with a different suggestion. I moved down the hallway examining the portraits because I didn't know what to do and once I got to the door, if it was locked, I'd have to accept that I was in deep trouble. Until then I could pretend, at least a little.

One portrait stopped me in my tracks. Esmeralda Grimes, wearing only a rosary and a golden aura, stared out at me, her hand lifted as if in benediction. Here was the portrait Esmeralda had filed suit and argued with Trevor over. He'd painted her as a gorgeous woman. And I remembered the rosary in the painting as the one I'd found beneath Trevor's bed.

The one I believed belonged to the journalist.

Somewhere behind me, something creaked. A hidden door, no doubt, that had allowed whoever it was to snatch up the two men who'd been with me. I put the phone in my pocket and waited in the darkness, struggling to control my breathing.

Soon I would find out what had happened to Tad and Thomas, and to Tinkie, Coleman, and Kitten. Where were the witches? And Malvik? Coleman had taken him more to remove him from the hotel than for any other reason, so he had to be on the dairy grounds. I wished strenuously that I'd been smart enough to bring Sweetie Pie and Pluto with me. They would have hunted down the hiding place of all the missing humans. Now I was on my own, and I was almost paralyzed by fear. It didn't make sense that fully grown humans could simply vanish. Without a sound. I thought of Jitty's last incarnation and her determination to make me believe that magic was possible. She'd been trying to warn me. Any minute now, something would likely reach for me. I could almost feel the bony fingers on my shoulder.

I had to get a grip on myself, and the quickest route was anger. Where in the hell was Coleman? He was the lawman, the person who was supposed to protect me from danger. Of all times for him to disappear, now wasn't a good one. Beneath my anger was worry. For him and for

Tinkie. My partner was mighty but small. She was also fearless and would put herself in danger to protect someone she loved. And Tad and Thomas had simply vanished. I felt responsible for Harold's cousins. I'd brought the brothers along, even though I now realized I shouldn't have. If they were hurt, it was on me.

Kitten was also missing, though I wasn't much concerned for her. But what had happened to the man I loved and my best friend?

Inaction gained me nothing. I walked to the door at the end of the hallway and turned the knob. Unexpectedly, the door opened on smooth, oiled hinges. I found myself in the ladies' parlor near the front of the house. I'd come through not a doorway but a panel. The hallway was one of the many secret passages in Musgrove Manor. Instead of heading to the front door, I took another right and made my way toward the kitchen.

I tried the light switch in a small serving room off the kitchen, but the power was still not working. There'd been no storms, no normal reasons for an electrical outage. I could only deduce, as Tad had stated, that someone had shut the power off deliberately. There could be no good reason for doing that.

I had to be very careful, or I would find myself snatched up. And while it might be the quickest way to find out what had happened to all my friends, it might also put me in a position where I couldn't help them.

I opened the door to the kitchen, hoping I would find them all around the table, waiting to spring their surprise. Then I could gleefully pistol-whip the bunch. But the room was empty, except for dozens of burning candles. They flared on the table, the stove, the counters, and the windowsills that looked out on the outline of the old dairy where a single, solitary figure trudged through the gathering dusk toward the outbuilding.

Pressing my fingertips to the kitchen window to be sure the figure wasn't a reflection or distortion, I looked for clues that would tell me who the black-clad figure might be. It was tall and slender, and could be either gender. It moved quickly, almost more shadow than solid entity.

"Who are you?" I whispered. "What do you want?"

As if it could hear me, the figure spun around and faced the house. I felt as if its gaze was drilling straight into me and I ducked instinctively. Who was that? Could it be one of the sisters? Or maybe Bob Fontana? I couldn't see clearly enough to be certain.

The logical thing to do was rush outside, track the figure, take it down, and find out its identity. But something about the way it moved, the uncanny knowing that it seemed to have, made me afraid. The very fact I was calling it "it" made me uneasy. Was it a human, or did the Harrington sisters truly have an ability to conjure something up that was less than human and possibly evil?

The bottom line, though, was I could cower in the kitchen, or I could take action.

Before I changed my mind, I went out the back door of the manor, crossed the porch, and stepped into the yard. A gibbous moon hung just above the tree line at the back of the pasture. When it rose higher, it might provide better light. Now, though, it was virtually useless. I angled to the front of the house and got my pistol and a good flashlight out of the trunk of my car. I checked Tinkie's trunk and got her pistol, too. And I hunkered down beside my car, where there was plenty of service, and called Harold. I could not call Oscar and tell him that I'd lost his wife. Harold, though, wouldn't chastise me or hold me accountable. He would come to my aid.

He picked up on the third ring. "Sarah Booth, what are you up to on a brisk February evening?"

Though a chill wind had sprung up, Harold's assured voice warmed me. "I'm at Musgrove Manor. Tinkie, Coleman, and your two cousins have disappeared. Would you pick up Sweetie Pie and Pluto and come help me?"

"An adventure. Of course. I was a little on the bored side waiting for Tad and Thomas to return."

"Harold, bring a gun. I don't know what's going on, but you should come armed."

"Have you called DeWayne?"

"He was supposed to meet us here, but I haven't seen him." Was it possible he'd arrived and disappeared, too? What had he found in Malvik's rooms?

"I'll bring Budgie." Harold sounded firm.

"I don't know . . ."

"We'll be there in twenty minutes. I'll get the animals and I'll bring Roscoe. Find a place to hide and stay there."

"Okay." I sounded uncertain even to me.

"You have to stay safe so we can work this together. If you disappear, Sarah Booth, I won't know where to begin."

Harold knew how to pull my strings. "I'll be in the front yard."

But I wouldn't be waiting. I would go to the dairy and see what was happening there. The lone figure had disappeared in that direction. If I couldn't apprehend the person, then at least I could spy upon it.

When I arrived at the dairy, my frozen toes and fingers felt like they might snap. I crept to one of the old windows that had long ago lost all the panes. The barn had been remodeled sometime in the 1960s to allow more natural light and air, but years of neglect had left the glass shattered and the building open to the elements. The Harringtons had begun work, putting in new flashings, sills, and doorjambs and adding flooring. I held my gun in my left hand and had Tinkie's tucked in my waistband. The flashlight was in my jacket pocket.

The soft murmur of voices came to me, and I felt my heart jolt. Had I found my missing friends? When I peeked into the dairy, I saw Hope and Charity seated at a table in front of a large silver bowl of liquid. Behind them were rows of feeding troughs and, at the far end, a milking machine.

Additional voices drew my attention. Leaning against the wall was Bob Fontana and the man from the Pickingill Society, Marlow Spurlock. There was no sign of my missing friends, or of Kitten, for that matter.

"Get to it," Bob commanded. "Where are those legal documents? Kitten went to a lot of trouble to get Trevor's signature on that deed."

"He couldn't have known what he was signing," Hope said angrily.

"Oh, I have witnesses to the contrary. Now, get after it. You said you could find them. So find them."

"We need help. We'll have to call upon the Master," Hope said. She was using the sting technique Tinkie and I had come up with, but the setup was all wrong. I had no idea where

Tinkie or Coleman might be. And it looked like both Hope and Charity were more prisoners than powerful witches.

Hope continued talking, following my script. "But I warn you, Mr. Fontana. When you accept the help of the Dark One, you are his for eternity. He has powers to do the unthinkable, and he will have his payment."

"I'll take my chances," Bob said.

"Or we can just kill you both now," Spurlock said. "Neater that way."

Spurlock, who'd taken money from the Pickingill group to save the witches, wasn't interested in saving them at all.

I wondered where Faith was and why she wasn't part of the tableau. And I was pretty certain Spurlock or Malvik had stolen the documents from the chest in the secret room. Why didn't Spurlock just give them over? Unless a coup was taking place!

"You may have us, but never think we're powerless." Hope was intimidating. Yes! "We aren't alone, Mr. Fontana. You forget that."

"Faith can't help you." There was a certain smugness to Bob's tone. "She isn't really a Harrington, after all. Your mother gave her up. What a fib to say she was stolen. She was left behind, and some people just can't get over that."

"We love Faith," Charity said, but her voice was tremulous. "She wouldn't betray us."

"Are you sure?" Bob pushed off the wall. "Get to work. I want to know where those papers went. Scry for them or whatever witchy thing you do."

"No." Hope wasn't going to be pushed around. "You lied about Trevor agreeing to sell you this property. These documents are forged or at least were signed under duress. I won't help you steal the land from us."

Hope started to stand, but Bob brought a gun from his side and pointed it at her.

"Sit down."

She almost collapsed back into her chair. "Esmeralda was onto you. That's why you killed her, too."

Bob laughed. "You jump to conclusions just like Kitten. She was certain I was sleeping with Esmeralda. She's done everything she can to cut me out of this deal. She thinks she can develop this property on her own. Hey, maybe you should ask *her* what happened to that hack writer. And that old fool Trevor, trying to play both ends against the middle. Just sayin', Kitten has a mean streak a mile wide. And she's good at finding scapegoats."

"You didn't kill them?" Charity asked.

"I'm not the only villain working this scheme," Bob said, completely comfortable with a cabal of villains. "I'm probably the best looking, but not the only one. Now find those damn papers or I'm going to put a bullet in your brainpan and end this. I'll have this property one way or the other."

Hope and Charity joined hands on either side of the large silver bowl and closed their eyes. They began to mumble softly.

"Stop the bullshit and tell me where to find those papers." Bob put the barrel of the gun to Hope's temple. She opened her eyes, but even from the distance of the window, I could see something was wrong. Her eyes were rolled back in her head, showing only the whites.

Bob stepped back. "What's wrong with her?" he asked Charity. "Make her stop." He was clearly unsettled. Even being on the outside looking in, I was shaken.

"She's in a trance," Charity said. "Leave her alone. She's communicating."

"With who?"

Charity rested her blue gaze fully upon Bob. "Magic comes at a price, Mr. Fontana. A heavy price. We seek our answers and influence from the Dark Lord. We may be the conduit, but you will pay the price."

"Stop this bull and tell me where those documents are. And if you see my wife, tell her when I get my hands on her, she is going to suffer. Betraying bitch."

Hope began to rock back and forth, and then jerked several times. "He is here with us," she said. "He will help you, but at a price."

"What's he going to demand?" Bob asked. "My soul?" He laughed.

"He'll demand too much," Hope said, and her face was bleak in the candlelight that illuminated the room.

She and Charity joined hands and began chanting in what sounded like Latin. The incantation made the hair all over my body stand on end. The water in the silver bowl seemed to swirl, as if a storm were brewing within the tiny confines. I wasn't in the best position to see, but something was happening. Hope and Charity bent forward, staring into the depths of the liquid.

"I know where the papers are," Hope said, looking up at Bob. "And you aren't going to like it."

"Spit it out," Bob demanded.

"They're at the sheriff's office. The deputy found them at the Prince Albert and confiscated them."

"Get up." Bob waved the gun between the sisters. He backed up and opened the trapdoor that led into the tunnels. "Get down there," he said.

"Just let us go," Hope said. "You can have the dairy. We'll move back to Louisiana."

"It's not going to be that easy," Bob said. "Now get down there."

I wanted to stop what was happening, and even though I had a gun, I didn't trust that Bob wouldn't shoot one of the sisters if I challenged him. Harold and DeWayne were on the way. It was smarter to wait for backup.

If Bob took the sisters into the tunnels, we could find them, perhaps when we had an advantage.

The trapdoor closed behind Bob and Spurlock, and the dairy barn was empty.

25

The lights of a vehicle swept across the front of the manor, and I knew Harold had arrived. I had to get back to the main house and warn him before Bob or some of his henchman—and I was positive he had henchmen—saw my friend. I also needed to move. I was freezing. My warm barn coat hung in the mudroom of Dahlia House and I wished for it with the same passion I'd wished for a bicycle for Christmas when I was seven. I got the bike, but I doubted Santa Claus would deliver my coat. I should have asked Harold to grab it when he got the pets.

I pushed off the wall and ran fast toward the manor, which was still dark and foreboding. I arrived just as Harold walked up the steps, flashlight in his hand. He was a perfect target.

"Harold," I whisper-yelled. "Harold!"

He heard me and snapped off the light. "Why is the power out?" he asked.

"Someone shut it off deliberately."

"Let's find the breaker box." Harold was a practical man. And a smart one.

When I reached his side, he grasped my arm and quickly blinked the light in my face. “Are you okay?”

“Everyone is missing. They just vanished. I was in the house with your cousins. Thomas disappeared first, then Tad. I don’t know what happened to Coleman, Tinkie, and Malvik.” My voice broke. I hadn’t realized how close to an emotional outburst I was. “Bob Fontana forced two of the witches into the tunnels in the dairy at gunpoint. He may kill them.”

“First things first. We have to find Tinkie and Coleman and my cousins. They’re here somewhere,” Harold said. “We’ll find them.” He walked to his sedan and opened the door. Sweetie Pie, Pluto, and his bad little dog Roscoe leaped to the ground, sniffing like crazy. Roscoe reminded me of one of the Marx Brothers running in a frenzy.

“Find Coleman,” I said to Sweetie Pie.

She snuffled over to the patrol car, circled it, and headed up the front steps to the open front door. When she disappeared inside, Harold nudged me. “We can follow or we can find that breaker box.”

“We need light.” I offered him Tinkie’s gun from my waistband.

“Brought my own,” he said, pushing back his jacket to show the Glock he’d brought. “And I brought this.” He opened the back door of his car and handed me my barn jacket. “I figured you’d be freezing.”

“You are a friend indeed.” I slid into the coat with a sigh of relief.

I was worried about Sweetie Pie, but we had to get the lights back on in the manor. Somehow, the scenario that Tinkie and I had planned had gone terribly awry.

“Where’s DeWayne?” I asked.

“He’s called in some help, Sarah Booth. He found a deed in Malvik’s room assigning the Musgrove property to the Fontanas. Apparently, Kitten had somehow gotten Trevor to sign the deed over to the Fontanas. DeWayne saw the signature.”

“How did Malvik end up with the deed?” I was certain I’d seen it in the secret room at the manor.

“I believe Spurlock took the deed after he conked you on the head, and somehow Malvik took it from Spurlock and hid it in his hotel room, thinking we’d never look there. Either he’s in on this or he was intending to blackmail the Fontanas.”

“What a snake pit.” I really couldn’t worry about property right now. My focus was my friends and Harold’s relatives. And then Hope and Charity. I had no clue where Faith might be, or what side she was working. I told Harold my suspicion that Faith was working the Arlington Woods land deal with the Fontanas. I was positive she'd negotiated the sale of the Keel land. I had no proof, though, only assumptions. Bob Fontana's implications were that Faith had abandoned her sisters and gone renegade, but Bob wasn't known to walk hand-in-hand with the truth.

Harold and I made our way around the manor to the power lines. The breaker box was on the side of the house, and the shrubs around it indicated someone had trampled them. Sure enough, when Harold flipped the breakers, lights came on in the manor. Mission accomplished.

If only finding our friends would be as simple.

"Should I call Oscar?" Guilt was eating me alive. Tinkie's husband had a right to know his wife was in danger.

"Why don't we hunt for her first? That's what Tinkie would suggest."

"Thanks." That was what I wanted to hear. If only we could find her safe and sound, then Oscar wouldn't have to be panicked. "Let's find Sweetie."

Even with the lights blazing, the manor filled me with trepidation. It was beautiful architecturally, but there was something sinister in the dragon motifs, the snakes on the lintels, and the fearsome claws of the table and chair legs. The house had been filled with totems. I reminded myself that these embellishments had been created long before witches moved into the house.

I filled Harold in on what I'd seen and heard at the dairy.

"It's safe to bet the Harrington sisters are being held in the tunnels, just like Budgie was."

"I thought you were bringing Budgie." I'd forgotten all about the former teacher. I was somewhat relieved he wasn't in tow.

Harold started up the stairs.

"Wait a minute! Where is Budgie?" I had a terrible feeling. He had to have gotten out of the car before Harold made it to the manor.

"He's in the tunnels, Sarah Booth."

"You let him go down there alone?" I couldn't believe Harold would do that.

"He knows what he's doing." Harold inhaled. "And he's armed."

"Oh crap." This whole thing was totally out of control.

The sound of gunshots came from somewhere in the upper floors of the manor, followed by Sweetie Pie's howl. Harold and I both bolted up the stairs. I had to find my dog and my friends. Pluto and Roscoe were also missing. This case, which had started out as a simple fact-finding mission, might prove to be the conclusion of my career as a private investigator.

At the top of the stairs, I led Harold to the sliding panel that revealed the secret room. I'd failed to truly explore the interior passageways and where they led. The panel was open and blood was splattered across the floor. Someone had been injured, possibly shot. “Wait for DeWayne, please.” I had to find my friends and dog. “Please, Harold.” Where in the hell was the deputy anyway? He should have arrived by now, even if he had to drag the Mormon Tabernacle Choir behind him.

“You shouldn’t go in there alone.”

“You know where I am. You and DeWayne can follow as soon as he arrives.”

“I’ll wait for a little while.” That was as much as Harold was willing to give, and I had to take it.

“Thanks.” I pushed the panel open wider, blocked it again with some heavy books, and stepped into the musty darkness.

My high-beam flashlight was a tremendous help as I moved to the end of the narrow dark room. As I suspected, a door opened onto another passage, this one wider and sloping down. I was somewhere in the interior of the house, moving toward ground level. Twice I saw passages that led off the main one, but I ignored them. They were narrow and filled with cobwebs.

The walls of the passage were wood and rough limestone block. Budgie would appreciate this architectural detail, but I wasn’t in the mood. I wanted only the safety of my friends. I couldn’t think about Coleman. What if I lost him just after we’d decided to act on our feelings?

A noise somewhere in the darkness ahead of me made me pause. It sounded like feet dragging on the floor. I turned off the flashlight and felt my way forward. When my fingers tangled in some kind of rope, I stopped. Clicking on the light for just a moment, I realized I held a hangman's noose in my hand. It was harmless, but the sight of it was chilling. What had gone on at Musgrove Manor over the long years of history?

A low whine came from up ahead and I pressed on. Sweetie Pie! Was she hurt? And where in the heck were Roscoe and Pluto? "Sweetie!" I whispered for my hound. I couldn't stop myself. Toenails scrabbled on the floor, and Sweetie came up to me, whining. Blood covered her head and back. I wanted to cry out, but I knelt beside her instead, my hands feeling for the wound that would produce such blood.

She licked my hands and then my face, and I couldn't detect any serious injury. I clicked on the light again and gasped. The beam caught Tad and Thomas. They were bound and gagged and tied in an upright position against the far wall of a room. Tad was bleeding from a cut to his forehead, and I couldn't tell if he was alive or dead. Thomas's wide eyes let me know he was conscious. His eyebrows jumped up and he shook his head.

Before I could turn to look behind me, I felt

a sharp blow on my left hand that held the gun. It flew across the floor. I rolled out of the way of the next blow, and Sweetie Pie dodged, too, and just in time. I still had the flashlight, and I swung it at the dark-clad figure that came at me with what looked like a fireplace poker. The heavy iron tool came down on my forearm and I thought I heard bone crack.

From out of the darkness a small black body hurled itself through the air. It landed on the attacker's head with a shriek like a soul escaping from hell. Pluto was on the scene. Sweetie Pie lunged at the off-balance figure and knocked it against the wall. As it slid to the floor, Roscoe arrived. He was a take-no-prisoners kind of dog. He went straight for the face and caught the person's nose and shook it like a dead rat. Blood exploded and Spurlock screamed and dropped the poker. I picked it up and clocked him on the head. And then there was silence.

My arm throbbed like red-hot flares were shooting through it, but it wasn't broken. I went to Thomas and untied him and removed the gag. He bent over his unconscious brother. "Did you see Tinkie or Coleman?" I asked.

"No. Someone snuck up behind me, put a cloth soaked in something over my nose, and the next thing I knew I was being dragged down these halls in the dark. Who is that man?"

"Depends on what role he's playing. Help me tie him up."

By the time we had Spurlock bound, Tad was coming to. Sweetie, Roscoe, and Pluto were fine. It was Tad's blood on my dog. "We have to find the others," Harold said. His tone worried me. "And the other sister, Faith? Did you see her?" he asked Thomas.

"No. We only saw that guy." He indicated Spurlock. "He never said a word, either."

"Get your brother outside," Harold urged him. "Put him in the car." He gave Thomas the keys. "Take him to the hospital and tell Doc Sawyer to be on alert. We may need him here."

"I can't leave you," Thomas said to Harold.

"You can and you will." Harold motioned for him to get Tad's other arm and lift him to his feet. "Now go."

We lit their way down the tunnel and to another panel that opened onto the dining room. Many of the candles were now guttering in puddles of wax. I had no idea how long we'd been making our way through the bowels of the house, but it was plenty of time for DeWayne to have arrived. Yet he hadn't. Something truly strange was happening at Musgrove Manor, and Harold and I were on our own. With the help of the dogs and Pluto.

"Sweetie, find Coleman and Tinkie," I said to my faithful hound. She could track like nobody's business, and she adored Tinkie and even liked Coleman. "And don't forget, Malvik is around here somewhere."

She gave a mournful howl and started out of the house. Her direction took me by surprise, but Harold and I followed as fast as we could run. Sweetie was out the door like a streak and bounding down the path that led to the creepy apple orchard. Roscoe was at her side and Pluto loped just in front of us. I'd never seen my cat move with such speed, which only made me go faster.

The moon had finally risen high enough to light the path that twisted through an open pasture, then took a slight downward turn into a protected orchard. Before we even reached the apple trees, I saw the feral cats. They were lined up on both sides of the path. Pluto rushed forward, and, as he passed them, they fell into line behind him.

"He's like the king of the cats," Harold said. "That is chilling."

"No kidding. He's like their ruler." I didn't want to think how that might be possible since he'd really only met these cats in the past two weeks. I wondered if they voted like the cardinals in the Vatican. That was an even more disconcerting thought as I imagined the cats in red capes and pointed hats. My fantasies were definitely getting away from me.

In the distance, Sweetie Pie set up a cry. She

was on a scent. At last Harold and I reached the orchard and stopped dead in our tracks.

"Oh, no." I couldn't believe what I was seeing. "This can't be."

"How did they get the bodies out of the morgue?" Harold asked. He was as taken aback as I was at the sight of three bodies hanging in the apple trees. Trevor Musgrove, Esmeralda Grimes, and Faith Harrington all had been hanged from the crooked branches of the leafless apple trees. It was like a tableau out of a horror movie. The bodies swung gently in the breeze, the ropes creaking with the weight. At least Trevor and Esmeralda had been dead before they were strung up. Faith, I couldn't say one way or the other.

"Doc wouldn't have released those bodies." But now, at least, I had a clue where DeWayne might be and what he was up to. If Doc reported two bodies stolen and no one could find Coleman, DeWayne would have to take action.

A muffled groan came to me and Sweetie Pie came dashing out of the trees with something in her mouth. When she dropped it at my feet, I saw it was a patch from Coleman's official sheriff's jacket. It looked like Sweetie had torn it from the sleeve. "Coleman is around here," I said to Harold. "Take us, Sweetie."

Back in the woods Roscoe barked his evil little troll bark, and Sweetie took off. I went after her.

"Should we cut these bodies down?" Harold asked.

"Coleman and Tinkie first. Bodies second."

Not two minutes later I saw a strangely shaped tree trunk and hurried to where Sweetie had sat down, howling softly. "It's Coleman," I called to Harold. "He's tied to a tree."

"Tinkie is here," Harold called out. "She's alive. Just gagged. And hopping mad."

The same was true for Coleman. I could barely get the tape off his mouth before he started barking orders. I was so glad to see him I just took it all in stride and hurried to do as he asked.

"Have you seen Budgie?" I asked him as soon as he was on his feet.

"No. Where are the sisters? And that bastard Malvik. As soon as we walked in the manor, he disappeared. He knows the secret passages in the house."

This was the hard part. "Faith has been hanged. Along with the bodies of Trevor and Esmeralda. They're just ahead in the apple trees."

Coleman looked at me as if I'd grown a second head, but he followed me back the way I'd come. We collected Harold and one truly pissed-off Tinkie along the way. "I cannot believe that devil Spurlock got the jump on me and knocked me out with chloroform or something of that nature," Tinkie complained. "Coleman went after Malvik, and Spurlock came out of nowhere."

"So Spurlock and Malvik are working together." I wasn't surprised. What I was shocked about was that Malvik had evaded Coleman. "At least Spurlock is out of commission. He's tied up in one of the secret rooms. He plays a role in this whole attempt to steal the dairy and land from the witches."

"Let's get back to the manor. I have to find the sisters."

I had to tell her before she saw it. "Faith Harrington is dead."

"What?" She stopped and Coleman nearly ran her down. "What are you saying?" She blocked the path.

"Someone hanged her in an apple tree. We need to go and cut her down. And Trevor and Esmeralda, too. Someone stole the bodies from the morgue." I didn't say it out loud, but I couldn't help thinking, thank goodness it was bitter cold. Decomp would be at a minimum, but it was still going to be keenly unpleasant.

26

"Oh no!" Tinkie really set up a wail when we were close enough to see the bodies. They turned slowly in the chill breeze. All around us the night was silent.

"Where are Hope and Charity?" Tinkie asked.

"We don't know. Bob Fontana had them the last I saw." That answer wouldn't satisfy Tinkie for long.

"Were they alive?"

"They were fine." Somehow I had to minimize her grief and panic. Even in the moonlight I could see she'd gone a pasty white and she clutched her stomach as if she might be sick. She turned away and dropped to her knees, gagging.

"Tinkie." I put a hand on her shoulder.

"I'm okay," she said, struggling to regain her composure.

Coleman lifted her to her feet and turned her away from the swaying corpses. "Just don't look. There's nothing you can do."

I hugged her close to shield her from the gruesome sight just as the sound of voices came to me.

"It's Bob. And Spurlock!" I couldn't believe he'd gotten free. "Hide."

We scattered and took cover in clumps of weeds and fallen limbs, and just in time. Bob and the alleged cunning man came toward the hanging corpses. They stopped short. "What the hell?" Bob asked.

"Who did this?" Spurlock sounded genuinely puzzled, and he walked with a distinct limp where I'd kicked him. "Was it that crazy Kitten? I told you months ago not to count on her. I'm not going to take the fall for this, Bob. I did your dirty business with that Jackson development that turned to crap. I won't be implicated in murder. You'd better find that crazy wife of yours and see that she takes responsibility." He sounded more desperate than dangerous.

"Where are Charity and Hope?" I whispered to Coleman.

He shushed me and found my hand. My fingers were freezing, and the warmth of his palm closing over mine gave me comfort. I pressed Tinkie against my other side. We would all get through this, and we would make the guilty parties pay.

"We have to get rid of Kitten," Bob said as he walked up to Esmeralda and set her body on a more vigorous spiraling swing. "We can hang her here, pretend she was strung up with these others. Blame it on Charity and Hope. And we have to get that deed away from the deputy.

You're responsible, Spurlock, running around those passages and tunnels like some kind of secret agent. You had the land deed and you let Malvik steal it from you. You're the idiot who put them in that trunk. Now we have to get them back."

"Okay, just get off my back. I've done the grunt work in most of this deal and I don't need you treating me like your toady. You brought me in on this, promising I'd get a position in your development company. I can't go home. The Pickingill Society is out for blood. If we don't get control of this situation, you're going to prison and I'm going to skip the country."

"Shut up." Bob drew back as if he might slug Spurlock, but he stopped. "We can pull this out. We just have to keep our cool. We can lay all of this at Kitten's door, and if she's dead she can't dispute it. We just have to stay calm." Bob nodded, agreeing with his own assessment.

Spurlock drew in a long breath. "Okay. We'll make that deputy give up the deed, and I'll take care of your wife. Then I want my cut and I want to get out of this godforsaken state." Spurlock was ready to be done. "Where did you stash Kitten? I want this over with."

"Pantry off the kitchen. She's a hellcat. Use the Taser if she gives you too much trouble."

"Will do." Spurlock ambled back up the path, leaving Bob alone with the bodies. Bob went to them, one by one, looking up as if he had no clue who they were or how they had gotten there.

"Let's take him out," I whispered to Coleman. "He's alone. We all have guns. Let's just shoot him."

"Good plan, except that would be murder. We have to find out where Hope and Charity are. We may be able to save them."

I wasn't in the mood for rational behavior. I wanted action. "Okay. What's the plan?" Tinkie and I had plotted to use the witches and a pretend magic spell to get the truth out of Bob and Kitten. All of that was out the window. It was up to Coleman now.

The sound of Latin chanting came from the darkness. I knew it was Hope and Charity, even though I couldn't see them. Somehow they'd gotten loose and were . . . casting a spell? That was really freaking helpful—not. Why didn't they just bring more guns? How did they get away from Bob and Spurlock? What the hell was going on?

Bob took a stance and sighted his gun on the path. "Come on out and I'll make it quick. If I have to chase you down, you'll regret it."

The incantation grew louder and more passionate.

"Stop that shit right now." Bob was losing patience.

The two women appeared at the top of the path.

They were dressed all in black, the gauzy fabric of their outfits floating around them. Somehow, they'd had time for a costume change. They chanted louder and harder, switching to English, and swirls of mist began to form around them. I was riveted in place.

As the mist grew thicker and swirled faster, they continued chanting. "Return the life to those who have been cheated. Fill the empty vessels with your power. Hecate, Goddess of the Moon and the feminine, give back what was wrongly taken. Esmeralda Grimes, Trevor Musgrove, Faith Harrington, return from the land of the dead and demand payment from the one who took your life."

"You don't scare me." Bob started for them. He didn't want to shoot them—too obvious, but I had no doubt he would kill them. The two witches took off back down the path, and I gathered myself to jump at Bob. Coleman held me back.

"Be still," he whispered.

Just as Bob passed by Esmeralda Grimes's gently swinging body, she began to buck and quiver. My heart almost stopped as I watched the dead body reanimate. "Bob Fontana." The words were spoken by the corpse in a deep, almost masculine voice. "I name you, Bob Fontana, as the taker of my life. I have come to claim what's mine."

Bob jumped away from Esmeralda like he'd been snakebit. "I didn't touch you, you crazy bitch. I should have killed you the way you were meddling in my affairs, but I didn't. You stay away from me."

My heart almost stopped at the words that seemed to come from the dead journalist. It was impossible, but the corpse seemed to be talking—and moving.

"Let me down, Bob. We have business." Esmeralda began to kick and struggle on the end of the rope.

Tinkie buried her head in my shoulder and I buried mine in Coleman's chest. Esmeralda had come back to life! We were in an apple orchard with a murderer and a zombie.

Bob stumbled away from the animated body and cursed a blue streak as he fumbled to find his gun. In his retreat, he backed into Trevor's dead body. The artist's corpse began to buck and twist at the end of the rope and make grotesque strangling sounds. "Bob! Bob! You want my land, don't you?"

"Get away from me!" Bob pushed at the body, setting Trevor to swinging.

"Bob, still want to make a land deal?" Trevor asked. "We can work something out."

"Aaaahhhh!" Bob launched himself away from Trevor.

The body of Faith Harrington began to twirl,

and she sang in a clear contralto the song "Witch Hunt" by Rush. "Vigilantes gather on the lonely torchlit hill . . ."

Bob stumbled backward, tripped over a fallen apple-tree limb, and began sobbing.

The ground beside Bob opened up and Budgie Burton appeared with a baseball bat and a flashlight. He shined the light in Bob's face and then brought the bat down across his shins. Bob howled. "Leave me alone. Leave me alone. I confess to everything. The land deal, everything. Just get me out of this orchard."

Coleman stood up and walked over to him. Bob scrabbled on his hands and knees to Coleman and grabbed his legs. "Help me," he said. "Please, help me. They've come back to life and they're going to kill me."

"Why would they do that?" Coleman asked, his voice so reasonable I wanted to slap him myself.

"They're going to drag me to hell. I didn't poison them or kill Faith, but I was involved. I'm guilty. I'll tell you everything I know if you stop them from taking me to hell."

"Good things happen to bad people," Coleman said as he snapped the cuffs on Bob. Roscoe, Harold's little evil dog, rushed over to Bob and peed on him. Roscoe had a way of getting his point across.

"Harold, DeWayne, let them down," Coleman called out. Slowly Faith began to descend to the ground. She gained her feet and stood up, removing the noose from around her neck.

"Thank goodness," she said. "My feet are asleep and stinging like I'm standing in a fire-ant bed."

"You're alive?" Tinkie didn't believe it and neither did I. We both stayed far back.

"Do I look dead?" Faith snapped.

"I'm not going to answer that," Tinkie said. She was right. If Faith wasn't dead, someone had done a great makeup job on all three of them. Their skin was pasty white with a bluish tint, their eye sockets hollowed. They were pretty damn creepy.

Slowly Esmeralda's feet touched the ground, and then Trevor's. They all stood up and began unhitching themselves from some kind of harness beneath their clothes.

"How did you do that?"

"It's an old hangman's trick. Body harness that stuntmen use in movies, cable, fake noose." Faith was brusque. "Once we figured out that someone had tried to poison Trevor and then Esmeralda, we knew we'd have to trick him into a confession. He knows who gave them the poison and we'll get it out of him. Now, let's get Malvik and that weasel Spurlock and make them tell us where my sisters are. If he's harmed one hair on their heads . . . I'll cook him in the caldron in the front yard."

• • •

Torturing Malvik turned out not to be necessary. When we arrived back at the manor, Doc, Charity, and Faith were waiting on us. Budgie had found them in the tunnels and released them. Doc had come when DeWayne called him—and had helped prepare the hanging scenario and then searched the tunnels with Budgie. Now the only person locked in the pantry was Spurlock. Doc had gotten the drop on him.

We could only deduce that Malvik had found Kitten trussed up off the kitchen and released her. They were both gone. They'd realized the poop was about to hit the fan and teamed up, at least for the escape attempt. DeWayne's roadblocks caught them on a backroad to the interstate. They were being returned to Sunflower County jail.

Coleman loaded Bob and Spurlock into the backs of two cruisers and DeWayne and Budgie, who'd been officially sworn in as a deputy, took them to the jail. The rest of us trudged into the manor, where Faith built a roaring fire in the men's parlor and we all lined up to warm our bones.

Trevor and Esmeralda were beside themselves, and I felt only slightly mean as I congratulated them on not being really dead. Someone should have told me. My plan for the big sting to get Bob to confess hadn't involved dangling corpses, but then again, neither Coleman nor Doc had bothered to tell me that Trevor and Esmeralda weren't really dead.

Faith washed the makeup from her face and joined Charity in mixing a round of Purple Zombie Cosmopolitans. It was an appropriate drink for the evening we'd just survived. Everyone was exhausted, but I had a bone to pick with one lawman. And Doc Sawyer, who kept shooting glances at me.

I sidled up to Coleman, who put his arm around me and hugged me close. "Not so fast," I whispered. "You could have told me they weren't dead."

"I needed you and Tinkie to believe it. You're an actress, Sarah Booth. You could have known the truth and pulled it off. But no one else involved in this has acting chops. You and Tinkie have a psychic connection that astounds me. If you had known the truth, Tinkie would have known the truth. She might have given our plan away."

That was a crock of rancid butter. "When Esmeralda started talking, I almost croaked. What if I'd had a heart attack?" I asked.

"It would have been my pleasure to perform CPR."

"You aren't going to get out of this with cheesy sexual innuendoes."

"He might," Doc said, grinning.

"Be careful, Doc. You're on my list, too. You

had to know all along they weren't dead. You could have told me."

"It wasn't my place to tell anyone," Doc said. "It was a lucky stroke that I recognized the poison used on Trevor. Back in the day, when I did some work for Doctors Without Borders in Haiti, I saw a case of poisoning that showed many of the same symptoms as Trevor, and don't feel badly, Sarah Booth, his heartbeat was undetectable without a stethoscope."

"Thanks. I could have sworn he was dead."

"All part of the poison. At any rate, I was able to get the antidote and use it before he actually did die. The poison left both of them in a zombie state—not dead but not really alive. The antidote came from those thorny trees you cut down, Coleman. Devil's walking sticks. When I saw that patch of trees in the backyard, I knew exactly what to do. Trevor and Esmeralda are both terribly lucky. For a time, I didn't know if they actually would live."

"So no one trusted me to keep a secret." I whirled on Coleman. "Or to be able to act. You didn't believe in me." That was a bitter pill indeed.

Coleman looked a little worried. "I made a judgment call. Don't blame Doc for this. It wasn't about trusting you with information or believing you could act. I did what I thought was best for everyone, Sarah Booth. I'm sure you've been there before." There was a hint of sadness in his tone. "I didn't expect we'd have to keep the secret as long as we did."

"You let me think you were in harm's way. And Tinkie, too. If Harold hadn't been willing to come with me . . ." I was getting really mad.

"Sarah Booth, you're being a little . . . unfair." Harold lifted one eyebrow at me.

"People in glass houses . . ." Doc threw in. I glared my response at him.

Tinkie cleared her throat. "The important thing is that the case is resolved. No one is dead. An innocent woman will be released from prison and the guilty will be punished."

"And the price of my art will skyrocket." Trevor laughed. "I saw the headlines of my death. Suddenly all the critics are lauding my work as masterpieces. This is how the art world works. You're alive and you're nothing. When you die, suddenly you're a genius. Well, I'm going to have my cake and eat it, too, thanks to all of you."

"Are you still selling the manor to the Harringtons?" I asked.

"No, I never intended to sell to them. We're partners. That's what sent Bob and Kitten over the edge. When I told them flatly that they would never get their hands on this land for a golf course, Bob lost his grip on his sanity." He frowned. "I never thought he or Kitten would try to kill me. And why Esmeralda?" He turned to the writer. "Why did they try to kill you?"

Esmeralda had been unnaturally quiet, and when the attention was focused on her, she seemed to withdraw even further. "I don't know."

"Did you find something?" Tinkie pressed.

"I found a lot of interesting things." She looked at Trevor, and I thought I caught a glimmer of some real emotional connection. It was gone so quickly I couldn't be sure.

"You came to the manor to retrieve your personal belongings," I said, remembering the sequence of events. "I told you I'd get them for you, but you didn't wait. Why?"

She inhaled but didn't answer.

"Why, Esmeralda?" Tinkie asked. "We need to know."

"The rosary beads I left hanging on the bedpost were from my modeling session for Trevor."

I remembered the necklace—and I knew where her painting was—in the secret hallway with a number of other valuable paintings. But I could keep a secret, too. "And?"

"Kitten gave me the rosary for that portrait. She thought it would be provocative. You know, a nude saint wearing a rosary. I thought she was very clever."

"And?" Would this woman never move on to the nut of the story?

"I saw that Fontana brat at the school board

meeting. I was wearing the rosary Kitten gave me, and he laughed about how the beads themselves were made of a poisonous plant. That's when I noticed that a couple of the beads were missing, and it occurred to me that was the poison used to kill Trevor. It was the perfect frame. I would have been blamed for his death. As it turned out, when I had a drink with Kitten she poisoned me, too. I would have also been dead so I couldn't even defend my reputation."

I hated to give her credit, but I suspected she was onto something. "So you came back for the necklace, and . . . ?"

"Malvik came out of the wall. I was feeling sick, and the room was spinning. That's the last thing I remember until I came to in the morgue at the hospital."

So Esmeralda hadn't fallen from the third floor, she'd been hauled down there and dumped in the koi pond to make it look like she'd fallen. It was a miracle she hadn't drowned.

"I was just about to start the autopsy," Doc said, "but I'd been through a similar scenario with Trevor, so I was better prepared when I detected a very weak pulse. I gave her the antidote, and she finally came around."

I turned to Trevor. "And you? How did you get to the orchard?"

"I found a note from one of my models to meet her in the apple orchard. It was a cryptic note but the orchard was a place I sometimes rendezvoused with women, so it wasn't an unusual request. When I got there, Kitten was waiting with a bottle of wine and the promise of some frisky fun. That's all I remember. I woke up with Doc Sawyer's ugly mug hovering over me. I have to say, I saw the crime-scene photographs of my face. Complete and abject fear. It's given me inspiration for a whole new series of paintings—something along the lines of *The Scream* that shows the inner turmoil of landscapes. Of course, I'll never abandon my female models. The female form embodies compassion and love and nurturing. These paintings will have tremendous commercial appeal."

And I didn't doubt that for a single second. "Obviously Bob and Kitten want the dairy property, and I can see killing Trevor, if they thought he might testify that he and the Harringtons were in a legal partnership regarding the future of the land, but I don't get this total crime spree. Why kill Esmeralda? And Faith?"

Harold shook his head. "That I can't answer. But once you figured out the land scam in Jackson with that subdivision and implicated Bob and Kitten, they had to know the jig was up. They were willing to sacrifice anyone who got in the way."

At least Tinkie and I were getting credit for finding Claudell Myers and the multimillion-dollar scam on the Pearl River. "Coleman and Doc should have told me what was going on."

"We took your original plan to use the witches to scare a confession from Bob and . . . elaborated a little," Coleman said. "It came down exactly the way you'd envisioned."

"Except that I was left in the dark and nearly had a heart attack."

"I think your heart's a lot more durable than you think," Doc said.

"Were you in on this?" I asked Tinkie.

"No. Not until Coleman told me."

"But you were," I said to Doc. "You knew Trevor and Esmeralda weren't dead."

Doc's grin disappeared.

"If it's any consolation, we didn't know," Hope said, putting a hand on Charity's shoulder. "I really thought they'd killed Faith. They were going to pin the whole real-estate mess on her, just like they did with that Meyers woman who's still in prison. Faith did help Mr. Keel sell his land. It was one of the last things she did as his broker and financial advisor. It was all above-board. But if you and Tinkie hadn't stepped in," she put a hand on my shoulder, "they would have gotten away with this and put the whole blame on Faith." She turned to Coleman. "If anyone has a reason to be mad, it's me. They let me think my sister was dead."

"The good news," Coleman said, striving for

a positive note, "is that I've called the Rankin County district attorney and filled him in on the Fontanas and the subdivision land scam. Claudell Myers should get a new trial if the charges aren't dismissed altogether." He approached me but I backed up. "You and Tinkie broke the case, Sarah Booth. I just engineered the confession."

My gut was in such knots that I didn't know what I felt—except pain. I understood the need to leave people out of the loop sometimes. I'd been guilty of it myself. But Coleman was . . . my lover. The man I'd just let into my bed and my life. And Tinkie was my partner. The closest thing to family I had, other than Jitty.

The knots in my stomach tightened even more.

"I know that look," Tinkie said, coming toward me. "Just stop. Right now. You can't hold it against everyone that we did what we thought was best when you do it all the time and expect us to understand. I remember last month when there was a dead body in your driveway—and you decided it was wet and cold and safer for me not to know until morning. Ring any bells?"

I looked to Harold for support, but he drained his Cosmo and refused to be pulled in. At last I looked at Coleman. I saw only hope. And that was the one thing I couldn't refuse. "Okay. I get it. But what role does Malvik play? Was it him or Spurlock who slashed up my door and window and tried to scare me?"

"It wasn't Malvik," Faith said. "He was a double agent. He was working for us. Once we realized the Fontanas had 'killed' Trevor, we knew they'd try forging a deed. You found the deed in the old trunk in the secret room. Spurlock stole it from you and knocked you out. Then Malvik stole it from Spurlock and took it to his hotel room to hide it until we could prove it was a forgery. Now that Trevor is alive, all of that is moot."

"Malvik is a good guy?" That one was hard to swallow.

"He is," Faith assured me. "So now it's all tied up. We know what happened and who is responsible. The nightmare is over."

Tinkie rushed me and pulled me into a hug and Coleman hugged us both. The Harrington sisters refilled our glasses, and we drank a toast to putting the Fontanas and Spurlock behind bars. After we'd had a chance to warm by the fire, Coleman motioned us to circle round.

"Let's put all of the pieces in place," he said. "Sarah Booth and Tinkie have information I don't know. Faith knows a few things."

A knock on the door made us all jump, but Coleman went to open it. He returned with a grinning Budgie. "Man, when I found Charity and Hope in the tunnels, I thought they were dead. Thank goodness they weren't really hurt." He took a drink from Charity and grinned wider.

He wore the brown uniform of a Sunflower County deputy and it was clear he was proud to be a member of Coleman's team.

"To Budgie," Coleman said, holding up his glass.

"To Budgie," we all echoed, sipping the Purple Zombie concoction that would be sure to extract a price in the morning.

"Where did you hide Esmeralda and Trevor?" I asked Doc. The logistics of this great deception intrigued me.

"In the morgue for a while, as they were recuperating. They were badly dehydrated and needed medical care. But when I kept 'eating' three hospital breakfasts and three lunches, I had to move them out. Cece took them in after the first twenty-four hours."

Ah, I wondered where my journalistic friend might be. Afraid of the consequences of her betrayal, she was lying low. And well she should. "Cece knew and didn't tell me!"

"She didn't have a choice," Doc said. "I put her in a tight spot. She didn't want to do it without telling you, Sarah Booth. I called on her journalistic code. There's a bond between reporters, or at least good reporters, that they will help another journalist in trouble. I asked Cece to honor that bond with Esmeralda."

"She made it clear she didn't really consider me a journalist," Esmeralda said, "but she protected me anyway. She showed me what a sisterhood journalism is."

"And Cece and Esmeralda are going to work together to create a blog," Trevor said. "They'll explore the world of celebrities, in art and entertainment, and spice it up with gossip and a few alternative facts. Millie is going to contribute."

I couldn't put a damper on the obvious enthusiasm in the room. "Okay, but remember this. I get five free passes on screwing up by not telling people things. Five. And no one had better fuss at me. Got it?"

"To Sarah Booth," Coleman said.

"To Sarah Booth!" And we all took a drink.

"What will happen to Bob and Kitten?" Harold asked. "I mean, they're going down on fraud and embezzlement and god knows what else in the Jackson subdivision case. But what will you charge him with?"

"I always knew Bob was willing to do whatever was necessary to get ahead. His whole tenure on the school board was about locating new schools near his developments," Coleman said, "but I truly never figured him for a killer. He'd cheat his mama out of her heart medicine if he could make a buck, but a killer . . ." He shook his head. "He was involved in the plot to kill Esmeralda and Trevor. Bob will face at least two counts of conspiring to commit murder and kidnapping on Hope and Charity for sure. I'll have to get with the district attorney to see what additional charges we can support. Kitten is in this up to her ears. She supplied the rosary made from the poisonous beads, and she slipped the poison in Esmeralda's drink and Trevor's wine. She'll face attempted-murder charges. Spurlock will be charged with first-degree assault for certain. It will take some digging for Budgie to suss out the role he played in Fontana Construction and Development's business dealings, but he's tied into that Jackson land deal."

"Malvik has always been weird, but he's not a bad guy," Hope added. "I hope you don't charge him, but if you do, I'll help with his bail."

"There's one thing I don't get." The tangled thread of this case had taken me through snarls I'd never foreseen. "How did you sisters find out about Musgrove Manor?"

Faith refilled her glass before she answered. "Mr. Keel introduced us, though I never met the Fontanas and only dealt with a woman named Lisbet Bailey, who I now know is Claudell Myers. At any rate, Mr. Keel was getting too old to manage the timber cuttings and replantings, even with his foreman. It looked like a good price to unload the land, but we were always very clear about the floodplain. The development company chose to ignore the truth."

So the last connection became clear. "Why did you leave your career?"

“I was tired of the pressure of the money world, and when I found out about my two sisters in Louisiana, we reconnected and I left the investment world behind.”

“Did you know what the Fontanas were up to?” Tinkie asked.

Faith shook her head. “I did not. But who would believe me. I knew if there were a true investigation, I’d be caught up in it. It was so much easier to just disappear and become someone else. Faith Harrington instead of Ophelia Marsh. But in working with the Fontanas, I learned about the dairy here and when my sisters wanted to start a boarding school, I knew this was the perfect place.”

“Plus, you could put it to Bob and Kitten Fontana by getting the very property they wanted so badly,” Esmeralda pointed out. “I like that. Revenge is always a fine motivator.”

“I admit it. We had what Bob wanted so badly. He went on and on about how this was close enough to Memphis and the football weekends at Oxford, Mississippi, to be a premier development. He envisioned a golf course that would host championship games. The PGA. That’s all he talked about. The houses around the course would be only for billionaires. It was a huge dream, an obsession.”

“One that he was ultimately willing to do anything to achieve,” Tinkie said.

I didn't feel sorry for Bob one whit. Given the chance, I would get Roscoe to pee on his head again. "Is Faith going to be charged with anything regarding that land deal?" I asked Coleman.

"Not at this time. But there's a lot of investigating left to do. If she violated investment laws, I'll have to report it to the Florida authorities."

"That's understood," Faith said.

"But she didn't do anything illegal," Hope said. "We know that."

It was nice they had confidence in their half-sibling, but I wondered if it was misplaced. Coleman would get to the bottom of it. Tinkie and I had earned our paychecks, and I could only say I was glad I'd deposited the money from Kitten and the Pickingill Society and that the checks had cleared.

"What about that painting of you?" Harold asked Esmeralda. "You were so hot to get it from Trevor that you sued him."

"I just wanted an excuse to be around him." She simpered as she looked over her shoulder at Trevor. "I've loved him for a long time. Now that we've shared a near-death experience together, we're going to work out the kinks in our relationship."

Tinkie and I both made the sign of the cross—used to ward off vampires—with our fingers.

"Do not give a single detail of those kinks," Tinkie said to laughter.

"The painting is here at the manor," I said. "There's a short hallway—"

"Loose lips, Sarah Booth," Trevor said, and I knew he meant to show Esmeralda the painting in a more private setting.

"What about that rosary? Is it really poisonous?" I asked.

"It is." Doc had the floor. "An interesting history. Budgie told me all about it." He nodded at the new deputy.

"The plant is *abrus precatorius*, also known as rosary peas, the devil's licorice, and a number of other names. In the past, they actually made rosary beads from the peas of the plant. It was high art to be able to carve and decorate the peas without damaging them, and I guess the poisonous nature of the bead made the religious use more powerful. They're highly toxic if the pea is broken. And several peas were missing from Esmeralda's necklace."

"That's the poison used on Trevor and Esmeralda," Doc said. "Faith wasn't poisoned, just sedated. Trevor had no knowledge of the deadly beads, but Kitten and Bob did. They gave the rosary to Esmeralda, another ace in the hole if they needed to set someone up for murder."

"If Faith wasn't poisoned, why was she hanged?" I asked.

"We pretended to hang her to give the whole zombie reanimation more gusto," Coleman said.

"Plots within plots within plots. You're sure Bob and Kitten are the source of all of this?" I asked.

"Yes," Coleman, Budgie, and Doc all answered at once. "And they're now locked in the hoosegow, along with Spurlock. Malvik is awaiting judgment. It's finally over."

Exhaustion hit me without warning, and I suddenly felt as if my spine had turned to Jell-O. I noticed Tinkie hadn't touched her drink, and yet she looked tired and pale. It was time to get home.

"What about the boarding school?" Harold asked. "Is it still a go?"

"Without a doubt," Hope said. "We'll be in business full swing by September. We're hoping for at least fifty students. Millie at the café has agreed to train a cook for us and help us get going. The county agent is coming out next week to help us lay out our summer garden. Everything is fine."

"Good." I was happy to hear the focus on nature would actually happen. "I'm heading home." But doubt still lingered. There were just too many timelines that didn't jibe, too many motives that seemed skewed. I'd have to sit down and lay it all out. But who had shot at Kitten and Bob the night Tinkie went over? Bob was drunk—he wasn't pretending. And Kitten was the one who called Tinkie. Of course, she could have made it up.

And I supposed Spurlock had been clawing up my door and window. It would just take more sorting than I had energy to provide right now. I wanted to take the victory and go home.

We all stood. Faith put her arm around her sisters as they started to bid us farewell. I had only one more question.

"Who untied Spurlock? I left him in the room where he had Harold's cousins."

Before anyone could answer, a sharp report sounded and the window shattered. Red bloomed on Faith's chest and her eyes widened. She tried to step forward, but she sank to her knees and then fell over.

"She's been shot!" Hope cried, kneeling down by her sister.

"Everyone on the floor," Coleman ordered.

27

Doc rushed to attend Faith, and her sisters scurried on their hands and knees to collect towels and whatever Doc said he needed. The wound was in her chest, but I had no idea if it had damaged her heart or lungs. Doc applied pressure to stanch the flow of blood.

"Budgie, Sarah Booth, come with me," Coleman said. "Harold, Tinkie, guard the sisters. Use a coat hanger and a broom and make a figure that you move back and forth in front of the window. See if you can draw the shooter's fire and keep him occupied. Just keep your heads down."

"What are you going to do?" I asked, though I knew the answer.

"Someone is out there trying to kill the Harringtons or one of us. We have to find them."

"Who could it be? Everyone is in the jail or in this room!"

"Obviously not."

I had a terrible feeling. "Do you think it's Gertrude Strom?" The former owner of Zinnia's fanciest B&B had developed an irrational hatred of me and had tried more than once to kill me.

"I don't know," Coleman said, "but I'm going to find out."

He headed to the front door, gun drawn and flashlight at the ready. Budgie and I followed. At the porch we were joined by the dogs and cat. "Roscoe, stay with Harold," I told the pup. "He needs you." Whining, Roscoe remained in the hall as we stepped into the night.

Coleman seemed to get a sense of the area and then he was down the steps and headed toward the old dairy barn. Budgie and I were right on his heels. We gathered behind the barn, and Coleman signaled us close together. "The shot came from that clump of trees."

It was a location that offered a good vantage point to anyone watching the house. The disadvantage was that we could easily slip behind the shooter, if he or she was still there. The overgrown pastures now provided plenty of woods and cover. Coleman signaled us forward, and as soon as we were in the trees, we fanned out. There hadn't been time to go over exact instructions, but I knew enough to call for help if I saw or heard anything. As we moved farther apart, I lost sight of Coleman and Budgie. My entire focus was on listening and looking for someone hiding with a gun.

It didn't seem possible that the woods could be so quiet. Each footstep brought a crackle of leaves or the snap of a twig no matter how hard I tried to be silent. Yet I couldn't hear anything of Coleman and Budgie. I was reminded of walking through the hallways of Musgrove Manor, thinking Tad and Thomas were behind me, only to discover that my friends were gone and I was all alone. Being left alone was one of the things that truly preyed on my fears.

Clouds had blown up and sometimes covered the moon, leaving the woods in blackness. I would stop and wait for the clouds to shift and allow the moonlight to illuminate the stark trunks and fallen limbs. I didn't want to use my flashlight—it was a dead giveaway should anyone be watching. Slowly, yard by yard, I moved toward the vicinity where the gunshot had come from. While I wanted to catch the shooter, I also didn't relish the idea of being a target. Besides, Coleman was out here and I wasn't about to abandon him without my backup, Budgie notwithstanding.

A noise ahead made me pull up short. I listened and realized it was the soft buzz of a cell phone vibrating. Coleman wouldn't be so careless. Or Budgie. But would a killer be so careless?

Aware the phone could be a trick, I waited. The buzzing came again, followed by an exasperated curse. Male voice. Not Gertrude. The relief was intense, but I was also aware that Gertrude could have hired someone to shoot me. She was that kind of nemesis. Pushing Gertrude from my mind, I inched forward until I caught a glimpse of a person in a blue and red jacket. He knelt on one knee, and he watched the manor with binoculars. I knew him instantly. I recognized the jacket his mother had brought him when we'd rescued him from the old Crenshaw place.

I'd been blind to his role in the whole thing—because he was a kid. A very bad kid, and one I'd sorely underestimated.

"Corey, drop the rifle." I pointed my gun at him. Now it all made perfect sense. He'd been spying on the Harringtons for weeks, at his mother's behest. "Put it on the ground. I don't want to hurt you."

"You're all going to die." He didn't release his grip on the rifle.

A rustling in the underbrush made us both pause. Five cats, lead by Pluto, walked toward Corey. Five more followed. Then another five from a different direction. They formed a circle around him.

"Don't make me hurt you," I said. "Coleman!" I hollered. "Over here."

Corey swung toward me with the rifle in his hand. I shot just above where his hand gripped the stock. Sadly, I'd been aiming at his leg.

"I will shoot you," I said. "I won't shoot to kill, but I'm not a great shot."

The cats moved in closer. Pluto yowled a serious warning.

"Those witches should never have come here. They screwed everything up. Everything. We had a plan. A great plan. We could have been rich."

"We can figure this out, Corey. Just put the gun down. Do it now."

"I can't," he said. He started to roll on his back and take aim at me, but the cats mobbed him. He never had a chance. Pluto went for his eyes while the others clawed and bit his hands and face and head.

He dropped the rifle, screaming, trying to protect his exposed flesh.

"Sarah Booth!" Coleman called. "You okay?"

"Here. I have the shooter. Better hurry or there won't be much left of him."

The cats stopped as suddenly as they'd begun. I grabbed Corey's rifle and pulled it out of his reach. I didn't have to worry, he was bleeding profusely and he was blinded by his own blood, if not cat scratches.

"Why, Corey? Why did you do all of this?"

"Those witches. They came to town and ruined everything. Mom and Dad had a plan to get stinking rich. They were a team, and it worked. Until those witches moved into the old-fart artist's manor. Then everything changed. Mom and Dad started fighting. It's like the witches put a spell on my dad. He said I was a spoiled brat. He was going to disinherit me. And it was all because those witches came to town and interfered in everything. I couldn't let those witches get away with it." He looked at the rifle, considering a lunge for it. I kicked it farther away.

"Don't do anything stupid, Corey."

"They are witches, you know." He stared straight at me. "They really are. They're wicked and filled with Satan. Everything they touch they've destroyed. They conned that old artist into investing in a stupid school."

I followed a sudden hunch. "You left a threatening note in Trevor's boot in an attempt to implicate Esmeralda?"

"She came over here, so stuck on herself, talking about the food she could get in the city but what a pit Zinnia was. Mom and I bought the ingredients to make that black grape sauce she was so stuck on. And so what? It wasn't that great. But then I knew Esmeralda had been talking about recipes with that woman who owns the café."

"You were framing Esmeralda."

"Yeah."

"And the second note was setting up an alibi for your mom?" The kid wasn't stupid. Too bad he'd never learned the difference between right and wrong.

"Yeah."

"Why did you have to kill Esmeralda and Trevor?"

"That guy's a lying SOB and a scumbag. He told Mom he'd sell the dairy to us. And that Esmeralda was just using my mom to get to Trevor. She was a cheap user. With her interfering, Dad would never get the land for his big development. He was already in trouble. Big financial trouble. These guys were threatening him. He needed the dairy land to get back on top."

"You attacked Trevor and Esmeralda. You poisoned them."

"I knew about the rosary pea beads. The witches thought they were the only ones who could make a potion. I gave some to Mom and she put it in Trevor's wine and Esmeralda's tea." He glared at me.

Bob Fontana might not be guilty of attempted murder, as I'd assumed, but Kitten and Bob were guilty of something far worse. They'd created a homicidal teenager, a kid so determined not to lose his wealth that he'd been willing to poison and shoot whoever got in his way. "You'd better pray Doc can keep Faith from bleeding to death."

"Why?" he asked. "I'm already a murderer."

"Because Trevor and Esmeralda are alive. You haven't killed anyone yet. But if Faith dies, that all changes. I have a bad feeling you're going to be tried as an adult if she dies. Mississippi still has the death penalty."

He didn't react. "Dead is better than being poor, you know."

I didn't answer. I didn't have to. Coleman and Budgie broke out of the trees. In a matter of moments, Corey was handcuffed and walking toward the manor. When I stumbled, Coleman sent Budgie on ahead with his prisoner.

"You okay?" he asked me.

"No."

"Some sleep will make all the difference."

"No." I didn't think it would, though I was more than ready for my bed.

"I know you're tired, but will you drop me at the courthouse?"

"Sure."

"Breakfast in the morning?"

I nodded. "I'd like that."

"Good. I'll have the case sorted by then with all the details. I heard what the kid said about concocting the poison. The whole Fontana family is going down."

When we arrived at the manor, everyone was on the porch, including Oscar. Harold had finally called him. Doc had taken Faith to the hospital, and the initial report was that the bullet had gone cleanly through her shoulder. She'd lost a lot of blood but was recovering. It could have been a lot worse.

Tinkie, looking a little green, was ready to go home. As we got in our vehicles to leave, she gave me a thumbs-up. "Tomorrow," she mouthed.

I nodded.

After dropping Coleman at the courthouse, I enjoyed the company of Sweetie Pie and Pluto on the drive home. I was surprised my hound was awake. She'd had a busy evening, but not as busy as Pluto's. My black cat and his feral buddies had literally taken Corey down. It was truly over. Coleman would have to decide on the charges, but it was clear to me that Corey had been responsible for many of the strange happenings. He'd been in the manor, frequently. He knew the secret passageways and tunnels. He'd been the person who attempted to frighten me with claw marks. The shocking part of it all was that Bob had intended to take the blame for his actions. I didn't realize he had a parental bone in his body, but on that I'd misjudged him. While Bob would escape attempted-murder charges, Kitten would not be so lucky. And Bob would spend a long time in jail for his financial shenanigans.

And the Harringtons would open their Wiccan school.

Tinkie and I were in the black with the money we'd been paid—which all came from the Fontanas. In their greed to paint the witches as evil, they'd sown the seeds for their own downfall.

Only two issues remained unresolved. My hand went to the little charm pouch hanging between my breasts. Had Coleman come to me because of spellcasting or had he come on his own? And what of Tinkie's pregnancy? I honestly didn't want an answer to either question. It was better to simply accept the stories we told ourselves. Coleman had made love with me because it was what he wanted. There was no external magic involved. It was just the culmination of a long road we'd both been traveling.

I didn't believe Tinkie was pregnant, but I also didn't want to live in that world where she found out she wasn't. Right now, she had her fantasy. And I had my man. Let sleeping dogs lie, as my aunt Loulane would wisely say.

I pulled into Dahlia House and, even though it was closer to dawn than midnight, I went to the barn. I'd give the horses a little grain to tide them over until the morning. I never skipped a feeding—and I felt guilty as hell as I trudged over the frozen grass that crunched lightly as I walked.

Strange, the light in the tack room was on, and when I opened the door, I found a note in the feed barrel.

"Coleman sent me to feed and blanket for you, Sarah Booth." It was signed DeWayne.

I checked the horses, who were indeed warm inside their blankets and were munching hay that DeWayne had put out for them. "Bless you, DeWayne," I said under my breath. Only a person with horses could truly appreciate the generous action that Coleman and DeWayne had demonstrated.

I headed into the house with Sweetie at my side. Pluto was already inside—likely on the kitchen table waiting for his chow. He was a demanding kitty.

I entered the back door and stopped at the sound of "White Christmas" filtering through the house. The scent of cinnamon permeated the air, though there was no evidence of cooking. Sweetie barked joyously and rushed through the swinging door into the dining room and I followed. I had no doubt who was responsible—and I was going to put a stop to her.

"Jitty!" When I entered the dining room, it was like stepping back in time. Red and green candles burned on the table and sideboard, and garlands of holly and cedar decorated the table. I went into the front parlor and found a Christmas tree alight with the old multicolored bulbs my mother had adored. One bad light would kill the entire string, and my parents had bickered pleasantly over retiring the old string and buying new ones. My mother had always won, because it was part of our family tradition.

Ornaments that I hadn't looked at for a long time hung from the branches of a beautiful, full cedar. The pang of past memories hit me hard. "Jitty." But this was more a cry of submission than reprimand. "What are you trying to do?"

There was a swish of fabric and Gillian Holroyd, as portrayed by the glamourous—and barefoot—Kim Novak, walked into the room. "I didn't start the magic," she said, "but I'll finish it."

I remembered the movie *Bell, Book and Candle*. Gillian Holroyd lost her ability to use magic when she fell in love with a mortal. Her cat, Pyewacket, had run away, but thank goodness Pluto was sitting in the foyer doorway licking a paw. He had no intention of hitting the road. I couldn't take a runaway kitty; an out of control haint was enough to handle.

"Jitty, I'm not in the mood," I said. "I'm tired."

"Like you're the only one who works." That sounded a lot more like Jitty than Gillian.

"It isn't a competition," I said. "Now put away the Christmas décor, though I do appreciate the true-blue adherence to the setting of the film. I'm going to bed."

"Alone?"

"No, with my shadow." Jitty could aggravate the horns off a billy goat. "Everyone is worn out. Even if Coleman was here, we'd just conk out."

"Not with that magic charm you're wearing. *Still* wearing," she said with emphasis. "You do believe in magic."

I reached beneath my blouse and my fingers closed on the silk sack. I was tempted to pull it off my neck and throw it at her, but I didn't. The little charm gave me great comfort.

"See." Kim, who was slowly turning into Jitty, goaded me.

"I don't believe in magic."

"But you *are* superstitious, which is just another kind of believin' in magic."

I did not want to argue the subcategories of magic, good or bad. "Can we talk about this tomorrow?"

Jitty was completely Jitty now, though she still looked gorgeous in the little black dress she wore. Not even her bare feet could detract from her glamour. "Do me one small favor."

Pluto trotted over to me and figure-eighted around my ankles. "What?" Sometimes it was easier to give in to Jitty than to argue.

"Hold that little charm and make a wish for Coleman."

"Like I wish he'd win the lottery? Or suddenly discover he had a four-week vacation he could take?"

"Maybe somethin' a little more intimate." She grinned. "I know what you need, even if you don't."

She would not be satisfied until I'd done as she asked. "Okay, okay." I brought the little sack out of my shirt and wrapped one hand around it. I closed my eyes. "I wish Coleman was here."

The knock on the front door made me gasp, and Jitty disappeared with a cackle. "I will get you for this," I said. She had to have known Coleman was outside when she started her foolishness. It could be no one but Coleman. The weariness seemed to drop away from me as I went to the door and threw it wide open. Coleman stepped in out of the cold and caught me in his arms. His kiss seared through me, and far in the back of my mind, I realized that Jitty knew me better than I knew myself. This *was* exactly what I needed.

"Am I forgiven?" Coleman whispered against my neck as his lips teased my skin.

I would have forgiven him for almost anything at that particular moment. But I'd learned a bit from my haunted friend. "Maybe."

He chuckled. "Maybe? That sounds very . . . conditional."

"And it is." Our gazes locked.

"What must I do to earn your forgiveness?"

"Take me upstairs and I'll tell you. I have a long, long list."

He swept me into his arms and carried me up to the bedroom. I clutched the little charm bag and remembered my wish, which had just been answered. Maybe I did believe in magic. Maybe everything would work out. Maybe the

Harringtons were real witches. The only thing I knew for certain was that I had at least three hours to be with Coleman Peters, and I wasn't going to waste a minute.

Center Point Large Print
600 Brooks Road / PO Box 1
Thorndike, ME 04986-0001 USA

(207) 568-3717

US & Canada:
1 800 929-9108
www.centerpointlargeprint.com